WITNESS TO SLAUGHTER

BY

K.A. Lugo

Tirgearr Publishing

Published by Tirgearr Publishing
Ireland
www.tirgearrpublishing.com

ISBN 978-1-910234-57-0

A CIP catalogue record for this book is
available from the British Library.

10 9 8 7 6 5 4 3 2 1

DEDICATION

Always for Peter

ACKNOWLEDGEMENTS

There are so many people I want to thank for making this book possible.

First, the biggest thanks goes out to my husband who is my greatest fan. At least, that what he tells me! He supports and encourages me throughout each project. He listens to me rant about plotting issues and cheers with me when I find my way over stumbling blocks. And he makes sure I'm fed when I get so busy that I forget to eat. I love him to the moon and back, infinity times.

I want to thank family and friends who supported me through this project. They never doubted that I could successfully transition from romance to thrillers and have cheered me on all the way.

I want to thank my production team: editor, Lucy Felthouse; proofreader, Jessica Corra; and Cora at Cora Graphics for creating the perfect cover for this book and set the theme for the series.

And, of course, a huge thank you goes out to my cover model, Rocco Benedetto, lead singer for Oraillegale – www.oraillegaleligabue.it. Ladies, if you haven't heard him sing, rush to his website and check out his videos. Trust me on this!

A very special thanks goes out to sensitivity reader, Elyssa Bolt. She was encouraging and supportive of the LGBTQ elements of my story, and she offered positive suggestions where I could tighten up. I can't thank her enough!

Also a big thanks to Kate Welch who gave me the name for one of my characters, Ginnifer/Ginnie. I was looking for something that stood out as unique and Kate came through with flying colors!

I can't close this without recognizing the help and support from two fantastic guys:

Detective Adam Richardson who runs the Writers Detective Bureau. Adam is a technical consultant for writers and screenwriters, and he runs a weekly podcast where he answers writers' questions. The podcast is linked from his website at Writer's Detective – www.writersdetective. com. You can join his group on Facebook at: facebook.com/groups/ writersdetective

Retired police sergeant for the City of Milwaukee, Patrick O'Donnell, who runs Cops and Writers. Patrick has published two books for writers that focus on police procedure to give crime writers' books street cred.

Check out the Cops and Writers series where you normally buy books. Links on Patrick's website - www.copsandwriters.com. You can join his group on Facebook: www.facebook.com/groups/copsandwriters

Witness To Slaughter
By
K.A. Lugo

CHAPTER ONE

San Francisco, California

Black Friday

"Police! Don't move."

Jack froze. The hairs on the back of his neck stood to attention as the officer's light silhouetted him against the brick wall.

"Slowly. Clasp your hands behind your head and turn around."

He pivoted in his crouched position to face the officer. She had her weapon aimed at his head, and he knew she wouldn't be afraid to use it if he made any sudden moves. He squeezed his eyes shut, flinching against the light trained on his face. Even though he knew the routine, his heartrate kicked up a notch.

"Help her," he said.

"Help is on its way. Right now, it's about you and me. Move away from the victim." Loose debris ground under his boots as he shuffled sideways. "Far enough. Put your chest on the ground. Arms wide out to the side. Cross your ankles."

Her tone of voice was clear and to the point. There was no mistaking what she wanted and he did exactly as instructed. He held his head just above the pavement, but even with his face turned away, the smell of motor oil, rotting debris, and what was probably piss filled his nostrils, as did whatever else had been spilled, dragged, or dropped in the near-dark alley. Overlaying it all was the metallic scent of the woman's blood. His stomach cramped and he swallowed hard to force back unspent puke. He tried breathing through his mouth, but it didn't help.

The officer radioed her position, and a moment later, Jack heard someone approach.

"What've we got here, partner?" a male officer asked, perhaps a bit too eagerly.

For a split moment, an image of Paul Travers flashed in Jack's mind. He shook it off and concentrated on the moment.

Squinting through the light's glare, Jack saw the partner's feet stop beside the first officer. He was sure a second weapon was aimed in his direction by the additional light now flooding his vision. He spun his head away to protect his eyes.

"I've got this," she told him.

"Are you sure? He's a big fucker."

"I said, I've got this. Watch your language, boot, and if you call me partner again, I'm writing you up."

So, she was his field training officer. There was no mistaking the irritation in her voice. Trouble in Paradise? Certainly not a partnership made in Heaven. This guy wasn't Travers, but he still sounded like an asshole.

"Sorry, Officer Massie. Just eager to help."

"You can help by doing your job," Massie told him.

Jack heard shuffling but the officers stayed where they were.

"So far, so good," Massie continued, her voice directed at him again. "Officer Jesse here—"

"It's William, Officer Massie. William James," the boot corrected.

"That's what I said. Officer Jesse James here is going to keep his weapon on you while I cuff and bag your hands. He's a bit excitable, so any trouble and I'm sure he won't hesitate to aerate your skull."

"Roger that," Jack said. He wasn't ready to take a bullet, but when he was, it would be by his own hand.

"Have we got ourselves a smartass?" asked James.

Jack remained silent. The last thing he needed was to piss off a gung-ho rookie with the nickname of an outlaw who was scrambling up the food chain.

James kept his light trained on him while Massie moved forward. At his side, he heard her holster her weapon before grabbing and twisting one wrist upward in a control hold. Her knee came down hard on his shoulder and she practically sat on his head, which forced his face onto the filthy pavement. Gravel bit into his cheek. He didn't want to think about what he'd picked up in his whiskers.

The officer firmly grasped his hand, pressing the wedding ring he still wore against his fingers, then quickly snapped a cuff onto his wrist. It hurt. She had his attention.

Jack knew she'd want the other wrist and presented it to her. His heavy leather jacket creaked in protest as she pulled up on his wrist to snap on the second cuff.

"I see you've done this before, so you know how this is going to go. Don't fight me and everything will go smoothly. I'm going to bag your hands now, then conduct my pat down. We good with that?"

"Absolutely."

After sliding sterile bags onto his hands and securing them, she lifted off his back. She pulled on the cuffs to roll him onto one side and then the other as she patted him down. She shifted her weight onto the back of his thighs and ran her hands along the length of his legs and checked his boots. She bagged those too before rising off him and moving away. He heard her weapon come out of the holster again before she returned to her partner's side. Both lights were back in his eyes.

Hand and foot preservation bags were essential for safeguarding evidence in cases like this. Besides the obvious blood DNA, it was possible gunshot residue could have transferred onto him when he checked the victim's vitals. He was sure they'd eventually take his clothes.

The process took only a few moments and was all done by the book. At any other time, with anyone else, he'd be impressed. But the woman beside him was bleeding out. She needed help.

"Will you help her now?" Jack asked.

Massie nodded to James to check on the victim. Jack angled his head and through the light shimmers in his vision, he met the victim's frozen gaze. James crouched down to check her vitals then shook his head as he returned to Massie's side.

"Wanna tell me about this?" she asked.

What *had* happened?

It had been six months since he'd discovered the awful truth about his daughter's murder. It ate at him worse now than the previous year. Any evidence he'd hoped to preserve from that night had been destroyed when Travers had taken Maria Navarro there, and Jack had been forced to kill him. What Travers' blood hadn't contaminated, the forensics team had. And Jack still didn't have any answers about his family. Zoë and Trax were dead, and Leah was still missing.

Was it possible Leah was still alive somewhere and remained hopeful he'd come for her, or had she given up hope . . . given up on *him*?

As much as he hated thinking about what Father Nick had suggested, could Leah have done *that* to their daughter, and Trax, and just walked away? Or, if she was dead too, was she buried someplace she'd never be found?

Questions burned in Jack's head like slow drip acid. He was sure he was going a little insane from it all. Wasn't that the purpose of torture?

The holidays were always the hardest on him. Not because his case load wound down to almost nothing, but because of the long, dark winter nights alone with nothing but his dark thoughts. There were days when it all sounded like buzzing and his head was the hive. It ate at him bit by bit until it got the better of him.

This time of year, the small apartment above Tommy Wong's Chinese Restaurant closed in on him, the walls pressing in like a vice. He had to get out; he didn't care where he went. He just needed to move, sometimes run, as if escaping the emotional prison he felt within himself. The physical exertion helped dissipate the ball of anxiety that made his body cramp in pain.

Tonight had been particularly rough on him. From the time he and Leah started dating, they'd always gone to the Union Square Christmas Tree Lighting Ceremony, held every year on the day after Thanksgiving, Black Friday. After Zoë was born, they'd brought her too.

Even after losing his family, he still attended the tree lighting ceremony. If by some miracle, however slim, Leah was still alive, was there a chance she might be there? For the last three years, he'd lived in hope he'd find her there, but he now believed hope had abandoned him.

This year, he told himself he wasn't going. If Leah *was* alive, Union Square was probably the last place she'd be. Hell, he doubted she was even in the city. He hated entertaining the thought she'd destroyed their family, but after so long and absolutely no clues to go on, her guilt seemed the only conclusion.

He wasn't convinced though. He still had questions. Like why didn't she drop off Zoë at a neighbor's house with an excuse she had to run a quick errand, then just walk away? If she'd gone, why leave her car behind, dinner still cooking on the stove, and her purse with her phone and wallet still inside?

That right there told him Leah hadn't killed their child. But if someone had come into their home, why kill Zoë and take Leah? And why wasn't there a ransom demand? Why not kill Leah too? Or why not take them both? He couldn't see Leah leaving their only child behind. Then again, he couldn't see her involvement in any of it, yet . . .

It all churned inside him until his blood was on fire and burning through his veins. Boiling pressure built to a point he couldn't breathe, and his heart pounded hard until he felt it would explode.

The intense, throbbing headaches were the worst. He felt like his skull was being forced open from the inside; the pain of it nearly blinded him.

The black dog of depression had become his constant companion; its gnashing teeth gripped his soul and played tug of war with his guts, pulling him, dragging him toward his ultimate goal—that small silver Parabellum round that would end it once and for all. Many times he'd sit at his desk, turning the round in his fingers, tears streaming down his face. Would he do it before he discovered the truth about that night? *Could* he do it just to end his torment?

When Jack felt himself giving in to the bullet's temptation, he forced himself out of the tiny apartment, with its oppressive walls squeezing in, and the Beretta screaming out at him to cradle it against his temple.

Tonight, he'd very nearly spent that round. The only thing keeping him from making the ultimate decision was the fact he hadn't found his daughter and Trax's killer. And he still didn't know where Leah was. Whether she was guilty or not, he had to find her.

Find Leah, find the truth.

Jack didn't remember leaving the apartment, much less the path he'd taken. The black dog pulled him along, and he hadn't paid attention to where *they* were going until Union Square loomed before him, with the tree aglow in the center of the plaza. He vaguely remembered pushing his way through the thousands of people, desperately searching for Leah—even knowing she wasn't there, and even after he'd told himself he was going to stop going. So, he'd kept walking.

It was when he stopped to get his bearings—looking for telltale landmarks—he heard a distinctive POP and instantly became alert. Another POP. Then screaming.

Instinct had driven him toward the gunfire. He knew it was the right direction by the crowd of frantic people rushing against him.

Down a narrow opening between buildings, the alley light had just barely shone onto someone lying on the ground against the brick wall.

Part of the problem when you don't care what happens to you is you make poor decisions. Jack's was to rush down the alley toward the figure disappearing into the shadows. He was lucky he hadn't been shot too, but the darkness living within him always hoped his luck would run out.

Not tonight.

He'd crouched beside the body. A woman. She was dressed in a long gown. He couldn't tell the color from the poor lighting, but there was no mistaking the dark stain growing across her abdomen and the pool of blood flowing out around her shoulders.

When he'd checked the pulse at her throat, his fingers slid across her carotid artery. Images of Zoë flashed in his mind—slumped in the highchair, warm blood still oozing from the wound in her neck. He'd just missed her killer, but by how long?

Jack swallowed hard and forced himself to concentrate. The woman's pulse was almost nonexistent, but she was alive. Her eyes slowly opened to look at him. Dark hair framed her heavily made-up face. She was beautiful, in a 1940s glamor kind of way.

"You're okay. I've got you," he'd told her, trying to keep his voice hopeful, for both their sakes. Inside, he could barely breathe and his mind spun at breakneck speed.

He'd examined the hole in her gown. Blood oozed freely. He had to stem the flow if she was going to survive. He'd pressed the palm of one hand over the wound and felt around his jacket for his Samsung cell phone with the other. He didn't know if anyone had called 9-1-1 yet, but he couldn't take the chance no one had.

Where's the goddamn thing?

Then he remembered the phone still sat on his desk. He'd been in such a rush to get out of the apartment, he hadn't thought to bring it with him.

"Damn it!" He'd gazed around him. The alley was empty. Anyone who'd heard the gunfire had run away from it. He was alone. Surely, someone had to have called for help.

Goddammit!

Something caught his eye beside the body. A kid's toy? He leaned over for a better look. "What the fuck?" It looked like a gasoline nozzle—white plastic with a black grip—but what the hell was it doing in the alley?

Sitting back on his haunches, a flash caught Jack's attention. He thought he saw someone in his peripheral vision, standing at the edge of the shadows at the corner of the building. Just as he inhaled to call out, to ask the person to call 9-1-1, light had flashed around him from the other direction—the same light the officers still trained on him.

He gazed again at the victim. Her blue eyes held their blank stare. She was dead. At least she hadn't died alone.

His senses played tug o' war with the black dog. When he swallowed the Parabellum round, he'd die alone. The reality hit him hard.

"Hey," Massie said with a raised voice, pulling Jack out of his head. "I asked you a question."

"I found her like this." He tried suppressing the irritation he felt.

"You're covered in blood. Start again. What happened here?"

"I told you. I found her like this. I was walking home. I heard two distinct gunshots. When I got here, she was on the ground but still alive."

"And the blood?"

Instinctively, he rubbed his fingers together, the plastic bags crunching. His hands were still slick with the woman's blood. "I checked her pulse and tried stemming the flow of blood from her abdomen with my hand." Jack heard sirens. "I didn't shoot her."

"That's what they all say," James said.

"You just patted me down. Did you find a weapon on me?"

"Doesn't mean you didn't stash it somewhere before we arrived."

He took a long, slow breath to try calming himself. "Look, Officer. I'm ex-Homicide. Jack Slaughter." He always hated when people pulled the *Do you know who I am?* card, but in this case, he'd make an exception.

Massie's tone noticeably changed. Was she surprised? "I've heard of you. I also heard you lost your shit after your wife was murdered."

He squeezed his eyes shut, trying to suppress the lump of bile in the back of his throat, once more threatening to eject itself. "My daughter was murdered. My wife is missing."

"And your shit?"

Was she baiting him? "Yeah, I kinda did that. But it doesn't mean I killed this woman."

Sirens echoed in the street before the cars screeched to a halt. Footfall in the alley told him the posse had arrived. A moment later, he was roughly yanked to his feet by a new pair of officers.

As he was led down the alley toward a waiting patrol car, he shouted over his shoulder, "Call Inspector Ray Navarro!"

CHAPTER TWO

Jack had no idea where he was.

According to the dash clock in the patrol car where he still sat, he'd been detained more than two hours. The officers who put him in the back of the car without so much a by your leave hadn't even left the radio on so he could listen in to the calls. That would have helped him understand the situation and what they intended on doing with him.

The crime scene was now awash with light. Jack realized the alley was a driveway leading to a parking lot behind the building.

Forensics had been called out and were now conducting their technical examination. Not Jon Cutter but one of the city's other medical examiners, Harold Baxter, among them. The rotund, balding old man ambled around the scene with a look on his face that Jack took as disinterest. Or maybe exhaustion. It was late.

Other than Baxter, only a few people were allowed within the cordoned-off crime scene while vital evidence was being gathered. By the looks of it, that kids' toy had been included.

Not long after Baxter arrived with his forensics team, CSI Gordon "Gordy" Chase had been accompanied by an officer to collect evidence from Jack. It had been a quick process that included taking blood samples and scraping under his nails, as well as bagging his boots and leather jacket. Without his jacket, he shivered against the late-night cold.

And he'd definitely had blood on him. Even with his bloodied clothes in an evidence bag somewhere and the window beside him cracked open, the metallic smell still filled the car's interior. It had imbedded in the back of his sinuses, too. It prickled like tiny bee stings and made him want to sneeze, but he forced it back. Gordy had given him a few wipes for his hands, but they hadn't been enough. Jack didn't want to run the risk of getting something that might still be on him into his own bloodstream.

Spinning red and blue lights from the other patrol cars reflected off the vehicle's interior, intensifying the stabbing pain in his head that had returned. The longer he sat here, the more he thought he was going to puke. He squeezed his eyes closed and swallowed repeatedly, trying to calm his stomach.

Where the fuck is Ray?

Had anyone heard him as he was being hauled away from the scene? If they had, did they even try making contact with his former partner? This was a homicide. *Ray should be here*, his brain screamed.

The door opposite him opened. Jack watched Lieutenant Dick Haniford slide in beside him. Over a white button-down shirt, he wore a blue pullover sweater with white snowflakes raining down on patrol cars and snowmen dressed as cops. In the center, a bold *POLICE NAVIDAD* was stitched into the knitted fabric.

A crisp new pair of dark jeans, clean, white Reeboks, freshly shaved head, and the scent of spicy cologne told Jack: a) the LT had probably been out for the evening when he got the call, and b) Nancy Haniford was almost certainly one pissed off wife right now.

"Fancy meeting you here." Jack grunted his reply. "Wanna tell me why I'm sitting in the back of a patrol car with one of the city's finest rather than still out with my wife?"

Jack huffed. "In that sweater? And in case you forgot, Lieutenant, I'm no longer on the force."

"Maybe it's you who's forgotten where you belong . . . Detective." Jack narrowed his gaze on Haniford before refocusing his attention on the crime scene. "You should be out there overseeing this, Jack, not sitting in the back of a patrol car. You wanna tell me what's going on? Or will I just let this run its course—Miranda, arraignment, court appearance, orange jumpsuit, a frisky roommate in a long-stay hotel . . .?"

Jack shifted in his seat and looked directly at Haniford for a long moment. "What did they tell you?"

"I want to hear it from you."

"I didn't do it." Haniford remained silent, waiting for the details. "I was walking home and heard the shots. By the time I arrived, the assailant was fleeing down what I thought was an alley. I don't know what's in the parking lot, but that's the direction he ran." Jack gestured toward the deceased still lying where he'd found her. "I saw someone on the ground and I went to assist. I checked her pulse. She was still alive. I tried stemming the flow of blood until help could arrive, but she died anyway. Then this." Jack jerked his head toward the activity in the driveway.

Haniford stared at him for a long moment. "Is that it?"

Jack nodded. "Pretty much."

"*Pretty much?* What aren't you telling me?"

"What do you mean?" Jack scowled.

"Don't bullshit a bullshitter. I know you play your cards close to your chest. What are you doing over here this late at night?"

The last thing Jack wanted to do was tell Haniford what dark shit lurked in his head. *Sharing isn't caring, goddammit.*

He lifted a hand to run through his hair then hesitated, reminding himself the hand wipes had done a piss poor job. Instead, he rubbed his hand down the length of his thigh, partly to get the blood off, but more in an anxious gesture to ease some of the tension coiling inside him. He'd been sitting too long. He needed to move. Glancing behind him through the side window, he wanted someone to let him out so he could walk. Maybe run.

"Well?"

I'm losing my mind and I want to put a bullet through my skull. Is that what he really wanted to say . . . what he wanted Haniford, or anyone, to *know*?

Cringing, he finally said, "It's the holidays. I—"

"I get it, Jack, and I'm sorry. You need to talk with someone. I'll put you in touch with the department shrink."

"I don't want a goddamn shrink. Besides, I've been talking with Father Nick."

"I thought you lost touch when you left Sunset."

Jack shook his head. "He's been over at St. Frank's for a while now. Look, I just wanted to take a walk. People walk, man. I heard gunfire and here I am."

Turning his gaze back to Haniford, Jack saw the man's jaw muscles tense. "Okay, Jack. What else can you remember? Any last detail at all?"

"There was something near the deceased. It looked like a gasoline nozzle but plastic, like a kid's toy. I don't know. It just seemed odd and out of place."

"We got that. Anything else?"

Had he really seen someone in the shadows or was his mind playing tricks on him? "I'm pretty sure I saw someone watching from the corner of the building."

"Do you think it was the shooter?"

Jack shook his head. "I don't think so. Like I said, when I arrived on the scene, I thought I saw someone running toward the driveway. I'm assuming the assailant or why run?"

"Do you think the shooter could have come back?"

"Why risk it? If it were me, I'd be across the Bay by now, not hanging around watching a crime scene investigation."

"Did you get a look at your witness?"

Jack shook his head again. "They stood in the shadows at the corner of the building. As soon as the officers showed up, whoever'd been there disappeared."

"Did you tell the officers you had a witness?"

"No. They weren't listening to me. It all went down quickly— light, cuffs, car. I don't think anyone heard me asking them to call Ray." Nodding toward the dash clock, he said, "That was more than two hours ago. Seems a bit long to hold a suspect if you're not taking them to the department for questioning," he added.

Haniford relaxed in the wedge between the seat and door. "They heard you. I asked them to detain you on the scene until I could get here."

Jack nodded his understanding. "They could have told me."

Ignoring the comment, Haniford said, "I asked Ray to stand down on this when I found out you were involved. You know . . ."

"Yeah-yeah. Conflict of interest. But I'm telling you, I didn't kill her. How could I? You know I don't carry a weapon. I have no reason to. Shit! The last time I used one was six months ago—"

Haniford put up a hand to silence him. "Don't go there. I'm sure we'd both like to forget that night." Jack couldn't agree more. "What do you *think* happened here?"

Things seemed to be winding down. Baxter had finally directed the woman's body to be lifted onto the gurney and Jack watched as it was wheeled past the patrol car. When his gaze met Baxter's, the ME gave no indication that he'd seen Jack. Asshole. There was certainly no love lost between him and the old man. Jack thought he was lazy and insensitive, and that he probably should either retire or *be* retired by the department.

"Really? I don't know. Maybe an argument or robbery gone wrong. All I know is I didn't do it. I tried saving her life."

"Baxter told me she was already bleeding out by the time you got to her. She had a through-and-through in the abdomen—survivable—but the shot in her neck nicked the carotid. There was nothing you could have done, Jack."

"Still doesn't make me feel any better." Jack inhaled long and slow then heavily exhaled. The adrenaline racing through him was returning to normal, exhaustion replacing anxiety. Ironically, what he really wanted now was to hit the sofa he still used as a bed and crash out until . . . later. Much later. Maybe sometime in March. April also worked.

"How much longer am I going to be cooped up here?"

"You know the process. We'll get you down to Mission Station to give a formal statement. And please, make sure they have *all* the details." When Jack lifted an eyebrow in Haniford's direction, the man chuckled. "I know you, Jack. You give up just enough to let investigators start from the ground up, while you're miles ahead of everyone else. Don't look at me like I'm talking a load of horse shit. Two words. Bonnie Boyd."

"Hey, that was to keep Travers off my back."

"Didn't work though, did it? Anyway, just do me a favor and give the detectives what they need. This isn't your case. Or Ray's. You just happened to be in the wrong place at the wrong time."

Jack nodded his agreement. "Now, are you ready to tell me what you're doing in this part of town?"

"What do you mean? I walked over to Union Square to see the lights."

"Is that where you think you are?"

He couldn't see much from where the patrol car sat just inside the driveway; the building blocking the street. He hadn't intended on going up to Union Square. After that was a blur.

"No idea. Like I said, I just wanted to go for a walk. When I heard the shots, I didn't stop to look for landmarks as I ran."

Haniford eyed Jack up and down, "Do you normally go walking in full leathers?"

Full leathers?

He squeezed his eyes shut, forcing himself to remember where he'd gone earlier in the day.

"I went to Marin," he mumbled. "Up Wolf Ridge."

"To the missile base?" Haniford asked.

Jack nodded, memories trickling in, his mind wandering. "I took my bike. There's no one up there this time of year."

America's Cold War defenses had stretched along the west coast from Alaska to California. There were some forty or more batteries and forts around San Francisco Bay Area alone.

Fort Barry lay at the foot of the mountain known as Hill-88 in the Marin Headlands beside Rodeo Beach, also known as *Nike Missile Site SF-88*. Officials were in constant contact with facilities on nearby Mount Tamalpais which networked with all ground-controlled interception radars in the region. Site SF-87 on Hill-88 had been one of them.

Located on Wolf Ridge above Fort Barry, several domed structures looking like giant golf balls had dotted the hilltop plateau and housed some of the most sophisticated radars and computer guidance systems of their day, and were used to guide Nike missiles launched from Fort Barry.

Back in the day, the twelve-inch guns mounted on disappearing carriages were capable of firing eleven-hundred-pound artillery shells up to eight miles. Jack had been to several of the now-defunct batteries around the city, including the original and still mounted disappearing gun at Battery Chamberlin on Baker Beach, but they were long gone from most other batteries.

In 1976, the Army had ordered all Nike missile sites to be shut down. While Fort Barry remained largely intact and had become a tourist attraction in more recent years, the radar facility on Wolf Ridge had been completely dismantled. What remained looked like a ghost town. It had become a destination for serious walkers, but Jack knew he'd have the place to himself on a cold winter day on the busiest shopping day of the year.

While closed to public vehicle access, Jack had maneuvered through the wide pedestrian entrance and used the old military road to reach the hilltop. He'd parked his bike on the concrete pad where the largest radar had once perched on the cliffside then waited for the fog to clear. Once it had, the entire breadth of the San Francisco Peninsula opened up before him, from the TransAm Building near his apartment in the east to the Sunset District and Ocean Beach near his house in the west. That high up and on a clear day, the west coast opened up nearly thirty miles south to Pacifica. And to the west, the sea stretched so far, he could very nearly see the curvature of the earth.

Being so removed from everything familiar in the city, with the near silence and only the chilly air blowing around him, Jack thought he could clear his mind and extinguish the fire flowing in his veins.

He'd been wrong.

He recalled being angry the whole journey back to the city, and once in his apartment, his anxiety coiled tighter until all he wanted was to get out again.

Gazing down, he realized he hadn't changed after his ride to the Marin Headlands. Only now his leather jacket, a gift from Leah, had been taken into evidence with his boots, leaving him with little more than his T-shirt, leather pants, and threadbare socks.

Anger ignited again. The ridge over his eyes tightened with an approaching migraine.

"What does it matter what I'm wearing?" he snapped.

Haniford chuckled as he knocked on the window, indicating to the waiting officer to open his door. He stepped out of the car then bent back in to look at Jack, a grin stretching across his face. "Because you're at The Majestic Lounge. In the Castro!"

CHAPTER THREE

Sunday

"Why don't you come back to Mass, Jack?"

Father Nicholas Morrissey sat across from Jack in the small office at the back of the Shrine of Saint Francis of Assisi Church, which locals lovingly referred to as Saint Frank's.

Jack had known Father Nick from the time his family attended Saint Gabriel's Church in the Sunset District and had sought the priest's counsel when he'd lost his family and through the years of being stalked by text. As a result, the two men had developed a close bond. Even though he'd brought down Travers, Jack still found himself at the church seeking the old man's counsel. Jack never attended Mass—he'd lost faith in God—but he enjoyed the camaraderie he had with Nick. The priest had no idea how many times he'd talked Jack down off his emotional ledge.

Whenever Jack wanted to see Nick on a Sunday, as he'd done today, he waited outside the church, then found the priest after Mass when everyone was gone.

"I'm not ready for that, Nick." He gazed at the glass of whiskey in his hand. As was tradition, Nick only poured them the one, even when Jack brought the bottle. Jack would only drain his glass when he was ready. He never came here to drink.

"You're showing up on Mass days more now than ever. Perhaps you're working your way back to God," the old man suggested. *Is that what I'm doing?* "What brings you to my door today?"

"Can't a couple of old friends meet for a drink and lively conversation?" Nick chuckled lightly at the last word. They both knew Jack wasn't a talker, so undoubtedly the comment brought on the short fit of coughing which reddened his friend's otherwise pale complexion. Jack leaned forward, ready to help if needed. "You okay?"

Nick nodded as he withdrew a kerchief from his coat pocket and dabbed his lips. "Fine, but less of the old bit, eh?" he said with a now low, raspy tone.

Sitting back, Jack persisted. "Are you sure? You look tired."

"Stop fussing. I'm doing just fine for a man in his nineties, thank you very much." He stuffed his kerchief back in his pocket and inhaled long and slow to catch his breath.

Nick had never told Jack how old he was before. Why now?

"Nineties, huh? You certainly don't look it. You must have seen a lot in your life." He hoped Nick would reveal a bit more about himself, though if Haniford thought Jack held his cards close to his chest, he had nothing on Father Nick. He wondered what secrets the old man kept to himself.

In spite of all the years they'd known each other, Jack still knew very little about the priest he now considered a friend. Nick had only ever insinuated he was from "back east"—he never specified from where—and had come to San Francisco in the sixties. Jack had no idea who Nick was or what he'd done for work before San Francisco, but he only ever implied he'd always been with the Church since his arrival.

He did some quick math in his head—Nick would have been in his mid-thirties in the early sixties. Had he been a priest before coming west? Wasn't Morrissey an Irish name, and didn't some Irish Catholic families encourage a son to join the priesthood? Maybe Nick had come from such a family.

"About as much as one can see from behind the Church's doors. Life comes to me. I don't go to it," Nick said.

"You need to get out more. Give me a few minutes and I'll bring up my Harley and a spare jacket and helmet. When was the last time you saw the city?" In his nineties, the man wouldn't have many more opportunities. "There's nothing like the wind in your face. Come on."

As he moved to rise, Nick put his arthritic hand on Jack's arm to still him. "These days, it's enough just to keep my old bones warm. You're a good friend and I appreciate the offer, but I'll pass." He patted Jack's arm before pulling away.

Jack looked at the man's hands for a moment—long fingers jointed by marble-sized knots; thin, pale skin covered with liver spots; brittle but manicured nails. Not a workman's hands, but the hands of a wise old man who'd given his life to the Church. And in the last few years, his guidance and counsel to a grieving friend.

Gazing at his own hands, Jack's heart sank, knowing that he wouldn't live long enough to see them change so drastically.

"Are you going to tell me the real reason you came to me today, Jack?" Nick repeated.

"A drink and comradery."

"Try again. I'm old, not ig'nrint."

Jack told him about Friday night—the body, his detainment, trip to the Mission District PD, and, after spending most of the night being questioned and giving his written statement, finally being allowed to go home as the day shift was coming in.

To his credit, Haniford had followed him to the station and hung around for support. Once they'd taken the rest of his clothes into evidence—swapping them out for a SFPD T-shirt that was too small and a pair of dirty sweatpants that had probably come out of lost and found . . . at least they let him keep his socks and jocks—Haniford drove him home where he immediately took a long, hot shower before hitting the sofa.

While he'd washed at the station, the blood had been dried on for so long that not even the scrubbing in the hot shower got it all off. Gazing at his hands again, he saw some was still embedded under his nails. He cringed. He hadn't realized he'd walked as far as the Castro, but given the neighborhood and the club, and the amount of blood on his unprotected hands, he couldn't take the chance he'd pick up anything.

He'd already scheduled a nucleic acid test for a week from tomorrow, which often detected HIV as early as ten days after exposure. At the same time, he'd be put on antiretrovirals. He'd also scheduled two follow-up tests—three weeks from exposure and then three months later, as was routine in cases like this.

His stomach soured instantly, forcing him to swallow hard. Just what he *didn't* need. HIV.

"Why were you out walking so late? The Castro is practically on the other side of the city. Do you normally walk that far?" Nick asked.

Jack shook his head. "It's a tough time of year. You know—" Nick patted Jack's hand again to say he understood. "Leah was so into Christmas—the lights, food, music . . . all of it. The gingerbread house in the Fairmont and the Union Square Tree Lighting Ceremony had become a family tradition. When Leah disappeared, I kept going, hoping I'd find her. Wherever she's gone, I keep hoping she'll come back for the holidays, if nothing else."

"And she's not there." It wasn't a question.

Jack shook his head. "I promised myself I wasn't going anymore. I'm just torturing myself. Then the apartment started closing in on me and I had to get out. It wasn't late when I left. I honestly don't know how long I was walking, or even where I was until Haniford told me. I'd stopped to get my bearings, heard gunfire, and ran toward it."

"And you don't remember getting there?"

Jack shook his head, wondering why his memory had such a black spot. "I've been trying to figure out the timeline. After Union Square, I don't remember where I went before winding up in the Castro. It was after eleven when Haniford found me in the patrol car."

After a brief pause, Nick asked, "I have to ask—had you been drinking, Jack?"

"No. One of the things they collected from me was a blood alcohol level. I was out on my bike earlier in the day and hadn't been home for long before I had to get out of the apartment. I hadn't been drinking. Though right now . . ." Staring at the glass in his hand now, he very nearly downed it in one gulp. Instead, he sat the glass on Nick's desk in front of him.

"Have you considered talking with someone?" Nick suggested.

Jack chuffed under his breath. "You sound like Haniford."

"Perhaps we're right."

"That's what I have you for." Jack gave Nick a side glance.

Nick sat slightly forward. "I'm happy to talk with you, Jack, but you need to tell me why you're really here. If you need my help, tell me what you want."

Nick was right. Jack wasn't a talker. He was so tired of talking with himself that when it came time to talk with others, he was often short on words. Or maybe he just wanted some company.

He thought about Friday night and his rising anxieties. And the goddamn black dog.

He scrubbed the back of a fist across his eyes. "It's been nearly four years since I lost my family. Why can't I get over it?"

"Loss is not something you get over. We never forget tragedy," Nick softly said.

"I can't live like this, Nick. It's eating me from the inside. What am I supposed to do?" He felt frustrated anger rising.

Nick turned his chair to fully face Jack. "Look at me, Jack. You will never get over this. You can only learn to live with it. You *must* find a way to live with it or it will destroy you. You're a good man. A strong man. You *can* get through this."

Jack squeezed back the knot coiling in his gut that threatened to strangle him. "I don't know how."

"Let me help you. Will you let me help?" Nick asked. "Do you trust me?"

"I do."

"Do you really?" he asked more forcefully.

Jack nodded. "I absolutely trust you, Nick."

He watched Nick extend those frail arthritic hands in his direction. "Take my hands, Jack. Pray with me."

Jack's back stiffened. He didn't come here for this. "I'm just here to talk with a friend."

"You said you trust me. Take my hands."

"God gave up on me four years ago. I'm not doing this." He heard anger edging his words. He wasn't angry with Nick. He was just angry. At everything.

Nick's hands shook but he never lowered them. "Perhaps God

hasn't given up on you, Jack, but you've given up on God."

Jack gazed down at the man's hands for a long moment. Then reached out.

CHAPTER FOUR

Wednesday, ten days later

"I want you to follow my husband."
He'd just returned from the doctor's office for the results of the nucleic acid test. Negative, thank God, but he wouldn't be totally out of the woods until the end of February when he had the last HIV result back. But this was good news.

No sooner had he returned, he heard footfall on the steel steps leading to the apartment. At the door, the woman inspected him up and down with a judgmental glance before pushing past him and moving through the room to perch herself on the chair in front of his desk.

"Sure, come on in," he mumbled, closing the door. He went to his desk, slunk back in his chair and folded his arms in front of him, not bothering to disguise how much he wanted to be alone.

The woman looked like she'd stepped from the pages of a fashion magazine. And he knew she had.

Ginnifer Whitney-Cummings, the model formerly known as Jennifer Morgan, was the city's darling. Her fair complexion, jet-black hair, and blue eyes so light they seemed to glow—along with her heavy bosom, tiny waist, and legs that went on forever—had made her popular with fashion designers and photographers. Seemingly overnight, her image had appeared on billboards all over the city and filled the top fashion magazines.

During Jennifer Morgan's short but illustrious career, she had attracted one of the city's most affluent socialites, Franklin Whitney-Cummings III.

If the stories were true, Franklin the Third had first seen Morgan at a fashion show he'd been attending with his then-girlfriend. It had been love at first sight, and after a handful of dates, their wedding had made all the tabloids. As had the rock he noticed she still sported on her delicate finger.

When she'd taken the Whitney-Cummings name, Morgan took the opportunity to recreate herself. She changed the spelling of her name to Ginnifer, retired from modeling, and dedicated herself to her new life as Mrs. Franklin Whitney-Cummings and all it entailed. Her fans loved her even more, as the tabloids couldn't get enough of her and her exploits with her rich and handsome husband.

From the moment they first appeared in public as man and wife—from yacht races on the Bay to political fundraisers—Franklin the Third and the now-Ginnie portrayed a couple very much in love and enjoyed the jet-setting lifestyle.

Everything about them seemed perfect.

Seemed being the operative word. Jack knew all too well how that assumption played out. Seeing her in his office now only solidified his belief that nothing was ever perfect. Even for the rich and famous.

What had Leah said about the famous? *It's unicorns and rainbows on the outside, baby. Inside, they're squirrels fighting in a sack.*

Jack nearly chuckled as he gazed across the desk. With her classic beige pantsuit with matching pumps and wide-brimmed sun hat, and the oversized Louis Vuitton handbag, Ginnifer Whitney-Cummings emulated the epitome of classic fashion. Nothing screamed squirrels fighting in a sack, but he wondered why she wanted her husband followed.

And why him? If she suspected her husband was cheating on her, she certainly could afford an investigator who moved in her own circle.

As if reading his mind, she continued, "I know I must seem out of place . . . here." She quickly cast a heavily-mascaraed derisive gaze around the small room and settled on the sofa, which looked like someone had recently been sleeping there. He hadn't been expecting anyone so hadn't bothered to put the blanket and pillow in the backroom.

"You could say that."

She smiled but it didn't reach her eyes. "I'll get to the point. You're a man who can get the job done. That's what I need."

"There are many good investigators in the city who can *get the job done*. Why me?" He leaned back in the chair and wove his fingers over his abdomen.

"If rumors are correct, you did what the San Francisco Police Department couldn't. They sat on a serial killer and got nowhere. You solved the case within days."

"I got lucky."

"Luck or not, you accomplished in those few days what a whole department couldn't do in years, and who didn't even see fit to warn the public, I might add. Really, I have no idea why we continue to donate to police charities. Anyway, I need someone like you."

"Mrs. Whitney-Cu—"

"Ginnie. You'll be working for me, so there's no need to be so formal," she told him.

Jack cocked an eyebrow. "I haven't agreed to anything."

"You are. I'm paying double your normal fee."

That made Jack sit up straight, if only on the inside. Outside, he remained calm—*unicorns and rainbows, baby*. She didn't need to know she'd piqued his curiosity.

"Money aside, Mrs. Whit—Ginnie," he corrected when she scowled. It was a look, he was sure, that got her whatever she wanted. "Money aside, why don't you speak with investigators who . . . cater to celebrity?"

Leaning forward, her breasts against the oversized handbag in her lap. A muffled whimper came from within. She reached inside and pulled out a small dog that looked like a Yorkie dressed in a similar fashion to herself and deposited it on the floor. It shook then scampered across the floor, sniffing as it moved.

Without missing a beat, Ginnie said, "Because this must be kept confidential. I'm sure you can appreciate one in my position,"—

Jack knew she really meant, *Because I'm rich and famous—*"wanting to keep certain things private. I don't trust other investigators. They're too quick to name-drop when they have big cases. I mean, really, they're no better than the paparazzi."

"I'm sure that's not true." Jack watched the little dog scratch at the outfit's collar and nip at the fabric, earning it a sharp *stop it* from its mistress. It returned to sniffing the floor and promptly squatted, creating a sizeable puddle for a dog its size before scampering away.

Ignoring what her dog had just done, the woman continued. "If you're going to work for me, I would appreciate you not calling me a liar."

"I'm sorry if I offended you. I'm just not sure what I can bring to the table that another investigator can't." Jack kept his gaze on the dog who looked like it was trying to find a place for its other business. Before it did, he rose and went to the dog. He grasped it by the back of its outfit and deposited it in Ginnie's lap. He used an old newspaper to soak up the piss. He'd sanitize the spot after she left.

After disposing of the soiled broadsheet in his waste basket, he leaned his hip on the edge of the desk, recrossed his arms and gazed down at her. "Why don't you fill in the blanks and let me decide if I'm even interested in this case? What's so secretive that you're afraid it'll get out? You want your husband followed. I'm assuming you think he's cheating on you. Yes?"

She looked away for a moment. Jack lost sight of her face beneath her hat's wide brim. When he heard her sniffle, he thought she was crying and went to the other side of the desk to pull some tissues from a box in his desk drawer. He handed them to her then returned to his chair.

When she gazed up at him, he saw she hadn't been crying at all. Everything about her shouted *fury*.

"It's more than that," she said through clenched teeth.

"Why don't you explain it to me?"

"I just want you to follow him. Tell me where he's going. Take your usual photos so I have proof of what he's getting up to."

"I'm not taking cheating spouse cases at the moment. Any investigator can do what you're asking."

The hat's wide brim managed to force a gust of air in his direction when she shook her head. "As I said, I need discretion. The Whitney-Cummings have a reputation to uphold. If it was just a matter of him fucking other women, I'd call him on it and cut him off at the balls . . . so to speak."

Jack was shocked at the woman's language, but given the fire in her eyes, he assumed she was so furious with whatever her husband was getting up to that language didn't matter.

"Of course. A woman in your position could hire someone to cut them off for you . . . so to speak." He only half-joked. The rich always assumed a certain level of power. Money talks and all that crap.

"When you solved the serial killer case, you effectively cut off the city's balls and handed them to the Chief of Police and the Mayor on a silver platter. That's why I'm hiring you."

"Explain it to me, then."

"It's really quite embarrassing. Humiliating, really. Not just for Franklin, or me, but for the city. The Whitney-Cummings' are as much a part of the city as . . ." She waved her hand in the air as if dismissing the subject. "Well, as any other city icon. As such, his behavior will be an embarrassment to the city, possibly on a national scale."

Jack's curiosity was scrambling around like a couple squirrels looking for trouble, but he wasn't sure how one man could bring down the city's reputation. If Travers hadn't done it, Jack didn't see how Franklin the Third could.

"Infidelity isn't a city problem," he told her.

Ginnie sat up straight in her chair, forcing the little dog to sit still in her lap. "You *do* know who we are, don't you? I mean, you aren't . . . rich. Certainly you must know of my husband's family."

His ancestors dated back to the Gold Rush, having owned Whitney General Stores that, among other things, sold overpriced equipment to miners and paid below average prices on gold.

Over the decades, those rustic stores had developed into Whitney Department Stores and rivaled the likes of Saks Fifth

Avenue, Neiman Marcus, and I. Magnin. Upon seeing the decline and ultimate sale of I. Magnin, the Whitney-Cummings' also decided it was time to get out. Their department store chain was sold and folded into another big-name company, then the family turned their attentions, and wealth, to hobbies of the elite.

It had been in the late '90s when tech start-ups in Santa Clara, now commonly referred to as Silicon Valley, became popular places for those with more money than sense to invest that the Whitney-Cummings' saw an opportunity to boost their waning bank balances. Investing in the likes of Dell, Apple, and Hewlett-Packard rocketed the family back into the social stratosphere.

Nodding, he said, "Of course, I know the family history, and your own. But I don't see how your husband cheating on you will bring down the city."

"In our circle," she assured him, "whatever he's up to can undoubtedly send shockwaves through the city, and beyond. Probably as far as Wall Street. He could be the complete ruination of the Whitney-Cummings name."

"Do tell." Just fucking tell me, he wanted to scream.

She leaned toward him and dropped her voice to a near whisper, as if the room was filled with prying eyes and big ears and she only wanted him to hear her.

"My husband has been wearing women's clothes."

CHAPTER FIVE

Jack tried calming the squirrels. He opened his mouth to say something, then closed it again.

San Francisco had been synonymous with a free lifestyle well before the '60s. Over the years, her citizens got up to a lot of crazy shit. And yeah, the more money, often the crazier the shit. Money bought whatever freak they wanted to try out. Cross-dressing paled in comparison to some of what he'd read about.

Was he surprised to hear Franklin the Third was wearing women's clothes? His mind quickly ran through the images that flashed through his mind. Franklin the Third was an athletic man with a form to fit—something akin to a runner or cyclist; lean but tightly muscled. Jack tried imagining the man wearing a strapless evening gown. Or was he into something tamer?

"Cat got your tongue, Mr. Slaughter?"

"Squirrels."

Her face screwed up as she asked, "What?"

He shook his head slightly. "Just a phrase my wife used to say." By the look on the woman's face, she had no idea who Jack really was—how was that for irony? She was probably only basing her decision to hire him on recent news. "What do you mean he's a cross-dresser? If his public persona is anything to go by, nothing screams out that he has, shall we say, freer self-expression. Why don't you start at the beginning? When did it start?"

She sniffed again, but this time her liquid blue eyes pooled, giving them a glassy sheen.

"I walked in on him last year. I thought he had a . . . a woman in his home office. I heard a woman's voice as I passed the door. It was late in the evening and I knew no one had come to our home for a business meeting. I thought he . . . he might have sneaked someone in. When I opened the door—"

She buried her face in her hands and wept a little too dramatically in his opinion. Her little purse pooch leapt to the floor and scurried off to the puddle it had previously made and sniffed. Jack shot a look between the dog and the weeping woman and back again. If that dog pissed on his floor again . . .

"Please, continue."

Using the tissues he'd given her moments ago, she dabbed at her eyes. "When I opened the door, he was the only one in the room. Except it wasn't him. I could only stare. At first I thought he was wearing one of my dresses, but he couldn't be. He's so much larger than I am. It was then I realized what he was wearing had been custom made. It occurred to me that he hadn't *just then* decided to wear women's clothes. He has his own seamstress, for god's sake."

Jack eyed the custom outfit her purse pooch wore and suppressed a snort. "He must have been doing this for a while if he decided to have tailored garments made." She nodded, dabbing her eyes once more and then her nose. "What happened next?"

"What do you think? I screamed at him. I demanded he remove the dress. Asked him what the hell he was thinking. Dresses? Really!"

"Let me ask you this. Do you appreciate a man in a kilt?" By the look on her face, his question was absurd. Of course, it was. "Humor me. What do you think of Scottish kilts?"

"They're okay, I guess."

"Just okay? I'm sure you've seen your share of kilted models in your day. I'm a hetero guy, but even I can appreciate the look."

Ginnie nodded. "Yes, I've worked with many men in kilts. Pretty sexy. Especially if they have an accent to match."

Jack nodded toward her. "And what about your own pantsuit?"

She quickly gazed over her outfit. "What do you mean? There's nothing wrong with what I'm wearing."

"Exactly. But aren't pants for men?"

"N-no." Her face screwed up slightly. "What are you getting at?"

"If men can wear kilts, effectively skirts, and women can wear pants, what's wrong with men wearing dresses?"

Her mouth opened and closed several times, as if she fought for a reply. He waited.

Finally, she said, "That's not the point, Mr. Slaughter."

"Then tell me, what *is* the point?"

"The point is that he's a Whitney-Cummings. He has a reputation to uphold. He's a man. A *virile* man. Nothing about him led me to believe he had this . . . this other side. He's been lying to me our entire marriage and I told him as much. We argued and shouted, and he cried like a little girl—" She stopped abruptly, probably realizing she was getting angry at the wrong person. Then more calmly, "He *was* not the man I married."

Jack was still trying to understand why she wanted Franklin the Third followed. She knew his secret, so why all the cloak and dagger?

"I'm sure you have secrets you don't tell him."

"Nothing like this." Her voice rose again. "Are you defending him?"

Jack shook his head and put his hands up defensively. "I'm a neutral bystander in this. I'm just trying to get some idea of why you want your husband followed."

"I told you. If this gets out, I'm . . . *we're* . . . ruined. We'll lose *everything.*"

"Let's back up a bit. You said you discovered his proclivity for women's fashion last year. You're still married to him. Why?"

Her back noticeably stiffened. "Because I'm being forced." Jack waited for her to continue, rolling his hand in a hurry up motion when she stalled. Finally, she said, "The prenup."

"You signed a prenup. What did you agree to?" This was getting good. Jack was glad he'd switched on the record app on his phone the moment she'd walked in.

"When we married, modeling was starting to become lucrative. I didn't need his money. But his lawyers insisted on the prenup to protect the family's fortune. He told me he loved me and the prenup didn't really matter . . . it didn't mean anything. He said he wanted me to quit modeling and gave me a dozen reasons why it made sense—he would take care of me. So, I quit. Everything was perfect and the prenup had been forgotten."

"Until last year."

She nodded. "When I told him I wanted a divorce, he reminded me of the prenup. My own lawyer said it couldn't be breached."

"What does it say?"

"Basically, I get nothing until his natural death. Unless I can prove that he's cheating on me. It says nothing about . . . *this*." She sobbed into her tissues again. "I loved my husband. How could he do this to me?"

"Loved? Do you not still love him?"

Her gaze shot up. "I—I guess. I don't know. I love the man I married, but he's not the same man."

"Perhaps he *is* the same man, but you just didn't know this side of him."

"There you go again, defending him."

"I'm just trying to understand the situation. There's nothing in the newspapers or tabloids about there being trouble in Paradise for either of you."

"That's because we came to an understanding. He refused to stop dressing in women's clothes, but I demanded that he keep it at home—private. In public, nothing changed. No one must know." She paused a moment, then looked him square in the eye. Her features softened; a delicate smile appeared. "You have to understand, when he's himself, he's every bit the man I fell in love with. He's strong, handsome, gregarious. He makes me laugh like no one else can. And when we're in bed . . ." She trailed off, her eyelids pressing together, as if remembering her husband's performances. "In bed, he's magic." Looking back at Jack, she said, "That's the only word I can use to describe how he makes me feel. Like I'm the only woman in the world, and only my satisfaction matters. He makes that *thing* inside me ache so much with love it brings me to tears. Have you ever made a woman feel that way?"

Her question was shockingly direct. That *thing* inside Jack squeezed, remembering the times Leah had wept after their lovemaking. He always tried showing her how much he loved her when they made love. Was that the reason for her tears? When he'd asked, she only told him it was because she was so happy.

Happy. Was killing their daughter her way of showing him how happy she was?

"I can only hope," he replied. "What about Franklin? If everything about him is perfect, couldn't you forgive this small part of him?"

"I've tried. I really have. At first, he agreed to keep it within the confines of his office. Curtains drawn. Private. I didn't want to see it. I wanted the man I'd married. I didn't want to know that other side of him."

"Something changed."

She nodded. "One night, he came to bed in a negligee. I told him to take it off. He refused. It must have been hours that we argued before I kicked him out of our bedroom. I told him in my bed, he needed to be a man. All man. Whenever he wanted to play dress-up, he needed to stay away from me. I didn't want to know that part of him. I didn't want to *see* that part of him. He agreed, but from that night on, he never came back to our bedroom."

"When was that?"

"Two months ago."

"Why come to me now? What's changed?"

"He breached our agreement."

"What happened?"

"He started walking around the house in women's clothes. We had another argument. Instead of retreating into his office as we'd agreed, he got in his car and left. In the dress. He went out dressed as a fucking woman! He's been going out every night since then. *Oh my God!* What if someone recognizes him?" Angry tears flowed down her inflamed cheeks. "Every fiber in my body that screams how much I love the man he *was* also hates the woman he pretends to be."

"Why don't you follow him yourself?"

"I don't want him to know he's being followed. For God's sake, if I followed him, I'd end up confronting him there and his secret would be outed, as would mine. I'd be more than just the betrayed wife." The words jerked out of her mouth as she suppressed her sobs. "I'd be a laughingstock. I would never be able to show my face in public again."

"Cross-dressing doesn't mean he's cheating on you," Jack pointed out.

Ginnie's eyebrows knit together with her scowl. "I'm hiring you to make sure he's caught in a compromising position. I just need you to get me the photos."

"Because he doesn't know me so wouldn't be looking for me taking pictures of him."

"Right. So, when can you start?"

"I never said I'd take the case," he reminded her.

She gazed around the room, then back at him. "Really? I'm paying you double your normal rate and you're going to protest?"

CHAPTER SIX

Thursday

"What did you tell her?" Ray asked, stuffing fries into his mouth.

Jack agreed to meet his friend across town in the Haight, near where he'd been investigating a suspected suicide.

Burger Urge was in the heart of the district and had always been a favorite spot when he and Leah double-dated with the Navarros. With Leah being a vegetarian and Jack needing somewhere to satisfy his carnivorous cravings, why not at the funkiest burger joint in the city? Leah had loved the place with its extensive vegetarian menu.

And he couldn't fault the atmosphere, from the quirky interior wall paintings and a ceiling covered with hand-painted ukuleles, to the extensive mural on the building's exterior, featuring iconic images of Janis Joplin, Jimi Hendrix, George Harrison, and others. Along with the '60s music coming through the speakers, it was all a garish tribute to the Summer of Love. And they all loved it.

Jack's chest tightened with the memory of the many evenings they'd spent here. He could almost see them all sitting at the next table, laughing so hard they had tears in their eyes.

He inhaled long and slow to calm his racing heart. It had been a long time since he'd been here—because of those memories— but in a way, coming back also felt comforting. Like visiting an old friend.

He filled his mouth with vanilla malt shake, soaking in those memories.

"What could I say?" he finally said. "She had a point. I couldn't afford to be picky. I handed her a contract and told her my fee. She whipped out her checkbook and wrote out a check double that without flinching. And I'll get a bonus if I get her the photos she wants by the weekend."

Ray whistled under his breath. "Nice. Now you can afford to pay for lunch." He gave Jack a wide grin.

Chuckling, he said, "Sure, why change tradition now?"

"Hey, man, I've got a bambino on the way."

"By the way you're eating for two, I can tell." Jack nodded at the belly starting to push its way against Ray's button-down shirt. His new mustache made him look like Cheech Marin from the old days.

Ray rubbed his stomach. "Maria calls it my sympathetic pregnancy."

Jack chuffed. "Keep telling yourself that. You need a new partner to get you out of the office more. You're spending too much time at your desk."

All humor went out of Ray's features in a blink. "Don't even go there, Jack. I'm a one-partner guy. I tried other partners, but I'm waiting for *the one* to come back to me."

Ray had blown through nearly a dozen partners in the last four years. Jack knew his friend was waiting for him to get back on the job. "You're like a love-struck teenager."

With a tender look on his face, Ray said, "I only have eyes for you, *cariño*."

Chuckling outright, Jack said, "I love you too, brother," as he stuffed the last onion ring in his mouth, then sucked down the remainder of his shake. After wiping his mouth and making sure he didn't have anything stuck in his whiskers, he pushed away his plate and sat back in his chair, folding his hands over his abdomen. If he wasn't careful, he'd be sporting a belly like Ray's. He probably would have, if not for the late-night tension that forced him out of his apartment for long walks.

Jack flinched. The last time he'd taken to the streets on foot, he'd found himself the center of attention in a homicide.

"Just don't try kissing me with that *thing* living on your lip," he said, flicking his fingers in the mustache's general direction.

A crease formed between Ray's eyes as he stroked the thing like a pet. "You should talk."

Jack chuckled. He'd given up shaving long ago. It was enough just keeping the resultant beard and mustache trimmed. Ignoring Ray's jibe, he asked, "Hey, who did Haniford flip that homicide to over at the Majestic?"

Ray leaned back in his chair, crossing his arms. The scowl remained. "Wash and Harry."

Jack knew them. Othuleyo "Wash" Washington had transferred over from Oakland two years ago when Debra "Harry" Callahan's partner had been killed in the line of duty.

Wash's mother had escaped South African apartheid when she was pregnant with Wash and settled in Chicago. He'd earned a full ride to college on the back of his exemplary football record in high school. In his second year, he'd been drafted to play for the San Francisco 49ers. He'd still been living at home, and when his mother heard the news, she moved them to Oakland to fulfill his dream.

No one had thought just a couple years later he'd be taken out by the same freak accident suffered by 1930s NFL All-Star, Albert "Turk" Edwards. Dubbed the *Turk and Surf*, it was after the coin toss at the start of the game when Turk turned to run back to the sideline when his cleat became entangled in the grass and sent him surfing across the field. He'd blown his knee and his career in that instant.

Similarly, Wash's cleat had caught in the grass, but it was during a tackle. He'd been hit from three sides—the first blow ground the cleat into the grass, the second blow forced his body to spin where he was planted, and the third slammed him into the ground. He'd blown his knee and also dislocated his collarbone. The collarbone had healed within a few weeks, but the knee required surgery which led to months of painful rehab.

The recovery time gave Wash some perspective—continue playing ball and suffering repeated injuries or finish his degree and find a new career. Three years later, he'd finished college and graduated from the academy, and was fast-tracking his way up the food chain. By all accounts, Wash was a standup cop who worked by the book. It didn't hurt that he still had the build and speed of an NFL lineman. And with his penetrating gaze of a pitbull, perps tended to give up quickly.

Wash's dark complexion was a sharp contrast to Harry's fairer one. Average height with a runner's physique, she'd been given the nickname by her late partner, David Perry. Not because of any references to Harry Callahan from the *Dirty Harry* movies, but because he'd said she reminded him of the singer Debbie Harry with her striking blond hair and toothy smile. Harry came from a long line of officers, from her great grandfather who joined the force in New York City after immigrating from Ireland, to her grandfather who followed in his father's footsteps, to her father who did the same. Harry was the first female cop in the family, and the first to leave New York for the sunnier west coast. She opted for college in California and stayed after the academy.

Perry had lost his life when he and Harry performed a routine door-to-door inquiry in relation to recent neighborhood break-ins. They'd no more than knocked on the resident's door when shotgun fire blasted through the cheap hollow-core timber, hitting Perry in the hip. As trained, they'd flanked the door while waiting for the occupant to respond. Investigators had determined the shooter must have known this and deliberately fired lower—he couldn't take the chance of hitting a vest and only winding the officer. It hadn't been a warning shot. It had been deliberate murder.

To Harry's credit, she'd pulled Perry down the few front steps to the lawn and behind some porch hedging before calling for backup. But the bullet had passed right through his femoral artery and he'd bled out before help could arrive. At least he hadn't died alone—one of a cop's worst nightmares.

After Perry's funeral, Harry accepted Wash as her new partner without issue, and they went right to work. For her, the job came first. Any anguish she felt over losing her partner was done in private.

Jack knew the loss had hit her hard. He'd agreed to meet with her where she asked how he coped with the loss of his wife and daughter. She confided in him that she and Perry had been more than work partners, so Jack better understood her loss. He'd locked the black dog in the back of his head and told Harry what she needed to hear.

"They're good detectives," he said. "What's the 4-1-1 about what happened up there? Have they ID'd the woman?"

"She was a *he*." Jack's eyes widened but he let Ray continue. "The victim's stage name was Pepper Mint. When he wasn't performing, his real name, Bob Johnson. Originally from Lubbock, Texas. His holy roller parents disowned him after he came out at fifteen. He lived in West Hollywood but traveled to the city for the Majestic's annual Drag Queen of the Year event."

"Sounds innocent enough. Any speculation on what preceded the murder? Any cat fights or full-on off-stage brawls?"

Ray shook his head. "Nothing's being speculated at the moment. I think they're going with hate crime. That's all I know."

Jack nodded. It wasn't Ray's case so his knowledge would be sketchy at best.

"You ever gonna tell me what you were doing up there?"

Jack knew he meant, *What were you doing at a gay bar?* Not just in the Castro. "I was just out walking, man."

Ray cocked an eyebrow. "That's a long walk from your place."

Jack agreed. At the time, his mind hadn't been on the destination, rather how far he could get away from the dark thoughts growing in his mind. "Yeah, I know."

"So, what gives?" Ray pressed.

Jack took a long drag of air. They'd had a great lunch and he was feeling better about being in familiar surroundings. He didn't want to spoil it by going back to that night. By the look on Ray's face, he wasn't going to get out of the question. What could he say that wouldn't dredge up all his internal shit?

"It's just the holidays."

"I get it. By why the Castro?"

"Trust me. That wasn't my destination. I wasn't thinking about where I was going. Or anything else. I just needed to get out of my place for a while. I was feeling . . . antsy." Yeah, that was a good, neutral word. "I needed some fresh air. Walking helps clear my mind."

Ray nodded as if satisfied with his answer, and didn't press any further. "You're still coming for Christmas." It wasn't a question.

"Absolutely." After a long pause, Jack asked, "Why pensive all of a sudden?"

"Maria hasn't said anything, but I see how tired she is. Her due date isn't until after the New Year, but she's struggling. She's really looking forward to Christmas. She says she's okay, but—"

"No worries. You and I can handle it. It won't get you out of buying her an expensive present, but she'll appreciate the gift of the day off." Jack tossed his friend a grin.

Ray scowled. "Don't mention presents. I have no idea what to get her."

Jack whistled low and long. "Think of something she really wants that's not practical—no clothes, no appliances, and whatever you do, do *not* get her baby stuff. Buy her jewelry. All women love sparkly things. Find something that shows her how much you love her."

"I get it, but I'm still clueless."

"We can talk about it later tonight when I come over." Thursday was dinner night with the Navarros. "While I'm there, I need to pick up my car. I can't tail Franklin the Third on my Harley."

CHAPTER SEVEN

Friday

From where Jack sat at the top of the bend on 27th Avenue in his black Jeep Grand Cherokee, he had the perfect view down to the Whitney-Cummings' home on Sea Cliff Avenue.

When he decided to get his investigator's license, he knew he couldn't follow clients and do stakeouts on his Harley. The bike was too noticeable. If the sight of it didn't turn heads, the loud muffler did. And he couldn't very well sit on it for hours at a time in the cold night air. He'd freeze his balls off.

His natural inclination for a four-wheeled vehicle would have leaned toward the classics, but staking out a house in a cherry '69 Chevelle SS, his dream machine, would certainly be out of place anywhere in the city. These days, few classics remained on the road, and those that did had most often been restored and were attention-getters even more than his Harley. Silicon Valley money hadn't just turned around the face of the city. Many of those new millionaires converted their wealth into flashy cars—exotics and classics alike.

He'd chosen the Jeep for a number of reasons, but mainly because it could handle the city's hilly landscape, and that it didn't stand out among the thousands of similar vehicles. Yesterday's people carriers and mommy-daddy family wagons had been replaced by today's comfortable SUVs—stylish workhorses. Gazing in his mirrors up 27th, he counted six other SUVs in or alongside driveways, which told him even the affluent preferred them, though he doubted any of these people actually took their vehicles off-roading.

Jack looked back at the Whitney-Cummings home. He didn't have to be inside to know what it looked like. The remodel had made *Architectural Digest*, and ultimately TV reality shows, having been transformed into one of the residential jewels in the city's crown.

Built on the cliff-edge in 1913, the house had been luxuriously modernized not long after Jennifer Morgan had landed Franklin the Third. On the outside, the house retained most of its Italianate architecture, with high-arched windows and bracketed cornices.

Inside was another story.

Magazine photos revealed each of the rooms had been remodeled in *wabi-sabi* design—clean, minimalistic lines emphasizing the simplicity of open space rather than lived-in clutter.

Walls had been removed to create wide, open-plan spaces, featuring only a few pieces of bespoke contemporary furniture in neutral colors that blended with the just-off-white walls. Most surfaces were devoid of objects or held bold statement pieces designed to stand out.

Those huge rooms didn't need clutter to beautify them. Wall-to-wall, floor-to-ceiling windows dominated the space; white walls framed the view like massive murals.

In the Whitney-Cummings house, views looked across the mouth of San Francisco Bay to the Marin Headlands and the Golden Gate Bridge. Who needed clutter with views like that? He'd only need a single comfortable chair facing the water, a tumbler of Jameson 12-year-old whiskey, and the peace and quiet to enjoy it all.

Jack knew from the magazine photos there was a wide glass-sided infinity pool on the cliff-edge—the type of pool that, when you were in it, seemed to merge with the sea.

He closed his eyes for a moment, imagining the view on a night like tonight—a partial moon against a deep blue sky devoid of clouds or fog, when everything seemed in sharp focus and so clear that the Tiburon lights sparkled clearly on the horizon just past the bridge.

Yeah, Jennifer Morgan had definitely scored herself an E-ticket to the good life when she married Franklin the Third.

His stomach tightened at the thought that so much regional beauty was only available to the wealthy, while others were forced to live on the streets because they'd been priced out of their own homes and had nowhere else to go. Even for those whose mortgages had long been paid off, the annual property taxes were crippling. That was something he understood as his mind raced to his empty house in the Sunset District. He wasn't just working to pay his rent over Wong's. He still had a mortgage and property taxes of his own. He really should sell it.

His house was little more than a hundred years old, and one of the few surviving examples of the small houses put up by developers to house the displaced after the 1906 earthquake. The selling agent had recommended they only buy the house for the land it sat on, but Leah had convinced him that tearing down the little Victorian-style house would be destroying another bit of city history, so they'd agreed to restore it.

There was nothing minimalistic or architecturally special about the house. A gentle grin tugged at his lips as he thought about how Leah had turned their house into a home, full of cozy furnishings and personalized touches. If there was a flat surface, she found a way to fill it with something—framed photos, shells she'd found on any of the beaches around the peninsula, plants, and knickknacks she'd collected through her life. Those had been some of the things he'd boxed up to keep, though he wasn't sure why. He hadn't unpacked them in the apartment, and it wasn't like he could take them with him when he pulled out his Beretta for the last time.

He rubbed his tired eyes, forcing himself to focus on his task. This was part of what he hated about stakeouts—all the random bullshit the quiet of the vehicle forced through his brain.

He checked the time. 11:23 p.m. Ginnie had told him there were times when her husband was *all* man. Maybe he'd surprised her tonight.

His stomach grumbled, reminding him that he'd missed dinner so he could get over here early. He should have brought snacks.

He took a swig from his water bottle, hoping to give his stomach something to concentrate on while he kept his mind on the job. He decided to give it another hour before heading back to his place.

From where he sat, most of the house was obscured by trees. Only the gate was immediately visible. If Franklin decided to leave, it would be through this gate.

Something diverted his gaze above the trees. The pale light cast by the partial moon was just enough to silhouette a figure in what looked like a glassed-in observation room on the roof. A second flash quickly illuminated Ginnie's face as she lit a cigarette, which meant she was facing the street. Could she see him in the Jeep, or was she watching for Franklin to leave?

His phone screen lit up and Ginnie's name appeared with the buzz of the incoming call.

"You okay?" he asked on answering.

"He's crazy. I don't know what to do."

"What happened?"

"The same shit, but I just can't get through to him. He won't listen to me. This is not the way *real* men behave. Every day the man I married is slipping away and this . . . this new *woman* he thinks he is comes out."

"Did he hurt you? Tell me what happened," he pressed.

He heard her take a long drag on the cigarette and the waver in her voice. "Tonight, he told me he's thinking of transitioning. I told him there was no way in Hell that was going to happen. He's my *husband*, and it'd be a cold day in Hell before I'd authorize that kind of spend."

"What did he say to that?"

Ginnie spluttered. "He told me there's nothing I can do about it. It's his life . . . blah blah blah. It's his money . . . blah blah blah . . . This is who he is . . . blah . . . he'll do what he wants . . . blah . . . I can leave if I don't like it . . . fucking *blah*. It's the same thing."

"You said he's getting worse. What's worse if this is your normal argument?"

"It's not necessarily something he's doing, but . . . I don't know. There's something in his eyes that's different. He's becoming more,

I guess, aggressive. When we argue, we normally just throw insults at each other. Then he cries like a little girl."

"And tonight?" he prompted.

"Tonight, he was stomping around, flailing his arms, shouting. Real drama queen stuff. Like this is how real women behave, for God's sake," she said dramatically. Jack laughed to himself at the irony of her words. "As we argued, I followed him into the kitchen. He pulled out a knife. I thought he was going to slice a lemon and lime for his regular evening G&T, but then he started waving the knife around while he yelled at me. I told him to put it down so we could talk like normal adults. He came toward me with it so I ran. He laughed but he didn't chase me. I came up here to the sunroom on the roof and locked both of the doors on my way up."

"Both doors?"

"Mmm-hmm," she said through another drag of the cigarette, her breath audibly shaking over the phone. "The one here in the room, and the other at the foot of the stairs. I know it's weird, but that's how my *husband* wanted it when we remodeled. Anyway, if I hear him breaking through the downstairs door, at least I have some extra time to call for help . . . or 9-1-1, or whatever . . . before he gets through the glass door."

There was a long pause on her end.

Jack asked, "Do you want me to call the department and have a patrol car swing by to check on Franklin? You can't very well stay up there all night. If he's drinking—"

"No." She cut him off. "I'll wait until he leaves before coming down. I need to figure things out. Maybe I can get him into therapy. He'll be the ruination of this marriage."

"Are you sure he's leaving?"

"He goes out every night around midnight. I know his routine . . . tarts up, has a drink, then leaves."

Just then, the gate slid open. "Must be midnight," Jack said without looking at his dash clock. "I'll follow him and see where he goes."

Ginnie moved closer to the window facing the street. Jack assumed from that vantage point she could see into the inner courtyard. "He's in his Mercedes."

Given the Whitney-Cummings' wealth and stature, Jack assumed the Mercedes would be one of the luxury models. What pulled out was a sleek, black Roadster, and Franklin barely missed the still-opening gate as he pulled onto 27th and sped past Jack's Jeep.

"Thanks. I'll get back to you later. Take care of yourself and don't hesitate to call 9-1-1 for help if you need it."

"Go get that son of a bitch!"

Jack disconnected. Ginnie certainly had a mouth on her. It probably didn't help her cause when she argued with Franklin.

"All right, then," Jack said under his breath. Finally, some action. Still wearing his seatbelt, he tossed his phone onto the passenger's seat and started the Jeep. He switched on the low beams and swung around to follow the Roadster up 27th. He caught up with it crossing El Camino Del Mar and heading toward Golden Gate Park.

Keeping a safe distance, he continued up 27th to Fulton where the Roadster turned left and paralleled the park. Jack forced himself to not think about how Travers had used Leah's disappearance to stage bodies around the park, just to get under Jack's skin.

He kept his gaze on the Roadster as it sped alongside the Panhandle and continued east toward the Financial District.

Where the hell is Franklin going? He certainly wasn't just blowing off steam or he might have diverted into Golden Gate Park, or he could have taken a shorter drive by turning right from the driveway and heading to Lands End. No, he had to have a specific destination in mind.

At Divisadero, just before the Painted Ladies at the Alamo Square Park, the Roadster slowed then hooked right without signaling onto Divisadero Street, now heading south and into the Haight District.

Jack knew the road forked at Waller Street—straight to remain on Divisadero or bank left for Castro Street.

The pit of his stomach tightened when the Roadster veered left as they neared the Waller junction. Jack knew then where Franklin was going.

The Roadster slowed to a stop at the traffic lights on Market

Street. On the green, it crossed the junction but didn't pick up speed. Instead, the Roadster swerved left into a driveway just beyond the Castro Theatre. *The Majestic Lounge* in glowing neon lights illuminated the front of the building. The Roadster just missed a crowd of people on the sidewalk who parted like the Red Sea. Jack wasn't sure if these people were waiting to get in or just dancing on the sidewalk. Even through the Jeep's factory soundproofing, thumping music vibrated through the vehicle.

He hung back for a moment before pulling into the club's driveway, instantly recognizing what he'd thought was an alley where he'd found Pepper Mint, aka Bob Johnson.

By the time Jack made it into the lot, Franklin had backed into a handicap parking space—*asshole*—as if he was entitled to it. The Roadster stood out like the proverbial sore thumb in a parking lot full of economy and other budget vehicles. His Jeep probably stood out too, so he stayed in the shadows a moment longer while getting his bearings.

A small Toyota pulled out just then, so Jack headed toward it. He slowed to let Franklin stride past the Jeep. He seemed clueless to the fact he was being followed.

Jack wasn't sure what look Franklin was going for. While his seemingly tailored outfit mimicked his wife's classic style, his makeup had been applied too heavily, and his wig looked like he'd dragged it behind the Roadster on its way across town. Jack thought he knew then what happened to Baby Jane. And she'd obviously been drinking.

He watched Franklin disappear through the club's back door before reversing the Jeep into the open space. Shutting off the engine, he looked at the dashboard clock. 12:15a.m. He logged into the Majestic's online site and checked business hours—2a.m.

"Great," he groaned under his breath.

How was he going to get the photographs Ginnie paid him for if he couldn't get near Franklin?

He swallowed hard at the thought of going inside. Not that he had any hang-ups over homosexuality. More that he didn't want to draw attention to himself as the only straight guy in the place, or worse, draw Franklin's attention.

"Fuck it!"

Before extricating himself from the Jeep, he grabbed his phone off the passenger seat and his spare black leather jacket off the backseat—the department still had the jacket Leah had given him.

He shoved his arms into the jacket sleeves as he strode to the door, then switched on the phone's video app and slid it into his breast pocket. If he couldn't get photos, he'd at least get video, and hopefully some stills from that.

CHAPTER EIGHT

If he thought the music outside the club was loud, what greeted him as he entered felt like it was splitting his skull, and it grew louder the further into the building he walked. The base beats thumped hard in his chest and the high notes whirred in his head.

Lights from one side of the room bounced off shiny Christmas decorations with the beat of the music, which was anything but festive. Already, he felt his head starting to ache.

God, he was getting old. Ten . . . fifteen years ago, he would have loved nothing more than going clubbing and to concerts. A few beers and some great bumping tunes would get him dancing and flirting with women.

He had to put all that away when he met Leah. She had a quiet but playful personality; she didn't like the loud stuff. And when Zoë was born, they both learned to enjoy the peace and quiet when they could finally get her to sleep. And he'd got used to the dull drone of street noise in his place above Wong's. Maybe too used to it.

Jack needn't have worried about attracting attention in the Majestic. He found himself walking past what looked like a gang of gay bikers. If anything, he felt over-dressed for the party, as many of the men wore little more than a leather jacket and heavy biker boots. Matching skinny black leather thongs just barely concealed their religion.

One man wore leather pants and matching jacket, similar to his own riding leathers. A black bandana with traditional paisley designs was wrapped snuggly over his head. He quickly looked away when he noticed Jack was looking at him.

One man stood taller than the group around him, though not as tall as Jack himself. He stepped away from his man-harem and stopped Jack in his tracks. The man didn't disguise his obvious critique of what he probably considered fresh meat. He looked Jack up and down, his gaze lingering on Jack's crotch before casting him a look of approval. Jack felt his spine stiffen under the scrutiny.

This guy was every bit the cliché gay biker Jack had ever seen pictures of—a look inspired by Glenn Hughes from the Village People. A dark, penetrating gaze shot out from beneath a small leather *crush cap*. His dark hair was short-cut with long sideburns, and a thick horseshoe mustache framed his mouth. His open silver-studded black leather jacket revealed the kind of hairy chest Jack didn't think anyone had seen since the 1970s—the hair was thick and spread across his whole chest and abdomen.

Thick biker-style chains looped around his neck and torso in a sort of bondage getup. A similar chain looped from his belt to his back pocket where it was probably attached to his wallet.

A quick glance further down revealed the man wore a similar style black thong as his friends, but his was studded and worn under black leather chaps that were similarly studded like a halo around the man's junk.

Absolutely no advertising here, Jack sarcastically thought. An outfit like this was designed for one thing and one thing only. *Here's my cock; you know what to do.*

Leaning in close, the man gazed intently into Jack's eyes. "I'm *Rod*," he said just over the music, emphasizing his name so there was no misunderstanding the double meaning. His voice was deeper than Jack expected.

"Good to know," was all Jack said, trying to move around the man, but he was blocked again. It was only a moment of scrutiny between them, but Jack felt if he didn't keep moving, it might give Rod the impression he was interested in a hook-up. He was not. He gave the man an abrupt nod and pushed past him.

It took all of Jack's will not to punch the guy in the face when he felt a hand grasp his ass. "Goddamn nice ass," Rod said over

Jack's shoulder, deepening his voice. "What time does it open?"

With cautious purpose, Jack grabbed the man's wrist and spun it in a control hold, pulling Rod closer. Jack stared him in the eye for a moment then told him in no uncertain terms, "Sorry, *Rod*." Jack similarly emphasized the name. "It's closed for business." He pushed the man back against his friends and continued walking.

From behind, Rod shouted over the music, "If you change your mind, you know where to find me."

Chuckling under his breath, he said, "You'll be waiting, Princess."

Normally, Jack's height gave him a slight advantage over shorter people, but the ridiculously high heels worn by most of the club's patrons made him feel short, and in a way, a bit intimidated.

He needed to find Franklin but didn't see a way around the people in front of him. Going through them was the next best plan. "Pardon me, ladies," he said, motioning to a vague location past the group.

In unison, several heavily mascaraed gazes turned his way. "Well, of course, Sugar," one woman dressed in a dark blue evening gown said. The group made a narrow path between them, each giving him the once-over as he passed.

On the other side, Jack inhaled deeply through his nose, both clearing his sinuses from the onslaught of perfume and trying to calm his racing heart. He gazed back from the direction he'd come. The woman in blue gave a wink and blew him a kiss. The phrase *fish out of water* hit Jack hard.

He kept walking. The sooner he found Franklin, the sooner he could get him on video, and the sooner he could get the hell out of the place.

Jack didn't have anything against the lifestyles of these men. It just wasn't *his* lifestyle. He felt like an intruder, and somewhat of a voyeur, in what should be a private place for people with alternative lifestyles. He didn't belong here. That alone made him nervous.

Near the stage, Jack's attention was drawn to two women having an argument. He moved in that direction as he circled the club and realized one of them was Franklin. He missed the start of the conversation, but by the time he was within earshot, it was obvious Franklin was not happy.

Jack could hardly believe his eyes when he neared the argument. The woman Franklin argued with—Jack pegged her as around five foot seven or eight—was so beautiful, he couldn't believe she was a man. Even with her obvious Adam's apple, she looked like she could have stepped off the big screen of a classic '50s film. Her short platinum blonde hair, floor-length pink satin dress, matching pink elbow-length gloves, and diamonds around her neck and wrists made her look every bit of the Marilyn Monroe she emulated.

Even her voice shouted *I'm a woman* as he . . . she . . . chastised Franklin. "How many times do I have to tell you, Carol, you can't go backstage?"

"What do I have to do to get up there? I want to perform." Franklin was adamant. He didn't appear to be taking *no* for an answer.

Marilyn crossed her arms under her bountiful breasts and stood her ground. A crease formed between her otherwise stunning eyes. "I don't know how many times I have to tell you; you're not getting backstage. You are *not* going to perform here."

Franklin's height was emphasized when he leaned in, practically bending over Marilyn like a vulture, his face full of rage. He'd made little effort to change his voice from his manly one. "I don't deserve this. I'm as good as every other girl here. I deserve the right to compete as much as anyone else."

Marilyn stopped Franklin from pushing past with a hand on his chest. "I own this club, don't forget, and I decide who performs. I said no. I saw your audition, Carol. You're not good enough. The women performing here are some of the best around the world. You," she paused, giving Franklin the once-over, "are not. And besides, we're halfway through the competition and not allowing new entries."

"You *bitch*. Put me on the stage and let the audience decide if I should be in the competition or not."

Marilyn shook her pretty head. "It's not going to happen. Don't make this harder than it has to be."

When Franklin tried pushing past, Marilyn let out a shriek that was barely audible over the music and shouting people in the crowded room. Without thinking, Jack stepped in and pushed Franklin off her.

"You heard the lady. No means no."

Franklin spun on Jack, narrowing his . . . her . . . gaze.

Jack forced himself to remember that when in drag or dressing as a woman, the pronouns were *she* and *her*, and she wanted to be called by her female name.

"Go back to your *butch boys* and leave us *ladies* alone." Carol made it sound like it was the girls against the boys in the place.

Jack kept his gaze on Carol. It seemed to Jack's untrained eye that Carol was trying to look like his . . . her . . . wife but failing miserably.

Jack grunted with confusion. When a married man decided to dress as a woman, how was the wife addressed? His wife, her wife, *the* wife . . .

Without diverting his gaze, Jack asked Marilyn, "Would you like me to show this *lady* the door?"

Carol's gaze darted between Jack and Marilyn and back again.

"I think she can find her own way out. But make no mistake, Carol, I'm not changing my mind. Another outburst like this and I'll bar you from the Majestic, and not just for the competition."

Carol growled before throwing up her arms in frustration and stomped off. She looked every bit of a man who hadn't learned to walk in high heels as she moved. When Jack was sure Carol was no longer a threat, he turned back to Marilyn.

"You okay?"

Nodding, she said, "Thanks for your help. I don't know what I'm going to do with that girl."

"You could bar her, as you suggested. Problem solved."

Marilyn glanced toward the door then back at Jack. "I could, but there are so few places for people like us. Even in San Francisco. She's confused and hasn't found herself yet. She's a duck out of water who's easily frustrated when she doesn't get her way. She thinks her privilege will open doors that she hasn't earned yet."

Jack jolted at the word *privilege*. Did Marilyn know who Carol really was? "What do you mean by *privilege*? Do you know who she really is?"

Marilyn shook her head. "No, I don't know her outside of the club, but I've seen her car. Anyone who can afford a ride like that has to have money. Money equals privilege in this city."

He releasing a slow breath then asked, "What doors are you talking about?"

Marilyn gestured with her arms and hands as she spoke, "It's not really doors, so to speak, but being accepted in the community. One doesn't just put on a frock, slap on some makeup, throw on a wig and call themselves a woman. It doesn't happen overnight. It's a process. Like puberty. One has to learn how to be a woman— how to dress, how to wear makeup, how to comport oneself. It takes practice—trial and error—before getting it right. So right that it becomes second nature. She isn't there yet."

"I'm sorry to hear that." Sounded like Franklin was still evident in the Carol he tried being—the successful businessman with a reputation of not taking *no* for an answer.

"You're new here." It wasn't a question. "What brings you to the Majestic? Certainly not for the ambience."

Jack chuckled. "I was looking for someone." He bit his tongue the moment he said it.

Marilyn laughed. "Aren't we all." She took him by the elbow before he could step away. He needed to follow Franklin . . . Carol. *Damn it!* "Come with me."

"I probably should go," he said as she led him to the bar where several young men raced back and forth serving drinks—all of them in nothing more than black short-shorts and black shoes of some sort. Jack couldn't tell in the shadows along the floor. Immediately, one of them trotted over.

"Whatever this strapping young man is drinking is on me." She leaned in close to Jack, brushing her breasts against him. "Really, on *me*, if you're interested. I must reward my knight in shining armor." Jack felt himself blush but hoped the club's lighting didn't show it. She let out a sweet laugh. "Cat got your tongue?"

"Well . . . umm . . . You see—"

Marilyn put a long-nail-tipped finger to his lips. "Wait here. I'll be right back." To the bartender, "Anything he wants."

With that, Marilyn dashed away toward the stage, then disappeared through the backstage door she'd been protecting from Franklin.

"What'll you have?"

"An exit stage left," Jack muttered.

"Never heard of it. Tell me what's in it and I'll keep them coming."

Jack waved away his comment. Franklin was gone by now and there was no telling where he was going. Home, Jack hoped. He gazed in the direction Marilyn had disappeared just as the house lights went down.

A moment later, she appeared on stage and launched into her rendition of *Diamonds Are A Girl's Best Friend. Cliché*. She mouthed the words, but her act appeared to mimic the original Marilyn's. Her boytoys wore what seemed to be the club's uniform—tight black short-shorts—as they carried her across the stage.

"Never mind. You have any aged whiskey?"

The bartender nodded. "Jameson do?" Jack nodded. "Coming right up. Rocks or straight up?"

"Very much straight. Thanks."

CHAPTER NINE

Saturday

His head throbbed.

Jack tried lifting himself into an upright position on the sofa but collapsed back onto his pillow. His body felt heavy, his eyes like they had sand in them, and he had to piss. He still reeked of perfume and sweat from the packed club and longed for a shower.

It had been closing time when Jack finally extricated himself from the club last night. No. This morning. He'd had too many whiskeys and ended up calling for an Uber to bring him home.

"*Great!*" He groaned aloud. That meant he had to find a way back to get his Jeep. Maybe Ray would drive him over, though he didn't want to have to explain to his friend why he'd spent an evening in a gay club. He was sure rumors were already circulating around the department after last week. He'd made a point of not going there to save himself from the ribbing he knew he'd get, good-natured or otherwise.

He forced himself to sit up and checked the time on his phone, but it was dead.

"Fucking brilliant." He'd forgotten to put it on the charger when he got back.

As promised, Marilyn had returned to where Jack sat at the bar, and they'd ended up talking about the club, the drag race, and the upcoming New Year's Eve Extravaganza. It may have been idle chat as far as Marilyn was concerned, but to Jack, she unwittingly gave answers to some of his questions about Franklin.

Marilyn didn't know *who* Carol was but knew *what* she was. She also said that while she didn't know Carol's real identity, Marilyn admitted she looked familiar. It wasn't Jack's place to inform her.

He forced himself to his feet; he really needed that piss and a shower. As he moved toward the backroom, someone knocked on his door. "Shit!"

"Fuuuck me!" said the small, thin man who looked about twenty-five, if that. He stood on the landing, looking Jack up and down with appreciation written all over his expression.

A quick glance revealed the man was dressed in white sneakers and a pair of skintight blue jeans with a noticeable bulge, telling Jack the man dressed left. A red pullover sweater with a big white snowflake in the center of his chest and a matching knitted red beanie on his head completed his holiday attire. *Christmas and all the shit that goes with it.*

There was something about his features Jack couldn't place but he definitely looked . . . manicured . . . for the lack of a better word.

The cold morning air pimpled Jack's skin, forcing his attention to the fact that he only wore a pair of sweatpants that had been cut off above the knee. His lack of attire in the cool breeze increased his need of the toilet.

Ignoring his discomfort and grogginess, he asked, "Can I help you?" Even to him, his tone sounded annoyed. He was.

The man chuckled lightly. "You don't recognize me, do you?"

"Should I?" To Jack's surprise, the man softened his voice and sang a line from *Diamonds Are a Girl's Best Friend*. "Marilyn!"

"You gonna invite me in, or will we give your neighbors something to talk about?"

Jack stepped back. "Yeah, sorry. I'm not awake yet. You surprised me."

"I can see that," Marilyn said, stepping into the apartment and giving it the once-over. "Nice place."

"Ain't it just?" he said, closing the door. "Give me five minutes. Have a seat." He didn't wait for Marilyn to sit down before disappearing into the backroom where he threw himself into the shower and pissed down the drain as water sluiced over him, soaping up as he went. By the time his bladder was empty, he was rinsing off.

Inside five minutes he was dressed in his normal black jeans and T-shirt, had put on the coffee, and padded into the front room with his socks in hand.

"Sorry about that. Late night."

Marilyn chuckled. "I guess you're not a night owl."

"Not anymore." Jack dropped into the chair behind his desk and slid into his black socks. "How did you know where I live?" He couldn't see his boots from where he sat. He'd find them later.

"I finally recognized you last night while we were talking. After the altercation with Carol, I knew you looked familiar. Then it hit me. I don't watch much of the news these days or I'd slit my own wrists, but I watch enough to know you're on it quite a bit. Jack Slaughter. Fallen homicide detective. The PI who saved the city from a serial killer yet can't find the person who killed his own kid."

"Hey, don't go there." He hated the reminder that his investigatory prowess didn't seem to include solving his own family's case.

"Sorry. Just repeating what I've heard on the news."

Jack only grunted a response but still felt the crease between his eyes tighten. "I put on some coffee. Want some?" He rose and moved toward the backroom.

Marilyn waved him off. "No thanks. I don't need the caffeine, but you go ahead."

A moment later, Jack was back behind the desk, his steaming mug on the desk and his boots now on the floor before him. He slid his feet into them but didn't lace them up.

"What brings you across the city?"

The man rose from the sofa and re-sat himself in the chair in front of the desk. "I wonder how many people sat in this chair before me. Forlorn wives who think their husbands are cheating," he said dramatically. "Disgruntled husbands thinking their wives are cheating, a parent looking for dirt on the other in their battle for custody of their victimized children . . ."

"Too many of all of the above, as far as I'm concerned, but it pays the bills. What brings *you* to my chair?"

Marilyn crossed his legs and folded his fingers over his raised knee. "I want to hire you." Jack sat back in his chair, rested his elbows on the arms, and threaded his fingers together over his abdomen. "It's become obvious we need some added security around the club. There are a couple bouncers at the front door and one in back. I've got three circulating in the main room. Isaac is our head of security and monitors everything from his office."

"Do you need extra security because of Carol?" he prompted.

Marilyn shook his head. He sat forward, sliding his ankle onto his knee and leaned his elbows on the uplifted shin. "Look, I know it was you who tried saving Pepper in the driveway." Jack winced. "She isn't the only one who's died."

"You have my attention."

"Pepper was just the first one at the club. Five other girls have been found dead where they lived."

Jack sat up. "*Five.*" He pulled a legal pad from across the desk and found a pen in the debris. *Shit!* His phone was still dead. He should be recording this. "Tell me about them."

"The first thing you have to understand about most drag queens is that sometimes we can be quite over the top. We love the drama and theatrics of dressing flamboyantly. It's all about the performance. Not just our costumes and makeup, but our names too. Names can be funny, ironic, or downright offensive. You don't see that in the trans community. They just want to fit in, so they'll take normal names—like Sharon, Barbara . . . or Carol. Drag is about performance and audience reaction—however we get it. This is part of why the Majestic hosts the annual drag race. It gives the girls a chance to really show off."

"Are you saying Carol is trans? I thought she wanted to be a performer," Jack said.

Marilyn shook his head. "I don't think Carol knows what she wants yet."

"Go on. About these five girls . . ."

"Okay, so we have . . . had . . . a group of performers, all Indian,

Bollywood-style dancers who went by the name the Indian Spicy Girls. And in the last two months, they've all turned up dead." Jack waited for him to continue. The subject obviously disturbed him. It disturbed Jack too. A whole group . . . five people . . . all dead. It sounded too suspicious to be coincidence.

"Who was the first?"

Marilyn inhaled deeply, rubbing the back of his hand across his eyes as he tried maintaining his composure. Jack handed the box of tissues across the desk. "Sorry. I was close to one of them. Her death hit me the hardest."

"Let's start there. Who was she?"

"She went by Sinner Minge . . . you know . . . it sounds like cinnamon, the spice. Her real name was Sai Joshi. Man, could that girl move." A smile crept across his face before he looked directly into Jack's eyes. "Police say she took her own life by putting a gun in her mouth. It blew off the back of her head. She was the last person I'd ever think would commit suicide."

Marilyn's words hit close to home. Too close. In his grief, Jack only thought about finding out what had happened to his family before eating his own bullet. He never stopped to think about what would happen after—who found him and how he'd *look*.

He swallowed hard and forced himself to move on. "How do you know how she died in such detail?"

"I had to identify her. She didn't have any family in the States. It was the same with all the girls. They all came over from India. Homosexuality at the time had been illegal there. They'd all been disowned by their families and had nowhere else to go. In America, they could be who they wanted to be. Well, at least in some cities like San Francisco. They've been performing in the Majestic for a couple years now. They get . . . got . . . a great vibe going when they did the Bollywood thing. That style of dancing is infectious. Anyway, I identified them all as their emergency contact."

"Are you sure Sai wasn't suicidal?" Jack asked.

Marilyn shook his head. "Absolutely not. Suicide is a sin in the Hindu religion. You can take the girl out of India, but you can't take India out of the girl. Besides, she loved her life here. She was happy."

"Tell me about the others."

"Nutty Meg—"

"Nutmeg?" Jack asked.

Marilyn grinned. "You're getting it. Her real name was Sanjay Bajwa. They found her hanging in her closet. The official report was accidental autoerotic asphyxiation. You know, strangling yourself during masturbation. I know for a fact that she wasn't into that. Wasn't into any kind of kink. She didn't do this."

Jack scribbled notes on the legal pad, occasionally glancing down just to be sure he could read his chicken scratch. "What about the others?"

"Nigella's real name was Dinish Ranganathan. No camp name for her. She was called Nigella because her skin tone was so dark, she was nearly black. Nigella means *black seed*. Residents in her building found her on the pavement, several stories below her apartment. The official report said she jumped."

"You said the whole group was found dead?"

Marilyn nodded. "The last two were the most disturbing. Not that the whole thing hasn't been."

"What happened?"

Marilyn squirmed in his chair a moment, pulled off his cap to run thin fingers through what turned out to be curly blonde hair—dyed the same shade as his Marilyn character. "Suicide pact. That's what the cops are calling it. They were found in bed with their arms around each other. Both had been shot."

Jack sat back a moment, taking all this in. "I've heard of that, but in all my years on the force, I never came across anyone who's done it. I know it happens. I just haven't seen it."

"Well, the first thing you need to know is that Cumon Myface and Star Anus—cumin and star anise, or Ramesh Patel and Krish Naidu—weren't lovers. They were brothers—fraternal twins. They lived totally separate lives. Even though they were twins and danced together, they barely tolerated each other outside of work."

"If they were twins, why did they have different surnames?"

"Fraternal twins may be born at the same time, but they have completely unique characteristics. They didn't even have that traditional twins bond. They were their own person, and going by different surnames helped them live separate lives outside their dance group. Unless you knew them, you wouldn't know they were related."

Jack scrawled Marilyn's comments and observations before tossing down the pen. He reached for his coffee, then realized he hadn't touched it and it had gone cold. He put it aside, his gut twisting. He hated thinking so many people were committing suicide, but he also hoped the city didn't have another serial killer on its hands.

"You said this all happened over the last two months?" Marilyn nodded. "Have detectives said how they're handling this?"

Shaking his head, he said, "No. I was only called in to identify the bodies. I'm not family, only the emergency contact . . . you know the drill. Frankly, I've never been questioned, so I don't even know if they're investigating. I mean, they're calling them all suicides, so what's to investigate, right?"

He had a point. "I'm going to make some inquiries and see what's going on. I'll mention what you said to my former LT . . . lieutenant . . . to see if he can share anything with me."

"Thanks. I appreciate it." After a moment, he added, "A couple days ago, one of our other performers was found dead in her apartment over in the Haight. She went by Minger Rogers—real name Michael Smith."

Jack's head shot up. Had that been the suicide Ray had been investigating when they'd met up in the Haight?

Marilyn noticeably swallowed hard. "That makes seven, if my math is right . . . including Pepper Mint. All drag performers at my club. And the cops don't seem to want to do anything about it because they're calling all the deaths suicides."

"I know for a fact that Bob Johnson's death . . . Pepper Mint . . . is being treated as a homicide. She was alive when I found her. She died before help arrived, but it was definitely murder. I saw the killer running away from the scene. Apparently across your parking lot. They didn't escape by car—"

"Yeah, there's a chain link fence back there. It's added security for the houses behind us, but I can't tell you how many times I've had it repaired. There's a service alley behind the theater next door and people love using it as a shortcut across the block to 17th Street."

Jack made a note to check the club's boundary and ask the neighbors if they'd seen anything that night. If he was lucky, maybe one of them had security cameras.

"Has anyone in the club been talking about the deaths?"

Marilyn shook his head with a, "Nuh-uh. Nothing beyond someone being shot on the premises, but chatter has died down and it's all about the competition again."

Jack made a few more notes on his pad then pushed it away again. "So, it's because of these deaths you're looking to beef up your security in the club?" Marilyn nodded. "If your friends are dying at home, homicide or suicide, how will beefing up your security help?"

"I figure whoever's doing it—and I do believe they've all been murdered—they're meeting the girls in the club. Doesn't matter what type of bar it is, gay or straight, people go there looking for hook-ups."

"Has anyone new been hanging around your club lately?" Jack asked.

"Not really, but how can I tell? I mean, people are coming from all over the world for the competition, like British Betty from London—Graham Stafford, Bunny MacTaversnatch from Australia—Tyler Dean . . . I know most of my patrons, even the out-of-towners, because they come every year for the drag race. You're really the only person who's been in recently who I didn't know. But," he added, "I'm glad I do now. Especially now that I've seen you practically naked." Marilyn bit his lower lip and gave Jack the once over before winking. "Oh, come on. I'm just flirting. I know you're as straight as the proverbial arrow."

"I might be straight, but I have nothing against your lifestyle."

"*Puhleeze!* Would I be here if I thought you did? Come on. I knew you were straight the moment you stepped between Carol and me. We had a nice chat last night, you and I. We need more people like you who accept us as we are. The world would be a more peaceful place."

"Take me down off your pedestal. I'm like you—I just want everyone to get along. And to stop killing each other."

"Right with you there. So, will you work for me?" Marilyn wiggled his eyebrows in Jack's direction. "Flirting!" he said with a snicker.

Jack ignored the gesture and turned to extract a contract from his file drawer. He filled in a few things, added his fee to the top, then pushed it in Marilyn's direction. "I don't work for free."

The man grabbed a pen off the desk and signed the contract without reading it. "I don't care what you charge. I just want my friends to stop dying." He looked directly into Jack's eyes and added, "And I don't want to be next." When Jack nodded that he agreed, Marilyn asked. "When can you start?"

"As soon as your check clears."

To his surprise, Marilyn stood up and dug into his front left jeans pocket, then pulled out a wad of cash and tossed it on the desk. The bulge instantly disappeared. "Will a grand do to get you started tonight? When you get to the club, I'll give you the balance."

Jack gathered up the money into a stack then slid it into the desk's locking drawer. "Yeah, that'll do it. And just to be clear, I'm not on your staff. I have my own way of working security and set my own hours; I don't just hang out at the door or stand in corners watching people. I'll probably be in and out of the club following leads. And I may also bring a partner with me or put him in the club when I can't be there. You good with that?"

"Right as rain."

"And it'll help if you reserve a space in your lot for my vehicle. I don't want to waste time or risk lives by having to hoof it down the street."

"Roger that. That's what cops say, right? Roger?"

With a snort, Jack said, "I'm not a cop anymore. I'm good with okie dokie."

"Your Jeep is still at the club. Come on. I'll give you a ride back. I'm sure you want to pick it up."

That solved that—no need to get Ray involved in this. "Thanks. Give me a minute." Jack laced up his boots, grabbed his jacket, and went for his phone. Damn it! He should have put it on the charger the minute he realized it was dead. He did that now before they left.

At the door, Marilyn asked, "Do you think you can wear your cop uniform in the club? The ladies will love it."

"Uhh, that's gonna be a hard no to that one, Marilyn."

He laughed. "By the by, when I'm in my street clothes, you can call me Chad. Chad Lucas."

"Roger that."

CHAPTER TEN

The Majestic was already slammed by the time Jack arrived at 9p.m.

He'd upped his game for his time in the club, choosing a pair of black dress slacks with comfortable matching shoes. He left his black button-down shirt open at the collar—this was not a suit-and-tie kind of place. He remembered how warm the club had been last night, so he left his jacket in the car. He switched on the Samsung's video and slid it into the shirt's breast pocket.

One of the features he appreciated the most with this phone brand was the long video record time . . . as long as it was on a lower resolution and the memory wasn't cluttered with too many unnecessary apps and photos. It wasn't. After each case, he cleared all the data onto discs that he kept with the hard copy files in his office cabinets, and he backed up the video and scanned documents to the cloud. Better to be safe than sorry when you lived above a greasy spoon.

Normally, he'd bring his field notebook, but it was too bulky to keep in his pocket, and in a place like this, he'd garner too much attention. Tonight, he'd keep as low a profile as possible and rely on the video and his memory.

As he approached the back door, Jack noticed Rod standing at the edge of the lot between the theater's wall and what looked like an old Toyota. The man was leaning back against the car, hands on the fender for balance and his head thrown back. Jack could just make out a bobbing movement at fender level and tried not being shocked at what he was seeing. He recognized the black paisley bandana covering the head of the person servicing Rod.

Suddenly, Rod stood up straight, pushed his friend away and gazed directly in Jack's direction. He'd been seen. *Great, and now Rod has a hard-on.* He kept walking.

At the door, the bouncer waved him through with a nod. He assumed Chad had informed his staff about the new security guy.

If it were possible, the club seemed to have packed in twice as many people than last night, and nearly everyone was in drag. The competition was in full swing. The current act took their bows as another contestant skipped onto the stage to perform her comedy act. Since she wore what looked like British flags, Jack guessed this was British Betty, aka Graham Stafford. She quickly got the crowd laughing with a few dirty jokes about Brexit—Britain's exit from the European Union.

Last night when they'd talked over too many Jamesons, Chad had told him Fridays were competition nights. Three acts were chosen who then returned the following night, Saturday, and competed to be that week's winner. The night he'd found Pepper Mint bleeding out in the driveway had been the first week of the competition. After tonight, there would be two more weekends of competition, making four semi-finalists who would compete on Christmas Eve night for Drag Queen of the Year. The winner would then officiate at the club's New Year's Eve Extravaganza, and also perform the official countdown to midnight.

Moving around the club, Jack kept his eyes open for signs of Franklin in his Carol guise, but he either hadn't arrived yet—Jack hadn't seen his Roadster in the lot, but that didn't mean he hadn't parked down the road—or he wasn't coming.

It wasn't long before Jack started drawing gazes, ranging from curious to appreciative, but everyone appeared to be enjoying themselves. Thankfully, no one tried hitting on him. He had a job to do and dealing with another Rod was a distraction he didn't have time for. If Chad had been right, that the killer was staking out his victims in the club, Jack needed to be on his toes. Six murders were six too many. Seven if Pepper Mint's murder was tied in with the others, and he thought it was.

He spotted Marilyn near the end of the bar and moved in her direction.

"Jack!" she called over the raucous laughter. She took him by the shoulders and stood on her toes, then planted a kiss on each of his cheeks. This was all a new learning experience for Jack; he didn't know how to react, so he didn't. He waited for Marilyn to continue. "I'm glad you made it. Grab a drink and we'll head into my office for . . . you know." Leaning in close again, she added with a whisper beside his ear, "For the rest of your money."

"We can settle later. I'd like you to show me around the building. I need to know what's behind or through every door, and I'll need a list of the names of everyone who works here and their job function."

"Is that really necessary? I mean, whoever is doing this will be in the club."

"You don't know that for certain. What if it's one of your performers eliminating competition, or someone on your staff with a grudge? And if the backrooms are easily accessible to anyone or if it's someone on your staff or a contestant, the suspect pool just got a lot bigger. Literally, the killer could be anyone in the building, or even hanging around outside," he added.

Marilyn considered what he said for a moment, then agreed. "Whatever you say. I trust you."

Jack glanced around. "The crowd looks like they're having a great time."

"Lots of liquor helps. Speaking of . . . what are you drinking?" She spun around and motioned for a bartender.

Waving away the offer, Jack said, "Thanks, but I don't drink on the job."

Marilyn arched a perfectly drawn-on brow. "Club soda, Coke, Virgin Mary . . . We don't just serve booze, ya know."

Jack chuckled. "A Diet Coke would be great."

Marilyn told the bartender to bring a double Diet Coke, then turned and looked Jack up and down. "I wouldn't have pegged you for diet anything." She flicked a long-nailed finger down his shirt buttons and added, "You're bursting out in all the right places."

Jack took Marilyn's wrist and moved it away. "Do I need to set some boundaries?"

She flashed him a disappointed grin. "Relax. I'm just helping you break your gay cherry. You look all uptight and nervous in a room full of queens."

Jack chuffed, then took a long swig of his Diet Coke when it arrived, draining half the glass. "Gay cherry, eh?"

"Sure. There's a first time for everything. Even for a straight guy hanging out in a gay bar."

"I'm not hanging out," Jack reminded her. "I'm working."

"Yeah, well . . . semantics." She sighed as they moved away from the bar. "So, tell me, what do you want to know? About the show, or the club, the lifestyle . . ."

Jack saw movement from the corner of his eye. The figure only stood out because he wasn't in drag. He downed the last of his Diet Coke, set the glass on the bar then followed Marilyn through the crowd to the backstage door. "All of it, but first tell me about this guy, Rod." He nodded in Rod's direction. Back from his liaison, he'd moved into the heart of the club with a keen eye on Jack.

Marilyn quickly glanced at the group and back. "Do I need to speak with him?"

"I can take care of myself, but I want to know what his game is. Last night, he let me know in no uncertain terms that he was available and didn't seem to want to take *no* for an answer. Is he going to be a problem? A heads up on *any* problem patrons will help make my job here easier." Jack tried not letting Rod know he was in the corner of his eye. If the guy started walking this way, he wanted to be prepared. That included getting him on video.

"Rod's like the popular girl in high school, only he's not a girl, and he's not that popular. But he *is* the center of his little clique, and all of his cling-ons want to be his bestie. Of course, he revels in the attention, but they don't give him what he needs. Apparently, you do if he's hassling you."

"Not hassling me, per se, but he was persistent to the point of grabbing my ass not two minutes after I walked through the door. And he's had his eye on me from the moment I walked in tonight."

"Do you want me to bar him until after the extravaganza?" Marilyn offered.

Jack shook his head. "I don't think that'll be necessary. Until this is over, everyone's a suspect. If he's involved, I'll need him here where I can keep an eye on him. If he *is* involved in this, barring him will only piss him off."

In his peripheral vision, he saw Rod weave through the crowd in their direction, so Jack opened the door for Marilyn then followed her through and firmly closed it behind them.

Backstage was as lively as the club, with performers rushing back and forth, shouting to their assistants as they prepared for their performance or practiced their acts. As Chad had told him earlier in the day, drag was all about performance.

In the first large room, if it was shocking seeing men dressed as women, it was more startling seeing some of the men who'd just arrived starting to remove their street clothes, and those men in the process of *the change*. Padded breasts and asses, accentuated hips, and corsets to draw in the waist all gave a male physique a more feminine form. Jack didn't want to look, but when he saw one performer manipulating his crotch into a tight-fitting body suit, Jack was curious where the guy put his junk, because the resultant disappearing act was surprising.

"Lots of tucking, my dear," Marilyn said with a grin.

Jack gazed away quickly. "What?"

"The only way men can pull off looking like women is hiding their penises." She bobbed her head toward the man Jack had been looking at . . . or perhaps he'd been staring. "It's all tucked back. The balls get squeezed up into an open space in the pelvis where the vagina would be, then the dick is pulled back on top. Spandex undergarments hold it all in place. Easy."

Jack glanced back at the man who was now doing his makeup. From the side, he was as flat as any woman Jack had ever seen. "Sounds painful."

"Not if you do it right. Try it when you get home."

"Thanks, but no thanks." His balls ached just thinking about it.

As Marilyn turned away, Jack was sure she was trying not to laugh at him.

He followed her through the building, drawing a mental map as they moved. Outside of the immediate backstage area and common areas, there were a couple other large dressing rooms similar to the one they'd just left, various storage rooms for props, overstock beverages and bar snacks, a plush green room for special guests, private bathrooms for staff and performers, and even a small kitchen. And of course, Marilyn's office with its own private bathroom.

In the last two rooms she showed him, one contained the usual electronics and computers that kept the lights on and music going throughout the building. Another was strictly for security—a small room that contained a bank of monitors along one wall that showed the interior and exterior of the building from several angles.

The moment Jack and Marilyn entered, a man dressed in jeans and a dark sweatshirt turned to see who'd interrupted him. He rose when he saw Marilyn, giving her a nod.

"This is our head of security, Isaac. He monitors all the comings and goings in the building through this system. Isaac, this is Jack. I've hired him as special security. He'll be reporting directly to me."

Isaac nodded his understanding and put out his beefy hand to Jack. "Let me know if you need anything." Isaac's voice was as deep as the color of his skin.

"Thanks." Jack looked at each monitor to see exactly what parts of the building were being observed. "You record all this?"

"Yeah," Isaac said, waving to the bank of machines on an adjacent wall. "These computers are dedicated to the security of the building and set up to record each camera independently. That way, if—"

"If one goes down, they don't all go down," Jack finished.

"You got it."

"How long do you keep the recordings?"

"It's all digital and we back up to the cloud on an hourly basis, so indefinitely."

"Thanks, Isaac." Isaac returned to his seat when Jack motioned to Marilyn that he was ready to leave. In the hall, once the door was closed, he asked, "Did the police get a warrant for any of your video?"

Marilyn shook her head. "No. Well, just the one for last week after Pepper was killed, but not the others. Since they're considered suicides, I don't think they even thought about our security videos. Why do you ask?"

"If the same person killed all of the girls, and you think that person is scoping out their prey in the club, your security cameras might have picked up something . . . or someone . . . unusual."

Marilyn gasped. "Sweet fucking Jesus," she said in her male voice. She cleared her throat, then Marilyn came through again. "What do we do?"

"Is there a way for you to get me copies of the video from, let's say, a week before Sai was killed and right up through last night?" If Rod was involved, Jack wanted to know. He seemed annoyingly persistent once he had his eye on someone, and as his group was the only one not in drag, maybe he had some grudge he felt needed satisfying. Or maybe he somehow felt left out because of the competition. The club operated as a gay club, but according to Marilyn, this was the time of year it was dedicated to drag, but everyone was still welcome.

"S-sure."

"Can you get it without alerting Isaac? The fewer people who know why I'm really here, the better. Can you do that?"

"Yeah. I can access our cloud from home. I'll get it copied and bring it over as soon as possible. Now, if you don't mind, the judging is about to begin. I need to fix myself up and get my tushie on stage."

CHAPTER ELEVEN

Sunday

Just because the Majestic closed at 2a.m. didn't mean he was able to leave then. It had been after 3:30a.m. before Jack was in his Jeep and driving back to his shitty apartment.

He'd stayed until everyone had cleared out of the place, and because he wanted to grab some photos of Franklin . . . Carol . . . exiting the building. She'd arrived just before midnight and spent most of the night at the bar and glaring at Marilyn. But she'd kept her distance. When she'd finally left, Jack noticed she hadn't left alone, but with a young man in street clothes who Jack didn't remember seeing before in the club. He'd have to ask Ginnie if she thought Franklin was sleeping around.

By the time Jack closed his apartment door, it was 3:54, and less than thirty seconds later, he was asleep before his body landed on the sofa.

It wasn't until the urgent need to piss woke him from a dead sleep that he realized three things: one) it was past noon, two) he was still fully dressed, including his jacket and boots, and three) he was getting too old for this shit.

Fortunately, his client's husband seemed to frequent the Majestic, so Jack could kill two birds with one stone—get the photos Ginnie needed while performing the job Chad hired him to do. However, it was blatantly clear to Jack he was no longer a night owl. The last couple nights had been hard on him, and he'd be back at it again tonight.

After showering and changing, he headed to his desk to

download last night's video and work on both case files.

Three hours later, he was so deep in concentration, going over club video and extracting still images of Franklin as Carol, that he jumped when the phone rang.

"'Lo," he grumbled into the phone.

"I take it you haven't eaten today." Ray chuckled down the line.

Jack put the phone on speaker then leaned back in his chair and stretched. He swiveled around to face the window and let the sun warm him. "What makes you say that?"

"You sound grumpy."

"Tired. Late start is all. What's up, brother?" Even to him, his reply sounded stilted.

"You still coming over to watch the game? It's nearly four and you said you'd be here at three. So . . ."

Jack spun back to the desk and checked the time on his computer screen. "Shit! I'm sorry. I picked up a new case, and a new security gig. I didn't get back until nearly four this morning."

"And?"

"And I've been working on case files and lost track of time."

"And?"

"And what?"

"And when are you getting your ass over here? The game is going to start soon. Maria has already made her famous nachos, salsa, and guacamole."

Jack threw back his head against the seat and squeezed his eyes shut. Maria Navarro was a damn fine cook.

"Of course, if you're going to be a no-show, I guess it means more for me, eh?"

"Like that's stopped you in the past." Jack didn't give Ray the chance to respond and said, "Give me twenty."

Streetlights appeared to chase him across the city as they seemingly popped on when he passed them. By the time he maneuvered the Jeep into a space directly across from Casa Navarro, the sun was just touching the horizon and casting the city in a dusky golden glow. The curtains in neighboring houses had been drawn across windows, the interior lights just visible where they didn't fully meet.

Jack grabbed the paper bag off the passenger seat, exited the car, then locked the doors with a click of the remote over his shoulder as he crossed the street.

Ray and Maria's house was located in the city's Excelsior District.

As with the rest of the city, the Excelsior District has its own unique history. At the southeastern edge of the city limits and practically in Daly City, the land had been registered with the city in 1869 as the Excelsior Homestead, part of *Rancho Rincón de las Salinas y Potrero Viejo*—Ranch at the Corner of the Salty Marsh and the Old Pasture—and had been part of the Mexican Land Grants of the 18th and 19th centuries.

After the 1906 earthquake, then owner, Emmanuel Lewis, had built two hundred homes for the city's newly homeless. A similar task at the same time was being carried out in the Sunset District where Jack and his family had lived—the same house was still sitting unoccupied.

Lewis' daughter, Jeanette, had her hand in naming the streets— north-south, streets were named for capital cities, and east-west, avenues were named for countries. Casa Navarro sat on the hillcrest on Dublin Street near Russia Avenue.

Casa Navarro was a relatively modern construction though, dating back to the '50s, and was one of the few houses on the street with a double garage. Ray parked his old red Silverado pick- up truck in the driveway so he could leave at a moment's notice if he was called into the station early or for emergencies—not that it fit in the garage—so Maria's car was the only one using the double space. When Jack mentioned he was going to rent a storage space, Ray had insisted he store his Jeep in the second bay rather than paying the extortionate prices traditional auto storage yards charged.

The missing Silvarado made Jack worry that Maria had gone into labor, even though it was still too early for the baby's arrival. He stepped under the nest of bougainvillea vines framing one side and the top of the door, devoid of flowers this time of year, and knocked. He hoped everything was okay.

"Jack!" Maria exclaimed when she saw him on her doorstep. Her extended belly looked very ripe, but otherwise she appeared fine. Relief shot through him.

He met her halfway for a hug and kissed her cheek.

"Come in, come in. Ray will be back soon." She pulled him inside by the hand and guided him into the kitchen. "He ran to the store for me."

Jack set the paper bag on the counter and extricated a small potted plant, a net of ripe avocados, and a six pack of Pacifico and set them on the counter.

"A little something for your collection," Jack said, handing Maria his gift. With as many houseplants as Maria had, he wasn't sure where she'd put this one, but he never arrived without a little special something for her as a way to say thanks for all the work she put into the Thursday dinners and the occasional special event gathering, even if it was just a Sunday ball game. "There isn't a label on it but the flowers reminded me of pink chilies."

"*Schlumbergera Bridgesii*—Christmas Cactus. I've always wanted one of these. Thank you, Jack." She kissed her fingertips and touched his cheek before moving to put the plant on top of the fridge and out of direct sunlight.

Jack hooked the net of avocados on a finger. "My contribution to the guacamole. Where do you want them?"

"I'll take them." Taking them and the beer in hand, she navigated the kitchen like a dirigible as she moved her rotund body methodically around the space. She set the avocados on the drainboard and put the beer in the fridge. Before closing the door, she took out two bowls and set them on the counter beside a large empty bowl. She removed the plastic lids then dropped a small spoon into each. "You're always so thoughtful, but you know, you really don't need to bring anything. You're family."

"All right. I'll stop then."

"Don't you dare! Especially with the plants."

"I'm sorry I couldn't get here sooner."

Waving his comment away, she said, "Ray told me you picked up two new jobs this week. That's good, right?"

"If by good you mean lucrative, then yes. I could really do without the long nights though. That's part of why I'm late. The hours are kicking my—" Jack stopped short. "My backside."

"I'm not a tender flower. You can say *ass*, Jack."

"Sounds like you're calling me a jackass." She glanced over with *the look* on her face. He could interpret it as he wanted.

Jack watched Maria retrieve a grease-spotted paper bag from on top of the fridge and take it over to the empty bowl. Instead of emptying the bag he knew contained her homemade tortilla chips into the larger bowl, she left it on the counter and turned to face him. Worry now filled her expression.

"Are you okay, Jack?"

"Sure, why?" He tried keeping a smile on his face.

"You look tired."

Jack crossed his arms in front of him. Was he putting up his defenses? "Like I said, I could do without the late nights, but I'm fine." *Please turn around and put the chips in the bowl. Do anything, but please don't press this.*

"Ray told me what happened the other night. I have to admit, I'm worried about you."

"I'm fine, really. There's no need to worry," he tried assuring her, but her worried look remained.

Maria rubbed her belly for a moment then looked up at him again. "The baby is kicking. Do you want to feel?"

He didn't. Not really. "Sure." He moved to stand beside her and let her guide his hand. His large palm nearly covered the side of her extended belly. He felt the baby kick the moment he touched her. Then another. He pressed his palm against the spot, his legs nearly collapsing from the memories suddenly flooding his mind, of Leah pregnant with Zoë and the hours he'd spent feeling his daughter growing in the womb. From the memories of the day she was born and the absolute joy of holding her in his arms for the first time. And the few short years of seeing her growing every day and learning and laughing.

He tried snatching away his hand when the vision of his daughter's lifeless body punched him in the heart, but Maria held him fast. He shot his gaze up and met hers, finding it full of steely determination.

"I know this time of year is hard for you. Look at me," she said, forcing his gaze back on hers when looked away. "I can't possibly know what you're going through, but I think I understand. I must tell you. I'm worried. Sometimes it feels like . . . like you're pulling away from us."

"I'm not—"

"Let me finish. We don't see you as much these days. Ray said he's tried calling you but you don't pick up. He's gone by your place and you're not there. You've started missing dinner nights. And tonight, he said you forgot to come over. This isn't like you, Jack. The two of you are practically joined at the hip. Even after all this time since you left the force. But these days— We need you, Jack."

His heart pounded hard as he blinked back emotion. He didn't want Maria seeing him cry. "I'm here." Did his voice sound as weak to Maria as it did to him?

"Jack, listen to me. We need you. We all do." She squeezed the hand he still held on her belly. "I know you still grieve for your family, but don't let it take over your life. You *can* have a normal life and still find whoever did those horrible things. It's okay to do both." She put her free hand against his face and used her thumb to smooth away the moisture now on his cheek. "We're here for you, Jack. Both of us. If you can't talk to Ray, talk to me. I loved Leah. She was like my sister, so it's been hard for me too. Ray and I knew we would have a family one day, and we wanted Zoë to be a big sister to our children. I meant what I said. We are family. Your loss is also ours. We should be able to turn to each other whenever we're in need. I want you to remember that."

He nodded. "I know. I appreciate it, but—"

"No buts, Jack. I know you talk with Father Nick. I just want you to remember you still have *family* to turn to."

Jack gazed at the tiny pregnant woman before him. Her face

was so full of sincerity that it took his breath away. He understood and believed everything she said. Had he been pulling away from the Navarros? He made a point of hiding his darkest thoughts from his friends. Hell, he didn't even tell Father Nick about the darkness, about the black dog and the Parabellum round with his name on it. No one needed to know that shit. Especially Maria.

"I know, Maria, and I appreciate it. But really, I'm fine." He slipped his hand out from under hers and bent to gently hug her. After a long moment, he leaned back and gazed at her again. He palmed her cheeks and leant in to place a kiss on her forehead. "I love you for caring."

Maria's smile was genuine. The tension on her face softened. "Don't let Ray hear you talking like that to me." They laughed lightly.

"Too late. Why do you love my wife?" Jack and Maria spun toward Ray. He stood at the kitchen door with a large reusable shopping tote slung over his shoulder.

Jack stepped aside to reveal the bowls filled with guacamole and salsa and bag of tortilla chips on the counter.

"Ah! Say no more."

Maria discreetly wiped the tears from her eyes and reached for the tote. "Put the chips in the bowl, *mi amor*, while I put these things away." After shooing away her husband, she pulled the items from the tote—bananas, pickles, chocolate ice cream, two six-packs of Pacifico beer, and a net of limes. She put the beer in the fridge beside the six-pack Jack had brought, and everything else onto the cutting board. She scooped some of the ice cream into a bowl and topped it with sliced banana and pickles. After slicing some limes, she put the rest beside the net of avocados. Moving past the men, she said, "I'll put the enchiladas in the oven in a little bit." Jack didn't miss the look she gave him before disappearing down the hall with her bowl and spoon.

Ray said, "Her crazy cravings are still sending me to the store at all hours. I thought this would be over already," he said, putting the ice cream tub in the freezer.

Jack chuckled. "Yeah, no—"

Ray's face screwed up when he saw the plant on top of the fridge and cast Jack a quick glance, but he didn't say anything as he reached in and extracted two bottles of Pacifico, popped them open then stuffed sliced lime down the bottle neck. Grabbing the chips in one hand and both bottles in the other, he motioned toward the living room.

By the time on the wall clock, the pre-game stuff should be over by now and the first quarter started. Jack stuffed a roll of paper towels under his arm and took the bowls of salsa and guacamole into the living room. Ray shoved over plants on the coffee table to make room for the bowls and beers before they both made themselves comfortable to watch the game.

"We need to talk," Jack said as the half time show began. He didn't bother looking to see who was performing, but he couldn't miss the smell of Maria's cooking filtering in from the kitchen. "I need help with something."

After a short pause, Ray said, "You always do this."

"Do what?"

"Every time you get a new job, you come to me for case files. If you're going to work cases that need department intel, you need to get your ass back in the office and get it yourself. Legally!" This wasn't Ray's first dig at him, and Jack knew it wouldn't be the last. Until his friend actually followed through with his refusal to help him, there was no reason not to maintain the status quo. "You hear me, Jack?" Ray spun to face him. "I'm not fooling around. I got a kid on the way and can't afford to get kicked off the force for supplying you with records. Or worse, get knocked down to . . . a desk job." He noticeably shivered.

Jack tried stifling a laugh as he asked, "Are you done whining yet? Even though you're a hard ass, Haniford loves you, so you ain't going anywhere. And I don't want you to *give* me the files." He paused, then innocently added, "I just need you to look at them and tell me what's in them."

"Same damn thing."

"Same but different," Jack offered.

Ray grunted. "I thought you were hired to follow that socialite's husband."

"It's become more—"

"Complicated. Yeah, yeah. Story of your life, *amigo*. And it always inevitably involves me."

"You're just jealous I can get away with shit you can't. And somewhere in the back of your mind," Jack poked his friend in the side of the head just above his ear, "you get some perverted satisfaction knowing you're involved, yet at the same time, you have total deniability because you're not actually the one skirting the law."

Ray smacked his hand away. "The hell, you say!"

"And . . . I think it involves your suicide in the Haight."

That shut Ray up for a long moment. "I'm listening," Ray said, casual interest now pouring from the tone of his voice.

"Huh! See? Secretly, you love it."

Ray huffed. "If I'm directly involved, it's a different story. Anything I can learn to help me solve a case . . . you know the score."

"Yeah, well I'm pretty sure this one is already closed, but it needs to be reopened. Along with a handful of others."

"Go on."

"Your victim's name is Michael Smith. Lived alone in the Haight. If you're as good a detective as I know you are, you will have seen the costumes in his closet, and a *lot* of makeup and wigs—"

"How'd you know?" Ray cut in. "We're still trying to locate the next of kin before releasing any information to the public."

Jack nodded. "Mm-hmm. It was deemed a suicide by shooting. Through the mouth, right? And no suicide note. Stop me when I'm getting cold."

"You're psycho or something."

"I think you mean psychic."

"No, man, you're psycho, but go on."

Without naming his client, Jack filled in Ray about following Franklin to the Majestic, what he'd learned from the club's owner about the first five victims, and that he thought the victim he'd found in the club's driveway three weeks ago was tied into a larger case that also now involved Ray's suicide victim because he also was a performer at the Majestic.

"Fuuuck me! If they weren't suicides, that would make . . ." he counted on his fingers.

"Seven, Ray. The five girls in the dance group, my homicide in the club's driveway, and your suicide in the Haight."

"Do you think there's another serial killer in the city who's targeting the club for some reason?" Ray asked.

Jack shook his head. "As much as I hate to say it, I think so. That, or gay hate crimes. If they're focused on the club, it may be because of the competition."

"Where do we go from here?"

"We?" Once partners, always partners, whether or not Jack was on the force. It made him all warm and fuzzy inside. "I'm going to see Cutter after the game. You can come along if you want."

"Whatever plans you two are hatching can wait," Maria said as she passed the living room. "Put the game on pause and come eat."

CHAPTER TWELVE

The city's Medical Examiner's office had moved from its longtime location behind the Hall of Justice building on Bryant Street to its new, dedicated, state of the art two-story facility on Newhall Street at India Basin in the Hunter's Point District.

Jack and Ray passed the city's latest sculpture called the *Alma* as they approached the public entrance.

Designed by renowned artist Richard Deutsch, the stainless-steel sails celebrated India Basin's rich boat-building past, having been an active harbor and shipyard in the 19th century. The Alma, a scow schooner, had been built by Fred Siemer in 1891 and named for his daughter. It was the last ever built in the basin and was the last one of its kind in all of America that was still on the water. Remarkably, the Alma had been purchased by the city from a private owner and restored in 1964, and ultimately named a National Historic Landmark in 1988 and was now moored off Hyde Street Pier as part of the Maritime National Historic Park.

In the smartly decorated lobby, Ray showed his badge at Reception and they were escorted through the building. They passed several offices down the long hallway before being led through large double doors and into the inner workings of the facility. Jack made a mental note to see if he could get access through the back of the building which was now protected by a high chain link fence with a large remotely activated sliding gate.

When they were led through the doors of the autopsy suite, Jon Cutter was just pulling a sheet over a decedent. After snapping off his soiled rubber gloves, Cutter met Jack and Ray with an extended hand.

"What brings both of you down here at this hour? I'd have thought you'd be home watching the game."

"Been there, done that," Jack said. "Best enchiladas in the city."

"Sorry I couldn't be there. I've been cooped up here all afternoon. How'd the Niners do?"

"Ray owes me twenty bucks."

Gazing at Ray, Cutter said, "Tough luck. Always bet on the home team."

"Yeah, well," Ray said. "The home team hasn't done very well until this season."

Cutter chuckled. "What can I do for you? If you're here together, it either means you've gone back to the job, Jack, or Ray's working on a case you've stumbled into again." He crossed his arms over his dirty gown and gazed between both men.

"The latter," Jack said. "Can we talk somewhere?"

Cutter removed the long gown and tossed it into the trash, revealing his Hawaiian shirt over scrub pants. He pulled off the protective booties from his closed-toe white Crocs and added them to the trash. He washed up before leading them back through the warren to his office. He cleared boxes off the chairs in front of his desk and stacked them against the wall beside some other boxes.

As Jack and Ray sat in front of Cutter's desk, Jack noticed the view behind the desk overlooked part of Heron's Head Park which included waterfront trails along India Basin and an ecological center. Jack thought it was a much nicer view compared to the freeway from his previous office.

"Still unpacking?" Ray asked, gazing around the room. "Where's all your surf stuff?"

A crease formed between Cutter's eyes. "New department, new rules. All by the book. Most of the personal stuff has to go." With a cock of his head toward the boxes, he added, "It all came over in the move, but I have to take it home at some point."

"Let me know when you're ready. I've got the Jeep out."

"And I've got the truck," Ray added.

Cutter gave a curt nod as he took his seat behind the desk. "Thanks, guys."

"Glad to see they let you keep the Aloha shirts." Jack nodded at the vintage yellow shirt festooned with surfers, hula girls, and other Hawaiian iconry.

The look on Cutter's face was unmistakable. "They'll have to strip my Kuu Ipos from my cold, dead body."

Jack would have chuckled if he didn't know how serious his friend was about his shirts. It could get him kicked out of Cutter's office. He couldn't afford that right now. They had important business to discuss.

"Coffee? I can't guarantee it hasn't been brewing a while, but it's hot."

Jack and Ray shook their heads in unison. "No thanks, Jon. If you don't mind, we'd like to get down to the meat of the matter." Jack pulled out the list of names Chad had given him and handed it to the ME. "You may have done the autopsies on some or all of these men. I'd appreciate you pulling up their files and having a second look."

Cutter leaned over the desk and scanned the list. A moment later he tossed it down and asked, "What are you implying here, Jack?" He leaned back and threaded his fingers together over his abdomen.

"I'm not questioning your work, Jon, but I think . . . *we* think there's more to this than the current evidence implies."

Jack told him exactly what he'd told Ray. When he was done, Cutter remained silent.

"Believe me, I was just as surprised. But what he said makes sense," Ray said. "We just need copies of the autopsy files so we can compare them with the police files. We need a justifiable reason to reopen each of these cases."

Cutter seemed to think for a moment, his gaze shifting between Jack and Ray, then spun to the computer on his desk. "I remember these cases being discussed."

"Discussed?" Jack asked.

"Yeah." He drew out the word while scanning the monitor in front of him. "Seemed like a lot of suicides coming in, but sometimes it happens. Give me a minute." Cutter rose and left the office, returning a moment later with a cup of coffee in one hand and a stack of folders in another. "Sure you don't want a cup?"

Ray shook his head. "What have you got?"

Cutter set the folders on the desk then scanned Jack's list. He rifled through the stack to find the folder he wanted and passed it over to Ray. "Harold Baxter performed the postmortems on each of the victims on your list—I grabbed these files off his desk just now. If Jack's list is in order, this should be your first victim. Sai Joshi. His remains were identified by Chad Lucas."

"Right," Jack said. "He was Joshi's lover and employer."

Jack took the report pages from Ray as he finished each, scanning them for the details he was looking for. Immediate Cause of Death was clearly printed on the page—GUNSHOT THROUGH THE MOUTH—Due To: SELF-INFLICTED— Ruled As: SUICIDE. Photos backed up the cause with extensive damage to the back and side of the head. Not waiting for Ray to finish reading through the file, Jack took the next folder from Cutter.

"Second victim . . . Sanjay Bajwa?" he asked. Cutter nodded. Jack went right to the same pages.

Immediate Cause of Death: ASPHYXIATION

Due To: HANGING

Ruled As: SUICIDE

Photos showed ligature marks around the neck.

"What do you make of these scratch marks?" Jack asked, handing Cutter the photo.

"Just a guess. Maybe he had second thoughts and couldn't get the noose off. There's nothing in the final report to suggest otherwise."

Jack decided to keep the information Chad had given him to himself until after he saw the police reports.

Jack's gaze halted along the page. Baxter noted hyoid bone fractures. "What about this?" He handed the report to Cutter. "Would an accidental hanging in this context result in numerous fractures along the hyoid?"

Cutter scanned the report. Shaking his head, he gazed at Jack.

"I'm not saying it's not possible to see these types of fractures in a hanging suicide—one where the body fell from a height. But in this context—slow asphyxiation from a closet rail—never seen it myself." He passed the report back to Jack who slid it into the folder and handed it to Ray.

Ranganathan's file was next.

Immediate Cause of Death: SUDDEN IMPACT WITH A HARD SURFACE

Due To: FALL FROM A HEIGHT

Ruled as: SUICIDE

He scanned the report which seemed standard but did a double take at the notes on the cranial diagram. "What's this?" Jack handed the page to Cutter.

Cutter read the report. "Baxter's notes say the victim died due to the impact with the pavement. He also noted there was a secondary laceration on the opposite side of the skull from the impact area. It exposed the skull and a grazing fracture is evident. The impact occurred prior to the victim's death and did not contribute to it."

Jack gazed at Cutter, focusing on his explanation. From his peripheral vision, he noticed Ray had come to attention. "You're saying this victim was struck before the fall?"

Cutter shook his head. "I'm saying there's another strike point on the cranium. Considering the height, my guess is he sustained it during the fall. He probably impacted with the building somewhere on his way down." Taking the photo from Jack, he added, "Given the amount of damage and blood, the investigators on the scene may not have seen it, but it was discovered during the postmortem examination."

Cutter handed back the report and photo which Jack replaced in the file before handing it to Ray, then took the last two files— Patel and Naidu—the suspected mutual suicide.

"What about the other two names on the list—the victim I found in the Castro the Friday after Thanksgiving, and Ray's Haight suicide?" Jack asked.

Cutter bobbed his head. "Still active. I can tell you that your shooting at the club was definitely murder. However, Ray's suicide falls in line with two of these victims." He motioned to the stack of files. "He was shot through the mouth. Once the autopsies are finished and cases are closed, I can give you access to them. Whatever you need, though, can probably be obtained in the active police files."

Both men gazed at Ray who nodded his agreement.

Jack opened the folder marked with Naidu's name and pulled out the autopsy report and a photo of the injury. He then did the same for Patel and set the files side by side. Both reports indicated the Immediate Cause of Death was PENETRATION BRAIN INJURY—Due To: GUNSHOT TO THE HEAD—Ruled as: MUTUAL SUICIDE.

Photos of the bodies confirmed the lovers' embrace and entry and exit wounds. Additional notes on each report indicated a possible mutual suicide.

So far, causes of death seemed to match what Chad had told him, but Jack wanted to see the full picture before deciding if the man's suspicions of murder were founded, or just an attempt to satisfy himself as to why so many people he knew were killing themselves.

It was all there before him in black and white, and color photographs, that these men had killed themselves, but something didn't sit right. He picked up each photo and held them side-by-side.

"What's up, Jack?" Ray asked, leaning over.

Jack cocked his head slightly, his gaze remaining on the images. "I don't know. Take a look. Maybe you can see what I'm not."

Ray focused on each image in turn. "The notes say the bodies were found together in an embrace. Looks like mutual suicide to me." He handed the files to Cutter who mumbled just under his breath as he inspected each image. A furrow formed between the man's eyebrows.

Tossing the images onto the open folders in front of Jack, he said, "They're still in the fridge. Let's take a look."

Cutter rose, grabbed the two victims' files and moved quickly through the door, leaving Jack and Ray exchanging wide-eyed glances before following him.

In the cold room, Cutter rolled out the first body from the wall unit. He laid one file on top of the decedent then spun and rolled out the second tray before placing the other file on top of that body.

Jack knew Ray didn't have a stomach for this part of homicide work and let him stand back. He never understood how Ray differentiated a victim on the street versus a cadaver on the slab, even if it was the same body, and probably never would.

Jack looked between the decedents as Cutter became animated. His hands and arms made arcing motions, as if he was acting out a scene in his mind.

"Jon—" Jack finally said, getting Cutter's attention.

"Ray, come here a minute," Cutter ordered. Ray hesitated but moved in beside Jack. "Stand face-to-face and put your arms around each other." Jack put his arms out, but Ray hesitated. "Come on, man, humor me a minute," Cutter said, his voice edged with impatience.

Ray slowly stepped into Jack's embrace. "No funny business, *esé*."

"As if I would," Jack remarked, pulling Ray against him. "Come on. Drop that macho Mexican bullshit and be serious. This is serious." Jack felt Ray trying to relax into whatever example Cutter had in mind.

"Say you two are lovers and going to commit a mutual suicide."

"They were brothers," Jack said.

One eyebrow lifted over Cutter's gaze. "Whatever. Put your hands up like you each have a gun and aim it at the other." Cutter made a finger-gun with one hand as an example and pointed it toward his own head. Jack and Ray did as Cutter instructed. "Now, where will the bullets impact?"

Jack and Ray gazed to where their finger-guns were pointed, then back at Cutter. "Side of the head, behind the ear," Ray said.

Cutter grinned. "Exactly. Now look at these two decedents. Tell me what you see."

Jack took the opportunity to plant a kiss on Ray's cheek before stepping away and moving in beside Cutter, leaving Ray cursing in Spanish. Anything to get under Ray's skin, Jack thought. Ignoring his friend's discomfort, Jack focused his attention on the bodies. He leaned into the one closest to him—Naidu by the name on the file.

"This wound is closer to the back of the head, but in the same general area as would be inflicted in a mutual suicide."

"Right," Cutter said. "Now look at this one."

Jack moved around the tables to the other side of Cutter to examine Patel's wound. His gaze shot up. "Through the mouth."

Ray quickly moved in beside Jack. "What does this mean?"

"If Naidu was shot in the head and Patel through the mouth, how could this have been a mutual suicide?" Cutter asked.

"Patel shot first before turning the weapon on himself," Ray offered.

Cutter shook his head. "If this was a mutual suicide, both men would have had similar impact locations, inflicted at the same time. But let's say Patel shot Naidu first. Would he have shot Naidu in the back of the head before putting the gun in his own mouth?"

"Sounds plausible, but that would make it a murder-suicide. Easily fixed in the paperwork," Jack suggested.

"What if Naidu's gun misfired, leaving Patel alive? Do you think he would have turned the gun on himself, shooting himself in the mouth? Or would he suddenly realize he didn't want to die and call for help? Most people who attempt suicide admit that at the last possible second, they had a change of heart. Seeing his brother dead and how he'd just missed being killed too, do you think Patel would have reacted differently and saved himself—a sudden, strong will to live—or go ahead with the plan and commit suicide? If I'm not mistaken, the Hindi religion forbids suicide."

Jack nodded. "Yeah, that's what I understand too. But could his grief have been so great that he would have killed himself anyway?"

"Look at the trajectory. There are two likely outcomes if he'd shot himself in the mouth. If he ate the barrel, he would have used his thumb to pull the trigger." Cutter demonstrated, using his fingers as a handgun. "The angle would have been awkward to use his index finger, so he'd be forced to use his thumb."

Putting his fingers under his chin, he said, "If he'd used his finger on the trigger, the gun barrel would have been pointed up and the bullet would have exited the top of his head, not the back of it as we see here. He would have bruising on his trigger finger." Cutter lifted the decedent's hands and showed them to Jack and Ray. "You can see both hands are clean. No bruising on either thumbs or forefingers."

Jack's back stiffened. He felt the other shoe was about to drop.

Cutter flipped open the file still lying on Naidu's body and pulled out the autopsy report and handed it to Jack. "It says here in the notes that the men were found in each other's embrace." He pulled out a photo indicating this. "What else do you see?" Both men scanned the image. "Look carefully. There isn't any comment on the report of blowback on either decedent, nor was there any GSR on their hands." Cutter looked between Jack and Ray, then added, "And there's only one weapon."

Jack's back stiffened, knowing he wouldn't like the answer to his next question but asked it anyway. "What are you saying, Jon?"

Cutter folded his arms across his chest and gazed between Jack and Ray, a furrow forming between his brows. "I'm saying there's no way these men shot each other. The wounds aren't consistent with mutual suicide. If they both were lying in bed, there's no way they could have shot each other."

Jack's heart felt like it was suddenly in his throat as he grabbed the photo from Ray and looked at every aspect of the image. He forced himself to breathe. Cutter was right. There was only one weapon, and it was on the floor beside the bed. The blood on the pillows and sheets wasn't as heavy as he'd expect for being shot in bed. And as Cutter saw on the autopsy report, no blood splatter on either body. Most importantly, there was no way they could have shot each other with the one weapon, then before they died, wrapped their arms around each other. And that crucial bit of information Chad had told him. Even though they were brothers,

Patel and Naidu barely tolerated each other. So why die by suicide pact?

Finally, Jack glanced at Cutter then gazed at Ray for a long moment. "The bodies were staged."

CHAPTER THIRTEEN

They'd taken two vehicles to the medical examiner's office so Jack could head straight back to his apartment after meeting Cutter, rather than having to double back across the city to take Ray home.

As it turned out, having two vehicles worked out perfectly.

After realizing they definitely had at least two murders on their hands, Ray went into the department to get copies of the police files for each of the seven victims, while Jack went home with copies of the ME's reports of the first five, the members of the Indian Spicy Girls group.

By the time Ray arrived ninety minutes after leaving the ME's office, Jack had already set up his murder wall. As per his typical MO, he'd tacked a fresh city map onto the wall, lined up the victims' headshots horizontally above it in the order of death, and linked each victim with colored string to the area in the city where they'd been discovered.

The folders Cutter had copied for him were spread on the floor in order of victim's discovery, with each postmortem image on top of their folder. Below were copies of the autopsy reports. Color coded cards had been quickly filled in with details of each death and personal notes as they applied, then were stacked beside the files on the floor.

"I see you didn't wait for me," Ray said, meeting Jack in the backroom.

After Travers had broken in earlier in the year, and later when Ray helped him put his murder wall back together, Jack no longer saw a need any longer to hide what he was doing in the backroom from his friend. And if he was going to solve this case, he'd need Ray on it with him. *Once a team, always a team.* It didn't matter that Ray would be the one earning the department's accolades. Jack knew that once they discovered the root of what was going on here, Ray would be made the lead detective on the case. Jack would just be the detritus stuck on his friend's shoe. It was always the same story though. If he wanted the accolades, which he really didn't, he needed to get back to the job. He didn't want that either.

"No need to wait. You were doing your part while I was doing mine. Now we can hit the ground running. Want some coffee . . . or a beer? I've got both," Jack offered.

"Better go with coffee. I suspect I'm going to need the caffeine."

Jack poured them both coffees then took the police files from Ray and sat on the floor in front of the ME files. "Don't stand on ceremony. Get comfy. This could take a while. And you better call Maria—"

Ray put his hand up. "Did that before leaving the department. She was already in bed. Get this, she tells me she already knows when you and I rush out of the house, she's already expecting the 'Honey, I'll be home late' call." Jack chuckled as Ray lowered himself to the floor and gazed over the postmortem folders already laid out. "So, where are we?"

Jack rifled through Ray's folders until he found the one for Sai Joshi. "This is our first victim." He pulled pages out of the folder and scanned them carefully. With the exception of the official police report, the rest of the file seemed to mimic the one Cutter had given him. There were some additional photos from the scene that were tied to the evidence report.

His eyebrows drew together. One image labeled as the weapon looked like the kid's toy he'd seen beside Johnson's body in the Majestic's driveway. He set the photo beside the police report on top of the folder and placed it below the ME's folder on Joshi.

He performed the task for each of the five victims until he had two rows of files—ME and PD—arcing in front of him.

Jack sat back and scanned his handiwork. His gaze kept being drawn to the weapons.

"Earth to Jack. Come in, Jack." Ray's voice cut through Jack's concentration. "If you're going to ignore me, I'll just head home now."

Jack flicked Ray a glance. "Sorry, brother. I'm just trying to figure out the angle here. Why these men? All members of the same group of dancers. And let's say they were all staged to look like suicides."

"It's hard to see some of these being anything other than suicide, Jack. Yeah, the last two guys definitely seem to have been posed. Once Cutter pointed out how it couldn't be suicide, murder was the obvious conclusion. Like one of those illusion pictures where you don't see the hidden image until you do, then it's obvious." Jack grunted his acknowledgement. "Do you think it's coincidence that all five members of the same group died in such a short space of time? Could the first three have killed themselves, but the last two were murdered?"

After a long pause, Jack finally said, "No, I think all of their deaths are related. We just need to find out how."

"Then let's look at the evidence. You have more in front of you than I do in the office. We should be able to piece together a working theory."

"Hmm," Jack muttered. A moment later, he looked over at Ray. "You brought the files on Johnson and Smith?" If he knew his friend, and he did, Ray had secreted copies of the two open case files out of the department—Bob Johnson, his victim at the club, and Michael Smith, Ray's suicide in the Haight. Jack was absolutely sure they were connected to the other five. The fact they were all involved with the nightclub wasn't enough for him. He just had to find the tie that bound them together.

He took the files Ray handed him and opened the first—Bob Johnson. As the investigation was still ongoing, there wasn't a final official police report. But there were a bunch of notes, some photographs, an incident report, and an evidence report that also included Jack's own fingerprints and personal details, as well as transcripts from his questioning, and a detailed list of items they took from Jack as part of the evidence, including his leather jacket.

"I want my jacket back once the case closes."

"I'll see what I can do," Ray said, downing the last of his coffee.

Jack hoped the look he shot Ray told his friend he was getting back his jacket, even if it meant him going down to the department, then breaking into the evidence locker and liberating the jacket himself.

Immune to Jack's intimidation, Ray ignored the threat and said, "Wash and Harry's notes are pretty thorough here. Everything seems to be in order. They went through the man's hotel room. Like the first five, Johnson also had a closet full of fancy dresses, shoes, and wigs. And a dressing table full of makeup and perfume to rival a Macy's counter, if the photos are anything to go by."

"What's this?" Jack asked, pulling a page out of the folder that looked like it had been torn from a notepad. Quickly scrawled:

"FAO LT Dick Haniford—Will have the final report soon, but decedent Robert Johnson's immediate cause of death was exsanguination due to two gunshot wounds . . . one to the abdomen and one to the carotid artery. He was already near death at the time of discovery. He would have survived the shot to the abdomen, but the second shot is what killed him. – P. Baxter, ME"

It didn't make Jack feel any better confirming what Haniford had told him in the back of the patrol car.

He watched Ray place the photo of the weapon on top of the folder before opening Smith's folder. That damn kids' toy.

Jack's brow tightened again as he pulled open Michael Smith's file—Ray's Haight suicide. Crime scene photos and field notes seemed to mimic Joshi's, and the weapon images were nearly identical to those of Joshi, Patel, Naidu, and Johnson.

Jack lifted the images of the weapons and looked at each in turn. What the hell were they?

"Please explain this to me. What are these? They look like kids' toys."

"Man, you've been away from the department for too long," Ray said. "These are *Imura* revolvers. They're the newest threat we're dealing with." Ray sat forward and looked at him with more seriousness than Jack had seen in a long time. "You don't need to *buy* a gun anymore. You can make one yourself at home on a 3D printer. Now, the only wait time to get a weapon is how long it takes to print out."

CHAPTER FOURTEEN

Monday

He lay awake for a long time, too wound up to sleep. Jack couldn't get out of his mind that in the time he'd been off the force, criminals had found a way to skirt the system by creating weapons with a simple home 3D printer. *What the absolute fuck!* When he woke, he planned on doing some online research into *Imura* revolvers.

It seemed like only moments later when pounding in his head forced open his eyes. Someone was knocking on his door. Still dressed in yesterday's clothes, he went to the door while rubbing the sleep from his eyes.

"Yeah?"

The young man on the landing was average looking, if not slightly effeminate, probably early twenties. His thin frame couldn't have been much over five feet and was bundled in a thick down-style jacket and washed-out jeans, the pale color of both matching his blue-gray eyes. A black baseball cap with bright orange SF lettering could have been a fashion statement, or maybe he supported the Giants.

"Are you Jack Slaughter?" His voice was about as soft as his looks.

What the hell was it with people? They have his address, climb the stairs, and knock on the door clearly marked *Jack Slaughter, Private Investigations and Security.* Who the hell did they expect would answer the door? Maybe he needed a bigger sign. Or one written in bolder letters. Or maybe flashing neon—

"Yeah." There was no reason to take his half asleep grouchiness out on the guy. Besides, he didn't look all that comfortable being here anymore than Jack appreciated being woken up from a deep sleep. "What time is it?"

The young man looked at his cell phone. "Just after ten. Mr. Lucas asked me to bring you this." He gave Jack a quick once over before handing him a small sparkling white gift bag stuffed with white tissue paper and tied closed with a red ribbon. Before Jack had a chance to thank him, the young man wished him a Merry Christmas and scurried down the stairs.

At his desk, Jack sat and opened the bag. He knew this wasn't a gift, but the holiday wrapping squeezed his heart, remembering all the Christmases, birthdays, and other special events that he no longer celebrated since his family had been taken from him. If not for Maria, who always remembered him at Christmas and his birthday, he wouldn't celebrate special occasions at all.

Which reminded him, he needed to get his shit together and dust off his plastic. Christmas was only a week away and he needed to shop for his friends. And the police gift drive for disadvantaged kids was this weekend.

He removed the bow, then upturned the bag and watched a handful of black flash drives tumble onto his desk. Each was marked *Xmas music* and were sequentially numbered.

He lifted an envelope that had also been in the bag and pulled out a Christmas card that had an image of two young men sharing a kiss beside a heavily decorated tree. *Merry Kissmas* was pre-printed inside the card. Below that read: *Let me know if you need anything else, sweetie. ~ Chad*

Sweetie. Jack grunted. He set aside the card then began sifting through the drives until he found the one marked #1 and slid it into the USB slot on his computer. A moment later, his monitor filled with multi-screen security video of the Majestic. He counted twelve screens in all.

Five interior cameras had been set up around the main room. Another camera had been positioned just inside the backstage door and showed the hallway leading to the changing rooms, security room, and Chad's office. Two cameras had been placed over the club's front door—one inside pointing down a short hallway leading into the club's interior and one outside with wide angle showing customers coming from what appeared to be a one-eighty-degree perspective along Castro Street. Similarly, two more cameras had been mounted at the back door—one capturing anyone entering, and one outside showing the parking area. The last two cameras showed the driveway from both perspectives.

The time stamp was from six weeks ago, 4a.m. The place was sealed like a tomb, and there was no outside activity, save the odd vehicle driving along Castro Street.

Jack fast-forwarded, then stopped when he saw someone walking through the parking lot and disappearing under the trees at the far corner. He scrolled back and caught the person turning off Castro Street and into the club's driveway. Perhaps it was a locals' shortcut. He made a mental note to check it out. And another mental note to recommend Chad put up a security gate to keep people out of his parking lot.

When nothing happened after a few minutes, he hit pause.

"I'm gonna need coffee for this."

Pulling off his clothes as he moved, he was naked by the time he set the coffee to brew. He stepped into the shower and started the water. The cold water instantly woke him. By the time he stepped out again, he heard the coffee machine spitting out its last drops into the pot. He quickly dressed then found his way back to the desk, steaming coffee mug in one hand and clean socks in the other. He clicked play and let the video run for a few minutes while he finished dressing.

Over the course of the next couple hours, Jack fast-forwarded through each thumb drive before popping in the next. Each drive appeared to contain several days' worth of footage from each of the club's security cameras. The multi-screens let him see all around the club at the same time, just as the club's head of security, Isaac, did.

Because he had a vested interest in the victim he'd discovered on Black Friday, he quickly found that drive and popped it in.

By now, he started recognizing club regulars. Not only Rod, but some of the performers, as well as the club staff. And Franklin Whitney-Cummings as Carol.

There!

He watched her move around the room, conversing with other patrons. Nothing seemed out of the ordinary. He flipped through his hand-written notes. Bob Johnson. From Lubbock, Texas. In the city for the competition. Jack had to admit, dressed as Pepper Mint, Bob certainly turned heads.

Jack watched her move from screen to screen and eventually she headed through the front door. Front door footage showed her stopping at the corner of the building to light a cigarette, then turning into the driveway. Was she heading to her vehicle in the parking lot, or did she just want a smoke in a quiet place?

Pepper Mint hadn't been followed, but a figure stepped out of the shadows and blocked her path. It was a short altercation before two shots were fired. Muzzle flash briefly lit up a sliver of the shooter's profile, as well as Pepper's. Shock instantly appeared on her face and her hands flew to her neck.

When she hit the ground, the shooter fired again. The abdomen shot he'd tried stemming the blood from. He hadn't known at the time she'd been shot in the neck, but his gut twisted just the same. Even though Haniford had assured Jack there was nothing he could have done to save her, it didn't make him feel any better. At least he now had more of the story.

The shooter didn't stick around after the second shot was fired. He turned into the parking lot and disappeared between two cars at the back corner. The same corner he'd seen pedestrians use. Now he was definitely going to check it out. The club was closed Mondays and Tuesdays so he knew he wouldn't be disturbed.

His gaze was drawn to the interior screen and the club's back door closing. He rewound the video to when the shooter ran into the parking lot and froze the scene. He knew someone had been there in the shadows. Would the video pick up who it was?

He slowed the video and scanned every inch of the screen as it progressed. *Damn it!* The angle pointed into the parking lot and not actually at the back door itself. He slowly scrolled forward . . . a little more.

Gotcha!

He watched a figure enter the club. He couldn't tell who it was. The light was positioned too close to the camera and cast a sharp glare over the person—another recommendation for Chad—but he caught the glare off her necklace. That's what had drawn his attention that night just as the officers were putting him on the ground. He scrolled back a few seconds and saw himself on the ground and the two officers standing over him.

Grumbling, he sped through the rest of the video. He remembered pushing past people as he ran in the direction the shots had been fired. People had been spilling out of the club in their rush to go the opposite direction from where they'd heard the shots. Now he saw the mayhem from inside the club, with everyone rushing to get out. His witness had disappeared into the melee.

"Damn it!"

He needed a break. He looked at the clock on the computer screen. 2:45p.m. Had he really been focused on the security video for more than three hours?

He stood and stretched in front of the window. The sun was too low in the sky to brighten the apartment, but the day was clear and the Bay Bridge was unmistakable down Broadway.

Reaching for the window crank to let a little fresh air in, he squinted at a woman walking up Columbus Avenue from the direction of the Transamerica Pyramid, aka the TransAm Building. As she got closer, he realized it was Ginnifer Whitney-Cummings. She stopped on the corner as the crossing lights changed to red. *What the hell does she want?* It hadn't even been a week yet since he'd taken her case.

He scanned the desk for his phone and quickly plugged it into his computer. He opened the record app and set it down again. He hoped she'd think the phone was just charging.

CHAPTER FIFTEEN

When Jack opened the door, he expected Ginnie to be standing on the doormat, waiting to come in, as any normal person would. Instead, what greeted him was her leaning out over the security railing. Her arched back pushed out her ass as she strained for a view he knew didn't exist on this side of the building. The only view from the landing was the Columbus Avenue side of the Condor Club. The pose might have been sexy if he was interested. He wasn't.

She slowly turned toward him. "Did I catch you at a bad time?" She looked up with a playful look on her face before pushing past him, her gaze never leaving his.

"No, come on in," he said to no one on the landing. By the time he'd closed the door, Ginnie had already seated herself in the chair in front of his desk and pulled out her purse pooch, which she deposited onto the floor. The dog instantly started sniffing around.

In the same stride, Jack lifted the dog by the back of its couture jacket and deposited it in Ginnie's lap as he moved to sit in his chair behind the desk. As before, the dog's outfit matched Ginnie's own—a pale yellow outfit with tan trim. Both owner and dogs' nails had been varnished yellow. They reminded Jack of a pair of Easter eggs. A bit early, but whatever.

"What can I do for you?" he asked, shuffling papers into a stack and moving them to the side of the desk. He pulled out his notepad and grabbed a pen in case he needed to make notes.

"Franklin has been going out every night, but you haven't called to tell me where he's going."

This woman has no patience, which probably gets her what she wants. That and money.

"These things take time," he calmly said.

She put the dog back on the floor and sat forward, plumping her breasts again. *Does she think sexual favors will get her anywhere?*

"You followed him the other night. I saw you go after him. You have to know where he went. Why haven't you called me?"

From the corner of his eye, Jack watched the little dog circling the room, sniffing everything. "As I said, it takes time. You hired me to get some photos. As a matter of fact, I was working on the file when you arrived." A white lie.

Ginnie scanned his desk. "Doesn't look like it to me."

Okay, so that's how she's going to behave.

He held his temper as he said, "Most of my files are digitized." He called up the files from the taskbar and spun the monitor around for her to see. "It's all on here." He returned the monitor back to its original position.

"When do I get to see it? I need to know where Franklin is going when he leaves our home."

"You'll see my report when it's finished." She opened her mouth to demand something else, but he put his hand up to quiet her. "But give me a minute. I was just going to print up some photos for the report. Since you're here, you can take a look now. Okay?"

Ginnie threw her back against the chair, recrossed her legs, then crossed her arms. "Fine. Whatever."

Just then, Jack noticed the purse pooch circle back to the place where it had pissed on his carpet on their first visit and rushed across the room. He nabbed the dog by the back of its jacket again and put it in Ginnie's lap. "I'd prefer your dog not keep pissing on my carpet like it's marking territory."

The dog yipped as she thrust it back in her purse as if it were a ragdoll and pulled out her wallet. Throwing some money onto his desk, she said, "Buy yourself another goddamn carpet. Just give me my photos!"

Holy shit! No wonder Franklin takes off at night. Dresses aside, if Jack was married to her, he'd probably start finding reasons to leave the house too.

He went to the printer and slid in some photograph paper,

then returned to the computer, selected a handful of photographs, and hit print. He waited beside the printer while it whirred and clicked, setting itself up to print and eject the photos.

He looked over at Ginnie. She'd refolded herself back into her protective emotional cocoon and stared out one of the windows. Her gaze didn't appear focused on anything in particular. More so, just not looking at *him*.

Complicated woman. First, she waltzes in like a call girl, then instantly turns into Cruella de Vil. It seemed to Jack's untrained eye there was more going on in their marriage than Franklin's cross-dressing. But what? Was he curious enough to find out? He didn't think so. As far as he was concerned, his job for her was completed.

When the printouts were done, he sat on the edge of the desk, one leg swinging, and gazed down at Ginnie. "I did follow Franklin the other night, as you rightly said." He noticed the woman's back stiffen. Jack knew what he had to tell her would probably change her life forever. Not that her husband dressing in women's clothes already hadn't.

"Get on with it." She'd lowered her voice; her body language remained guarded.

"I followed him across the city to the Castro. There's a club there called the Majestic Lounge—"

"He's going to a gay bar? Fucking great!" she huffed. She recrossed her legs and rolled her eyes back in their sockets.

"It appears so. At the moment, they're having a drag queen competition. I can't account for his whereabouts before you hired me, but it seems he's known there, at least by the management."

Ginnie spun her gaze in Jack's direction. "Known for what, exactly?" Her foot started bobbing up and down.

Jack shook his head. "From what I've gathered so far, he's just a patron. And they only know him by his trans name, not his real name."

"Are you going to tell me what name he's going by, or will that cost me extra?"

"Patience is a virtue, you know."

"Not when I'm paying you double your rate. Spill." She sat motionless for a moment.

"I don't know if he's using a last name, but I spoke with the manager, and she only knows him by Carol."

"Carol." It wasn't a question but came out more like an accusation. "Fucking Carol!"

"Does the name have any significance to you?"

"It's his fucking mother's name. His late mother. She was a nasty piece of work, but he was still a mama's boy. Dear God, I hope he's not turning into Norman Bates." She noticeably shivered.

"What do you mean?"

She shot a gaze of disbelief at him. "You have seen *Psycho*, haven't you?" Stifling a chuckle, remembering earlier when Ray called him psycho, he nodded that he knew the movie, and her reference. "It *all* makes sense now." The foot started bobbing again. Her shoe flipped off and landed on her handbag. Her purse pooch yipped again then scurried out of the bag and across the room to hide behind the sofa.

Poor dog. "Why do you say that?" Maybe she'd forget the dog when she left, and he could find it a new home.

"The wig, the drunk makeup, the attitude . . . it's all his mother. The couture is my style," she said, almost proudly. "I should be grateful for that. But the whole *Mommy Dearest* stuff makes sense. Let me see those photos." Before he could present them to her and tell her what he knew, she grabbed them out of his hand and flipped through them, tossing each onto the floor when she was done looking, interjecting comments ranging from *asshole* to *fucking asshole* to *what have I done to deserve this?*

"If it makes you feel any better, he's not competing in the drag race," he said.

Shaking her head, she said, "Not looking like that, he won't. He has absolutely no style."

Just to egg her on, he said, "Maybe you can show him how it's done?"

Tossing the last photo on the floor, she slowly turned her gaze in his direction, and under her breath, she made her feelings clear. "I'll kill him before that happens."

CHAPTER SIXTEEN

Before heading to the Majestic, Jack stopped at a store three blocks from the club. This store had been Leah's favorite place to bring Zoë, as many of the toys had been handmade and the clothes made with natural cottons and dyes. He tried pushing down the lump in his throat as he stepped across the all-too-familiar threshold and into the well-lighted store. Timber box-shelving and cabinets lined the walls and throughout the store, all displaying hundreds of toys, games, and clothes. An image of Zoë tottering back and forth across the store, giggling in her rush to see everything forced the lump in his throat to swell.

Taking a deep breath, he approached a woman behind the counter who helped him select some onesies in gender-neutral colors—Ray had told him he and Maria wanted to be surprised by the baby's sex—and several brightly colored playthings.

When he was done there, he stowed the sacks in the back of the Jeep, confident they wouldn't be visible through the heavily tinted glass, and ran into Walgreens across the road for some boys' and girls' toys for the annual department-sponsored toy drive. Every year, Santa's grotto was set up for the city's poor and under-privileged kids, each child having the opportunity to meet Santa and receive a gift. No one left emptyhanded.

By the time he reached the Majestic, the sky had darkened though it was barely six. Jack pulled into the parking lot and parked near the corner of the lot. He wanted to see where the path led through the trees. He grabbed his flashlight from the center console and exited the Jeep.

The driveway was kitty-corner from where he stood under

the tree in the far corner of the lot. Devoid of any vehicles, the lot appeared larger. From his position, he was able to scan the entire area, including the line of vision from where Rod had been serviced behind a car, to the cameras over the club's back door and this side of the driveway. Nothing of any significance stood out.

He switched on the flashlight and shone it along the length of the chain link fence that had been interwoven with thin timber slats used for added privacy for the neighbors behind the club. Jasmine vines covered most of the fence which was overhung by half a dozen tall Pepper trees. A California lilac had grown so large, it now blended into the rest of the trees and nearly obscured the corner parking space, disguising the break in the chain link.

Jack directed the light around the gap, then carefully maneuvered himself through it and into a narrow space between the back of the theater and the backyards of those living on Hartford Street. He followed the path behind the theater, through a broken gate, and between a pair of buildings, out onto 17th Street near the corner at Hartford. It seemed a lot of work just to not have to walk around the block, but for anyone who knew this gap existed, it made an easy getaway. One could, theoretically, hide in the shadows back here for hours if the police were looking for them.

Judging by the condoms and needles, it was also a popular place for sex and drugs. Rather than retrace his steps through it, he walked around the corner and back to the parking lot. Now he knew about the alley and where it led, it made things more interesting.

Before leaving, he checked out the security cameras, then tested the back door to ensure it was locked.

It wasn't.

Jack's heart kicked up a beat. His vehicle was the only one in the lot. Had Chad or Isaac forgotten to lock up, or had someone broken in?

His only firearm, the Beretta, was stowed in its lockbox back in his apartment, and he rarely used it except to renew his investigator's license and requalify to actually own the weapon. The last time it saw the light of day was when he confronted Travers.

Jack rushed to the Jeep, opened the back, pushed aside the gifts he'd bought, and extricated the tire iron. Killing someone was always a last resort, but that didn't mean he couldn't beat the shit out of an intruder. Breaking and entering didn't require a loss of life, just the use of his legs for a while.

He quietly opened the back door and entered the club, tire iron in both hands and just above his shoulder. Minimal lighting was on in the main room though the holiday lights were off, but he was able to see where he was going.

He checked the front door first—locked—then headed toward the backstage door and slowly turned the handle. The hall light was on. Was this normal?

He listened. Nothing. He checked the dressing rooms and Isaac's security room. All clear. He'd turned to check on the other rooms when he heard a noise and followed the sound to Chad's office door. He slowly turned the knob and eased himself into the room.

Chad stood with his back to the door while he rifled through his file cabinet. After extracting a folder, he turned back to the desk. Jack could only describe the screech the man let out as something he'd only heard in cheesy B movies. The contents of the folder went flying when the man clutched at his collar with one hand and put his other hand over his mouth to stifle a second scream.

He dramatically threw himself into his desk chair, then put his head onto the desk and covered it with his arms, gasping hard.

Jack lowered the tire iron, walked to the desk and waited for Chad to look up. When he did, there were tears in his eyes, and fury in his voice. "What the fuck is wrong with you?"

"Me?" Jack huffed.

"Yes, you. Jesus Christ, Jack. I thought you were a burglar and going to kill me. You scared the ever-living shit out of me."

"Your being here when the club is closed didn't exactly calm my heart, Chad. What are you doing here?"

"I own the place. What are *you* doing here? I thought you knew the club was closed early in the week. You're not expected to do your security thing when we're closed." After taking several deep breaths, Chad's body noticeably relaxed.

"I watched some of your videos. Thanks for sending them over. I saw a couple pedestrians using the parking lot as a shortcut, so I came over to check it out. You need to get that fence repaired and get a gate on the driveway."

Chad released an exasperated sigh. "You have no idea how much money I've spent fixing that damn fence. Do people really travel with bolt cutters on them? No sooner have I got the fence repaired, someone is back the next day to open it up again."

"Have you been back there?"

"Not recently, why?"

Jack sat in the chair in front of the desk and put the tire iron on the floor beside him. "You need to call the city and have HAZMAT get someone back there to clean up the condoms and needles."

Anger crossed Chad's face. "I've called. They tell me it's not city property. The theater says it's not their property, the residents behind us say it's not their property, and I know damn well it's not mine. Someone has to be responsible, but no one has stepped up. Everyone I talk to says it's the club's responsibility since they're coming through our fence, and that it's most likely my patrons using the space to hook up. Forget the fact that the city has a huge junkie problem, and of course the hookers. That's not on us. They don't all come from my place. That alley has two ends, you know." Jack nodded, having just walked the length of it. "The best I can do is keep fixing the fence and hope people eventually forget about it. And even if they do, people will still keep going back there from the 17th Street side."

Jack nodded that he understood. "I'll have a talk with my old LT and see if he has any suggestions. It's more than a health hazard."

"Don't I know it. So, what brings you here? I mean into the club."

Jack huffed. "I wouldn't be good at my job if I didn't make sure your doors were secure while I was here checking out that hole in your fence. I wasn't expecting to find the back door open. Mine is the only vehicle in the lot, so—"

"Sorry about that. I had lunch with some friends down the road and walked up. I meant to only be here for a few minutes, but—" Chad looked at the time on his phone. "Shit! I didn't realize it was so late." He threw himself onto his knees and quickly gathered up the folder and papers, then stood and tossed them onto his desk. Grabbing his keys and coat, he said, "Sorry, I need to run. I've got a date."

Jack picked up the tire iron and rose. "I'll give you a ride to your car," Jack said as they walked through the club. Jack stopped at the back door and adjusted the light beside the camera.

"What are you doing?" Chad asked.

"I noticed on the security video that the light is too close to the camera. The glare obscures anyone coming through this door. The night Pepper Mint was shot, someone I think is a witness came through the door but his, or her, face was obscured by the glare. Hopefully, this will solve any future problems." Jack exited the building and held open the door for Chad who then made sure the door was locked before they left.

"Your witness came into the club?" Chad sounded surprised. "I wonder why they didn't use the hole in the fence too in case they were recognized as having seen the shooting."

In the Jeep, both men secured their seatbelts and Jack started the engine. "When I arrived on the scene that night, one of the first things I saw was someone running into your parking lot. I'm assuming it was the shooter and they used that alley as an escape route."

Chad gasped. "If they knew it was there, they must be familiar with the club." He made an audible shivering sound. "I'm freaking out, thinking the killer is one of my customers. Gawd! I hope they're not a contestant."

Jack doubted it but didn't say anything.

Jack dropped off the toys at the department's donation station but didn't plan on sticking around. It was late and he knew Ray would be home by now anyway, so no need going to find him.

As he walked between the lobby and drop off point for this

weekend's event with Santa, he couldn't help noticing the new faces at Reception. The longer he was away, the fewer people he recognized.

Just as he turned toward the front door, he heard, "Jack, wait up."

"What are you still doing here?" he asked. Ray hadn't gone home yet.

"I just came from seeing Haniford. It didn't take much for him to agree to reopen those cases," Ray told him.

"Did you mention me?"

Nodding, Ray said, "Yeah, and he's cool with you being involved."

Jack lifted an eyebrow. Haniford was never happy with his involvement. It always came back to when Jack was returning to work. "Really? He actually *said* he's cool with it?"

"Well, not really. I told him what we suspected, and he agreed to reopen the files. Since he knew you and I talked, I'm assuming he expects you'll be involved."

"But did he agree to let me in on the case?" Jack knew he hadn't but wanted to see how Ray reacted.

"I wouldn't say he agreed, but he didn't specifically say not to involve you. You know how it is. You're an asset to the department and always will be. Just not officially. You know what you gotta do to be official, *homes*."

Jack chuckled. "Yeah, I do. Come on. I'll walk you out."

CHAPTER SEVENTEEN

Tuesday

Ray picked up Jack at his place just before 10a.m. After agreeing on a plan of action—marking the victims' residences on a map and hitting each one based on proximity rather than order of murder—Ray drove them to the apartment of the first victim, Sai Joshi.

Jack wasn't surprised the apartment had already been cleaned out. Housing in the city was hard to come by, so the landlord knew he could re-rent the place quickly. It didn't matter that someone had been killed in the place. Just clean it out, clean it up, and clean up on the rent. What the new tenant didn't know wouldn't hurt them.

What hadn't changed, to his knowledge, were Joshi's neighbors. Someone had to have seen or heard something. While Ray was interviewing tenants on the next floor up, Jack knocked on a door directly opposite Joshi's place. When it wasn't answered, he knocked again. Maybe they were at work. It was Tuesday, and by the time on his phone, it wasn't even eleven yet.

A long moment later, the door opened to the end of its security chain. A petite young Asian woman of average height, with dark hair and brown eyes appeared in the narrow gap. It looked like she'd been sleeping. The belt of her pink silk robe was loosely tied around her hips, causing the hastily donned garment to fall open around her bare shoulders. Paired with her bare legs, Jack didn't have to guess she wasn't wearing anything underneath. Her cheap security chain wouldn't protect her if anyone wanted in, especially dressed like that.

"Yes?"

"I'm sorry to bother you. My name is Jack Slaughter." He handed her his card. She looked at it then back at him. "I'm a private investigator and looking into the death of your neighbor, Sai Joshi." He cocked his head toward the door across from hers. "I'm wondering if you can tell me about the day he died."

"I didn't really know him."

"Not friends." She shook her head. "But maybe friendly? People always know something about their neighbors—notice their habits, see people going in and out of their places, hear things through the walls. Anything like that?"

"He was pretty quiet. We said hello in the hall, but that was about it. He was . . . different. We didn't have the same social circle, if you know what I mean."

"I don't. What do you mean, different?"

She thought a moment, perhaps carefully choosing her words. "I think he was trans or something. I never saw women going into his place. At least, not real women."

"What do you mean by real women?" he prodded.

"You know . . . born female. His friends were men but dressed like women. I don't know . . . does that make him gay? Sometimes, he dressed as a man too, but mostly when I saw him, it was in the evening and he was dressed as a woman. He seemed kinda weird, so I kept to myself. I don't know much about anyone in this building."

"You just keep to yourself," he repeated. She nodded.

Jack was taken aback. In this day and age, in San Francisco, did people still question the lifestyle of others? Sure, racism and sexism still existed everywhere, but were alternative lifestyles still criticized in a city with a large gay community going back decades? Maybe this woman was just naïve.

"The night he died, did you hear anything, see anything? Something that stood out as unusual?" Jack referred to his notes and gave her the day and date.

She shook her head. "I work late. And sleep late, in case you can't tell." She waved her hand from her bed-tussled hair, down the length of her barely-clothed body. "I don't remember anything."

"He was shot. Did you hear gunfire? That's pretty loud," he suggested.

She shook her head, then said, "I was sleeping. But . . . now that I think of it, I do remember being woken up by something. I listened but didn't hear anything. I thought I might have dreamed it, so I went back to sleep. It wasn't until later I heard a lot of people in the hall that woke me up again. I went to the door to ask them to keep it down so I could sleep, but when I saw the police, I closed the door. Whatever they were doing over there wasn't any of my business."

"Do you remember what time you were awakened by the sound, or when you heard the people in the hall?" he asked.

She thought again. "I think I woke up the first time around three-thirty or four." Her eyes went wide. "Do you think that's when he killed himself? Do you think the sound that woke me up was him pulling the trigger? Ohmygod!" Her hand covered her mouth to stifle her sharp gasp.

Jack pushed on. "It's possible. Is that all you remember?" He'd check the police report about their arrival time and their investigation. At least he had a more accurate time of death. He'd check that against the ME's report.

The woman's mind wandered before she looked up at him. "If I'd gotten up, do you think I could have saved him?"

He shook his head. "No. He died instantly. You have my card. If you remember anything else, please call." Before she could close the door, he added, "You might want to get a better security system installed if you're going to answer your door half naked."

A scowl instantly crossed her face before she slammed the door on him.

Jack knocked on the door at the end of the hall, Joshi's next nearest neighbor. It was the last apartment on this floor; there were only three. When there was no answer, he met Ray coming down the stairs.

"Any luck?" he asked.

Ray shook his head. "Most people work this time of day, but

I talked to one man who said he was dozing on the sofa while watching TV. He heard a shot that woke him up but thought it was the TV. He didn't hear anything else so got up and went to bed."

"What time was that?"

"He didn't know. Didn't look at the time, but thinks it was between three and four in the morning," Ray said.

"That jives with what the neighbor across from Joshi said. She pinpoints it closer to three-thirty. Same story. Sleeping, heard a sound, but thought she was dreaming so she went back to sleep. The police woke her up later; we can pinpoint their arrival time on the investigation records. Which apartment was your guy in?"

"The one directly above Joshi's place. What's next?"

Jack thought a moment. "Let's see if anyone's home below Joshi's apartment. Maybe they heard something."

Ray nodded and followed Jack downstairs. He found the relevant apartment and knocked on the door. When it opened, they were greeted by a tall, wiry old man with thinning grey hair and slightly stooped shoulders.

Presenting his card, Jack said, "Good morning."

Before he had a chance to continue, the man looked between him and Ray and said, "I'm not buying anything, young man, so you can just skedaddle. How did you get into the building anyway?"

"Perhaps you should talk to your landlord about hiring a doorman." The old man's response was pushing Jack's hand that held the card away from him and moving to close the door. Jack put his palm on the door and continued. "We're not selling anything. This is Detective Ray Navarro with the SFPD. I'm a private investigator. Jack Slaughter." He pushed his card forward again. Ray presented his badge. The man took it and gave it and the badge a close inspection.

"A P.I., eh?"

"Yes, sir."

"A private eye, private dick, detective, gumshoe, sleuthhound, an inquiry agent, a—"

"Yes, sir." Jack cut him off. The old codger must still watch a lot of cop shows.

"Sorry. It's an old habit of an old man. You see, I do crosswords. Synonyms have to be second nature if you want to finish those puzzles."

Jack chuckled. "Crosswords are a great way to keep the mind sharp. I'm wondering if you can help us. There was an incident in the apartment above you—"

"Yes, yes. Poor man. To take his own life like that. Crying shame."

"Yes, sir. Did you hear anything that night?" Jack asked.

The man shook his head. "I'm sorry, but no. I take out my hearing aids at night so I can sleep." The man turned his head to show Jack his ears.

"Gunfire is pretty loud. You didn't hear anything at all?"

He shook his head again, tapping a spot just in front of his ear. "Not a thing. Without these contraptions, I'm as deaf as the proverbial."

"All right. Thank you for your time. If you think of anything, please call the number on my card."

As Jack turned to leave, the man asked, "Don't you want to know if I *saw* anything? My eyes still work pretty good."

"You said you take out your hearing aids so you can sleep," Ray said.

"I do, but I didn't say I sleep well." He eyeballed Ray for a long moment, then looked back at Jack. "Sometimes I get up and go for a walk around the block. Walking helps keep me fit. That's why I'm ninety and still doing my crosswords," he said with pride in his voice.

"Did you go walking that night?"

"I did."

Jack couldn't help feeling a little impatient but reminded himself that many of the city's residents were old and lived alone. Maybe Jack and Ray were the only people the old guy would talk to today.

"Would you like to tell us about it?" Ray asked. "What did you see?"

"Sure-sure. I can't tell you about any shot because I wasn't home. It was quiet but I couldn't sleep, so I went for my walk. The air is fresher at that time of night. It's peaceful," he explained.

"Yes, sir. Is that when you saw something unusual?" Jack wanted to roll his hand at the man to hurry up. He already felt like the old guy was wasting his time.

The man rubbed his chin as he thought, his gaze wandering. "I can't say if it was strange, but certainly unusual. When I got back to the building, someone in a dark coat rushed past me in a fierce hurry. Nearly knocked me down the front steps. I don't mind telling you, there's no respect for the elderly anymore."

Jack's attention piqued. "Did you get a look at this person?"

He shook his head. "No, he had a big hat pulled over his face. I can't even tell you if he was white, Black, Chinese, or Howdy Doody. He was dressed all in black. Gloves too."

Finally, something to work with. "Can you give me an approximate height?"

"Oh, yes. He was tall but not quite my height. I'm still six-two, ya know," he said, again with pride. He straightened and put a trembling hand at chin level to indicate the height of the man rushing past him. Average height for most men was somewhere around five feet ten inches, depending on which survey one read.

"Impressive. You do look healthy," Ray told him.

"I am. Except for my damn hearing. I guess for ninety, I should expect something to fail." The man chuckled. "This man was skinny too, if that helps."

Jack nodded. "It does. Is that all you remember seeing?"

"I think so. If I remember anything else," he waved Jack's card in front of him, "I'll call you." As Jack stepped back from the door, the old man added, "Since I helped you with something, maybe you can help me in return."

"What's that?" Jack asked.

The man disappeared into his living room and returned a moment later with a crossword and pencil in his trembling hands. "I'm stuck on the last clue of this puzzle and can't figure it out. Are you either of you any good with these things?"

"Not really." Jack took a slow, calming breath.

"I just need an eight-letter word. Starts with P and ends with E. Something one can lose at the drop of a hat." The man looked up from his crossword, expectation in his gaze.

Yeah, he knew that one. It was something he was struggling with this very moment.

"Patience."

CHAPTER EIGHTEEN

Jack slid into the passenger seat of Ray's department issued unmarked vehicle. Once behind the wheel, Ray called Haniford to let him know he was getting a warrant to search Dinish Ranganathan's apartment. While they had the police report, Jack had questions. He wanted to know if Ranganathan was struck in the apartment and it caused him to fall; if he was struck and then pushed over the balcony; or if Ranganathan struck his head on the way down to the pavement, and if so, where? There had to be evidence. Since investigators assumed suicide, they didn't appear to have performed much of an investigation. Once they got the warrant to get into the apartment, they'd also interview his neighbors while they were in the building.

Jack checked the map. For as much technology as he used in his job, he didn't trust GPS for multiple stops. Not around San Francisco anyway. GPS had led him the wrong way down too many one-way streets, so for now, he went old school.

As they were visiting each victim's apartment, the next nearest on the map was Sanjay Bajwa's place. As with Joshi's apartment, Bajwa's had already been cleaned out and re-rented. There was one other neighbor on Bajwa's floor.

"I don't know anything," the man at the door said. Jack gauged him as middle aged, a little overweight and carrying a small paunch, and losing his hair in an obscure pattern. What he had stuck up at odd angles.

Jack let Ray take the lead on this one.

"Were you home that day?" Ray asked.

"I don't remember. If I was, I was sleeping. Didn't he off himself in the middle of the night? I sleep at night. Everyone sleeps at night," he said gruffly.

Jack knew Ray had little tolerance for people like this guy, so he stood back and tried keeping a chuckle to himself.

Admirably, Jack thought, Ray calmly continued. "You're the only neighbor on the floor. You must have seen or heard something. Anything unusual on the days leading up to Mr. Bajwa's death?" The man shook his head. Ray handed him his card. "All right. Thank you. If you do remember anything, let me know."

Halfway down the hall, the man called out, "Hey." Jack and Ray turned back. "I don't know if this is a thing, but there was some noise coming from inside the apartment. I think the guy was a dancer. I heard him in there all the time with his funny music. Once he had the door open and I saw him spinning around in girls' clothes."

"What do you mean by 'spinning around in girls' clothes'?" Jack asked.

The man's face screwed up in a disapproving way. "You know." He moved into the hall and twirled like a drunk ballerina. "Like a girl. Looked like he was wearing fancy drapes."

Jack gazed over at Ray, then back to the man. "He was Indian. Do you mean he was wearing a *sari*?"

"I don't know what you call it, but it looked like girl's clothes to me."

"What set his normal dancing apart from what you heard on the night of his death?" Ray asked.

"Normally, I only heard the one guy. That night it sounded like two of them. But it didn't sound like dancing. More like shuffling and stomping around."

"Do you remember the time?" Ray continued.

"Sometime after three, I think. Does that help?"

"Yes, sir, it does," Jack said. "Thank you. You have my partner's card. Please call if you remember anything else."

At the car, Jack said, "Shuffling and stomping around could have been the struggle between Bajwa and his killer, him fighting his attacker. Or even getting the body onto the clothes rail."

Ray scribbled in his notebook. Jack had his video. "Sounds like it to me, too."

Next up was Krish Naidu's apartment. While he had been killed in his brother's apartment, Jack and Ray still needed to talk to the neighbors.

No one in the building seemed to be home, or if they were, they weren't answering their doors to strangers. But they did speak to a young couple in the lobby as they entered the building arm in arm.

"We didn't know him," the man said.

"We didn't know him, but we knew *about* him," the woman corrected.

"Right. We heard he was a dancer, or an actor maybe. We saw him in costume a couple times. I think he was Indian so maybe he was in a Bollywood type movie," the man suggested. "There are a few film studios around."

"Thank you for your help," Ray said, handing the man his card. "If you remember anything—"

"Yeah. We'll call," the man finished.

As Jack and Ray turned to leave, the woman stopped Jack with a hand on his arm. "Sorry."

"Was there something else?" Jack asked.

"Is there anything you can do about the access to the building?"

"What do you mean?"

"There was this weird guy," she said. That drew Jack's attention. Ray's too by the look on his face. "I saw him earlier in the evening when we went out to dinner. He was lurking across the street," she motioned to where she'd seen the man, "under that big tree. It was dark, and he was wearing black. I nearly missed him standing in the shadows. Later, when we came home, he was running out of the building. When he saw us coming up the sidewalk, he turned and ran the other way."

"Could that have been the night Mr. Naidu died?" Ray asked.

The couple murmured between themselves, then the man said, "I think you're right. Do you think he killed him?"

Jack shrugged. "It's hard to tell. Do you remember what time you saw him . . . when you left and then returned?"

"We had plans to meet friends at eleven," the man said. "We walked so left around ten-thirty." The woman nodded her confirmation of the time they left the building. Still looking at each other, he said, "Came home around two-thirty." The woman nodded, agreeing with the time, and they both turned back to Jack.

"Okay, thanks. We appreciate the heads up. We'll definitely look into that. Unfortunately, we can't do anything about access to your building. You'll have to take that up with your landlord."

If the killer was skulking around, maybe one of the neighbors on the street had a security camera set up and they could take a look, but up next was Ramesh Patel's place.

Jack felt like they'd hit the jackpot at Patel's. They interviewed two separate neighbors on the victim's floor who both recounted shouting and scuffling in Patel's apartment that night. While the shouting stopped, the shuffling continued. Not long after, two loud bangs, then a few moments later, a third bang before it went quiet.

"Did you report the noise to the police?" Jack asked the neighbor he interviewed, a middle-aged man who reminded him a lot of Carl Boyd.

"No. Why should I? They just tell you it's a civil matter. Besides, whatever they were arguing about wasn't any of my business. A few slamming doors and then it was quiet. That's all I cared about."

Jack felt his anger flare and took a deep breath to rein it in. "Two people died—"

Just then, Ray came up beside Jack, cutting him off. He had finished his inquiry down the hall.

"Did you see anything unusual on the days leading up to the incident?" Ray asked. "Anyone who didn't belong in the building or someone suspicious hanging around outside?"

"Nah, I didn't see anyone inside, but there was a guy staring up at the building when I came home from walking my dog. It was like he was looking up at one of the windows, but I don't know which one. Who knows why people do what they do?"

"Did you get a look at his face . . . see what he looked like?" Jack asked.

The man shook his head. "He was all dressed in black and standing in the shadows. I only saw his eyes when he realized I was watching him. Then he turned around and walked up the street. Maybe he wasn't looking up at the windows. Maybe he was looking for an address. I don't know. What I do know is I never saw him again. Sorry, I can't give you more than that."

"You saw his eyes. That's something," Jack said. He shifted his balance onto his other foot, his body moving a little closer to the man. "Did anything stand out about them? Did you see what color they were? What about shape? Something!"

When Ray nudged him in the side, Jack realized he was raising his voice.

"What my partner means, is that if this man was Asian . . . Chinese, for example . . . his eyes would be longer and narrower, or even almond shaped," Ray explained. "If the man had blond hair, his eyes might have been blue . . . if you saw their color."

The man thought, then shook his head. "Definitely not Asian. I didn't see the color of his eyes, but what I did see of his face, he was definitely a white guy."

After doling out cards and thanks, Jack and Ray went back to the car.

"What was that back there?" Ray asked. "Is this getting to you?"

Jack ran his fingers through his hair, then pinched the bridge between his eyes. "I guess I'm out of practice. I'm not used to interviewing so many people back to back like this."

Ray nodded, checking the time. "Okay. Let's call it a day. I still need to get the warrant on Ranganathan's place. At this time of day, I probably won't get signed off on until tomorrow. Ranganathan's apartment is in the Haight near where my victim, Michael Smith, was discovered. We can hit both at the same time."

Jack nodded his agreement. "Drop me at my place and I'll get our findings up on my wall."

"Let's swing by the judge's chambers to see if I can get the warrant signed first, then I'll give you a hand."

Once all the cards and notes had been added to the wall, Jack grabbed a couple beers from his fridge, then followed Ray into the front room, handing him a bottle as he lowered himself onto the sofa. Jack flipped on the side table light, then the one sitting beside his monitor before dropping into the chair behind his desk.

Glancing at the monitor, he felt he really should be watching the Majestic's security camera footage but didn't switch on the machine. He felt more tired than he should after doing a few door-to-doors.

Ray broke the long silence. "You okay?"

Sitting the bottle on the desk, Jack scratched at his scruff. "Yeah, just tired. It's been a long few weeks."

"Are you working security at the club tonight?"

Shaking his head, he said, "Nah, they're closed Monday and Tuesday. But I was over yesterday checking out their exterior security."

"Find anything interesting?" Ray asked.

"There's a narrow gap between the theater and the neighbors off Hartford Street. I think it's supposed to be a service alley for the back of the theater, but it's just wide enough for the average person to use as a shortcut from Castro Street over to 17th via the club's parking lot. A security gate behind the thrift store on 17th was broken through a while ago, based on the rust on the broken hinges and the level of the scattered trash. I think Chad's given up on repairing the fence on his end." Jack downed the last of his beer and dropped the bottle in the trash basket behind the desk.

"Chad owns the Majestic?" Jack nodded in the affirmative. "Chad's a surfer name, not the owner of a gay bar."

Jack chuckled. "He does drag as Marilyn Monroe and is a pretty good performer too. Nice enough guy from what I can tell."

"Do you think the thrift store or neighboring stores have security video?" Ray asked.

Jack shrugged. "Possibly, but probably not into that alley. It's on my to-do list to check out."

"Seems like you have a pretty long to-do list these days.

Following the socialite, security at the club, now helping me investigate these murders. As your friend, I have to say you're looking tired. I'll get some help from Haniford so you can get some rest," Ray suggested.

"I'm okay. I'll try getting some extra sleep tonight so I can hit the pavement fresh in the morning."

Ray ran his gaze over the sofa, then looked back at him. "I don't know why you don't sleep in the backroom. This thing is *totalmente jodido, homes*. I can barely handle just sitting on it. I can't imagine what you're doing to your back."

Jack grinned. "Maybe I need to buy a new sofa."

"Maybe you need to get out of this *agujero de mierda* and into a normal house." Ray sat forward, putting the bottle on the side table. "You need a real bed . . . in a real bedroom. You need room to spread out. A proper place to bring dates—"

Jack cut him off right there. "I don't date."

"You should. You're a good-looking *hombre*. You attract all the bees to your hive, man."

Jack lightly laughed. "Are you calling me a queen bee?"

Ray threw himself back against the sofa. "You know what I mean. Living here," he waved his arm around, "in this place . . . you've been here too long. You need to join the rest of the population again. Find someone and make a life."

"I had a life."

"Make a *new* life. Do you think Leah would want to see you living like this?"

Jack's eyebrows drew together. "Don't talk about Leah."

"I get it, partner, I really do. But it's been four years. Something has to give. You need to—"

Jack shot out of his chair. "Stop telling me what I need to do." He stomped to the far end of the window, crossed his arms, and looked out at the Bay Bridge, her string of lights shining through the foggy night sky.

After a short pause, Ray lowered his voice. "I'm sorry, Jack, but you have no idea how hard it is for me seeing you like this. And Maria. Every night she asks about you. What do I tell her?"

"Tell her I'm fine," Jack said under his breath.

"But you're not fine."

Ray wasn't wrong. Jack had nearly four years of not being fine. Maybe he was getting used to it.

"I'll *be* fine . . . once I find Leah and find out what happened to our daughter. I'll be fine then." He'd told Ray the same thing over the years.

"I understand, but that doesn't mean you have to live here, like this. If you won't go home to your own house and if you won't sell it so you can buy another house, why not consider coming to live with us for a while?" Ray suggested.

Jack turned toward his friend. "Is this you making the offer or Maria?"

"Why can't it be both of us?"

"You have a baby coming any day now. You don't need me . . . cluttering your place," he hastily finished. He didn't need Ray knowing what he really felt. Instead, he used the excuse, "I need office space and room to spread out."

"Fine. Keep this place and turn it into a proper office. But come home with me. Stay with us for a while. You need to be with family."

Ray was nothing if not generous. It was just one of the things he admired about his friend. His offer humbled him, but Jack knew if he moved out of the apartment . . . even if he did keep it for a proper office . . . he knew he'd only bring down the atmosphere in the Navarro home. Ray and Maria had a wonderful marriage. They were happy and it showed. Ray's whole demeanor completely changed with the slightest mention of his wife.

Jack already knew what this baby was doing to his friend. He was already the proudest father in the city and his child hadn't even arrived yet. Jack didn't know how *he* was going to survive after the baby was born. If Ray was anything like himself, he knew his friend would talk the ears off anyone who'd listen about his new son or daughter. He'd done the same thing when Zoë was born. Putting himself into that situation—smack in the center of Ray and Maria's joy—was a bad idea. He couldn't subject his two closest friends to the darkness that lived inside him. He barely kept his shit together when he had dinner with them. And now that they were expecting...

Ever since Ray had told him about the baby, it brought everything back. All the happiness and joy he'd once felt that swelled in his chest until he wanted to scream to the world how much he loved his family. Only now, the lack of those feelings swelled in his chest until he wanted to explode with hurt and fury. It was just one of the reasons he threw himself into so much work. It was all distraction—the job of following Franklin the Third, the security gig, the murders, the door-to-door inquiries, and knowing most of it tied in somehow . . . trying to put all of the puzzle pieces together. Not to mention now that it was the holidays and all the shit that came with it.

He used to tease Leah about her love of Christmas. She became more obsessed after Zoë was born. It wasn't his thing, but he loved watching how excited his girls got when they went to see the tree lighting at Union Square and all the other big holiday events around the city.

He had to admit, he did enjoy helping her shop for and decorate the tree. They'd made love in front of the tree a few times. The sparkling lights danced over her perfect body and flashed in her eyes as she gazed up at him. He didn't need Christmas to bring him gifts. She was his gift. Every goddamn day of the year. *That* made him happy. Had, he reminded himself.

Working this hard meant he didn't have to remember those things. He wanted to work until he dropped his exhausted body onto the sofa, asleep almost instantly, despite the nightmares that still haunted him. The worn out piece of furniture didn't bother him. He was simply too tired to notice, or care. Then he'd wake up the next day, and as soon as his eyes opened, he'd bury himself in the work again. It was a cycle he'd repeat until he took out his Beretta for the last time.

"Jack," Ray said, pulling him out of his thoughts. His lowered voice nearly pleaded with him. "Come home with me. Be with our family. At least through the holidays."

He turned back toward the window, squeezing his arms tighter around himself. "Tell Maria I appreciate the offer. It means a lot. Honestly. You're both great friends."

In the window's reflection, he watched Ray rise from the sofa and come to stand beside him. He didn't look over; he was barely keeping things together as it was. Ray squeezed his shoulder, but neither said anything for a long moment. Jack breathed deeply to calm his racing heart.

"I didn't mean to upset you, Jack. We just want you to know we're here when you need us." All Jack could do was nod, indicating he'd heard what his friend had said.

Then the hand was gone, and Jack felt colder for it.

"Look, I'll catch you tomorrow."

When he heard the door open, Jack said, "Thanks, brother."

"No thanks needed."

"And hey," he said over his shoulder. "We can't forget to interview Bob Johnson's neighbors. The shooting victim at the club. He's part of this too."

"Good idea. We'll do that."

"If you're going to Haniford in the morning, suggest he get Wash and Harry to help out gathering surveillance footage from any of the neighbors where the victims lived."

"How about I pick you up in the morning and we see Haniford together? Maybe you can get your jacket back then," Ray suggested.

Jack really didn't want to deal with his former LT, but getting his jacket back was something he *did* want to do. "Good idea. I'll be ready by ten."

"You gonna be okay?"

"Yep. Never better." And it was the truth. Until he found Leah and his daughter's killer, nothing would ever be better than it was this very moment.

CHAPTER NINETEEN

Wednesday

As promised, Ray strolled through the door at 10a.m. Thankfully, there was no mention of their discussion the previous night.

"Marie sent this over."

Jack took the brown paper bag Ray handed him; it was on its side and rolled closed. He pulled out a thick paper plate covered with foil. "What's this all about?"

"She's been baking. She wanted to volunteer to help with the kids this weekend, but I won't let her. She's too close to her due date. So, she's baking *galettas* instead." Ray puffed out his cheeks and screwed up his eyes, as if he was going to vomit.

Jack chuckled, setting the plate on the desk. "By the look on your face, you've eaten more than a few."

"I told her she was starting too soon—they'll be stale by Saturday—so she sent these over for you. Enjoy."

Pulling off the foil, he found a mound of cookies in various shapes and colors. He tossed a powdered sugar covered ball into his mouth. His taste buds were immediately happy. Maria's culinary skills went far beyond her guacamole and salsa.

Beside him, Ray pointed to each type of cookie. "The one in your mouth is a *Polvorón*—Mexican Wedding Cookie. These are *Hojarascas*—a kind of citrus spice cookie," Ray said, motioning toward the round speckled cookies powdered with granulated sugar and spices. Then he pointed to the cutout cookies and said, "Those are *Mantecados*. They're made from toasted flour, cocoa, and flavored with flower sugar then covered in powdered flower sugar."

"What are these colored ones?" Jack asked, taking a bite out of a blue cookie. It seemed these came in a set, each cookie a different color of the rainbow.

"They're normal Christmas sugar cookies. Maria likes to add food coloring to each batch so they're more colorful than white cookies. Apparently, because they're so colorful, she doesn't have to ice them. She thinks the gay community will appreciate the rainbow colors on Saturday."

"You can tell Maria thank you from me. They're delicious. And yes, everyone will love them." He popped one of the *Hojarascas* into his mouth to hold while re-covering the plate, then he slid into his jacket. "Ready when you are," he said after finally biting into the cookie and grasping the remainder in his hand.

Ray's face screwed up again. "Are you sure you want to go out today? You still look tired."

Zipping up the jacket, Jack nodded. "I'm good to go now that I've had some of Maria's baking." In truth, Jack felt like he was coming down with a cold, but he had too much work in front of him to worry about getting sick.

Ray chuckled. "There's more where that came from. She made me go shopping for ingredients early this morning so she could bake all day."

Lieutenant Dick Haniford's office was at the top of the police headquarters building at the back, overlooking Pier 50 and the city of Alameda on the other side of the south end of San Francisco Bay.

The last time Jack had seen Haniford was in the patrol car on Black Friday. Then, he was in street clothes. Today was much the same. Only, instead of the blue sweater he'd worn that night emblazoned with *POLICE NAVIDAD*, today he wore a red sweater with an image of Santa's sleigh being pulled by police motorcycles, and the words *I CAME TO SLEIGH* stretched across his chest. Jack groaned.

"Navarro. Slaughter," Haniford greeted, waving them in.

"LT," Jack said.

Haniford must have seen some reaction on Jack's face, as he quickly glanced down then back up. "'Tis the season, or so the wife tells me. When I'm done here, I'm heading home to take Nancy Christmas shopping. I came in for this." He waved his free hand toward the chairs in front of his desk. "Have a seat. Fill me in. What did you turn up yesterday?"

Ray settled into his chair—the paper bag he'd carried in resting on his lap—and filled in Haniford. "Based on some of our witness interviews, there's a running theme focusing on a guy who lurks in the shadows across the street before gaining entrance into the buildings. He's our primary person of interest, but so far, no one has been able to give us a description other than he's about five-nine or ten with a slim build. He's always seen in black with a wide-brimmed hat to shield his face. One witness clocks him as Caucasian."

"That jives with the person I saw running away from the scene that night at the Majestic." Jack sat forward, elbows on his knees. "Given that all of the murders were patrons of the club, I'm not wasting anyone's time by saying we think it's the same guy. And we think this is the same guy involved in Ray's suspected suicide in the Haight. Especially as it turns out, he was also a performer at the Majestic."

A deep line furrowed between Haniford's eyebrows. "Have you pinned down who the first victim was?"

"We're working on information we gathered from the club owner," Ray said, glancing at Jack.

"Chad Lucas owns the Majestic Lounge. He approached me to do security for him during the holidays."

"Isn't that the place with the drag race?" Haniford asked. Jack nodded. "Explain. And Jack, don't waste my time by withholding details."

Jack sat back, crossed an ankle over his leg and wove his fingers over his stomach. Haniford knew Jack all too well. He'd left out a lot in The Butcher case.

"I was hired to follow a woman's husband and he led me to the club, which he's known to frequent, according to Lucas."

"No names?" Haniford asked.

Jack shook his head. "Not at the moment. They're well-known socialites, and she wants to keep this out of the headlines. It doesn't bear any relevance to this case though. Just letting you know how I got the club gig."

"Go on."

"So, I followed the husband into the club. I wanted to see what he was up to and try getting some photos for the wife's divorce . . . strict prenup and all that." Haniford nodded that he was following along. "While there, an altercation broke out between the husband—who's now a cross-dresser, by the way—and a man dressed as Marilyn Monroe. Turns out to be Chad Lucas, the club owner. Long story short, Chad came to my apartment the next day to hire me for added security for the event. We had a talk about what was going on in the club, and with his friends. He hopes with me there, we can prevent anyone else from being targeted. I intend on finding out what's going on and who's killing them."

"As we talked about a couple days ago, Lieutenant," Ray said, "there's strong evidence pointing to murder and not suicide. Cutter agrees. He took us into the fridge where he still had Patel and Naidu's bodies. Their deaths were deemed a suicide pact or murder-suicide, but Chad told Jack that while they were brothers and performed in the same group, they didn't actually like each other. The position of the bodies doesn't make sense based on that alone."

"Interesting," Haniford remarked. "But it doesn't mean they didn't kill each other. Could there have been something going on that caused them to end their lives together?"

Ray shook his head. "Nothing adds up here. The trajectory of the bullets was completely wrong for a mutual suicide, and body evidence doesn't match up for a murder-suicide."

"And only one weapon was found on the scene," Jack added. "Like the other shooting deaths, the weapon was also left behind at this scene, but just one. Not all were shot though. One was staged to look like a hanging and the other appears to have jumped to his death. But at all of the shooting scenes, similar weapons have been discovered."

Haniford's gaze widened. "That's gotta be expensive. Do you suppose it's someone weeding through his gun collection, or maybe he has a supplier of cheap weapons?"

Jack and Ray shared a look. This time Jack jerked his head toward Haniford for Ray to continue. "*Imura* revolvers."

"What the fuck?" Haniford's expression screwed up in disbelief.

"Handguns manufactured on 3D printers," Ray explained. "They're good for a couple shots. Our guy only needed one. Or two in the case of Patel and Naidu. Since the weapon is effectively worthless after that—the 3D filament degrading quickly after each discharge—he's leaving them behind as he exits the residences."

"Another clue that these men didn't kill themselves. I'm guessing if we go back through the evidence and investigator notes, there won't be any mention of a 3D printer in anyone's apartment. And I'm pretty sure Kinko's would never agree to that kind of job. Our perp owns his own home printer." Jack fidgeted in his seat then sat forward again, trying to get comfortable. His body was starting to ache. He looked over at the waste basket beside Haniford's desk and swallowed back the lump in his throat.

"We'll need to pull those weapons out of evidence and get them fingerprinted, if they haven't been already," Haniford said.

"I'm already on it."

"Thanks, Ray." Haniford shook his head in disbelief. "How did the investigators miss this. And the ME? Don't tell me Cutter is losing his touch. I know he's not happy with the new arrangement, but botching autopsies—"

"Not Cutter," Jack cut in, taking his mind off his queasy stomach. "Harold Baxter. He was the ME on all of these victims. The only one he tagged as murder was my shooting victim, Bob Johnson. He was the only one who wasn't killed in his place of residence. It's quite possible that because he was a visitor to the city and staying in a hotel, the perp didn't want to chance being seen."

"Goddammit! Are we talking about another serial killer?"

Jack shrugged. "That's not my call, but if that's what this is, he's only targeting performers at the one nightclub."

"This is not what I need right now. It's not what the city needs," Haniford exclaimed, pounding his fist on the desk.

"At least these victims' families will know what really happened to their loved ones," Ray said. Jack knew his friend was talking about the women Travers had killed, some of whom still were yet to be identified.

"I'm told," Jack continued, a knot growing in his belly, "a murder is easier to cope with than a suicide. Most people who take their own lives will leave a note explaining their actions to their families. While it's not uncommon, none of these victims left a suicide note. Knowing it was murder may not bring back their loved ones, but it can help them cope better over an unanswered suicide."

Haniford sat back heavily in his chair. "How many are we talking about?"

"Seven if you include my guy at the club and Ray's in the Haight. Chad didn't mention anyone else other than the first five—Joshi, Bajwa, Ranganathan, Patel, and Naidu." Jack explained who the Indian Spicy Girls were and how they related to the Majestic.

"What about the other two?" Haniford asked.

"Bob Johnson was from out of town. Formerly from Lubbock, Texas, lately of Los Angeles, here for the competition, as I said. Ray's guy was Michael Smith. We're not sure but he may have been another club patron based on the female clothing and makeup found in the guy's apartment."

"Could that stuff belong to a girlfriend?" Haniford asked.

Ray shook his head. "Didn't appear there was anyone else living in the apartment. Plus, it all seemed garish and loud. You know . . . sequins and feathers."

Jack added, "We're interviewing his neighbors today. I'll talk with Chad when I'm back in the club tonight, see if he knows anything about Smith. And if I can find out where Johnson was staying, we can swing by the hotel and talk to staff. Maybe on an off chance this mysterious suspect was seen there, even if he was only lurking in the shadows outside the building."

Haniford nodded before spinning in his chair to look out across the bay, his fingers steepled over his mouth. It was a long minute before he turned around again. "Okay . . . If I have it right, you'll be talking with Smith's and Ranganathan's neighbors today, and you'll be inspecting both of their apartments?" Turning to Ray, he asked, "You've got the warrants now?"

"The judge signed off on them this morning before I picked up Jack to come here."

Haniford nodded. "Jack, you're talking to the club owner when you see him tonight and asking about Smith." Jack and Ray nodded their agreements. "Hopefully, we can wrap this up quickly before the media gets hold of it. If all the victims are tied to that club, we may have to shut down the club until we can catch whoever is doing this."

"There's another thing," Jack said.

"Jesus!" Haniford cursed under his breath. "What?"

Jack and Ray exchanged glances. He expected Ray to take up the task but left it in his lap with a curt *you ask him* jerk of his head toward Haniford.

Jack nervously shifted in his seat. He wasn't a cop anymore, wasn't employed by the department in any way, shape, or form. He was only assisting Ray in an unofficial capacity. Yet, here he was, sitting in his former LT's office and asking him for help on an official police case. When he gazed back at his friend, Ray again jerked his head toward Haniford, widening his eyes and indicating Jack needed to get on with it.

"What, already?" Exasperation edged Haniford's voice.

Jack narrowed his gaze at Ray then turned toward the LT. "Since we've established Bob Johnson was part of all these suspected suicides, which I'm sure we can all agree are now murders, we think we need to bring in some help. This is bigger than the two of us. Especially because of the time of year. We need to catch as many possible witnesses as we can before they leave the city—Christmas is only a week away. And because I'm not officially on the case—this is Ray's case and I'm just helping in an unofficial capacity." When Haniford opened his mouth to speak, Jack held up his hand. "I know, I know. Old story, same answer. When I'm ready. But this case ties into the job I'm doing at the Majestic, so I have a vested interest in seeing it through."

Haniford thought and hesitantly nodded. "What do you need?" He gazed at Ray when he asked.

"Since Wash and Harry are already investigating the open Johnson case, we'd like to pull them in on this one too," Ray said. "We've interviewed most of the neighbors in the apartment buildings and will finish this afternoon. What we need is someone to interview all the neighbors on the streets and ask if anyone has any security cameras that might have picked up the suspect. If we can obtain some of that footage, there may be an angle that'll reveal his face. If there is, we can get the techies to do a facial recognition scan. If he's in the system, we can pick him up for questioning."

Haniford paused, then leaned over and pushed the intercom, connecting him with his secretary. "Helen, are Wash and Harry in the building?"

"Let me check, Lieutenant." A moment later, the intercom buzzed. "Inspector Callahan just clocked in. I'll send her up."

"Thanks. Send in Wash when he gets here."

"Also," Ray continued. Jack didn't miss the sharp lift of Haniford's eyebrow when he looked up at Ray. "We need someone to go around to all the places that sell 3D printer supplies. Whoever is doing this is using a hell of a lot of filament. If he paid with a credit card or check, we'll have an address on him. Since Johnson is their case, they've probably already been to his hotel, so it's one less thing on our to-do list. If we can get this guy's address, they can pick him up and bring him in for questioning."

Haniford nodded his agreement then sat back in his chair again and gazed between Jack and Ray, as if gauging what to say and to whom. He settled on Ray. "How's Maria doing?"

Ray grinned. Jack hated himself for grimacing at the way his friend's face lit up.

"She's doing great. She's more than ready to have this baby, but she's distracting herself with baking."

"Nancy is too. The baking," he corrected. "When she's not shopping. Why does Christmas have to be so goddamn expensive?"

"I hear that," Ray said. "Add a baby on the way and . . ." Ray didn't have to go any further. Everyone knew how expensive it was having a family. "Maria wanted to help out on Saturday, but she's too far along for her to be on her feet for so long. So instead, she's baking cookies for the event." Ray leaned over the desk and put the paper bag in front of Haniford.

"What's this?"

Jack watched Haniford open the bag and pull out the foil covered, festively decorated paper plate. Ray explained the various Mexican cookies while the man sampled them.

Jack eyed the Wedding Cookies but didn't say anything. He had his own plate at home. Though now his stomach twisted at the thought of food.

"If this is a sample of what Maria is making for Saturday, they'll be a hit. These are wonderful, Ray. Please give Maria my thanks."

Just then, a knock sounded and the door opened. "You wanted to see me, sir." Inspector Deborah Callaghan strode over to stand beside Ray.

"Grab a chair, Harry." When she did, Haniford told her about his conversation with Jack and Ray. She took notes while he spoke. When he finished, he asked, "Do you understand?"

"Yes, sir," she said. "Visit the victims' neighbors and obtain any security camera footage. Also, track down any and all shops selling 3D printer equipment and ascertain which customers have been bulk buying. Go back to the hotel to re-interview the staff about the guy dressed in black."

Haniford nodded. "Excellent."

A knock at the door and Inspector Othuleyo Washington entered the office. "Sir." He quickly gazed at the group sitting in front of the desk then focused on Haniford. Jack didn't register any curiosity, just waiting for instructions. He admired the man's confidence.

Haniford waved him into the room where he moved to stand behind his partner. "Morning, Wash. Another case ties into yours so I want you working together on this. Harry will fill you in."

Wash glanced at Harry then said, "Just tell us what you need us to do, sir. We'll help any way we can."

"I'll just say it sounds like a total clusterfuck of mistakes on this one, folks. We'll need to go back through everything with a fine-tooth comb. Going forward, we don't need any more mistakes, so be sure to take a CSI with you, Ray. And so we're clear," his gaze darted between Harry and Wash, "Ray is taking lead on this investigation. Everyone reports to you; that includes the two of you." He motioned to Harry and Wash. "Ray, you report to me." Haniford turned to Jack.

"Sir?" Jack asked.

With a deep sigh, Haniford said, "We both know where you stand here, Jack. I'm turning my head to your official involvement. I can tell you till I'm blue in the face to stand down on this, but I know you won't. So, keep your head down. Do the jobs you were hired to do by your clients. I know they tie into this case, but please let Ray take the lead . . . Or at least make it look like he is."

CHAPTER TWENTY

Dinish Ranganathan's apartment was located on Upper Haight Street, so named because it was on the hill part of the Haight District. They'd just come from Michael Smith's apartment in the Lower Haight where they hadn't learned anything new.

The building containing Ranganathan's apartment was modern construction that had been built to mimic historical architecture in the district. Ranganathan's place was four stories above what appeared to be an underground residents' parking garage. They didn't have access into the garage, so they parked on the street halfway down the block in the first free space Ray could find.

Jack followed Ray and CSI Gordy Chase through a heavy glass door into the building's lobby where they were immediately met with a bank of mailboxes against one wall. At the back of the lobby, two doors flanked a central stairwell and were marked GARAGE and MANAGER.

Ray knocked on the manager's door.

"Yes?" An attractive older woman stood in the doorway, looking between each man before settling her gaze on Jack. Her up-styled graying hair was more salt than pepper, and while her rosy features seemed youthful, the deep lines around her eyes and slightly jowly cheeks gave away her seniority. Her pink-slippered feet, knee-length floral dress, matching pink sweater, and reading glasses hanging from a pink cord around her neck completed her grandmotherly appearance.

Her piercing blue-green gaze unsettled him, but he couldn't say why.

Ray cleared his throat, drawing her attention. "Ma'am.

I'm Detective Reyes Navarro with the SFPD." Waving to Jack and Gordy, he said, "Private Investigator Jack Slaughter and CSI Gordon Chase. We have a warrant to enter Mr. Dinish Ranganathan's apartment."

She took the warrant and quickly gazed over it. "I thought you boys already did your thing up there."

"We did," Ray assured her. "We just need to double check a couple details and require access into the apartment."

The woman disappeared for a moment and reappeared with two keys. "This one," she held up a key, "is for the apartment. Please be sure the door is locked when you leave. I don't want to have to walk all the way up there just to check the door."

"We will," Ray promised. "And the smaller key?" He took it from her too.

"For the mailbox, over there." She pointed to the bank of mailboxes just inside the door. "Poor man. It doesn't seem right that he's still receiving mail, but maybe there's something in there you can use."

"Yes, ma'am. We'll bring it up to the apartment with us," Ray told her. "You can let the postal carrier know Mr. Ranganathan no longer lives in the building. They'll put a stop on his mail until a change of address has been filed by the family."

The woman nodded her agreement. "Be sure you bring both of those keys back to me."

"Thank you," Ray said. "May I have your name for our records?"

After one more lingering look at Jack, she said, "Janeen Baker," then stepped back into her apartment and closed the door. Jack had the strangest feeling she was still looking at him through the peephole.

After Gordy dusted the mailbox for prints—no stone left unturned—they grabbed the mail and headed for the stairs.

A sign that said APARTMENTS had an arrow pointing up the stairs. A smaller sign beside the first listed the apartments as 1st Floor – 201 and 202, 2nd Floor – 301 and 302, and 3rd Floor – 401 and 402.

It hadn't escaped Jack's notice that the address on the warrant said the victim's apartment was number 402 and the only way up was by the stairs.

He felt the tiredness push against him as he mounted the stairs behind Ray and Gordy, half pulling himself up by the handrail, his breath becoming labored the more stairs he climbed. He really needed to get more sleep. That was on his to-do list once this case was solved.

At Ranganathan's door, Gordy doled out new booties and powder-free nitrile gloves, aka medical-grade gloves that were quickly becoming the norm across all public service departments. They fit like a second skin and were nearly puncture resistant, better protecting the wearers from most contaminants, including bloodborne infections.

Ray turned to Jack, weaving his fingers together to make sure the fingertips fitted correctly. "You okay? You don't look so good."

Jack agreed. He didn't feel so good either. "I'm fine. Let's get this done."

Entering the apartment, Jack was surprised by the generous size of the place. His first instinct was to find the balcony and get onto it to check out the victim's fall trajectory and see if there was any evidence that had been missed the first time around. But he held back. This needed to be played by the book.

Jack gazed at Gordy. "Were you on the team during the original visit?"

The CSI shook his head. "First time."

"Good. Everything will be fresh to you. Keep your eyes open. Check everything. Treat this as a new crime scene." Gordy nodded and moved into the room, choosing a spot on a low table to set his kit. "Ray?"

Ray gazed around the room. "I'll check the bedroom and bathroom. Why don't you check the kitchen and living room? Get Gordy to collect anything you think looks unusual. You know the drill." Jack nodded and moved into the kitchen as Ray disappeared down a short hall.

If everything had been left *in situ* the night of Ranganathan's death, the kitchen was tidy except for two partially filled glasses of red wine on the counter beside an uncorked bottle. They'd been sitting out for so long, most of the water had evaporated and left dark streaks inside the glasses, and mildew was forming in the residue.

Did Ranganathan already have a visitor in the apartment, or had he been expecting someone? Three in the morning seemed a bit late to be entertaining, but Jack had to remind himself that the man was a performer in a late-night club.

Nearby, the countertop wine rack was full, minus the bottle beside the glasses. On closer inspection, it appeared Ranganathan preferred red wine, especially from the *Masked Rider Winery* down in Paso Robles. All of the bottles in the rack were from this winery, as was the bottle on the counter beside the glasses—*Gunsmoke Red.*

No lip marks were on either glass, but he'd get Gordy to check the smudges for fingerprints.

He glanced around the small kitchen—white cupboards, black countertop, stainless appliances, and the breakfast bar overlooking the living room—it all seemed clean. Even the interior of the oven was spotless, making Jack wonder if the man even cooked. A quick check inside the cupboards revealed several spices, chutneys, and prepacked naan bread, which were now out of date. Wilted and rotting vegetables in the refrigerator confirmed they'd been freshly bought before the victim's death. Fresh produce didn't give Jack a feeling the man was going to kill himself.

Stepping out of the kitchen area, Jack glanced around the living room. It was also well-kept. Timber floors and white-painted walls had been furnished with Indian décor—brightly colored scatter rugs, colorful cushions on a tan sofa, traditional wall hangings, and big leafy plants sitting on several pieces of dark timber furniture. Taller plants had been placed in woven baskets and placed around the room.

Overall, this part of the apartment showed a careful attention to detail that reflected the victim's heritage; it was one of the cleanest crime scenes he'd ever seen. He was surprised there wasn't any fingerprint residue from the previous investigation, but if those investigators were treating the death as a suicide, perhaps they declined that part of their search.

Jack's gaze settled on a large window overlooking Haight Street. In the corner between the bay window and a right-angle window sat a large palm tree. The window to the right was partially obscured by a tall leafy tree. On closer inspection, he noticed scrapes along the floor toward what revealed itself as a pair of long, narrow multi-pane glass doors onto the balcony.

"Gordy," Jack called to the CSI who had moved into the kitchen to dust the wine glasses and bottle. He looked up at the sound of his name. "I need this documented before I touch it."

Gordy came to Jack's side after grabbing his camera from his evidence kit. "Show me what you need photographed."

Jack pointed to the scratches on the floor, the tree, and the balcony doors.

Ray quickly appeared from the hall. "Find something?" He rushed to Jack's side.

Gazing around the room, thoughts spun in Jack's tired mind. "This tree has been moved. See the scratch marks? If the victim jumped or was pushed over the balcony, how could he have gotten out there if the tree was in the way?"

"Holy shit," Ray said with a sharp gasp. "Gordy, photograph the area so we can compare it to the original report. We need to rule out that it wasn't moved by the previous investigators or anyone else after the fact."

When Gordy was done, Jack said, "Help me lift this, Ray, so we can get onto the balcony." Jack didn't want to take the chance any evidence was hiding under the tree. He grunted as he lifted his side. The tree was much taller than it was wide—definitely a lot taller than he was—but it wasn't as heavy as he expected. "Who the fuck keeps trees in an apartment?" But it must have been too heavy for whoever moved it, or the floor wouldn't have been scarred.

After they set the tree a few feet away, Ray said, "Maria has one at home. I think she called it a Fiddly Fig, or something like that. She said they're supposed to be fiddly to keep alive, but you've seen the damn thing. It's like a triffid." Ray turned a leaf to show Jack.

"If it's a fig tree, where are the figs?"

"Don't ask me," Ray said with a whine, his face pinched. "My only job is to help her water the damn things. I just hope once the baby comes, she won't have time for her plants anymore and I can get back some of my house."

"*Ficus Lyrata.*"

Jack and Ray turned in unison to Gordy. "What?" They echoed each other.

"That tree is called *Ficus Lyrata*, or commonly, Fiddle Leaf Fig. They get their name from the shape of the leaves—fiddles. And your wife is right, Inspector. They are fiddly to grow."

"Explain," Ray said.

Gordy stepped over to the tree. "These plants are a pain in the ass to acclimate. They don't like direct light, but they do like it bright; it can take time to find a spot in a room they like. Typical of Ficuses, if they don't like where they are, they start dropping their leaves. Find a place they like, and they'll thrive. You can see where this one had originally been placed off to the side of this glass door. The floor timber is darker in this spot than the rest of the house, most likely from black stains coming off the bottom of the basket. The terracotta pot absorbed a lot of water that over time has leached into the basket and eventually mildewed the floor. This only happens over a long space of time. If you look around the apartment, you'll find other potted plants with similar damage on the floor where they've lived where they're happiest."

Jack and Ray agreed with Gordy's assessment. Ray scribbled notes in his pad while Jack made sure his phone captured the video.

Gordy waved his hand along some of the leaves. "Look here. You can tell this tree hasn't been moved, probably in years. See how tall it is? It loves this spot. And check out all the shiny leaves. You can tell the victim took care of it. What little dust on the leaves has settled since the victim's death."

Ray ran his fingers through his hair and groaned. "It looks like Maria's tree isn't going anywhere any time soon."

Jack didn't think so either. As long as he'd known the Navarros, their tree had been in the same place—in their dining room beside but not in front of the west facing window. Even when they updated their house and removed the carpets to put in timber floors, Maria directed the installers to work around the tree as much as possible—literally moving the tree only a few feet aside to remove the old carpeting and lay the new hardwood then immediately move it back to the exact same spot.

"Better check for stains on the floor, brother." Jack heard Ray groan again and suppressed a chuckle.

"You can also tell the plant was moved. Not just by the scratches on the floor, but see these leaves?" Gordy waved his hand along the browning leaves nearest the glass door. "They're sunburnt. If the plant hadn't been moved, they'd still be fully green like those on the rest of the tree, because they were out of direct light. Move it into the sun and it goes crispy around the edges. The longer it's in the sun, the crispier that side of the tree gets as it dies back."

"Holy shit, Gordy," Ray remarked. "Why aren't you an investigator? I never would have caught that."

Gordy chuckled. "I work best alone and in the background."

"I'm sure Ray will be happy to put in a good word with Haniford if you ever want to move up. Ray needs a new partner—" Jack started.

"Fuck you! You need to get back on the job."

"Keep glaring, brother. Look at me." Jack leaned back and postured with his arms spread, nearly falling over when his head felt like it wanted to spin. He caught himself and finished. "I'm not on the force, yet here I am," he said with a weak grin.

Ray scowled before turning back to Gordy. "Okay, so we know someone else was here because the plant was moved. Let's see what we find on the balcony. This tree was moved across the door for a reason."

As Gordy turned to go back to his previous task, Jack reached for the door handle. "Hey, Gordy, we're gonna need you back over here with your camera." Jack pointed at a broken pane of glass on the top corner of the multi-pane door, a partial hole still evident where a bullet passed through at the edge of the broken pane. "I think I know where the victim got the initial wound."

Gordy rushed over to take a few photos before Jack examined

the hole in more detail. "Yep, the round was fired from inside the apartment. Look at the spiderwebbing through the remaining glass. This must be the original glass. You can see the slight rippling where some of it's thicker than the rest. See here where the round left its imprint?"

"Hang on a sec." Ray withdrew his Glock and extracted a 9mm round then compared it with the partial in the glass pane. "Forensics will have to confirm, but it's either a .38 or a nine mil."

Jack nodded his agreement then turned the lock on the door and swung it open to inspect the other side. He was anxious to see if the lab results showed the same size round as the other shooting victims. "Gordy."

The CSI stepped over and snapped a few pictures before letting Jack and Ray continue.

"This too, Gordy." Ray pointed to the glass on the narrow balcony floor. Since the incident, leaves now littered the tiled flooring and partially obscured the broken glass. Had the first team missed it, or had there been leaves here that night too? Either way, it was poor detective work. Careful not to disturb this new evidence, he moved onto the balcony, Ray behind him. Jack's stomach squeezed as he looked over the side and down the length of the building to the sidewalk where the victim had landed. A shadow stained the concrete where solvent had been used to clean off as much of the blood as possible, but it wasn't evident that the victim had struck the building anywhere on his way down.

"Want me to get photos of this while I'm here?" Gordy asked, pointing to a bullet lodged in the horizontal frame over the door.

"Ya think?" Jack said. The headache growing behind his eyes made his reply harsher than it should have been. "Thanks, Gordy. Let's also pull the slug and get it to ballistics." Then he added, "And let's get a line of trajectory while we're here."

Ray turned, crossed his arms over his chest and leaned against the concrete coping. "What do you think?" Ray's face took on his customary pinched look when he was concentrating.

Stifling a grin, Jack unconsciously mimicked Ray's posture

and gazed into the apartment, watching Gordy work. "What I think is this was definitely murder. Something isn't fitting right though." Jack steadied himself on the balcony as a mild wave of nausea washed over him. He was definitely coming down with something. He wondered how much it was going to cost him to ask Ray to stand in for him at the Majestic tonight.

"What do you think it is? What's not fitting right?"

Jack shook his head. "I don't know, but I'm not going to figure it out here." He waited for Gordy to finish what he was doing then went back inside. Ray followed.

Something caught Jack's eye as he moved through the door. He stepped back out again. The late afternoon sun had moved past this part of town, and the tree beside the building was starting to cast the balcony in shadow. But as Ray switched on the apartment lights, something appeared on another pane of glass. One panel down and one over was a distinct smudge. Maybe not a smudge but an irregular shape.

"Hey, Gordy. What do you make of this?"

Gordy moved in beside Jack and looked at the print from several angles. "See this?" Gordy indicated with his finger to the bottom of the crescent shape. There was a mark in the center of it.

"What am I looking at?" Jack asked, studying the mark.

Gordy fingered his ear. "It's an ear print. This is the lobe, and it looks like he's wearing a stud of some kind. If the ME's report confirms the victim had an ear stud, then this looks like your victim's ear print. I'll get a print and you can compare it to the postmortem report." Gordy leaned in closer. "We might have a partial fingerprint too."

"Holy shit!" Jack exclaimed. "Excellent work, Gordy." He clapped the man on the shoulder then moved toward Ray. From the corner of his eye, he'd seen his friend moving around the room. He knew Ray did this to view scenes from all angles. He'd stopped now on the opposite side of the room from the balcony doors. His eyebrows squeezed so close together, they seemed to merge.

"See it?" Ray's gaze was fixed across the room near where Gordy worked.

Jack moved closer to Ray and looked at the room from this angle. "What am I looking at?"

Ray pointed to a tall cabinet. "There. It's going to be obvious when I point it out."

"Yeah. It's a highboy or something. It's on the same wall as the tree."

"Yeah but look down. Underneath. The feet are just tall enough for something to fit under it." Ray rushed over and got down on his side. Jack followed and crouched down to see what his friend was doing. "Hand me Gordy's camera. I want to get a shot of this before I touch it."

Gordy stepped over and handed Ray the camera. After taking the photos he wanted and handing back the camera, Ray slid his arm under the cabinet and rifled around for a moment before sliding back and sitting up.

Dangling from his index finger was an *Imura* revolver.

CHAPTER TWENTY-ONE

Friday

After a bit of bribing, Ray had agreed to take Jack's place at the Majestic Lounge Wednesday night. He was definitely sick—his head pounded, his body ached, and he felt weak as the proverbial kitten. He knew there was no way he could handle a long night at such an active club. He was sure it was just a virus and he needed rest, and lots of it.

"Take a couple days, Jack," Chad had told him when he'd called to let him know Ray was standing in for him. "Midweek is generally quiet, but it'll kick off again Friday. This is the last of the semi-finals and it'll be absolutely screaming."

Jack had sent Ray anyway.

When he hadn't felt much better Thursday, Ray had agreed to sub again. Not for the money Jack was paying him for his time. And not because Ray was technically still on the clock with this investigation—all of the murders tied into the club, so it made sense he check the place out.

Ray had only agreed to work both nights because Jack had relented and agreed to get out of his apartment and spend a few days at the Navarros' over the holidays. The thought of putting himself in the center of their holiday cheer made Jack's stomach twist more than it already did. But he needed the down time to get healthy so he could work at the club for the remainder of the competition and through the New Year's Eve event.

To Jack's surprise, Ray also said he'd shadow him the last few nights. He wanted to be close if something kicked off. Both men agreed there was another serial killer in the city, and they were both sure he wasn't done yet.

Jack hadn't wasted the last two days. When he wasn't sleeping, he was sitting in front of his computer, watching the club's security tapes. He'd discovered some interesting things. One of which was Franklin the Third.

When Jack had first encountered Franklin as Carol, she'd been angry and argumentative. Jack had been sure she was trouble. But while watching the video, he realized Carol was increasingly accepted by club patrons and she seemed in her element socializing with the others, and to Jack's surprise, she was a decent dancer too. Jack didn't know why it should surprise him. Years ago, when Leah was—he very nearly thought alive—when Leah followed the tabloids, several stories focused on Franklin and Ginnie's nights out. By the video clips he'd seen on television, Franklin kept up with the best of them.

Jack heard someone on the stairs and looked up at the door. He checked the time—just before noon. He wasn't expecting anyone. He reached for the mouse and clicked on the computer camera then swung it around toward the door.

Just as he rose to answer the knock, the door swung open, revealing Ray on the threshold. "Hey."

"You toxic?"

Jack chuckled. "No. I think it was just a twenty-four-thirty-six-hour thing. Come on in."

Ray stepped into the apartment, but he wasn't alone. The man with him was dressed in khaki pants and a blue polo shirt. He was clean shaven, and his normally unruly hair was cut close to his scalp.

"Jack," Rod said.

Jack's gaze ricocheted between the men then settled on Ray. He felt his brow tighten, and the dull ache he'd had in his skull for the last few days returned.

"What's this all about, Ray?"

Ray closed the door then both men met Jack at the desk. "Feeling better?" Ray asked.

"Cut the shit. What is *he* doing here?"

"You need to hear this, but I figured it was better hearing it from him—DEA Special Agent Roderick Henderson."

The silence falling just then felt like the air had suddenly been sucked out of the small room.

"DEfuckingA?" Jack drew out a slow whistle. "I think I need to sit down for this." He sat heavily in his chair. Ray motioned for Rod to take the chair in front of the desk then pulled over another chair from the corner of the room. Jack turned the camera toward the men then reseated himself, leaning back with his fingers woven over his tightening abdomen.

The men exchanged glances. Jack assumed they were weighing up who'd speak first. "Well?" he loudly prompted, slapping his palm on the desk, startling the men. "Out with it."

Rod spoke up first. "I tried getting your attention the first night you showed up at the club. I wanted to let you know I was on the job."

Jack chuffed loudly. "You were on the job all right."

Rod sat forward in the chair, elbows on his knees. "I wanted to get you alone so I could explain there was an ongoing investigation. I-I'd seen you the night of the shooting in the driveway, and I was sure when you showed up in the club that you had to be investigating."

"I was hired to do security," Jack said.

"Sure, but knowing your reputation, I was sure you'd be investigating that murder. And the other circumstances," Rod added.

"What other *circumstances*?"

"There's been an undercurrent of rumors going around the club about all the suicides. A handful of people taking their own lives across the city doesn't usually kick up a lot of dust in any department. But anyone paying attention can see so many of them are involved with the club. That's suspicious by any standard. Something is going on over and above the drugs," Rod explained.

Jack sat back again but felt the tension growing through his body. "And even though you know about the suicides, you're still only focused on finding . . .?"

Rod's spine noticeably stiffened as he sat up. "We, the agency, believe Chad Lucas is operating the club as a drugs front. I was sent in undercover to investigate that."

"And you saw me at the club in the driveway the night Bob Johnson was killed—Pepper Mint?" When Rod nodded, he said, "If you saw me, did you see the shooting?" His chest tightened at what he felt coming.

Rod shook his head. "Not the first shot. I was having a smoke at the back door when I heard it. When I looked up the driveway, I saw the second shot. The victim was already down. The shooter rushed past me, and before I had a chance to get to the victim's side, you were coming up the driveway. I ran in the direction of the shooter, but he disappeared at the back of the parking lot. By the time I got back to the driveway, I saw flashing lights. Since you were on the scene, I went back inside."

"Why didn't you make yourself known to me at the time? It would have gone a long way to my not being detained as a suspect, and everything else that's come with it."

"I couldn't risk blowing my cover. You were there for the police end of it. I'm still there to do my job—bring down a drug dealer. Six months of investigations would have been flushed down the crapper," Rod explained. "But when I saw you in the club that night, I tried getting your attention."

Jack's eyes widened. "Tried? The only thing I felt you trying to do was bend me over a car fender." By the look on Rod's face, he knew what Jack implied.

"I had to stay in character. I'd hoped you'd recognized me, even with all that gear on. When you didn't, I had to let you go. If you were going to be working the club, I knew I'd have another chance to get you alone. Of course, every time you saw me looking at you or walking in your direction, you found ways to ignore me."

"I didn't recognize you then, and I don't now," Jack said.

"I gathered that." Rod chuckled lightly, then more somberly, he said, "I was on the initial investigation when your family—"

"Yeah, okay. Fast forward to why you're here now." He spun his gaze toward Ray.

"I spotted Rod on Wednesday night when I walked in," Ray explained. "I knew him before he moved to DEA and know he's a deep-cover agent. He didn't see me come in and I didn't want to blow his cover, so I waited for him to spot me. When that didn't happen, I followed him into the bathroom last night." Jack lifted an eyebrow at his friend, but Ray ignored his little taunt. "Others were in the bathroom so I told Rod to empty his pockets. During a quick pat-down, I let him know I was working in the club and we needed to talk. We agreed to meet this morning, which we did, then came here."

"We decided we should share some intel . . . to help each other out. You and Ray maintain your security status in the club, and I continue with my investigation. Anything we feel crosses over, we let the other know." Rod crossed his legs just then, and a moment later, his arms. His body language told Jack that any information shared would be one-sided—PD to DEA only.

"Yeah . . . right," Jack drew out on a breath. After a long moment, Jack pulled up video from the night of the shooting and spun the monitor to face Rod. "This you coming in the back door?"

The video moved in slow motion as the person rushed through the back door, light bouncing off something shiny around the person's neck.

"Yeah. That glint must be one of the chains." Rod sat up again and motioned with his hands as he started explaining about his costume. "There's this chain thing that goes around—"

Jack put up his hand. "Yeah, yeah. But explain this to me. That night, I was sure I'd seen a woman at the corner of the building. It looked like she was in a dress. Admittedly, I didn't get a good look, because as soon as I saw her, the cops showed up and put their lights in my face. I was sure I'd seen someone in a long dress. Are you sure it was you?"

Rod nodded in the affirmative. "Yep. That was the night I'd ridden over on a bike—you know, part of the overall biker theme—and had worn a long leather duster. It could have looked like a dress in the shadows."

Jack spun the monitor around and made sure the camera angled back to face the two men.

It all made sense now, as much as he hated admitting it. While he could check that box off his list as being resolved, now what? Something still wasn't sitting right.

He gazed at Rod. It was hard reconciling that the trimmed back agent sitting in front of him was the scruffy biker he knew from the club. He had to admit, whoever staged the costuming did a damn good job. Right now, Jack could have mistaken him for an accountant or a realtor.

Jack's mind quickly ran through his time in the club—his encounter with Rod, his get-up . . . his harem.

He looked at the agent with a narrowed gaze. "Tell me about your harem."

Rod gave him a confused look. "What do you mean?"

"You're undercover in the club, gathering intel to take down Lucas, or whoever is dealing."

Rod nodded. "Yeah. I already said that."

"Right, but what about your harem? Are they all agents too?"

"Not all."

"How many? I've counted at least five of them. If they're not all agents, how many are? And if they aren't all agents, who are they? Exactly." Jack pushed for answers.

Rod shifted in his seat. "Where is this coming from?"

"I saw you in the parking lot last week."

Rod's eyes widened. "I—"

"What happened?" Ray asked. His gaze ricocheted between Jack and Rod.

"I saw our friend here in the parking lot behind some cars. It was obvious, even from where I stood, that he was getting a servicing," Jack said, his gaze never leaving Rod's.

"Is this true, Rod? What's going on?" Ray demanded.

Rod's face noticeably reddened as he broke his gaze with Jack and shot a look in Ray's direction. When he looked back at Jack, the man was obviously struggling for the correct answer. Jack knew it wasn't uncommon for undercover agents to get emotionally, and sometimes physically, involved with someone while on the job. Jack had no problem with Rod being gay . . . *if* he was. But a blatant sexual act in public could certainly put his undercover status at risk, and maybe even his career.

"Rod," Jack prodded.

The man pulled out his wallet and extracted a photo, then handed it to Jack. "My girlfriend."

Jack took the photo. The woman was attractive but not stunning. "She's a cop." It wasn't a question.

Nodding, Rod passed the image to Ray. "Inspector Susan Sharp. She works vice." He returned the photo to his wallet, then stuffed the wallet back into his pocket. "Giving that I wasn't going to doll up . . . you know, like the others in the club . . . I opted for the biker get up. I'd stand out on my own, so I enlisted Susan's help. It didn't take long before we picked up some cling-ons."

"They blow you too?" Jack wasn't putting on any kid gloves for the agent. His behavior was inappropriate, even if the person blowing him was his girlfriend. They were on the job and should have respected that.

"No, absolutely not. That night you saw us was the first time *that* had happened. You see . . ." Rod gazed between Jack and Ray again. A smile crept across his face when he said, "That morning, I'd asked Susan to marry me. I guess we were still feeling loved up when we met at the club that night. We wanted a few minutes alone before things got crazy, so we went outside to talk. And well—"

Ray shook his head. "I don't know whether I should congratulate you or tell you how wrong it was. You were on the job, man. If anyone else but Jack had seen you—"

"I know, I know. It's not hard to get lost in the moment. Susan was the one who spotted Jack. As soon as I knew you saw us, reality kicked in and reminded us both where we were. It hadn't happened before, and it hasn't happened since." After a long silence, Rod asked, "Are you going to report us?"

Jack gazed at Ray for a long moment before his friend lightly shook his head. Looking back at the agent, he knew he wasn't going to report the guy, but he'd certainly make Rod think he would. "I don't know yet. That depends on how much you're really willing to share with us. We know how you guys work over there. You promise to share intel if we share with you—we scratch your back first, then you leave us waiting for our scratch. If you want our help, you have to help us. Really help."

Nodding vigorously, Rod agreed. "Absolutely. Whatever you want."

"If either of us get the slightest feeling you're holding out . . ." Jack left the threat hanging.

Rod stood up and extended a hand toward Jack. "Whatever you want," he repeated.

After a moment, he rose and took Rod's hand, then watched him spin toward Ray to shake his as well.

Just then, Ray's cell phone buzzed. He pulled it out and his face screwed up at whatever appeared on the screen. After a couple more taps, he said, "Check your messages. You'll want to see this."

Jack pulled up the messages on his phone, then sent the data to his computer monitor. The image was hazy, but they had it now.

"Our mystery man." Jack fell back into his chair, gazing at the dark figure on the screen. Witness descriptions had been spot on—average height, slim, Caucasian. The person on his screen turned and raced up the sidewalk. When he looked over his shoulder to see if someone was following, Jack could have sworn he recognized that profile from somewhere.

"Yes," Ray exclaimed. "Harry and Wash came through with the neighborhood surveillance videos." Ray's phone sounded again. "Shit!"

"What is it?" Jack asked.

"We've got a body. Officers are on the scene. This one's ripe."

CHAPTER TWENTY-TWO

By the time Jack arrived at the scene on Hearst Avenue, crime scene tape had been stretched across each end of the block, and several officers were in place to protect the barricades and monitor the crowds. One of those officers recognized Jack and lifted the tape for him to walk under.

On his approach to the house, Jack saw the CSI van, ME's wagon, and Haniford's own police vehicle. Jack wondered if it was Baxter or Cutter attending the scene.

Ray spotted Jack and stepped away from the officer he'd been talking with. He moved forward with a scowl on his face.

"What's up?" Jack asked.

Thumbing over his shoulder, Ray said, "Haniford's inside."

"What brought him down here?"

"Victim number eight."

Damn it. Of course, Haniford was anxious the city might be facing another serial killer, so it made sense he'd want to be on the scene.

"Please, tell me Cutter is here." He jerked his head toward the ME's wagon.

Ray shook his head. "Baxter."

"Shit. We'll need to keep a sharper eye on this." Ray nodded his agreement. "Okay, what else do we know about the victim?"

Ray flicked through his notebook until he found the page he was looking for. "Adult male, twenty-three years of age, Caucasian. ID says he's Aaron Landon. He's been renting the converted garage at this address. He kept late hours, so no one knew anything was wrong until the landlords started smelling something coming through their floor."

159

"Has his family been notified?"

"Yeah. The officer I spoke with just now," he said, glancing at the officer across the lawn, "said he'd got ahold of the sister, Amy Landon. She said Aaron left home about five years ago. Their father kicked him out of the house when he told the family he was gay. They haven't seen him since. He's been run through the system—some scrapes but nothing serious. It all seems to stem from hook-ups gone wrong."

"Prostitution?" Jack guessed aloud.

Ray nodded. "His file says he was living on the streets. His trouble seems to have come from that time—new to the city and doing whatever he had to do to get by. Last year, he was hospitalized after a couple drunks kicked the shit out of him where he was sleeping in a doorway. Then nothing until this." Ray glanced over at the house.

"Poor kid." Unfortunately, this wasn't a unique story. In a city with an extraordinarily high number of homeless, the streets could be a dangerous place. More so for a newbie trying to fit in. Not all homeless camps accepted new people—they simply didn't trust anyone they didn't know. And a lot of them competed for the same johns. "Did he ever contact his family in the last five years? Ask to go home . . . need money . . .?"

"According to the sister, she and Aaron had emailed a few times in recent months. We'll go through all of his correspondence, but she said he'd told her he was off the streets and in his own place. She said he sounded happy and had invited her to come for a visit."

"What was the cause of death? Do we know yet?" Jack glanced up as the ME, Harold Baxter, appeared in the front yard, followed by assistants who wheeled the gurney out of the garage apartment and toward the ME's wagon. Jack grimaced to himself knowing Baxter was involved.

"Stabbing," Ray said.

"Stabbing? What makes anyone think this is part of our investigation?"

"There's nothing obvious alluding to suicide. Stabbing is

straight-up murder. According to Baxter, the blade pierced the heart and killed Landon almost instantly."

Jack gazed directly into Ray's eyes. "So, what tells us this is related to the other victims? Was he a contestant at the Majestic? Was he a cross-dresser, or is there anything obvious in the house tying him to the club?"

Ray shook his head. "We don't know any of that right now. The only thing we're tying to our cases is the knife used had been 3D printed. That tells us this could very well be linked to our cases. We just need to find out how." Ray snapped his notebook closed. "Now you know what I know."

"You said he was ripe. Do we know how long he's been dead?"

"According to Baxter, decomp puts the TOD around five days ago. We'll want everything confirmed by Cutter," Ray said.

"Absolutely. Given Baxter's failed postmortems on the last six of seven victims, I don't trust him with this one. Who knows how many others he's botched?"

Ray nodded. "Agreed."

"Let me see Landon's ID."

Ray pulled out his phone, brought up the photo app then spun it in Jack's direction. "This is his California driver's license. It hasn't been updated yet with this address, but it confirms his former Sacto address."

Jack took the phone and zoomed in on the victim's face. He narrowed his eyes, focusing on the young man's features.

"Do you recognize him?"

Jack shook his head. "I don't know. Maybe I've seen him before, but all this," meaning the current crime scene, "could be putting him out of context. Forward me a copy of the photo and I'll ask Chad tonight if he's ever seen him." Ray tapped the phone a few times and a moment later, Jack's phone beeped. "Thanks. Got it."

"Back on the job?" Ray asked.

Jack nodded. "Yeah, but I'll be happy when the competition's over and I can go back to spying on cheating spouses." Which reminded him that he needed to check in with Ginnie. He hadn't heard from her since he sent her his final report.

"Assuming Landon's number eight, we'll need to canvass the neighborhood to see if anyone saw anything the night of the murder," Ray said.

"I still have a copy of that mystery man on my phone." He pulled up the image, then looked toward the gathering crowd. "No time like now to see if anyone saw this guy hanging around."

"Good idea. I'll take this end of the street. You take the other. Meet me back here when you're done."

Jack agreed and headed to the end of the block.

Typically, everyone Jack spoke with said they hadn't seen anything unusual, and they hadn't seen the dark stranger. Not surprising for a neighborhood like this. Just two blocks up, there seemed to be a lot of theft and vandalism. Even if their places on this end of the street hadn't been hit in the past, people just didn't want to get involved. They certainly didn't want to attract attention and see their homes get vandalized or robbed in retaliation for working with the police.

As Jack turned to go find Ray, he spotted a boy of maybe sixteen or seventeen standing alone with a bike at the back of the group. He stared directly at Jack, as if he had something to say. Instead of approaching the police tape, he threw a leg over the crossbar and peddled away.

Jack rushed to the corner of the block and watched the boy ride a few houses up the road, get off the bike then wheel it down the breezeway. Now he knew where the boy lived and would visit after the excitement died down.

Once investigators were finished—crime scene tape and a DO NOT ENTER notice stretched across the door, street barricades taken down, and the crowd dispersed—Jack watched Haniford approach where he stood with Ray across the street from the house. This wasn't Ray's case yet, but Haniford must have felt this murder connected to the others somehow and had wanted them to stick around, even if the only thing tying Landon to the other victims was the 3D printed knife.

It was all a little too coincidental for Jack. If the other murders hadn't involved 3D printed handguns, the knife would have just been a curious clue to this young man's murder. But with six printed weapons having been recovered, and now a similarly printed knife, the case felt like it could spin out of control.

"You okay?" Haniford asked when he reached the men.

"Yeah, why?" Jack asked.

"You're scowling and breathing heavy. That tells me you're thinking too hard."

"Just trying to figure it out. 3D printed handguns, and now a printed knife," Jack said.

"If Landon's killer is the same guy who killed the drag queens, what's the link? Nothing in the house suggests he was a drag queen. That would have instantly put him at the Majestic. But there's nothing," Ray said. "Just a guy wearing a black leather thong and biker boot with a hole in his chest."

"What did you just say?" Jack spun on Ray. "What was he wearing?"

Ray's eyes narrowed. "A black leather thong and biker boots."

"Let me see that photo again." Jack grabbed the phone as soon as the image was up. Sparks raced through his body, and not the good kind.

"What?" Haniford asked.

Squinting, Jack forced the memory to the front of his mind of Franklin and the young man in his Roadster. One of Rod's harem.

Jack forwarded the image to his phone then pulled up his text app and sent the image to Rod. Less than a minute later, Rod responded.

"Fuck!" Jack exclaimed.

"What already?" Haniford demanded.

Jack ran his fingers through his hair and cursed again. "I sent the image to Rod—"

"Rod who?" Haniford asked.

Ray filled him in on the DEA agent. "I was going to call you about this."

Haniford spun back to Jack. "What about this Rod?"

"I sent him the victim's photo and asked if he recognized him.

He came back immediately, naming him as Aaron Landon. He was one of Rod's crew in the Majestic Lounge, but he hasn't seen him for a few days. You can add this one to the list. He's definitely victim number eight."

Jack found the house he was looking for on Ridgewood, just around the corner from the Landon crime scene on Hearst. The boy's bike was propped up against a rickety fence along the breezeway, around the corner near the front door. Jack stood near the hinge side of the door and pushed the doorbell. He didn't hear it ring or buzz inside, so he knocked. He heard movement and saw the curtain twitch in a nearby window, but no one answered the door. He knocked again.

"I saw you go inside."

"Who is it?" The male voice on the other side of the door sounded older than Jack would have expected from the youth on the bike. As if he purposefully lowered it to sound older.

"My name is Jack Slaughter. I'm a private investigator. I have some questions about a disturbance around the corner. I'd like to talk."

Jack was about to knock again when he heard the deadbolt click and saw the door handle turn. The safety chain was still in place but the young man he'd seen on the bicycle peered through the narrow opening.

The boy looked about five-ten, wiry with baggy dirty jeans and equally soiled gray T-shirt. His light brown hair was shaved in a fade at the sides with a tight crop on top. His dark brown eyes, thick lips, and light complexion told Jack he was from mixed race parentage.

"I'm alone," Jack said with a lowered voice.

"What you want?" The boy's voice now sounded normal.

"You looked like you had something to say back there." Jack thumbed over his shoulder.

"Nah, I ain't got nothing to say."

"Are you sure? It'll be kept in the strictest confidence. I'm not police. I just have a couple questions. May I come in?" Jack asked.

The youth looked like he was weighing his options. "I'm happy to do this at your door, if you don't mind your neighbors knowing you're talking with me. I'm sure they saw me over at the crime scene and will automatically assume I'm a cop." He let that settle on the boy for a moment.

A moment later, the door closed then reopened after the safety chain was removed. The door swung open just enough for Jack to slide through.

For the lack of a better word, the house was a dump. "Your folks home?" he asked.

"Nah. Moms is working."

"And your father?" The boy just shrugged. "I'm sorry. Sisters? Brothers?"

Anger crossed the boy's face. "I thought you wanted to ask me about what happened. I didn't know you were going to interrogate me. You think I did it?"

"Did you?"

The boy's back stiffened and he took on a protective stance. "Aw, hell nah! I mind my own business. What you want to know about me foe?"

"I'm just trying to get to know you. You know me—Jack Slaughter PI. All I know about you is you're home alone and let strange men into your house without asking for ID." Jack crossed his arms in front of him.

The boy's face screwed up as he stepped back. "You got any?"

Jack reached into his jacket pocket and withdrew a card. "A bit late to ask, don't you think?"

The boy took the card. "You could have printed this up anywhere. You got a badge or somethin'?"

Jack nearly chuckled as he pulled out his wallet and showed the boy his investigator's license which had his image on it. "Are we good?" His card was offered back. "You keep it in case you need it."

"You wanna sit down or somethin'?"

"Sure. Do you want to tell me your name? Just so I know what to call you while we're talking. It's off the record," Jack promised, sitting on a worn and filthy single stuffed chair. It might have matched the grubby sofa, but he couldn't tell from all the dirty, threadbare blankets covering it. The boy sat at the opposite end of the sofa, away from Jack.

"Dewayne."

"Just Dewayne?"

"Watkins."

"You live here with just your mother, Dewayne Watkins?" The boy nodded. So, single mother raising her son alone. Obviously not a lot of time to clean house. "Where does she work?"

Dewayne shrugged. "Around."

"Will she be home anytime soon? Maybe I can speak with her too."

He shrugged again. "She come and go. Don't know when she'll be home. I mostly take care of myself."

"Must be hard," Jack said, nodding to the garbage and dirty dishes scattered around the floor and on the table between them.

"I do awright. You gonna tell me what you want?" Dewayne asked.

"I just want to know if you saw anything. Over the last few days, did you see anyone around who didn't belong in the neighborhood?"

Dewayne shook his head. "Naw, I ain't seen nothin'."

Jack sat forward. "Out there, you looked at me like you had something to say. So maybe we can start again." He pulled out his phone and brought up the victim's image, then turned it in Dewayne's direction. "Do you know who this is?"

Dewayne nodded and handed back the phone. "That the dude that live round the corner. He get whacked?"

Jack nodded as he scrolled to another image to show Dewayne. "Do you recognize this guy?"

"That the dude that did it?" Dewayne asked as he gazed at the dark figure on the screen.

"We don't know yet. We're trying to find this guy to ask him some questions too. Did you see him around the neighborhood?"

"Maybe. What's it worth to you?"

So that's how he was going to play this, Jack thought, taking back his phone. "What's it worth to keep yourself out of juvie or being sent to CPS? Your mother obviously isn't taking care of you, Dewayne. That's child endangerment."

"Dude, I'm fifteen. I takes care of myself jus' fine. I'm the king of my castle." Dewayne threw an arm over the back of the sofa and took on a cocksure posture.

"King of the trash heap more like. You're a minor without parental supervision. You play ball with me and you can maintain your . . ." Jack gazed quickly around the room, ". . . luxurious lifestyle. Fight me, and I'll have CPS down here in a heartbeat. What'll it be?" The boy turned away and considered his options.

"Yeah, I saw 'em. They pulled up in a fancy black car."

"Them? Are you saying there was more than one person?" Jack's heart thudded hard a couple times. Did this just get harder?

Dewayne shook his head. "Naw, just one."

"Did you get a make?" Jack asked, feeling oddly relieved.

"Yeah. It was a fly Beamer."

"What was so *fly* about it?"

Dewayne sat forward and gestured with his hands, as if he was describing the shape of a woman's figure. "She was all sleek in the right places. Low to the ground with a tight, fat ass. Low profile treads, brushed aluminum wheels, blacked out windows . . . mmm-mmm."

Jack suppressed a chuckle. "Did you notice a license plate or any distinct markings? Hard top or soft top?" Jack asked.

"Naw, jus' black. Convertible, but the top was up. It was dark so I couldn't see nuttin' inside."

"So, you went out to the car?"

"Hell yeah. Sweet ride like that don't come round here too often. I hadda check it out. You feel me?"

The kid probably would have lost his shit if Jack had ridden his Harley to the crime scene. "I bet." His heartbeat kicked up several notches. "Since you saw the car pull up, you must have seen someone get out."

"Naw. I fell asleep watching TV. I saw it when I got up to take a piss. I heard something and thought it was my moms coming home. I saw the ride then, so I went outside to check it out."

"Do you know what time that was?"

"Nah, but it was pretty late. Maybe three or four in the morning."

"Your mother often come home that late?" Dewayne hesitantly nodded. "Didn't staying up that late make you late for school on Monday?"

"Christmas break, man."

Jack had forgotten about that. "What else can you tell me? You went out to look at the car . . . the Beamer."

"I made sure no one was in it then I got up close to look through the tinted windows. Sweet ride like that got to have leather interior and all that fancy shit rich people can afford, right?"

Jack nodded his agreement. "You said you saw the driver. If not when he pulled up, then when?"

Dewayne moved to the edge of the sofa and rested his long arms on his knees. "I didn't hear anyone coming back, but someone pushed me to the ground while I was trying to see inside. Pissed me off, man. I jumped to my feet, ready to fight whoever got up in my business. Got right in their face and told them don't nobody disrespect me for no reason. I wasn't doin' anything wrong. Just lookin'."

"Sounds like you were eye to eye with him. What happened? Come on, Dewayne. This is important," Jack urged.

Dewayne shook his head. "Someone came outta they house over the road and yelled at me, asked if I was awright. I turned to see who it was and by the time I looked back, the car was heading up the road like the devil hisself got its tail."

"No plate number?"

"Naw. Waited until they got up the road before turning on the lights."

"But you saw him. What did he look like?" Jack felt like he could throttle the kid if he didn't hurry up and give him what he wanted.

Dewayne waved in Jack's general direction. "Just like in that picture you showed me. Only it weren't no dude. It was a chick."

CHAPTER TWENTY-THREE

"Was he absolutely sure the person he saw is our suspect?" Ray asked.

There were ten other places Jack thought he'd rather be right now than the busy nightclub, even if things seemed somber. Another death of a club patron, especially this close to the competition finale, had to be wearing on everyone. At least Ray was with him and they could talk while surveying the crowd.

Jack nodded. "Yep. He confirmed the photo of our suspect was the same person he saw getting into the car in front of his house. He was eye to eye with her. Said it was definitely a woman."

Ray folded his arms in front of him. "Fuck me!"

"I know. I didn't see that one coming either. But given the circumstances, could it have been anyone here in drag?" Jack suggested.

"Is it my imagination, or did things just get worse?"

"When you figure it out, let me know."

"Do we tell Rod any of this?" Ray asked.

Jack shook his head. "Let's sit on it for a while, and see if he shares anything with us first. In the meantime, I want to check out everyone in the club to see if they even vaguely look like the person in the security camera image." He pulled up the photo on his phone. "Something hasn't been sitting right with me."

"What are you thinking?"

"I don't know. The profile seems familiar, but if this person really is a woman, I can't place her. If it's a man, he has to be able to pass himself off as a woman really well."

Marilyn crossed Jack's line of vision as she moved from the bar toward the backstage door.

"Do you think it could be your friend over there?" Ray nodded toward Marilyn.

Jack held up his phone and compared the image to Marilyn just before she moved through the doorway and shut the door behind her. "I don't know. It's possible." He closed the photo app and put his camera back in his breast pocket, video switched on as usual. "But why would she kill her lover? And the whole group? What's her motivation to kill the others? It's not like she's in the competition, and she's not a judge. It could be Marilyn, but it doesn't add up."

"If you don't think Lucas is the person in that photo, we better circulate to see if there's anyone else in the club matching your witness' description. Like you said, whoever's doing this must be hanging out in the club. All the victims are club-goers, so he or she has to be here somewhere, right?"

"No time like now," Jack said. "I'll check backstage and find Lucas. I want to get his take on Landon's killing. See if he's heard about it yet. By the looks on some faces around here, I'd say news has traveled quickly. You circulate out here and I'll meet you later at the bar." Ray nodded and moved into the crowd. Jack had to give his friend some credit. Once he'd settled into the investigation, he let go of his reservations and dropped his macho BS. Work was work.

Backstage, Jack took a quick look into the dressing rooms as he walked down the long hallway. It was relatively quiet, and most contestants were still changing into their costumes. Next, he peeked into the security room.

"Hey, Isaac." Jack stepped forward with an extended hand.

Reaching out, he said, "Mr. Slaughter."

"Please. Jack."

The man nodded, acknowledging the informality. "What can I do for you, Jack?"

He pulled up Landon's driver's license photo and showed it to Isaac. "Have you ever seen this guy in the club?" Jack already knew Landon hung with Rod's crew, but maybe Isaac could give him some added insight based on his screen viewing.

Isaac scanned the image for a long moment then handed back the phone. "Yeah, I've seen him in here. He hangs with the bikers, but I've never seen him circulate much. Seems pretty shy."

"The other night, I thought I saw him leaving with someone. Do you think you would have caught that on the parking lot security camera?" Based on the extensive footage Lucas had sent over, Jack was sure this footage would be there too. He'd seen the two leaving together, but he hadn't had the chance to view all the security video while he was sick.

"Do you remember what night it was?" Isaac asked.

"Last Sunday after closing," Jack said and watched the man go through his files.

A moment later, video of the parking lot came up. Jack saw himself sitting in his Jeep, watching club-goers leaving the premises. Some got into vehicles and left, some turned and walked up the driveway, and a few used the shortcut through the back fence.

Then he saw Franklin as Carol walk to the Roadster, followed by Aaron Landon. They both got into the vehicle before it drove away. It was definitely Landon.

"Thanks, Isaac. That's exactly what I was looking for."

"No problem. Anything else? I'm happy to find it for you," the man said.

"I appreciate it. I'll let you know."

"Hey, you think Carol killed that boy?" Isaac asked.

"How did you know he was dead?" Jack had never said Landon was dead.

"Are you kidding? It's all over the club. A lot of people have died who were connected with the club. Frankly, I'm surprised people are still showing up for the competition. I don't see how Chad is keeping it together, especially since—"

"Yeah, I know. That must have been really hard on him. I can assure you, everyone available at the department is on it. Ray is here tonight too." Jack wasn't telling anyone Rod was actually DEA. That was a whole other subject. Rod's role at the club didn't have anything to do with the murders, and Jack didn't want to tip off anyone on the off-chance Lucas really was dealing drugs in his club. "We'll get to the bottom of it. In the meantime, thanks for showing me the video."

"Like I said, whatever you need."

In the hall, Jack looked at Lucas' office door. He had to admit, he actually liked the guy. To each his own in his private life, but what little he knew about Lucas, he seemed straight up . . . for the lack of a better term. He hated thinking the guy had anything to do with Landon's death, or the others. But the profile of their suspect in the photo did bear a striking resemblance to Lucas as Marilyn.

Jack took a deep breath and knocked on the door. When it wasn't answered, he gazed down the hall to see if anyone watched him, then tried the knob. Locked. Probably just as well. The place was full of people, and the last thing he wanted was Lucas finding him rifling through his personal space on his own. If it turned out he was innocent, Jack didn't want to break that bond of trust they'd developed. But if he was guilty, Jack wouldn't hesitate to take him down.

He met Ray back at the bar as they'd agreed.

"I got nothing," Ray said, taking a swallow of the coffee he'd ordered while waiting for Jack.

Jack waved to one of the bar staff. A double Diet Coke had quickly become his usual, so it arrived quickly without him having to ask for it. "Me either. But I did stop in at Security and have a chat with Isaac. He showed me the video from last Sunday night of Landon getting into my client's husband's vehicle and leaving together."

Ray's eyes widened. "That's good. Now that he-she is tied to the victim, we can bring him-her in for questioning."

Jack chuffed lightly and explained, "It's *she* while in women's clothes, Ray." Ray just waved him off. "We'll definitely need to question him. Let's head over in the morning when we can catch both him and his wife at home."

"Is *she*," Ray emphasized, "here tonight?"

Jack shook his head. "Not yet, as far as I can tell. It's early yet," he said, checking the time. "Or maybe he's scared off because of his friend's death. I'm not putting all my stock on my witness' statement. Who he saw could very well have been a man in women's clothes. Landon left with my client's husband while he was dressed as his alter ego. He could be our suspect, so we need to tread carefully."

"I don't think we have enough substantial evidence to get a warrant yet, but we can certainly question him. If he won't play nice . . ." Ray let his suggestion hang. They both knew the next step to get a statement from an uncooperative witness.

"That's why I want to be with you when you go to the house. You can question the husband while I question the wife . . . my client . . . separately. I need to check in with her anyway."

Just then, the lights lowered throughout the club and the stage lights went on. Marilyn flounced onto the stage, wireless mic in hand, and began her rendition of *Diamonds Are a Girl's Best Friend*. Jack wondered if Lucas knew any other Marilyn numbers.

CHAPTER TWENTY-FOUR

Saturday

Jack was already sitting in his Jeep on 27th when Ray pulled up and parked behind him in his old red Silverado.

Ray had owned the pickup for as long as Jack had known him, which was a long time. While his friend made enough money to afford a newer vehicle, there were always excuses why he wouldn't upgrade the nearly thirty-year-old pickup—it could haul anything, he needed it while updating the Dublin Street house before they'd moved over from the Mission, and now that they were expecting their first child, he wanted to save money for all the things he was sure they'd need.

In reality, Jack knew Ray would never sell or replace the pickup because he was a sentimentalist. The old Silverado had been the first vehicle Ray bought as soon as he got his driver's license. Other vehicles had come and gone, but the Silverado was something he'd never part with. Jack was sure when the time came and it broke down for the last time, it would probably spend the rest of its days rusting out in his friend's driveway.

Ray slid into the Jeep's passenger seat and closed the door behind him. "What are you grinning about, *ese?*"

"Am I?" Jack kept his thoughts to himself. "I'm glad to see you found the place. I'm sure the neighborhood knows you're here now too."

"What's that supposed to mean?"

"I heard that big block motor of yours coming before I even saw you. Really, brother, you need to invest in a newer, and quieter, ride."

"Yeah," Ray groaned. "I'll make you a deal. I'll buy a new truck the day you get your ass back on the job."

"Not ready for that," Jack reminded him.

"Neither am I." The men sat in silence for a moment before Ray asked, "How do you want to play this?"

Jack turned slightly in his seat to face his friend. "I better catch you up first. You've heard of the Whitney-Cummings'?"

Ray nodded with a shrug. "About as much as anyone—spoiled, entitled assholes—like most rich people. Is that who your client is?" His eyes widened with surprise.

Jack explained the situation and briefly explained who Ginnie was before marrying Franklin, and who they'd become as a couple through the years.

"Then a few months ago, she caught him dressing in women's clothes and pitched a fit. They seemed to work out a new normal to maintain some semblance of normalcy—he agreed to keep it at home but would be, as she put it, *all man* when they were in public. But now he's going out as a woman called Carol and frequenting the Majestic. According to Ginnie, Carol was his mother's name, though he seems to be trying to style himself after his ex-model wife."

Ray let out a long and low whistle. "Sounds like someone has mommy and wifey issues."

"Undoubtedly. Anyway, she hired me to follow him so she can get past her prenup restrictions for divorce. She needs photos of him to prove he's the one not keeping the marital vows and all that. First night tailing him, he led me to the club. You know the rest."

"And at some point, Lucas hired you for security. A pretty sweet deal. The wife pays you to tail her husband," Ray said, lifting one hand palm up. "The club pays you for watching their customers," he said, leveling his other hand. "You clean up on the *dinero*." He slapped his hands together, motioned that he was adding stacks of money together, then shoving the invisible wad into his breast pocket. "Very sweet deal. Sounds like you can afford to buy me a real nice Christmas present this year." A wide grin lifted the edges of Ray's bushy mustache; his eyes crinkled at the sides.

Jack chuckled, ignoring his friend's comment. "I've been keeping their identity to myself per Ginnie's request. I have a strong feeling she's more afraid of losing the money than her marriage and is using the family reputation as her excuse for secrecy. That's why she came to me rather than going to an investigator who caters to the obscenely rich and grossly famous."

"I get it. And now that Franklin-Carol was seen leaving with our latest victim, you think he's somehow involved with the other victims?" Ray asked.

Jack shrugged. "Right now, I don't know anything for certain, only that he was probably the last person to see Landon alive. We know Landon left with Franklin, but where they went has yet to be determined. If he took Landon home, it would have been in his Roadster. I'm trying to figure in the BMW my witness said was in front of his house that same night."

"Was he sure it was a BMW? If it was dark, maybe he didn't see a maker's symbol."

"He was pretty adamant it was a Beamer."

"Maybe it was just coincidence. Maybe Franklin's only involvement was in taking Landon home that night, regardless of whatever they got up to at the victim's place," Ray suggested.

"Or maybe Franklin came back later in a different car. If he was the killer." Jack glanced back at the house. The gate had opened while they were talking, but so far, no one was leaving.

"Do you think Franklin was sleeping with Landon? He was pretty young, but it's not unheard of for young gay men to find a sugar daddy, or an older man to prefer barely legal partners," Ray said.

"Good points."

"Do you think this Ginnie woman knows if he's sleeping around? All this dressing as a woman means he's gay, right?"

"I don't know if Ginnie knows anything about her husband's extracurricular activities. What I do know is only what she told me, that he's no longer coming to their bed, so I'm assuming he's taking it somewhere else. Since he's frequenting the club, it's quite possible he is testing out his new identity in every way."

Ray nodded his agreement then asked, "If he killed Landon, do you think he was involved with the other victims . . . and killed them too?"

"Right now, everything is possible, but we need some strong evidence if the judge is going to sign off on a search warrant for this house." Jack nodded at the property. "It's my hope we don't need to go that far right now though. I doubt Franklin knows he's being tailed and thinks that his alternate identity is still secret to everyone but Ginnie."

"So, what do you suggest?"

"What I'd like us to do is go in as we normally would. You take Franklin to a quiet corner to talk and I'll deal with Ginnie. She's my client so I can catch up with her, but I'll make it look like I'm questioning her in an official capacity so Franklin doesn't feel singled out. If we play this right, Franklin won't be any the wiser and just think he's being questioned like anyone else from the club who knew the victim. We'll both get something out of the meeting."

Ray nodded again. "Good idea."

"If Franklin isn't home and it's just Ginnie, I'll explain you're helping me with security at the club. Maybe she'll let us take a look around. Then, if we see anything unusual, you can go for that warrant so we can get an official look. What do you think?" Jack suggested.

"Works for me. Are you ready?"

Jack took a deep breath. "Ready as I'll ever be."

Jack set up the video on his phone and slid it into the breast pocket of his jacket. He exited the Jeep and pressed the lock button on his key fob as the men strode toward the Whitney-Cummings home.

The gate had remained open so there wasn't any need to use the intercom on the pillar. This played to their benefit, as any delay in getting the gate open would not only remove the element of surprise, it also gave the occupants a chance to hide anything incriminating.

As they passed the four-bay garage, they saw one of the doors was open and the Roadster had been pulled out, as if someone was preparing to leave. They were just in time to catch Franklin at home, but was Ginnie?

At the door, Ray leaned in and rang the bell. Not only was the house pretentious, so was the bell that chimed inside like church bells. It certainly wasn't the common ding-dong in the average home.

They waited a long moment, staring at the heavy, white-painted timber door before it swung open. Jack was somewhat surprised when Ginnie answered the door and not a servant. *Great, she's home too. That'll save time.* By the look on her face, she was surprised to see Jack on her doorstep.

Ray showed her his badge and said, "Good afternoon, ma'am. I'm Inspector Reyes Navarro with the SFPD. This is my associate, Private Investigator Jack Slaughter. We're wondering if you might have a moment to speak with us."

Jack saw Franklin appear inside the house, watching from the back of the foyer. "Sir," he said by way of greeting.

Franklin stepped up beside his wife who flinched when he put his hand around her waist. "What's this all about?" He squinted at Jack. Did Franklin recognize him from the club, the night he broke up the argument with Marilyn? If he did, he didn't say anything.

"They're police . . . darling," Ginnie added, not looking directly at Jack.

Ray repeated his introductions.

"What can we do for you?" Franklin asked, looking back and forth between the men on his porch.

"This will only take a moment or two. Do you mind if we come in to talk?" Ray asked.

A furrow appeared between Franklin's obviously plucked eyebrows. "Is that necessary?"

"Not necessary if you don't mind your neighbors listening in." Ray nodded to an elderly man who'd stopped across the street with his little dog and who was obviously taking a keen interest in the interaction in the doorway.

Franklin thought for a moment then smiled and waved to the man before pulling open the door so Jack and Ray could enter. Franklin let them in only as far as the foyer. "What's this all about?"

"Sir, if I could have a word with you in private," Ray said.

"I really don't see this as necessary—"

Ray cut him off. "Please, sir. It's a delicate matter."

"Fine." Franklin led Ray through the foyer. Jack assumed by the magazine photos he'd seen years before that they'd gone into the living room. From what he could tell from where he stood, the house hadn't changed much since those photos. If anything, the walls could do with fresh paint, but otherwise it appeared the same.

"We okay to speak here?" Jack asked Ginnie with a lowered voice.

After checking to see where her husband had led Ray, Ginnie gazed up at Jack. "I think so. What's the meaning of this?" she whispered. "If you needed to speak with me, you should have called. I would have come to your office."

"It's actually better this way. I agreed to accompany the inspector in order to protect your previous business relationship with me. He now knows you hired me to work for you, and questioning Franklin privately means your husband may feel freer to discuss happenings at the club."

Ginnie was quiet for a moment then nodded her agreement.

"I also thought it would be a good opportunity to catch up with you as we haven't spoken since you came by for the photos. I haven't heard from you since I sent you my final report."

Ginnie pivoted slightly and looked in her husband's direction. Their new position also gave him a view of the living room and the men in it.

"I haven't talked with my attorney yet, but I'm sure what you gave me is fine. I've been a little busy. But you could have asked me this on the phone. What's the meaning of this? Why have you brought a detective to my home?" she demanded.

"Inspector Navarro brought me with him," Jack corrected. "There was an incident at the nightclub your husband has been frequenting and the inspector is questioning all potential witnesses who were at the club on the night."

"How does the inspector know Franklin was there? I thought our identity was safe, Jack." She kept her voice lowered, but the tone was saturated with annoyance.

"It is, for now. But there's been a death of a club patron, and Franklin was the last person seen with the victim. So—"

"Goddamn him!" she hissed under her breath. "Can he not do anything right? Everything he touches makes *my* life hell. Tell me everything."

"I'll tell you what I can. Ray is my former partner from when I was on the force. He's been assisting me with some event security at the Majestic Lounge, where your husband . . . spends his time. One of those patrons was found dead in his apartment. The club's security camera recorded the victim getting into your husband's Roadster and leaving the premises. The camera captured the car's license plate number which led the police here." Jack watched Ginnie's expression flash between anger and hatred and perhaps fear. Was it fear of losing her husband to prison, or anger that her private world could come crashing down around her when the media found out what was really going on behind closed doors? No doubt the media would be picking up on this sooner rather than later. He added, "Inspector Navarro is asking your husband about that now. Discreetly of course."

"He damn well better be. If anyone is going to ruin that man's life like he's ruined mine, it'll be me." Ginnie folded her arms over her breasts and flashed her gaze in her husband's direction.

Jack pulled out his notebook and pen. "Can you tell me where Franklin was six nights ago? That would have been last Sunday night, into early Monday morning."

"I don't know. Why?"

"That's when the incident took place. If you can tell me when he left and subsequently returned home, it would go a long way to establishing his whereabouts at the time of the murder. Honestly, I'd like to think this was just coincidence," he added.

Ginnie thought for a moment. "I can't say for sure. I'm usually asleep by the time he sees fit to come home."

"I know this is a difficult time for you, but do you think your husband has . . . how can I put this delicately? He was seen leaving with our victim after the club closed—"

"Do you mean, is he fucking men?" she asked.

"I was trying to be a bit more delicate, but yeah."

She glanced back toward the living room. From Jack's perspective in the foyer, Franklin looked visibly upset, not angry or defensive. Curious.

"I don't know. Sure, it's possible he's fucking men now. Was he fucking that boy? Probably. I mean, he's no longer in my bed, so he has to be going somewhere, right?" she spat. "That's really something you'll have to ask him."

Boy? Jack's spidey sense kicked in. Had Landon's murder already become public knowledge? "That's what I was hoping you'd tell me."

Ginnie glared at him. "He doesn't tell me what he's doing, so how the fuck would I know? It's not like he takes me with him."

Jack took a deep breath before he said, "I'm sorry to have upset you. Let's calm down."

Ginnie uncrossed her arms and stiffened her back, the posture meant to intimidate, but it didn't have any effect on him. "Don't you dare tell me what to do in my own home. I'll—"

"You'll do what? And if you talk any louder, your husband will know something is wrong here and your cover will be blown. I don't think you want that. Not if you want to walk out of your marriage with the nest egg you're hoping for." His words seemed to sink in, as she recrossed her arms over her heaving breasts and stepped back. "Now, as far as your husband needs to know, I've just been corroborating his alibi with you for last Sunday. Are we good with that?" When she refused to look at him, he repeated, "I said, are we good with that?"

She nodded curtly. "Yeah, sure. Whatever."

"Can you tell me where your husband was going just before we arrived?" Jack asked.

"I don't think anywhere. He likes detailing his car. He likes it clean when he goes out."

It was Saturday night, and the last of the club's semi-finals, so

Jack was sure he'd see Carol later tonight. Glancing around, he wondered where her little purse pooch was. "Where's your little friend?"

Ginnie's brows drew together. "What friend?"

"Your dog. Little dogs are notorious barkers, but the house seems pretty quiet."

Keeping her gaze on her husband, she stuttered, "Oh, he . . . he's at the groomers today. Besides, he was debarked as a puppy. He wouldn't stop yapping at every little noise or shadow."

Before Jack had a chance to comment, Ray and Franklin reappeared in the foyer. A calmness had settled between them.

"Are you sure you don't mind?" asked Ray.

Franklin waved his hand toward a hallway. "No problem at all. Happy to show you. Follow me."

Ray nodded for Jack to follow. "Mr. Whitney-Cummings is going to show me his Roadster." His friend smiled and rubbed his hands together.

"Please, call me Franklin."

Ray corrected himself. "*Franklin* is going to show me his Roadster. If you're done here, we can head out after we see the car."

Ginnie put on a false smile, but there was no mistaking the hint of animosity in her voice. "Franklin is very proud of his little car."

"Thank you for your time, Mrs. Whitney-Cummings," Jack said, then fell in line behind Ray and followed Franklin down a long hall and through a door, Ginnie behind them.

The long, four-bay garage space was cleaner than any Jack had ever seen. Everything had its place, and most of it was behind stylish cabinet doors. The polished concrete floor didn't seem to have a single spot of oil staining it. And the walls had been painted a similar neutral color as the rest of the house.

He wasn't surprised that a car filled each bay. Franklin flipped a switch and the remaining three doors opened to let in the natural light. "Let's go out this way." He moved between the wall and the first car, a sleek red Maserati GranTurismo. Once in the driveway,

Jack saw that all but one of the cars had been parked nose out.

Beside the Maserati, a black BMW Z4 convertible was parked nose in. Alongside that was a black Bugatti Divo. The last bay was open, and the Roadster was still in the driveway. What Jack had thought was a black Roadster was actually a dark granite.

All of the cars in Franklin's collection definitely fit in with his previous reputation as an elitist with rich tastes, and a man who loved his cars.

His gaze flashed back to the BMW and his heart started pounding. "Nice cars, Mr. Whitney-Cummings," Jack said. "Mind if I take a closer look? On my salary, this will be the closest I'll ever get to this kind of luxury."

"Sure. I'll see if I can get Chad to pay you more."

Jack's heart nearly stopped just then. "Chad?" Franklin *had* recognized him. And by the look on Ginnie's face, her husband's blatant mention of the club had angered her more than Jack knew she already was.

Franklin nodded. "I've seen you in the club. Everyone knows you're there for extra security during the competition." The tone of his voice dropped, telling Jack that Franklin was aware of what had happened to so many club-goers.

"Thanks, but that's only a temporary gig." He moved forward to check out the Bugatti, but his true intention was the BMW. If Dewayne had been out looking at the car as closely as he said he'd been, it was possible his prints would be on the window. "Bugatti, eh? Very nice."

"My husband fancies himself as Bruce Wayne when we take it out," Ginnie said.

Franklin chuckled. "She thinks it looks like the Batmobile."

Ray stroked his mustache as he circled to the other side of the vehicle. "Yeah, I can see that. Does that mean you have a Batcave under your house?"

"Very nearly, Inspector. Only it's a gym. Same view overlooking the outer Bay as the living room above it and opens out to the pool and patio. There's even access down onto Baker Beach," Franklin said.

While the men talked, which also distracted Ginnie, Jack

turned slightly to see if he could catch any smudges or prints on the Beamer's window. Unlike the other cars in the garage, the BMW hadn't been washed in a few days, so maybe—

Bingo!

"Hey, Ray, do you think after seeing Franklin's cars it will finally convince you to trade in your truck?" Jack asked, forcing a grin.

"You know, *esé*, if I had the money, I could very well trade in my old Betty." Ray said to Frankin, "You have some really nice vehicles. Thanks for letting us see them. I was admiring the Roadster, but these . . ." He let out a long and low whistle.

"We better get moving, Ray," Jack said. "I'm sure these folks have better things to do with their afternoon." Jack needed to get his friend out of there before Franklin offered to take them for a test drive. That in itself could ruin their chances of getting any evidence out of the Roadster, recently detailed or not, as well as prints off the Beamer's window.

Back at the Jeep, Jack said, "You need to get that warrant, brother. One of their cars matched my witness' description— the BMW—and there are prints on the driver's side window consistent with my witness' description. And if Franklin really did kill Landon, we need to get whatever evidence is left from the passenger seat of his Roadster."

CHAPTER TWENTY-FIVE

Jack followed Ray to the department. After parking, he scrolled through the video he'd taken at the Whitney-Cummings' house until he found the images of the cars in the garage. He wrote down the plate numbers on each vehicle and tore the page out of his notebook. Ray could run a trace on them while he was upstairs.

"I doubt they'll come back to anyone else, but better to be safe than sorry," Jack said.

"And you're sure they were fingerprints on the window?"

Jack nodded. "My witness ID'd a BMW parked in front of his house that night and the car at the Whitney-Cummings' matches his description. The tinted windows meant he had to lean in to look." As an example, Jack leaned toward the window on his Jeep and shielded his eyes as he peered in. "The smudges on the driver's side window are consistent with what he told me. Even if all we get is a print of the side of his hand, we can bring him in to get his prints and compare it to the one we get off the car's window. Palm prints are as unique as fingerprints."

"I'll be down as soon as I'm finished."

Jack thumbed over his shoulder. "I'm heading to the park." Ray nodded and trotted up the walkway and in through the department's main entrance.

Mission Bay Commons Park was located two blocks over from the department. It was a narrow green space stretching between 3rd Street and Terry A. Francois Blvd., across from the Pier 52 Boat Launch in the Central Basin.

The green space was flanked with tall leafy trees and box

hedging. In the summer, colorful flowers attracted bees, butterflies, and birds. Benches dotted along parallel footpaths separated the grass from the flanking roads, making the park a popular lunch spot for workers in the area. It was an oasis in the bustling city, and the perfect spot for the department's annual children's Christmas event. While the flowers were now gone and the trees slept for the season, the warm, sunny day made up for it—a bonus of living in California.

Jack had already dropped off his toy donations in the department last Saturday, so he headed right into the heart of the park, bypassing the donation station. He tried pushing aside the memories from the last time Leah brought Zoë down to meet Santa while he worked the event.

He spotted Haniford talking with what looked like some city officials at the police information tent and moved in that direction.

The park had been set up like a traveling Christmas carnival and was already thronged with families. Holiday decorations festooned the space and activities were in full swing.

He dodged several kids chasing each other back and forth across the grass. An apologetic mother forced a smile out of him as she spun him around while running after her son who was chasing a gull that was foolish enough to try settling in such a hive of activity.

A band played Christmas music which filtered through loudspeakers. Kids danced in front of the stage. He smiled at their lack of rhythm as they stomped to the beat. The sheer joy on their faces punched him hard in the chest, both remembering how Zoë would dance to anything vaguely musical, even when he sang to her, and missing all those times they'd shared but would never be enough.

He focused on the kids in front of him. Two of them spun together in quick circles, then fell down beside each other in a fit of giggles. He couldn't suppress a smile as he passed by.

Typical of carnivals, several games had been set up around the park that encouraged parents to play along with their children—squirt guns filled balloons to bursting, ring tosses onto old fashioned milk bottles, penny pitches onto plates, ping pongs into empty fish bowls, Whack-a-Mole, Skee-ball, and more. A big bouncy castle was set up in one corner, as well as the quintessential game of strength, Ring the Bell.

Every game offered a prize, and by the looks of things, everyone walked away a winner. All profits to play the games went toward the department's children's charity, along with all the donated gifts.

And at the center of it all, Santa's Grotto had a line of parents with their children waiting to get inside to tell the old man what they wanted under their trees.

This event was much like others he'd worked when he had been on the force. Only today, he didn't recognize many of the volunteer officers. His chest tightened at the thought of returning to work as a seasoned officer yet feeling like a rookie; having to get to know the new team that was developing without him.

He chuckled at the officers he did recognize, some who'd retired but always volunteered to help out. Jack wondered if it was his former LT's influence or his wife's who had each volunteer officer wearing a special uniform for the event—green elf shoes and matching cap, bright red pants, and a black holiday-themed T-shirt.

The whimsical shirt featured a cheery cartoon elf police officer who wore a green elf hat and matching green curly-toed shoes similar to the officers themselves, but instead of the green pants, the T-shirt characters wore red and white striped stockings. Directly across the center read: *POLICE ELFICER*, in big, bold letters.

"Jack!"

Haniford's greeting drew Jack's attention and he watched the LT approach.

"*SLEIGHIN' IT?*" Jack asked with a grin, looking at the man's latest garment—police motorcycles towing Santa in his sleigh across a full moon. "At least your theme is consistent. Is Mrs. Haniford to blame for this one too?"

Haniford nodded. "You have to admit, they've been some good ones this year."

Jack nodded his agreement. "Last year's Grinch theme was pretty good too."

"Yep, Nancy sure has some imagination. Kinda scares me to think about next year." Both men chuckled, knowing the LT's wife was creative by nature and loved lending a hand for special events. "Thanks to her, our volunteers have new uniforms this year. What do you think?"

Jack quickly gazed at the volunteers and tried not laughing. "I saw them. I'm kinda glad I'm not volunteering this year. Don't tell her that though." He gave Haniford a sidelong look he hoped told the man he was kidding.

The LT smiled and said, "I'm glad you made it down. By the look on your face, you're enjoying the event."

"It's nice seeing everyone having such a great time."

"Me too. I have to admit, I do enjoy this time of year."

Without thinking, Jack said, "Leah did too."

Thankfully, Haniford let the comment go. "Where's your sidekick?"

"Upstairs taking care of some business. We just came from my client's house where we did an informal Q&A. Ray's running some vehicle plates and filing for another warrant." Jack brought him up to speed about the evidence recovered at Ranganathan's apartment and the witness at the Landon crime scene.

It was also time to let Haniford know who his clients were, and how Ray convinced Franklin to show him his cars, including the Roadster. And that the BMW in the garage matched his witness' description.

Haniford dragged his hand down his face and rubbed his chin. He opened his mouth a couple times to say something, then closed it again, apparently not being able to find the words. Then, "Holy shit" tripped off his tongue. "Franklin? Are you sure—I mean, when I've spoken with him at some of the police events he donates toward, he's never given me any indication . . ."

"Now you see why his wife asked me to keep their identity private. If this had just been about the divorce, there would be no reason for her to hire a private investigator. But if this turns into something more, we'll have to bring them both down to the department for questioning. At that point, we won't be able to control the press once they get wind of it."

"We?" Haniford asked.

"Slip of the tongue. You know what I mean. The warrant will allow us to get prints off the Beamer, grab any evidence that might be left in the Roadster, and get us into the house. If Franklin's involved in all these deaths, we'll nail him to the wall."

Haniford nodded. "I don't have to tell you that I'd like to see the back of this yesterday."

"I'm just happy as a pig in shit that the wife paid me in advance."

"I bet," Haniford said. "Harry and Wash have been busy too. They canvassed the neighborhoods looking for other witnesses and CCTV footage, went back to the hotel—nothing there— and interviewed suppliers of 3D filament. They've also gone back through all the evidence from each crime scene with fresh eyes." He put up his hand, as Jack was about to tell the LT that he and Ray had already done that. "I need this done by the book. I know you and Ray have gone through everything. But your place isn't the department. When it comes time to file charges on someone, we need everything done in-house, by the book, and with my stamp on it."

Jack nodded. "Got it. I can bring everything down and we can set up my murder wall upstairs. I've got copies of just about everything. What doesn't double up with what's in-house, we can add it to the wall. I know Gordy collected a lot of evidence at Ranganathan's place."

"I'll let you know if we need to go that far."

Haniford's gaze shot past Jack. He turned to see Ray running toward them with a fist full of papers. When he reached them, he bent over with his hands on his knees and panted heavily.

"You okay, brother?" Jack asked.

"I don't remember the last time I saw you run like that, Navarro," Haniford said.

"Ha. Ha," Ray said, breathless. "You won't be laughing when you see what I've got in my hand." He pulled the pages away when

Jack grabbed for them. "Nuh-uh, *esé*. But you ain't gonna believe this shit."

"Out with it." Haniford put on his lieutenant's face and folded his arms in front of him.

Ray stood up and straightened the wad of papers. "I met up with Harry and Wash. They found a supplier of 3D filament. The owner said he has a client who's been buying it in bulk the last few months. Luckily, they didn't need to get a warrant in order to obtain the sales records for the buyer. The shop owner was very accommodating."

"Who was it?" Jack asked.

Ray shook his head. "Patience is a virtue." He shuffled through the papers and settled on the next. "Gordy put a rush on the new evidence from Ranganathan's apartment. The weapon I recovered from under the chest was a match for the ones recovered at the other scenes. Same brand and type of filament, same revolver pattern, *and* the same filament was used to make the knife that killed Landon. Gunpowder residue from the weapon and the window glass match that on the slug we pulled from the door frame on the balcony."

Haniford shifted from one foot to the other. "If you've got a name from the sales receipts on the filament and the filament is the same on all the weapons, let's have it. Who is it?"

Ray wagged his finger at Haniford. "Nuh-uh," Ray repeated. "There's more. The prints recovered from the door glass came back. One was definitely an ear print. Cutter confirmed it by taking a print off the victim who is still waiting for the family to collect his remains. Other prints were from the victim. It looks like he was held against the door. And there was a partial fingerprint not belonging to Ranganathan."

"Was it enough to run through the system?" Jack asked. Ray nodded. "Who the hell is it?" *Fuck Ray's dramatics*, Jack silently cursed. He wanted to see what was on the pages in his friend's hand.

Ray snatched them away again. Looking at Jack like a cat that got the cream, he said, "This will blow your mind. There was enough of the print to run through the system, and it brought up a name. Eleanor Mae Hogg . . . Ellie Hogg to friends and family."

In an instant, Jack felt as if a window had opened and all of his evidence blown out on a gust of wind. "Who the fuck is Eleanor Mae Hogg?" Jack asked through clenched teeth. "Sounds like a character off the *Beverly Hillbillies*."

"Not far off." Ray read from the page in front of him. "Ellie Hogg was born in Nameless, Tennessee—"

"What do you mean, Nameless?" Haniford asked.

Ray shrugged. "I did a quick search and found out that no one knows why it's called Nameless other than back in the day, no one could agree on a name. But get this. Back in the '30s, there was an article in the *Jackson County Sentinel* that said a local back in the 1860s wanted to call the place after their county attorney general, but it was rejected because the name reminded residents of the Civil War and the Confederacy a few years earlier. So, it was agreed to leave the town without a name."

"Ray," Haniford said sternly. "Are you ever going to get to the point?"

"This case has so many threads, it's like a drunk spider trying to spin a web."

"Pick a thread and follow it, brother. We're not getting any younger." Jack mimicked Haniford's posture, folding his arms across his chest, but in his case, he was trying to keep from throttling his friend.

"Get this. The attorney general was called George Morgan—"

"Morgan?" Jack repeated.

"Yeah. The guy everyone remembered from the war was Army General John Hunt Morgan. I didn't notice if they were related, but apparently, in 1863, General Morgan led a troop of men on a thousand-mile raid through Tennessee and into Kentucky, Indiana, and Ohio that became known as *Morgan's Raid*. Thousands of his men were either killed in battle or captured. One of his own brothers was shot down before his eyes. His anger made him reckless, but he was eventually captured and turned over to Federalists. Long story . . . interesting one, but long."

"How does this General Morgan tie into this case?" Haniford asked.

"Not General Morgan, but the attorney general, George Morgan. He was Ellie Mae's great grand uncle, maybe eight or nine generations back on her mother's side," Ray explained.

Jack shifted from one foot onto the other. "You still haven't explained how this Hogg woman is relevant to our case."

"When the prints came back on Hogg, it also brought up her police record. Her family were stereotypical backwater southerners. She grew up with three brothers and they all hunted with their father in the mountains. Squirrel, possum, turkey . . . They also participated in regional shooting competitions. By all accounts, Ellie Mae was a crack shot. She made the regional papers with photos showing her with her kills and awards." Ray waved a printout of a news clipping which Jack grabbed from him before Ray could pull it away.

The image was grainy, but it was easy enough to see a young girl posing with what looked like a turkey in one hand and a small trophy cup in the other. A big grin spread across her face. With the black and white image, it was impossible to gauge the color of her hair, but she had an otherwise pretty, heart-shaped face and wide eyes. The caption below the image said: *Ellie Mae, Age 15, Bags Another First in the Jackson County Turkey Shoot.*

"You said Ellie Mae had a police record. Where's that?" Ray finally handed over the printouts. Scanning them, he found this young girl had applied her shooting skills to a number of activities outside of hunting and turkey shoots, including firing her weapon within the town limits, as well as shooting at road signs and street-side mailboxes from a moving vehicle. All minor juvenile stuff, but none of it earned her any time in jail.

Jack focused on the next page—the arrest report. According to the report, neighbors said they heard gunfire and screaming coming from the Hogg property and called it in. On arrival, officers found Ellie Mae had trapped her brothers in a corner of the barn and was screaming at them. She'd been firing buckshot at any of them who tried escaping. The boys were covered in blood and bruises, and one was cowering on the ground, crying and shaking uncontrollably.

When the officers made their presence known, Ellie Mae had turned on them and fired. She claimed she didn't know they were police and fired out of reflex. She said her brothers had tried raping her. The boys denied the accusations, and the officers arrested her for a number of infractions, one of which included firing a weapon at the officers and intentionally causing bodily harm to her three brothers.

She was eventually released when the brothers decided not to press charges. Ellie Mae dropped off the radar not long after. A missing person's report had been filed which said Ellie May had left a note for her mother that read: *No one is ever going to hurt me again. I'm going to do something better with my life.*

Jack looked at the girl's details on the arrest report. It appeared the incident with her brothers had happened a couple weeks before her eighteenth birthday. Was it possible she ran away from home as soon as she was eighteen? He didn't doubt it.

He gazed at the young woman's arrest photos. Again, in black and white, but these were much clearer. The report noted brown hair and blue eyes. At nearly eighteen, it was easy to see there was natural beauty under all of her grime.

Something about her eyes though.

Jack scratched his cheek through his beard and asked, "So you're saying the partial print Gordy found at Ranganathan's belongs to this girl? The report is dated, what . . . fifteen years ago? That would make her about thirty-three now. What's she doing in the city, and how does she know our victim?"

Ray rifled through the pages in his hand, pulled up another photo and handed it over. "This is Ellie Mae now."

For a long moment, Jack compared the images of the young girl and the grown woman. Had they stood side by side, they would have appeared two different people. But they shared one common feature that instantly told Jack they were the same person. While she'd dyed her hair black and shed her Tennessee roots, as well as shed some weight, it was her eyes that gave her away. Both versions of herself had the same defiant and angry liquid, blue-green gaze.

Ray added, "And I ran the plates on the Whitney-Cummings' cars. The BMW comes back to Eleanor Mae Hogg with an address up on Grenard Terrace, as do the credit cards used at the store selling the 3D printer filament. Legally, this woman is still Eleanor Mae Hogg. I'm not surprised she changed her name for work but it's not something she had to do through legal channels."

Jack looked back at Ray. "Are you shitting me?"

"Would I ever?" Ray tapped the photo in Jack's hand. "That there is Ellie Mae Hogg. Aka Jennifer Morgan—"

Jack finished for him. "Aka Ginnie Whitney-Cummings."

CHAPTER TWENTY-SIX

Sunday

Jack checked the time on his cell as they approached the residence—9:47a.m. He wondered if the couple were up yet.

Ray had had trouble last night reaching the on-call judge, despite repeatedly trying his cell number throughout the evening. It had been nearly midnight when his friend had finally received a call back. The judge explained he'd taken his family out for dinner and had forgotten his cell phone in his overcoat pocket. The overcoat had been left with the hatcheck clerk, so he hadn't heard it ringing.

Ray met the judge first thing this morning to sign the search warrants on both residences on the Sea Cliff Avenue and Grenard Terrace before picking up Jack, and now they were on their way to the Whitney-Cummings' home to perform the first search.

When they arrived five minutes later, patrol cars were already lining the top of 27th Avenue and awaiting the warrant Jack held in his hand.

Ray slowed beside an unmarked department vehicle containing Harry and Wash, nodded then proceeded to the residence where Ray parked in front of the closed gate. Harry and Wash pulled up beside Ray's vehicle, completely blocking access to the road. Patrol cars fanned out on the street behind the inspectors, effectively surrounding the front of the property.

This was all done quietly and professionally. No lights or sirens, and chatter was kept at a low level. It was a quiet Sunday morning and both Jack and Ray hoped to keep it that way.

At the back of the gathering group of officers, Jack recognized two familiar faces—the officers who detained him at the scene where Bob Johnson had been shot at the Majestic. They saw him too, and other than glancing at each other, they made no effort to acknowledge him.

Standing at the gate, Ray repeated the same instructions he'd given the officers at the department on what he wanted to see accomplished with the search, and what they were looking for.

"I can't emphasize enough how much we need that 3D printer. The dark clothes witnesses described would be helpful too. And don't break anything," he added. "The department can't afford replacement costs on anything inside this residence. Got it?" When everyone nodded their agreement, Ray turned to the intercom on the gate pillar and pushed the button. When it went unanswered, he pressed it again several times.

"Who is it?" By the sound of his voice, Franklin must still have been sleeping.

"Hey, Franklin. It's Inspector Ray Navarro. I was here yesterday—"

"I remember. What can I do for you, Ray?" Franklin asked. "I was out late last night and I'm still in bed. Can this wait until later?"

"I'm sorry, it can't. We have a warrant to search the premises."

"A *warrant?*" There was a long moment of silence before the gate slid back on its tracks. "Let me get dressed and I'll meet you at the door."

Ray turned to the waiting group behind him. "Kid gloves, folks." Jack followed Ray to the front door. Franklin was opening it just as Ray leaned in to ring the bell.

"What's this all about, Ray?" Franklin looked like he'd pulled on whatever he could find off the floor—rumpled khaki pants and an equally wrinkled blue and white striped shirt of which he was just fastening the last button. He hadn't bothered to slide on a pair of slippers on his rush to the door. He quickly gazed at the group of officers spilling in through the gateway. "I don't understand. Is this because I gave Aaron a ride home the other night?" He gave his hair a quick finger comb.

Jack handed the warrant to Franklin who only gave it a cursory glance before setting it on the hall table.

"The warrant allows us full access to your home, property, and vehicles," Ray explained. "Is Mrs. Whitney-Cummings at home? We'll need to speak with her as well."

Franklin quickly glanced behind him, then back again. "I don't know. She has her own room—"

Ray held up a hand. "We need to come in now. Jack will accompany you up to your wife's room while our officers get started. We'll be as quick and as careful as possible."

The look on Franklin's face was a mix of fear and embarrassment. "Please, Ray. Is there anything you can do about all the cars out front? My neighbors—I'll do anything you want, but please, can you make this look less obvious?"

Jack swore the man was about to cry. He gave Ray a quick nod.

Ray turned to Harry. "Get those vehicles out of the middle of the road." She nodded and moved off to give instructions. Ray turned to Wash. "I want you to oversee the search. No stone left unturned."

"You could have just asked, Ray," Franklin said, as Wash led the officers inside. "You didn't have to go to this extreme."

"I'm sorry, Mr. Whitney-Cummings," Jack said. "Yes, you were the last person to see Mr. Landon alive. As he was in your vehicle, we need to search it for evidence. Anything collected must be done by the book or will be inadmissible in court. I'm sure you understand."

"If you just need to look in the car, why are your officers going through my home?"

"If you ever brought Mr. Landon home with you, or—"

"He was never here. I never bring anyone home with me," Franklin asserted as he watched officers going through to the living room and spreading out through the house. "Besides, I've detailed the car since that night—"

"We understand," Jack continued, "but we'll be going through all of your vehicles as part of this search. Now, I'll accompany you up to your wife's room and we'll bring her down here to wait for the team to finish."

Jack followed Franklin to a set of stairs beside the open plan kitchen and up two floors to the top of the house. At the end of the long hallway, Franklin stopped and knocked on the door. When there was no answer, he tried the knob, but it was locked. He knocked again.

"Ginnie," he called, but there was no reply. He knocked again. "Gin, we have guests. You need to get up." Again, there was no reply. "I've got a key. Give me a moment." Jack waited at the door while Franklin went to find his key. Jack pressed his ear to the door and listened for movement. Nothing.

Franklin returned in less than a minute, having also stopped for a pair of loafers which he wore sockless, and put the key in the door. When it swung open, the first thing Jack noticed was the wall to wall windows overlooking the mouth of San Francisco Bay. Golden Gate Bridge connected the city to the Marin Headlands to the east and Point Bonita Lighthouse along the headlands to the west. A cargo ship moved under the bridge toward the city, and early risers already sailed their yachts into the open waters of the Pacific.

Yep, all he needed was a glass of top shelf whiskey, a comfortable chair, and a view like this.

Jack's reluctant gaze fell on the contemporary square frame canopy bed. It was clear it hadn't been slept in. He performed a quick search of the room and en suite bathroom, including her walk-in closet. Much like what he'd seen on the way upstairs, the décor here mimicked the rest of the house with clean lines and neutral shades. A large antique armoire was set against a wall. Its hand-carved wood and intricately painted details made the wardrobe stand out among the ultra-modern furnishings.

"Does your wife sleep anywhere else in the house? Or does she have a private study or any other place where she likes to spend time? What about the sunroom on the roof?" he asked. "Does she have a hiding place in the house? What about a panic room?" Jack knew the uber-wealthy often had a hideaway in case someone broke in.

Franklin nodded. "We have a secure room down on the lower

level in the gym room. I don't know where Gin is, but why would she be hiding? Honestly, I don't even know if she's home. If her car is here, she's here."

"We'll look for her. Let's start by looking in the rooms on the way up to the sunroom upstairs."

Moving through a warren of halls and working room by room, they made their way to the sunroom stairs. Jack pulled out his phone and dialed Ginnie's number. It went to voicemail. "This is Jack Slaughter. I need to speak with you. Please call me as soon as possible."

He then called Ray. "Send someone out to see if the Beamer is in the garage. Ginnie's not in her room. Franklin and I are searching the upper floors for her now, but he tells me if the car is gone, so is she."

"Hang on." Jack heard Ray shout to an officer to check the garage for the car.

At the top of the stairs, Jack stepped out of the glass-sided sunroom and onto the flat roof that was hemmed in by a waist-high solid stucco wall. While he waited for the officer to come back to Ray, Jack made a circuit of the space. Maybe Ginnie knew they were onto her and she was making a run for it.

The front of the residence had a wide view in both directions along Sea Cliff Avenue, as well as up 27th Avenue. There was also a panoramic view of much of the city, from the Presidio to the east, across Twin Peaks, and the treetops along most of the three-mile length of Golden Gate Park to the western horizon.

Each side of the structure had views into neighboring properties, much of which was obstructed by mature, leafy trees.

He crossed to the back of the house which had an even more impressive panoramic view of the outer bay.

A long moment later, Ray said, "Nope, not there. Just the other three."

"Thanks." Jack disconnected. "Car's gone. Do you know where she might have gone so early on a Sunday?"

Franklin shook his head. "No idea. Despite the press, things haven't been great between us for a long time now. I know she doesn't like me spending so much time at the club—"

Jack raised his hand. "You don't need to explain." In reality, he just didn't want to hear about the man's personal problems. He wasn't a therapist and there was nothing he could say that would make the guy's situation any better or easier. "I get it. But your wife . . . Maybe you both need to see a professional." He hated making the recommendation. He'd been advised to see a therapist a number of times over the years since losing his family. And rejected every suggestion. He had a plan. Franklin didn't appear to though. "Or maybe you need to do one of those projection things—where do you see yourself in five years, then work toward it."

Franklin shrugged and moved over to lean a hip on a large timber planter box containing an overgrown Agave and gazed at the water. Large, dusty blue-green leaves edged with variegated yellow to red spilled over one side of the planter in an impressive display.

Phone still in hand, Jack dialed Ginnie's number again. Voicemail. "Ginnie, Jack again. I really need to speak with you. It's urgent." He disconnected.

"What's that all about? Why do you have my wife's number?" Franklin demanded, his voice edged with concern.

Did he tell Franklin why his wife had come to him? Since he'd completed his job for her, did the confidentiality clause still apply? And if it did, could it morally be waived in the current situation?

"Oh, wait. Yesterday, Ray introduced you as a private investigator. Did she hire you to follow me?" he asked, folding his arms across his chest. When Jack didn't reply, he continued, "That bitch. She's been threatening to divorce me if I didn't stop going to the club. But you knew that, didn't you?" He spun his gaze back to the sea.

"Look, I was hired to do a job. One that was completed a couple weeks ago. Yeah, she wanted to know where you were going, and wanted photos to prove it. The job was done within a couple days and I hadn't seen her again until yesterday." Mostly the truth. "My involvement with the PD has nothing to do with what she hired me to do."

Franklin looked Jack square in the eye now. "What do you mean by weeks ago?"

"Ginnie came to my office a couple weeks ago. Why?"

Franklin chuffed under his breath. "She knew where I was going long before two weeks ago. She's been threatening divorce for months. I wonder why she waited so long before hiring a PI to spy on me."

"She told me about the prenup, that she needed photos. Really, I don't care why she hired me. I've got rent to pay, so I take the jobs I can get." Why did Jack feel the need to justify why he chose this occupation? If he wasn't careful, this guy was going to piss him off. He took a deep breath and let the silence fall between them. *Wait.* "What do you mean she knew where you've been going before she hired me? She told me she didn't know."

A knowing look crossed the man's face. "Oh, she knew. She's followed me there a few times. A few weeks ago, she made a horrible scene in the parking lot. One of the bouncers had to escort her to the front of the club while another drove her car onto the street. She was told never to come back. Then you show up."

This revelation changed everything. Ginnie knew where Franklin was going. She'd been to the club herself. And since the bouncers eighty-sixed her from the premises, she hired him to follow her husband. Were her reasons true? Did she really need the photos for a divorce settlement, or was it something else? Nothing about this case settled well with him—she'd lied to him about the reasons she'd hired him, she'd lied about her real name, her prints had shown up at Ranganathan's apartment, and now he knew her car was registered to a separate residence.

"Does your prenup say she can't collect on your assets unless she can prove you've cheated on her?" Jack asked.

Nodding, he said, "Yes, but it's the same for her. It works both ways. I can't claim on her assets either unless she's cheated on me. She came to this marriage with a substantial portfolio, no matter what the tabloids would have you believe." Franklin's cheeks reddened. "To be honest, she had more money than I did. And after the house renovations, which she dictated and I paid for I might add, my accounts were edging near the red. All these years, she's barely touched any of her own assets, I can assure you."

So, Ginnie knew her husband was cross-dressing long ago. She had more money than her husband. She wanted a divorce, but what did she hope to gain by claiming any part of the pittance he had left after she'd spent most of his money?

"If she has more money than you, why would she worry about the prenup? Why not just leave the marriage? She'd still have what she came into the marriage with," Jack asked.

Shrugging, Franklin said, "She's a selfish bitch, that's why. Yes, she needs photos of me cheating on her. Even through all her bullshit . . . her nagging, her verbal and physical abuse, her stalking me, her threats . . . she still can't prove I've cheated on her."

"What about Landon? You gave him a ride home. Was that all there was to it? Just a ride home?"

"Just a ride home."

"Nothing else? Nothing that could be misinterpreted as cheating?"

"Just a ride home," he repeated. "Yes, I did go inside. We talked, then I left," Franklin said.

"May I ask what you talked about?"

"You probably know it already, but Aaron was a troubled young man—"

Jack nodded. "Right. His family disowned him after he came out about his sexuality, then he relocated to the city for a fresh start that didn't go well. Somehow, he was able to get off the street and into that garage apartment. That's about all I know."

"I gave him the money."

Jack's eyes widened. In his wildest imagination, he hadn't considered Landon had a benefactor. "Did Ginnie know about this?"

Franklin shook his head and shrugged. "I don't know. We've been staying out of each other's business a lot over the last few months, except for when she's been drinking and gets volatile and decides to chase me across town. You know, I would probably go to the club a lot less if her tantrums were under control. I just don't want to be anywhere near her when she's like that. There are days when, thankfully, I don't see her at all."

"Where do you think she goes?" Did Franklin know his wife held a residence in her real name?

"No idea. And really, I couldn't care less. The only reason we haven't filed for divorce is because she makes more than I do just on her royalties alone, and if I filed, she knows she'd be paying *me* a monthly alimony rather than the other way around. Probably why she's fighting so hard to find proof I'm the one who's sleeping around. I've thought about filing on her, but I know that would really set her off and I don't need that kind of drama in my life. I have enough on my plate with what she's already dishing out." Franklin grunted lightly.

Jack's stomach twisted tighter with each revelation about his wife. "What did you know about your wife before you married her? By all accounts, very little time passed between meeting her and putting a ring on it, so to speak."

The corners of Franklin's lips rose slightly. "I think it was lust at first sight. Jennifer Morgan was every guy's wet dream, right? For me, I loved her sense of style, her professionalism. She was gregarious and we had fun together. Sure, we had sex. She was aggressive—maybe a little too aggressive—but at the time, it was exciting. The tabloids started hinting at marriage, but we hadn't talked about it. Then one day, she said we should give them something to really talk about. So, we did. And for a while, it was a lot of fun. Until it wasn't. Her aggression became more volatile and harder to predict."

"What about the club? Your change in . . . persona," Jack said with delicacy, "didn't happen overnight."

Franklin was quiet for a moment. He continued gazing at Jack, as if weighing what to say. "No, it didn't. I always felt a little uncomfortable in my own skin, but I was forced to live up to parental expectations. You must know all about my family."

Jack nodded. "The Whitney-Cummings' are part of city history. Who doesn't know about them? And you."

"Right, but then I met someone. The old cliché. I left one night after one of Ginnie's unreasonable tantrums and went up to the Fairmont to drink it off in the lounge."

Jack knew about the Tonga Room & Hurricane Bar. Back in the late '20s, the hotel had installed a deep lap pool for hotel guests, called the Terrace Plunge. In 1945, it underwent a million-dollar refurbishment at the hands of an MGM set director called Mel Melvin. While the pool remained, the rest of the room had been transformed into a Polynesian-inspired restaurant and bar. Tables and chairs surrounded the pool under numerous strung lights, faux palms, and big lamps with shades that looked like grass skirts. A grass-roofed boat floated on the pool, serving as a band stage. City officials gave the venue high praise as the best, and Jack thought only, tiki bar in the city. Visiting chef Anthony Bourdain had said it was *the greatest place in the history of the world.*

"I know of the place, but can't say I've been," Jack said.

"You won't see anything else like it in the city. You should go at least once in your life. The food is fabulous."

"Thanks. I'll think about it." Leah certainly would have loved a place like that. If things had been different, he'd have a lifetime to take her to places like the Tonga Room. If she were still alive and if he found her, he'd take her anywhere she wanted to go. "Go on. You were at the bar, and . . ."

"A guy asked if I'd share my table with him. It was busy and other tables were full, and we were both on our own, so why not? We got talking and found we enjoyed each other's company. No biggie."

"But—" Jack prompted.

"I went back the next night, to get out of the house. He was there. We had a laugh, shared the *pupu platter,* and—"

"Wait, what?"

Franklin chuckled. "It's a platter of meats with a small hibachi so you can cook at the table. Anyway, afterward, we went up to his room for a drink, and well, one thing led to another." Franklin's face turned a bright pink. "It was my first time . . . with a man."

Jack held up his hand. "You don't need to elaborate. I can fill in the blanks myself. I thought you said you never cheated on your wife."

Franklin winked. "I said she never caught me."

CHAPTER TWENTY-SEVEN

"Besides, it was only with Jim," Franklin continued. "He was from Monterey. We only met up when he came to the city, and we stayed within the hotel walls. We both knew it wasn't serious; it was just a bit of fun. He made me forget about Ginnie and all of her drama. Plus, he didn't know who I was other than a guy he met in the bar. I was free to be . . . me."

Jack nodded he understood. "Didn't anyone in the hotel recognize you?"

Franklin shrugged. "I'm sure someone must have, but Jim and I never made it obvious we were anything more than friends meeting for drinks."

"You speak in the past tense. How long ago was the affair?"

"Maybe two years ago. It only lasted a few months, certainly less than a year. I was heartbroken, of course, but he introduced me to a whole other world."

"One that included adopting another persona?" Franklin nodded. "When did that happen?"

"Jim wore me down. He didn't understand why I refused to go out on the town with him. Right up to the end, I never told him who I really was. He only knew me as Frank, and I only knew him as Jim. In fact, there's no chance I can look him up if I ever go to Monterey to try finding him. For all I know, he's married with kids."

"What changed?" Jack asked. "What happened that you agreed to go out in public with him?"

"Jim wanted to go clubbing but I always refused. Then Halloween came and dressing up was the best way to hide my identity, so I reluctantly agreed. We went as Bette Davis and Joan Crawford from *What Ever Happened to Baby Jane*? Jim was scarily perfect for the role of Baby Jane Hudson. He could recite lines from the movie with amazing accuracy, including the timbre of his voice. His attention-seeking allowed me to fade into the shadows where there was little chance I'd be recognized," Franklin explained.

"Then what happened?"

"It wasn't long after that Jim's job changed, and he stopped coming to the city. But that night, putting on that ugly dress . . . I saw another side of myself I wanted to explore. Being with Jim opened the door, and dressing as a woman allowed me to walk through it." Franklin laughed lightly. "I know you won't understand. Guys like you are utterly self-assured about your heterosexuality. I thought I was too. I was raised to be the man my parents expected of me. I'd accepted it for most of my life, learned to work around any self-doubts scratching under the surface. But once through the door, I realized I'd been lying to myself. At first, I only wore women's clothes in the privacy of my own home."

"Ginnie explained it to me the day she hired me. She said when she discovered what you'd been doing, she'd thought you had a woman in your office," Jack said.

"I think she would have been happier if there *had* been a woman in there with me."

"Do you think Ginnie knew about Jim?"

Franklin shook his head. "If she had, she wouldn't have hired you."

"At what point did she know something was off in her marriage?"

"I can't say for sure, but the day she found me in my office certainly tipped the scales. Her tantrums grew more intense, so I started going out nearly every night. Not just to get away from her, but to see where the new me was leading. Then one night I found the Majestic Lounge."

"Has anyone there recognized you?"

Franklin shook his head. "I don't think so. The drag race has nothing to do with how I present myself at the club; I never go there without Carol. And it's the only place I go now. Places like the Majestic are safe havens for people like me. Even if anyone has recognized me, I'm sure they're keeping it to themselves, as I would their real identity. If anyone *had* discovered who I am behind the makeup and wig, it certainly would have been splashed all over the tabloids by now."

"How did Ginnie know where you were going?"

"She got in her car and followed me. Like I said, she knew where I was going long before she hired you. She just wanted the photos for the divorce because she couldn't get them herself."

"Is there any reason you wouldn't just grant her a divorce to get her and her drama out of your life?" If Ginnie was that much of a bitch, why stay with her?

Franklin glanced out to sea for a long moment, then settled his gaze back on Jack. "Good question. I've asked myself that same question every time she starts getting wound up over nothing. I have offered to tear up the prenup, but with her assets being much higher than mine, and California being a no-fault divorce state, she'd end up owing me money. She wants it all."

"Wouldn't you just let her have the house so you can get on with your life?"

Franklin shook his head. "It's my name on the deed. She told me she couldn't qualify for some reason. The house is my only real asset anymore."

"And the cars?"

"Leased. I can barely afford the monthly payments. Once the leases are up, they're going back to the dealers. And Ginnie knows it. She's been bleeding me dry, yet she still wants the house."

The more time Jack spent with Ginnie, not that it was a lot, the more he realized she wasn't quite the person she wanted people to see. Early on, she seemed every bit the estranged and hard-put-upon wife she claimed she was. He'd almost felt sorry for her, even if her language was antagonistic and coarse. Then her attitude quickly became more volatile and downright rude when she didn't get her way.

Now, based on Franklin's confessions here on the roof, Jack gave himself a mental pat on the back for still having great spidey senses that something wasn't quite right with the woman. She threw money around like it was confetti, even to the point of buying him off when her purse pooch pissed on his crappy old carpet.

Those instincts also told Jack he didn't think Franklin had anything to do with Landon's murder, and probably not the others either. But what did Ginnie have to do with it all? He was sure it had been her car Dewayne had seen parked in front of his house. Had she followed Franklin to Landon's house? Or had Franklin been driving his wife's car that night, and if so, why?

Jack was fuming because now that they were here to print the Beamer, the car was gone. He cursed the judge for leaving his cell in his jacket pocket. It was his fault they might be wasting this warrant, and all of their time.

"I have to ask. Do you ever drive Ginnie's car?"

Franklin shook his head, his eyes widened. "Absolutely not. She won't even let me in it long enough to pull it out of the garage so I can detail it for her. That's why it was so dirty yesterday when you were here. Come to think of it, maybe she's taken it out to have it cleaned. She does that, but she never lets me touch it."

"On a Sunday?"

"We're a twenty-four-hour, seven-day-a-week society these days. Even car washes." Franklin shrugged. "To be honest, I'm not even sure she was here when I got home last night. Come to think of it, I don't remember seeing her car in the garage."

In most any other situation, Jack knew there were questions one didn't ask just anyone, especially if they were suspects. But Franklin had been blatantly candid with him. He didn't get any sense that the man was deflecting or hiding anything, so he chanced his arm. "What do you know about the suicides tied to the club?"

Franklin glanced up at him again for a long moment. "Am I a suspect in those too?"

"In a spate of suicides? Why would you be?" Jack asked.

Franklin gestured his chin toward the house. "That's a pretty sizable warrant just to search my car, don't you think?"

Nodding, Jack asked, "Did you know any of the victims?"

"I know a lot of people from the club."

"What about these people specifically?"

He paused, as if choosing his words carefully. "Is any of this on the record?"

"We're just talking here. I'm not a cop . . . not anymore. Just a private investigator with a huge chip on his shoulder and barely making ends meet. I have a vested interest in the suicides because of my job at the club. And I'd like to find some closure for Chad," Jack said.

Franklin nodded. "I'd been with most of them the nights they died."

Jack hoped his surprise didn't show itself on his face. "Do the police know about that?"

"I don't think so. I've never been questioned."

"What can you tell me about those nights?" Jack asked. "Do you mind if I record this?"

"What for? I thought you said we were just talking."

"We are, but I forgot my notebook." He hoped Franklin would work with him. "I've been off the force for too long and old habits are starting to slip." When Franklin nodded his agreement, Jack felt a pressure ease off his chest. He switched on the phone's record app and held the device in his hand. "Let's start with the first victim, Sai Joshi. I understand he and Chad were seeing each other. Do you know if they had any problems or disputes?"

"You mean, was there anything that would make Sai put a gun to his head? No. That night, he'd come to me for advice on what to get Chad for their two-year anniversary. We left the club and went to his place. We had some wine, talked about some gift ideas, then I left. He was happy. Even excited. He was looking forward to their anniversary. The next day, I heard he'd put a bullet in his head. To say I was shocked is putting it lightly."

"What about Sanjay Bajwa?"

"Coming to terms with this new lifestyle hasn't been easy.

You don't wake up one morning and suddenly know what you're going to do, or how to incorporate yourself into the community," Franklin said.

"You mean being gay?" Jack asked.

Franklin shook his head. "I don't know if I'm gay or bi or whatever. Being with Jim was an eye-opening experience and I enjoyed my time with him. But am I gay? I don't know. I do still like women, so maybe I'm bi. But honestly, I'm taking my time trying to figure it all out. And Sai and Sanjay and the others were helping me. I'm not looking for partners, even if my wife has turned against me. Jim was the only person outside my marriage I've been with."

"If you weren't sleeping with Bajwa, what was your relationship?"

"Makeup. Like I said—"

"You don't just wake up one morning and know what you're doing." Franklin nodded. "And Bajwa was teaching you how to apply makeup?"

"Yes. When I left his place, I felt I had a better handle on something I'd been struggling with."

"And Dinish Ranganathan?"

"Hair." Jack chuckled. "What's so funny?"

"Do you remember the night a couple weeks ago when you argued with Chad in the club about performing?" Jack asked.

"Wait. That was you!" Franklin's eyes widened with surprise. "I'd forgotten about that night. But yeah, I remember. What about it?"

"Your hair wasn't exactly screaming high society."

Smiling, Franklin said, "I don't suppose it did. I'd just had a huge fight with Ginnie. As I was leaving, she grabbed at my wig and tried pulling it off. It was pinned to my own hair. While it stayed put, it was a little worse for wear by the time I got out of the house. I must have looked a fright on the receiving end."

Franklin wasn't wrong. "More wine and conversation there too? With Ranganathan, I mean."

Franklin shook his head. "No. It was a relatively quick visit. He said he had a date afterward."

"That late at night?"

Nodding, Franklin said, "People like us often socialize at night. Clubs are open late, and when you're jazzed up after closing time, it's not uncommon to keep the party going at home."

Jack had asked the question because he knew there'd been a second wine glass on the counter, but that it hadn't been touched yet. Perhaps it was for Ranganathan's date. He wondered who it was. "Do you know who his date was?"

"No. It was none of my business. He didn't volunteer the information and I didn't ask."

"Fair enough. What about Patel and Naidu, the brothers?"

"It took a lot of convincing. Even though they were twins, they didn't like spending much time together outside their dance group. But they agreed to help me with costume and a dance routine. That night you found me arguing with Marilyn . . . Chad," Jack nodded he understood, "I tried telling her that I'd been working really hard on my persona. Sure, it would have been fun to perform, but it's all been finding myself, and finding my place in the community. I wanted to participate. Somehow."

"You worked on your makeup and hair, got a new wardrobe, and learned how to dance in an effort to fit in." It made sense to Jack.

"Correct. Hearing they'd shot themselves . . . well, I didn't think they hated each other that much, but you never know."

"What can you tell me about Michael Smith? He was the out-of-town contestant, wasn't he?" Jack asked.

"No, that was Robert Johnson. I didn't really know him, but we'd had a couple drinks and talked. He'd come out recently, so we talked about that. He seemed nice. He even hugged me and kissed me on the cheek and thanked me for listening to him. When he said he was feeling apprehensive about getting back to his hotel on his own—country mouse in the big city sort of thing—I offered him a lift. I told him I'd meet him on the street when he'd said his goodbyes, but when he didn't come out I figured he got a better offer, so I went home. I can't tell you how upset I was hearing he'd been shot in the driveway. If we'd walked out together, I could have been shot too." He noticeably shivered.

"And Michael Smith?"

"I'm ashamed to admit this, but since this is technically off the record—" Jack nodded it was. "Ginnie and I have enjoyed our share of coke over the years. It had been a while. I guess once I was getting recognized as a club regular, Mike approached me one night and asked if I wanted to do some lines. I agreed."

"Were you doing them in the club?" Rod told Jack he thought it was Chad dealing in the club, but maybe it was Smith who Rod was looking for. He'd be shocked to find his main suspect was already dead.

Franklin shook his head again. "Once, but I didn't want to get Chad in trouble. We went back to Mike's place to do it."

"Just the once?"

"A couple times. I stopped going when he made it clear he wanted sex."

"Understood. Do you think Mike is dealing in the club?"

"No, I don't think so. If he was Isaac wouldn't have let it last very long."

"Why would he? Isaac is head of security. It's his job to keep drugs out of the club," Jack said.

"Isaac protects his own interests. He might be tucked away in his office most of the night, but he has a couple guys that circulate on busy nights. If you're looking for drugs, everyone knows you talk to Isaac, or one of his boys."

Isaac. It made sense. Who better to control the drug trade in the club than the head of security? Sitting in his office monitoring entrances meant he could dump any stash he had on him once he saw officers approaching and tip off his guys on the floor to do the same. As much as he hated to think about it, he was going to have to find Rod.

"The last night I saw him alive, I'd let him know I appreciated his offer of drugs and sex and would keep him in mind. The truth of it is, I have enough on my plate with everything else. I didn't want to develop a habit like that as a coping mechanism."

"That's commendable. You left on good terms?" Jack asked.

"Absolutely." Franklin cocked his head. "You know, it's hard trying not to take any of this personally. We all know each other at the club. I've been going long enough that I feel like others are starting to trust me. But knowing that so many people I've turned to to help me transition have died . . . killed themselves . . . well, I'm sure I don't need to tell you what an emotional blow this has been for me."

Jack saw Franklin's hands noticeably shake. "I get it."

Franklin looked Jack squarely in the eye. "Do you really? I'm starting to feel like anyone I get friendly with ends up dead. That's pretty hard to accept."

"I do get it. Four years ago, I lost my family—" Jack's throat swelled, cutting off his air. He gazed over the outer bay and took deep breaths to calm the rising panic. He rarely used the loss of his family as a way to connect with suspects, so it surprised him that he'd blurt it out now.

Jack felt Franklin's hand on his shoulder and gazed over. The man just looked at him for a long moment, then said, "I'm sorry." His earnestness poured out in two simple words, making Jack's throat swell again.

He swallowed hard and looked toward the water, but he didn't pull away. "I am too." He forced himself to compartmentalize his emotions then stiffened his back and stepped away slightly, letting Franklin's hand fall away from his shoulder. "What else can you tell me about your wife before you married? Other than her being a model?"

"Honestly, only what she's told me, which hasn't been much. I know she's from back east and doesn't have any family. She told me her life was the quintessential rags to riches story, having been discovered by chance and all that, but even those details are scarce. It's a pretty sad state when a husband has to resort to the internet to find out more about his own wife. Ginnie's always been a bit of a mystery, which I think also appealed to me. I've always been in the news, no thanks to the paparazzi, even when I'm not doing anything, simply because of my name. But I've always relished the thought of being a nobody. Even for just a day. Now, Carol gives me that anonymity."

"Understood." Jack did, too. He'd been a successful homicide detective, which, to a degree, meant he'd been known around the city. It was when he lost his family that he became recognized nearly everywhere he went. His face and story had been plastered in more tabloids and newspapers than he cared to count. Even theorists jumped on the bandwagon. Not just in San Francisco, but across the state. He was the homicide detective who may have killed his own family, and if he had, where had he buried his wife?

The phone, still in his hand, buzzed. He checked the time before answering Ray's call—nearly 1p.m. Had he and Franklin really been on the roof for the last two and a half hours?

"Yeah?"

"Where you at, *ese*? Did you ever find Ginnie?" Ray asked.

"I'm on the roof with Mr. Whitney-Cummings—"

"Franklin, please."

"With Franklin. Ginnie isn't here and she's not picking up her cell. What's going on down there?" Jack asked.

He heard Ray inhale deeply. "We got very little. That's to say, nothing. No 3D printer, no weapons, and nothing tying Franklin to Landon's murder. His car is spotless, as he said. And with the Beamer still MIA, we can't get prints off the window, which was the main purpose of this exercise. We're ready to wrap things up."

"We'll be down in a minute." Jack disconnected and looked over at Franklin. "They're nearly finished downstairs."

"Did Ray find what he was looking for?"

Jack shook his head. "I'm sorry we've intruded."

"I really do hope you find out who killed Aaron. He was a really sweet kid who didn't deserve how he'd been treated. And he certainly didn't deserve to die like that. That's part of why I helped him get into the apartment. He couldn't get a job without a fixed address, and he couldn't get a place to live without a job. Classic Catch-22."

"That was generous of you to help him," Jack said.

"What a shit way to go though, just as he was getting his life straightened out." Franklin stood upright and moved toward the sunroom door, then turned back toward Jack. "Do you know if his family are coming to claim his remains? If not, I'd like to pay for his burial."

"I'll look into it and let you know," Jack said. "And before we head down, I wanted to ask you if you know a woman called Eleanor Mae Hogg."

Franklin looked confused. "I can't say that I do. Why do you ask?"

"Eleanor was from Tennessee where she was raised with three older brothers. She ran away from home after they tried raping her," he said.

"The poor girl, but what does she have to do with me?"

"A lot, as it turns out. She has a rags to riches story. She came to California where she began a modeling career under the name of Jennifer Morgan." Jack let that settle for a moment while Franklin processed the information.

As the reality of what Jack just told him sank in, Franklin's eyes widened, and shock crossed his face. With a raised voice full of incredulity, he said, "Wait. Are you telling me I married a woman called . . . called Eleanor Mae *Hogg*?" He swayed on his feet before dropping onto a deck chair. "How . . . when . . . What the fuck?" He shot a confused gaze up at Jack.

"It's no secret Ginnie changed her name when you married, but we discovered it's not the first time she's reinvented herself. Jennifer or Ginnie, legally she's still Eleanor Mae Hogg. We have credit card receipts and a Tennessee arrest record under that name that includes her photo. It's her." Jack watched Franklin scrub his fingers through his hair and down his face. He could very nearly hear the wheels grinding in the man's head as he processed the information. It was clear to him Franklin knew nothing about his wife's past. "Yesterday, we ran the plates on all the vehicles in your garage. The BMW isn't exactly a luxury car like the others, which stood out as unusual. It seems strange she wouldn't have registered it as Morgan or Whitney-Cummings, but it did come back to Eleanor Mae Hogg. That makes us wonder what else might be still in her legal name."

"Why wouldn't she have told me? Any of it?"

"I'm sure this has come as a shock, but anything you can tell me will really help. We know she also has property. We ran the plate on the BMW and found it's registered to a place on Grenard Terrace. Do you know anything about that?"

Franklin nodded. "She was living there when we met. She told me she sold it."

"We're heading there once we've finished here," Jack told him. "By the way, I didn't see her little dog when we were here yesterday. Would she have taken it with her this morning?" Jack asked.

"What little dog? We don't have a dog."

It didn't happen often, but just then, Jack felt at a loss for words. He distinctly remembered the dog, and it pissing on his carpet. "Are you sure? She brought it with her whenever she came to my office."

Franklin raised an eyebrow at him. The smirk told Jack that a bit of Carol had surfaced. "I think I'd know if we had a dog. Besides, I'm allergic to them." Franklin stood up and reached for the sunroom door, then turned again. A coy grin crossed his face. "I need to call my lawyer. If she hasn't legally changed her name, her things could be out on the street by sunset." With that, the man flounced—that's the best way Jack could describe it—down the stairs and back into the house.

CHAPTER TWENTY-EIGHT

Grenard Terrace was a private cul-de-sac off Greenwich Street in the Russian Hill District, surrounded by traditional apartments and a handful of exclusive condos. Ellie Mae's condo was at the top of the circular driveway. Her BMW Z4 was in the carport.

"Pardon me!" A middle-aged woman called out from across the communal driveway. She was dressed in a beige pencil skirt suit, and the glasses attached to a sparkling necklace bounced off her small breasts at the same tempo her beige heels clicked on the paving bricks. She must have recognized Ray as a person of authority and navigated toward where he stood among the assembled officers who'd followed Jack and him over from Sea Cliff Avenue.

As she approached, Ray said, "Just a moment," and turned back to Harry and Wash. "Same as before. You know what we're looking for. If you're met with any resistance by the occupant, let me know."

Jack watched the inspectors move toward the two-story Spanish-style residence with big windows and a red tile roof.

"Wash," Jack called. "Be sure to print the vehicle too." Wash gave Jack a mock salute and continued toward the residence.

"It's Inspector Navarro." Ray said when he faced the woman. "How can I help you?"

The woman's gaze followed the officers toward the house, then she looked back at Ray. "Are you here to do something about that woman's dog? It barks constantly. I've called the police on numerous occasions, but I feel like I'm being ignored."

"We're here now, so we'll have a talk with her," Ray assured the woman.

"She's not home."

"Her car is in the carport, missus . . ." Jack said.

"Miss. Mary Duncan. And yes, she was here, but you just missed her. I saw her head down the alley just before you pulled up." Mary pointed to a narrow gap between the residence and the boundary fence. "There's a narrow path some of us use that cuts through to Lombard rather than having to walk all the way around the block. Anyway, as you can hear, she's left that poor little dog alone. Again. I mean, why get a dog if you're just going to leave it cooped up and alone all day?" Mary's face screwed up in disbelief. "She could have at least taken it with her. She won't even take it with her when she goes out in the middle of the night."

"What do you mean 'when she goes out in the middle of the night'?" Jack spoke up.

Mary gazed up at him. "Just what I said. As soon as she backs out of her carport, the dog starts barking. And howling."

"What time does she usually go out?" Jack asked.

"I don't know. I'm not keeping a log of her comings and goings!" Ray folded his arms across his chest. Jack recognized his look of exasperation. Mary must have got the message too, as she took a deep breath before continuing, "It varies. She goes out, perhaps around one or two in the morning and won't return until after five or so. If at all until the next day." Mary leaned in and lowered her voice to nearly a whisper. Her eyes darted between Jack and Ray. "You don't think she's a prostitute, do you?"

Jack cleared his throat to muffle a laugh. "I don't think so, Miss Duncan."

Ray took out his notebook and made several detailed notes. "Can you tell me about when she's home or not during the day?"

Shaking her head, Mary said, "Not really. I work around the corner at the bank. I often come home for lunch; it's more affordable than going out to eat, you see. If it's quiet, I know she's taken the dog away with her. Honestly, I keep hoping she'll leave the dog wherever it is she goes, because when she comes back, it's usually just to drop the dog and go. And the barking starts *all over* again."

"Yes, ma'am," Ray said. "Can you give me your neighbor's name?"

Good question, Jack thought. The property search showed Ellie had bought the house not long after she started making a name for herself as Jennifer Morgan. But did her neighbors know her as Ellie or Jennifer? Or did they even recognize her as Ginnie Whitney-Cummings?

Mary shook her head and folded her arms across her breasts. "No idea. She's lived here for years and has never talked to anyone that I'm aware of. That one is a bit strange; I don't mind telling you!"

Jack chuckled to himself. Mary had no idea how right she was. "We'll try locating her. And while we're here, we'll do a welfare check on the dog."

"A welfare check?" Mary's voice rose slightly with indignation. "Is that all you can do? Can't you take the dog to . . . I don't know where . . . maybe a shelter or something? It's disturbing our quiet enclave." She nodded to the surrounding apartments and duplexes. Some of the apartment dwellers had stepped onto their balconies and others were milling around the perimeter of the driveway, having taken an interest in all the patrol cars.

"I'm afraid that's all we can do unless we can prove the dog is in danger. Barking is a civil matter. If you've spoken with your neighbor and she won't remedy the situation, your next course of action is to seek legal advice," Ray explained.

"Isn't that what I'm doing now?"

Ray breathed deeply. "I mean, talk with a lawyer."

"That seems a bit extreme. Is it really too much to ask for some peace and quiet? It's not just barking. The howling is heartbreaking, like the poor thing is literally crying out for attention."

Jack glanced at Ray then to Mary. "Would you be interested in taking the dog in, or at least looking after it while its mistress is away?"

Mary's face contorted. "Hell, no. That dog isn't my responsibility and I don't want it to be. I just want my quiet life back."

"How long has this been going on?" Ray asked.

"I don't know. A year or so. Seems like forever."

Harry appeared at Jack's side. "The door's locked and no one's home. We need a locksmith."

Ray turned to Mary and said, "Thank you for your time. We'll see what we can do about the dog."

"What are you going to do about the other noise?" Mary asked.

Jack lifted an eyebrow at Mary's comment. "What other noise, Miss Duncan?"

"As if the barking wasn't bad enough, there's some kind of machine running over there. It's constantly on, whether she's home or not," Mary explained. "I can hear it from here."

Jack cocked his head and agreed there was a low-level hum coming from the direction of the condo, along with the dog that was intermittently barking and howling.

"Thank you, Miss Duncan," Ray said, adding the last detail to his notebook. "We'll take a look when we check on the dog."

Without waiting for her response, Jack and Ray followed Harry across the driveway and up the steps leading to the front door. Ray knocked to be sure no one was home, then checked the knob to confirm the door was secure. "Yep, we'll need a locksmith. Harry, call—"

"Give me a minute," Jack said. He'd noticed a door at the back of the carport and retraced his steps to the driveway. He side-stepped between the car and wall as he edged to the door and tried the knob, but it was locked too. Pulling out a small leather case from inside his jacket, he gazed around to make sure Mary Duncan had returned home. From this angle behind the car, and the surrounding patrol cars, he was sure none of the onlookers saw him either. Kneeling, he extracted the tools he needed from the case then inserted them into the lock. It sprang instantly. *She really should have had better locks on the place.*

After replacing the tools in the case and sliding it back into his inner pocket, he quickly went inside and closed the door behind him.

He knew Ginnie wasn't home, as the dog was barking somewhere upstairs. Even if she had been home, she probably wouldn't have heard him above the racket the machine was making. It was no wonder Mary Duncan complained about the noise.

A long, narrow hall connected the carport to the rest of the lower level of the residence, which included a laundry room, a small guest bathroom, and two bedrooms, the first of which was the master with an en suite. The décor was practically the opposite of Ginnie's bedroom over on Sea Cliff. No contemporary minimalism here. This room had been designed with antique furnishings and finished off in floral patterns with ruffled curtains. It made sense to him now why the antique armoire was out of place over on Sea Cliff. It was definitely part of this matching bedroom suite.

The second bedroom had been converted into a sort of office-cum-workshop. A built-in wraparound counter filled three walls opposite the door. Built-in cabinets were under the middle portion of the worktop, and above that was a blacked-out window, the sliding panel of which was partially open.

The counter to the left was set up as desk space with three oversized monitors encircling a keyboard and mouse, and a plush swivel chair.

On the counter to Jack's right, there wasn't just one, but three professional size 3D printer machines set up against one wall, each of them creating various pieces Jack recognized as parts of a handgun.

He tapped the edge of the space bar on the computer keyboard. The monitors flickered and came to life. Designs for various components for an *Imura* revolver were spread across the screens.

Jack felt gut-punched. A ball of acid forced its way to the back of his throat. He wanted to throw himself into the swivel chair to catch his breath but didn't dare disturb any evidence on it.

Until yesterday in the park when Ray had told him and Haniford about Eleanor Mae Hogg, Jack couldn't understand what she'd have to do with Ranganathan and why she'd been in his apartment. Had she been the date Ranganathan told Franklin about?

It started coming together when Ray dropped his bombshell and revealed Ellie Mae had recreated herself as Jennifer Morgan, long before meeting Franklin Whitney-Cummings.

Now, standing here and watching the machines create the elements needed to make another *Imura* revolver, it rocked him to the core.

His client—the former top model and currently the unhappy wife—was the one who'd been killing patrons of the Majestic Lounge. But why? Certainly not just to obtain a divorce.

He needed to get Ray in here now. They had to find Ginnie before she knew they were onto her.

Jack rushed up the stairs to the main floor and through the open plan room to the front door. It barely registered that her choice of antique bedroom décor was the same throughout the residence. He snatched up the little dog on his way to the front door, both to quiet it and to keep officers from letting it out once the door was open. It instantly quieted but he felt it shivering against his arm.

Jack flung open the door then grabbed Ray by the front of his jacket with his free hand and pulled him through the house. "It's her," he said as he moved.

At the top of the stairs, Ray jerked out of his grasp. "What are you talking about?"

"It's her. Goddammit, it's her!" He flew headlong down the stairs and returned to the office. "Hurry up!"

"What the absolute fuck . . . " Ray said under his breath when he entered the room.

Jack spun, gesturing at the printers. His heart pounded so hard in his ears that he scrubbed his fist across his forehead to force back the pressure building there. He took a couple deep breaths to keep from shouting out his realization.

"Look. She's creating another weapon. The plans are on the screen. The noise Mary Duncan is hearing is Ginnie printing out handgun components." He waved his free hand toward the computer monitor. "It's her, Ray. Ginnie-fucking-Ellie Mae . . . she's the one staging the suicides. She's our killer."

Just then, Wash appeared behind Ray. "Umm, guys—" A hanger dangled from a beefy, gloved index finger. Upon it was a long, black coat and matching scarf. In his other gloved hand, he held a black, wide-brimmed hat. "These were in the closet near the front door."

Jack and Ray stared at each other for a long moment. Ray opened his mouth to say something, then shut it again. Jack had a hard time finding words himself.

Harry squeezed past her partner. "Holy shit!" Another officer pushed in behind her.

Ray gazed up and spread his arms. "Okay, everyone. Out. We need to protect the scene."

"Wait. What's that?" Jack asked, stopping at the door, the last to leave the room. He cocked his head. Something squelched, followed by low level voices. He gazed at the partially open window. Was it someone outside? He moved toward the window and listened. He heard the sound again. Not outside. He gazed across the full length of the counter. There. Behind one of the monitors.

"What do you have, Jack?" Ray stepped back into the room.

Jack leaned over and turned up the volume. "Motorola."

"What the hell?"

"She's been monitoring police calls, Ray. She knew we were coming before we got here. There's no telling what else she's been privy to."

CHAPTER TWENTY-NINE

Jack and Ray stood on the open plan main floor beside the sliding door that led onto a private patio surrounded by a high, vine-covered wall. As with the interior furnishings that focused on a single occupant, seating outside was also for one person. Several tall, potted leafy trees added privacy from neighboring windows. It appeared nothing about this residence welcomed visitors. Probably intentional, as Ginnie had been keeping the place as her secret hideaway.

"How do you want to play this, Ray?" Jack asked. "Put out a BOLO and an ATL?"

"What do you think, Jack?" Ray asked, sarcasm dripping from his words. His scowl darkened.

"What I *know* is we can't waste time rushing all over the city trying to find her. She's on foot and there are a million places she can hunker down."

"Right," Ray agreed, tossing his hands onto his hips. "Based on what you told me about your conversation with Franklin, I'm guessing she won't go there either."

"He's probably changed the locks already."

Ray chuckled. "I'll get a warrant to monitor her phone activity."

"Good idea. She can't stay on the street all night, so she'll definitely be back for her car."

"What about getting it over to forensics? We're not just talking about fingerprints on the window. If she's really the one who's been killing these people, there's going to be a shitload of evidence inside the car," Ray pointed out.

Jack shook his head. "Agreed, but for now, let's just take the prints off the window. She's going to need a vehicle. If we leave it here, we can grab her inside the Beamer and kill two birds with one stone. If she knows we've been in the car, she may not take it. Same goes for the house. If she heard the call on the radio, she only knows we were coming to question an Eleanor Mae Hogg. There's a chance she may not be aware that we know who she really is. And unless she has spares," Jack added, "she'll want this new weapon too."

He never would have guessed the beautiful former supermodel would have been capable of anything like this, but now knowing she was crack shot Ellie Mae from Tennessee, it made sense that she'd know how to handle weapons. Even ones made from plastic.

"You're right," Ray said. "Her only choice is coming back here when she thinks it's safe. Even if it's just for her car. We'll put an unmarked vehicle on Greenwich Street and post a couple plain clothes officers on Lombard in case she comes back through that alleyway."

Jack's gaze tracked a pair of officers as they moved through the upper floor. "I know just who we should put out on Lombard." He shifted the dog into his other arm and crooked his finger at the officers.

"Inspector," the male officer said to Ray as the pair approached, neither looking at Jack.

The male officer's name tag said W. James. The female's said G. Massie.

Were they embarrassed by their treatment of Jack the night of Bob Johnson's murder, or discounting his presence at this scene because he was no longer on the force?

"You know Jack Slaughter," Ray said. "He's consulting on this case. I want you to afford him the same respect you have for any of your senior officers." The pair glanced at Jack then back at Ray. "Is that understood?"

"Yes, sir," Massie said.

"Is that all, sir?" James asked.

"No." *Not by far.* Jack felt a little comeuppance creep through him. "We want you both in plain clothes and over on Lombard to stake out the street entrance to the side alley." He thumbed in the direction of the alley beside the house. "If our suspect returns for her car, or anything else," Jack said, shifting the dog to his other arm again, "we need to know."

Massie bobbed her head that she understood. "Yes, sir."

"Sir," James said to Ray. "I—"

"Yes?" Ray lifted an eyebrow at James' tone. "Do you have somewhere else to be, officer?"

"Yes . . . I mean, no. I mean—"

"When you graduated from the academy, did you swear to protect this city?" Ray asked.

"Yes, sir. Of course."

"Did you swear to protect it only when it's convenient for you?"

"N-no, sir."

"This woman has killed eight people. And by the looks of things, she's preparing for number nine." Ray crossed his arms over his chest. Jack knew his friend struggled to keep his cool. He'd seen this posture before many times. "If you want to stay on this team, you'll get into your civvies and get your ass out there."

"Let's go, newbie," Massie ordered.

"But—" James started.

"But what?" Ray leaned closer to James and stared him in the eye. Jack recognized this tactic of intimidation. James didn't budge though, making Jack wonder if the man had a set of balls on him.

"Sir, I don't agree with having to take orders from a civilian," James finally said, barely glancing Jack's way.

"Officer," Ray said so calmly as he stepped toe to toe with James without breaking eye contact that even Jack couldn't tell how much anger was boiling inside his friend. James pressed his lips firmly together but held his position. "This man remains the most decorated officer the city has ever seen. We're lucky he's agreed to consult with us on this case. Whether he's on the force or not, he's still one of our brothers. We take care of our own. Got it?" James' back stiffened but he remained silent. "I said, got it? Because if you don't, you can hand in your badge now and go home."

James quickly glanced at Massie. He wasn't getting any favors from his TO. A long moment later, he stepped back. "Yes, sir. Tell us what you need. We'll get it done."

A grin crept across Ray's lips. "Right answer. Jack?"

"As I said. This is a plain clothes stakeout. You'll be on foot so you can follow our suspect if necessary." Jack handed the dog to Ray then pulled out his phone and brought up the most recent photo he had of Ginnie. "Give me your numbers so I can send you the suspect's details." When receipt of the suspect information was confirmed by the officers, Jack continued. He explained how Ginnie was portraying herself publicly, and her true identity. "Witnesses have all confirmed someone dressed in black has been casing the homes of our victims. While we've taken some of those garments into evidence, our suspect may have more than one change of clothes. Massie, take your TO over to Mary Duncan's and see if she remembers what our suspect was wearing when she left."

"Yes, sir. She's pretty famous," Massie said. "She should be easy to recognize."

"If and when you see her, get on the horn immediately. Inspectors Callahan and Washington will be in an unmarked vehicle on the street and monitoring the driveway to see if she comes up that way," Jack said.

"Sir," James said to Ray. "Any chance we can be in the stakeout car?"

Before Ray could speak, Jack pulled himself upright, put his hands on his hips and looked down on the officer. His height packed as much of a punch as Ray's steely gaze. "You're a whiner, aren't you?"

James flashed an angry glare at Jack. "No. *Sir*."

Jack couldn't figure out what this guy's beef was with him, but this wasn't the time or place for it. "Good. You both can head back to the department now to get changed. Be back here in half an hour to get started. I'm guessing we should be wrapping up here about then." Ray nodded in agreement.

"We can get started now, if you'd like. We have street clothes in the car," Massie said. James frowned; his disapproval evident.

"Good plan. Change out then head down to Lombard. And, Officer Massie?" Ray added. "Get your rookie under control."

"Sir!"

"Dismissed."

Jack and Ray watched the officers walk away. It was obvious by their body language they were arguing.

"Think James'll be trouble?" Jack asked.

"I hope not. Here," Ray handed the dog back to Jack. "Deal with this. I'll let Harry and Wash know they're on stakeout detail down on Greenwich, then we can wrap things up here."

"What? After what you told those dimwits, you're putting me on doggie detail? If you think I'm sitting out Ginnie's arrest to doggie sit, you have another think coming."

"We can't very well leave the dog in the house. What if Ginnie . . . Ellie Mae . . . finds out we're staking out the place? She may never come back. Even for the weapon. We have to consider her in the wind. Which means that dog could die of starvation. Better to take it out now. If there's the slightest chance she's onto us, she may never even notice the dog's missing when she comes back."

Jack shifted his weight onto one foot. "And just where do you want me to take it?" It's late in the day and shelters are closed. I know Franklin won't take it. He's allergic."

"Take it to your place. Drop it in a shelter tomorrow when they open," Ray suggested, shrugging.

"I live above a restaurant. I can't have pets up there." In reality, Jack didn't know if he could or not. He just knew he didn't want the dog in his place.

Frustration deepened the stress lines forming across his friend's face. "Look, I really don't care what you do with it. I've got other things to deal with." Ray called Harry and Wash over. "Why not spend a night in your own house? No rules about dogs over there, I bet."

That cut Jack to the quick. "Seriously, Ray? You're going there?" Ray just rolled his eyes and turned toward the approaching inspectors. *Okay, Ray, if that's how you want to play it.*

To Harry and Wash, Ray said, "Let's get that outfit back in the closet. If and when she returns, I want things exactly as she left them. Then I want you both down on Greenwich, watching that driveway. It's the only way in and out of this complex." Ray gave them the details of what he wanted, including Massie and James over on Lombard keeping an eye on the alley.

"You got it," Harry said.

"Jack, you're with me. I'll take you back to your place then head over for the warrant on Ginnie's phone." Ray froze for a second, then moved to the sliding door onto the small patio and opened it a couple inches. "In case she wonders what happened to her dog. Maybe she'll think she forgot to close the door and it got out."

Before Jack could say anything, Ray headed toward the door.

Jack held up the little dog in his palm to face him. Its little black eyes were canopied by overhanging hair. He gave the dog a scratch on its head and neck, which seemed to make it happy.

His finger caught on the collar hidden under a layer of hair. A tiny disc dangled from a light pink collar that said *Butch*. He'd naturally assumed it was a female based on its doggie haute couture. But, holding the dog up for inspection, he said, "Well, Butch, it seems your mistress may be having an identity crisis of her own. You are clearly not the Fifi she's making you out to be."

Jack hadn't bothered turning on the light when he got home. It was late, not quite midnight, but blissfully quiet. Even the lack of street noise seemed to give him some respite.

He'd stripped off on the way to the bathroom for a piss, put on a pair of sweatpants, then threw himself onto the battered leather sofa. He cursed when a spring caught him in the ass. He moved over to settle against the cushion then tipped back his head and closed his eyes.

He was body weary and mentally exhausted. It had been one long-ass day. He still tried wrapping his head around Ginnie being the killer all along.

He let his body relax and his mind followed, but rather than sleep, he felt himself being pulled into a half-awake/half-asleep vortex of confused thoughts.

If Ginnie had killed those men, why hire him in the first place, even if all she needed were photos for her divorce?

And what was her motive for killing so many innocent men? In that her victims were all patrons of the Majestic, was she trying to frame Franklin for the murders? If so, why stage them as suicides? Why not just shoot them outright and plant evidence incriminating Franklin?

None of it made sense.

At the tinkling sound, he turned, expecting to see the little purse pooch. Instead, it was the black dog. A silver disc suspended from its collar sounded like a windchime, winking like a suncatcher with a promise of respite. The dog sat gazing at him, as if waiting for its moment to pull Jack along its dark path, its promise of relief unfulfilled.

The dog moved toward him. Beyond it, Leah stood with her arms folded in front of her, a look of longing across her beautiful face. No, not longing. Was it fear, or perhaps sadness? Jack certainly felt her disappointment. His heart ached for her. He reached for her—

Ringing.

Reluctantly, he turned from Leah and saw Ginnie. Beneath her wide-brimmed designer hat was the grinning face of the crack shot teen, and she held a flailing turkey by the legs in one hand.

Ringing.

When he opened his eyes, the room was still dark. Light from the Condor Club across the road formed soft lines between the gaps in the blinds.

Ringing.

His phone screen flashed Ray's image with the incoming call.

Jack rubbed his palm down his face in an effort to clear his mind, then clicked receive to answer the call. "*Jack Slaughter, Private Investigations and Security.*"

"Cut the crap, Jack." Even over the phone, Jack could see his friend's face in his mind and knew he was one pissed off dude.

"What's wrong?" Jack sat up and finger-combed the hair out of his eyes. He needed a haircut but would worry about that once the case was solved.

A quick check of the time showed he'd been sleeping less than thirty minutes.

"What do you want to hear first? That Massie and James fucked up and Ginnie got past them? Or that she also managed to get past Harry and Wash? Or that after one of the longest days of my life, I get home to find a little dog in my bed and sleeping on my pillow?" Yep, Ray was pissed. Jack grinned that he had a little part to play in that.

"Let's hear about Massie and James first."

"They're not offering up any excuses or explanations. Simply that they didn't see Ginnie enter the alley leading up to her place," Ray said.

"Maybe they didn't. She could have made her own path through a neighbor's garden. Is the alley the only entrance onto the property, other than the driveway? Did anyone check or just take it that it was?" Jack asked.

Ray grumbled. "Fuck if I know. It's possible. Or just maybe, we're dealing with a lot of fuckups on this."

Jack kept his voice calm in the hopes Ray would relax a little. "Let's assume there's another way onto the terrace and it wasn't through either of the known entrances. Ginnie's on the property now?"

"No, and we don't know how long she was at her place either."

"Has anyone gone back into the house to see if she's taken anything?"

"Someone is on their way there now."

Jack got up and went into the backroom. "I'm putting you on speaker so I can get dressed." He pressed the speaker icon and set the phone on the table under his murder wall. It needed updating now that he knew Ginnie was at the heart of the case, but he hoped they'd catch her before he did. "Tell me about Harry and Wash." In reality, he couldn't imagine them fucking up anything. By all accounts, they were fine inspectors.

He kicked off his sweats and pulled on the black jeans he'd left on the floor earlier. While Ray talked, he slid into a clean black T-shirt.

"We don't know what Ginnie did while there, but she definitely came back for her Beamer. Harry said a vehicle came down the driveway dark. It turned onto Greenwich before the lights went on and it sped up the road. As the car passed, they realized it was the suspect and gave pursuit."

Jack took the phone back in the front room where he slid his feet into his boots. "Did they catch her? Tell me they got her." He propped one foot on the sofa arm to tie the laces, then the other.

"In an ideal world . . . They followed her across the city, trying to get her to pull over, but she eventually lost them in heavy fog in the Presidio. It looks like she might be heading to Sea Cliff, so I have officers heading that direction. I'm nearly there myself."

Jack went to his desk, unlocked the side drawer, and pulled out his gun case. God, he hated this part of investigations. Nothing about PI work should be dangerous, but lately it seemed he was being pulled into situations that went much further than cheating spouses, missing children, and surveillance.

"I'll meet you over there," Jack said and disconnected the call before Ray could ask him about the dog.

He gazed at the box for a solid minute before punching in the password. The red light flashed green on the first try and he heard the lock open.

The barrel edge of the Beretta glinted in the dim light coming through the blinds. He was almost afraid to touch it.

He cleaned the weapon monthly. That wasn't the problem. There was no intention of using it. Just keeping it in working order. Taking it out now, as a means of defense, was another story. If Ginnie was armed, he needed to be too.

For the last four years, he'd hoped the next time he pulled out the Beretta would be his last. But this wasn't that time. He still hadn't found Leah or the person who killed his daughter and Trax. Knowing where he was taking the weapon tonight didn't make the task any easier. He never went out with the intention of killing anyone—he'd always hated that part of his job, as a cop then homicide inspector and now private investigator—but it was always a possibility, and one he had to be ready for. Kill or be killed.

When did he start becoming afraid to do his job? Was he really getting too old for this shit? Or was it that he was just ready to hang it all up and call it quits for good? Would it matter that he hadn't found Leah, or the person who'd destroyed his family?

He took a deep breath and held it for a moment before pushing the air out of his lungs. Forcing himself to focus, he quickly lifted the Beretta from its custom foam insert. He pulled back the slide and snapped the full 19-round magazine into place. The slide closed with a sharp snap. He checked the safety was on before sliding the weapon into the jean's waistband in the center of his back and headed for the door.

"Fuck this shit and the horse it rode in on," he cursed, grabbing his jacket, then slammed the door behind him.

CHAPTER THIRTY

Monday – Christmas Eve

"You gotta help me." The voice on the phone was barely a whisper.

"Dewayne? What's wrong?" Jack had just turned onto California Street and raced for the Whitney-Cummings residence on Sea Cliff. The fog had come in thick and stuck to the pavement, making the speed he was going dangerous, but he wanted to be there when they took down Ginnie.

The dash clock read 12:33a.m.

"Someone's in my house. You gotta help me."

Jack heard the fear in the youth's voice. He pumped the brakes, put the phone on speaker and set it back in the phone caddy, before pressing the record icon. "What do you mean someone's in your house? Did you call the police?"

"Fuck no. You told me to call you if I needed you. I need you!"

"Where are you?"

"I'm in the attic. Come on, man. You gonna help a brother out or you gonna let me die?"

Jack pumped the brakes again, looked in his mirrors for traffic and pedestrians, then took the next left turn, accelerating again. "Stay where you are. Stay quiet but don't hang up. I'll be there as soon as I can."

It seemed to take forever getting the few miles across the city, most of which had been along the 101 then 280 which practically dropped Jack at Dewayne's front door. But within a few minutes, he stomped on the brakes and screeched to a stop in front of

Dewayne's house. The Jeep still rocked when Jack threw himself out of it and rushed to the front door, pulling the Beretta from his waistband as he moved.

"I'm here, Dewayne." He whispered into the phone. As he'd turned onto Rockwood, he connected the hands-free device to the phone and slid it into his breast pocket and stuffed an earbud into his ear. "Where are you?" He checked the knob with his free hand—locked—then heard scrambling on the line. "Dewayne, where are you?" Jack rushed down the breezeway to the back of the house and reached for the backdoor knob, but the door was partially open. "Dewayne," he whispered loudly down the line. More scrambling but the boy was silent. Had the intruder found him?

Jack pushed open the door with his foot, cringing when it creaked on its hinges, and entered the kitchen. He double fisted the Beretta, flipped off the safety, and listened for intruders, but the interior of the house remained quiet. Keeping the weapon angled toward the floor, he chose his moves carefully, hoping the floorboards allowed him silent passage across them. He stuck to the perimeter of the room where he'd be less likely to make noise or cast shadows from the streetlight coming in through the open door.

His gaze darted around the living room as he creeped into the hall, keeping an eye open for an attic hatch. His pounding heart forced blood into his ears as he went room by room. Kitchen, clear. Living room, clear. Bathroom, clear. First bedroom, clear. Hall closet, clear.

Where's the fucking hatch?

He heard a sound behind him and spun just in time to catch the short pipe in his hand. "What the fuck, Dewayne?" He pulled the weapon from the boy's hands. "I could have shot you, goddamn it."

"I thought you were her," Dewayne said.

"Her who? What's going on? I thought you were in the attic."

"I was, but I thought I heard her leave, so I came down. Then I heard noises and grabbed the first thing I could find to defend myself," the boy explained.

Jack pushed the boy into the living room and set the pipe on the coffee table. Safety on, he tucked the Beretta back in place at the base of his spine. "I thought I told you to stay put."

"I did."

"Stay put in the attic until I got here."

"Naw, you didn't say that."

"I'm pretty sure that's what I implied. Tell me what happened," Jack demanded, throwing his hands on his hips. He quickly gazed around the room. It still hadn't been cleaned.

"I was watching TV. I thought I heard a noise, so I turned it off so I could hear better. I saw the doorknob turn—"

"Maybe it was your mom coming home," Jack offered.

Dewayne shook his head. "Naw, she gots a key. Besides, she hasn't been home in months, and I ain't expecting her neither."

Jack gazed around the room again. Months? "So, you ran to the attic. Sounds like you've been up there before." Dewayne gazed away from Jack and moved to the other side of the room to flip on the overhead light. It was so dim, it barely made a difference. "Well?"

"Well, what?"

"Tell me about the attic."

Dewayne clearly thought about if he should tell Jack anything, but finally relented. "I used to go up there sometimes when I was little, when Mom's boyfriends got mean."

"What about tonight? Do you know who was trying to break in?"

With obvious reluctance, Dewayne jerked his head in the affirmative. "It was that woman who killed the guy around the block."

For a moment, Jack couldn't breathe. "What do you mean? How do you know who killed Landon?"

"I—I saw her do it."

Jack moved forward, his gaze firmly on Dewayne. "*What?*" His body started vibrating with shock and anger. "Why didn't you tell me?"

"I didn't want to get involved."

"That's a copout. But you're involved now, so I'd recommend filling me in so I know how to handle this situation." Dewayne threw his arms around himself and looked away. When he turned back a long moment later, Jack saw fear in his eyes, but his tightly pressed lips and grinding jaw suggested he wasn't going to give in to it. Jack had seen this before in other suspects—scared shitless but trying to disguise it with false bravado. "Dewayne . . ." Jack hoped his tone was enough to tell the boy his patience was wearing thin.

"I went up the road on my bike to score some weed. On my way back, I heard yelling coming from that house. There was a gap in the curtains, so I looked to see what was going on."

"What did you see?"

Dewayne looked away. "I saw a woman stabbing the guy. He couldn't have been much older than me." He looked at Jack when he said that.

"He wasn't." Jack kept his voice neutral. He wasn't going to lie but he didn't want to add to his already high anxiety. Calmly, he said, "Tell me what you saw."

"She was mad. I mean really pissed. Dude was already on the floor when I looked in. He looked dead; he wasn't fighting back. But she just kept stabbing and yelling at the guy."

"Did you hear what she was saying?"

Dewayne shook his head. "She wasn't making any sense. Just crazy talk. But she was mad. I don't know if it was him or someone else, but that poor guy—"

Jack put his hand on Dewayne's shoulder. "Then what happened?"

He shook his head. "I don't know. She suddenly stopped. Didn't move. Like she was listening for something. She turned toward the window and must have seen me. I got on my bike and got the fuck outta there."

"What about the car? You told me you saw it in front of your house. Was that the truth?" Jack knew it had to be, as he saw the prints on the window that corresponded with someone having looked through the window.

Dewayne nodded. "When I got home, I saw the car. What I said before, that was the truth. I ditched my bike and went to look inside. I didn't know it was hers. When she came around the corner and saw me at the car, she ran over screaming at me to get away. She still had blood on her hand when she grabbed at me. If that guy across the road hadn't come out when he did, I probably woulda been killt too. She just got in the car and took off."

"You said it was the middle of the night. How do you know she still had blood on her?" Dewayne disappeared down the hall, then came back with a hoodie. There was a streak of dried blood across the front where she must have grabbed for him.

Jack took the hoodie, then carefully folded it and tucked it under his arm, then gazed around the room for a moment.

Dewayne's a witness.

Not just someone who could ID the suspect as a woman, and not just seeing a random woman getting into a black BMW near the scene of a murder. He'd seen the murder and could ID the perpetrator. He pulled up Ginnie's photo on his phone.

"This her?" When Dewayne nodded, he asked, "Why do you think she was trying to get in your house?"

"She was in the house. No doubt. She gots in the same way you did. After I heard her trying to get in the front door, I went up in the attic before she could go round back. I heard her in the house. She kept saying she was going to get me and shut me up." Dewayne crossed his arms again, shifting his weight between his feet.

"Are you sure it was the same person?" When the boy nodded again, Jack pulled out his phone and disconnected the call with Dewayne's phone and tapped the icon for Ray. "Ray—"

"Where are you?" Ray asked, panic in his voice. "I'm standing here with Franklin. He hasn't seen Ginnie. She's not here."

"She was never going there. I'm over on Ridgewood at Dewayne's house. Ginnie was just here. And Ray . . . Dewayne just told me he witnessed Landon's murder." Jack heard Ray's sharp curse in Spanish. He felt the same. "I'm going to take him to my place. Meet me there." Before Ray could reply, Jack disconnected the phone.

"What do you mean you're taking me to your place?"

"Listen to me carefully." Jack gazed directly into Dewayne's eyes and spoke as calmly and clearly as he could to make sure the boy understood the seriousness of the situation. "I need you to pack some clothes and whatever you think you'll need for the next few days. I'm taking you into protective custody."

Dewayne's face contorted. "Protective custody? Naw, man!" His voice was filled with disbelief.

"Yeah, man," Jack echoed. "You're the only person who can tie her to your neighbor's murder. We know that murder is linked to seven others. Without your eyewitness statement, everything else we have on her is circumstantial . . . evidence that suggests she might have killed these people, but nothing that absolutely links her. *You're* that link. She was here to kill you to protect herself." He let it sink in for a minute. When Dewayne didn't say anything, Jack repeated, "Please. Get your things so I can take you with me." Dewayne clearly thought about his options. "Don't make me get CPS involved. You've just admitted your mother has been gone for months, and I know you're a minor. I can't and won't leave you here, not under these circumstances. So, please."

"Okay, already."

Jack watched the boy move around the house. First to the kitchen for a brown paper bag, which he seemingly dumped random stuff into. While he gathered his things, Jack secured the back door. Out of curiosity, he checked the fridge and cupboards. Both were practically empty. Back in the living room, after checking all the windows in the house, it seemed the place was full of cardboard pizza boxes and a few Chinese takeout boxes. Dewayne was lucky if he didn't have rats with all the filth he was living in.

A scattering of envelopes spread across the dining table. He pushed them around with the nail side of his finger. All were addressed to Denise Watkins. Ones with government seals on them had been opened. *Looks like Dewayne has been cashing his mother's welfare checks.* Made sense. How else could he have lived here for so long? It appeared he'd kept up the rent, paid the utilities, and fed himself.

Just then, Dewayne appeared in the living room, a stuffed bag in his arms.

"Got everything you need?" Jack asked.

"Man, if this house burned down tomorrow, I gots everything I need right here." He shifted the bag in his arms.

Jack's heart squeezed. "Get your house keys anyway." Dewayne grabbed a set off the coffee table. "Ready to go?"

"Do you have room in your ride for my Xbox and TV?"

Jack chuckled. "Yeah, sure. And on the way to my place, you're going to tell me about your mother."

Ray had already let himself in. He was pacing in front of the windows when Jack pushed open the door. "Come on in, Ray. Make yourself at home."

Ray spun. "Fuck you," he said, striding forward. "This our witness?" He looked Dewayne up and down.

"Dewayne Watkins, meet the biggest pain in the ass in my life, Inspector Ray Navarro. He's also the best detective in the city and in charge of finding the woman who killed your neighbor. Dewayne, tell the inspector what you told me back at your house while I grab the rest of your stuff from the Jeep."

By the time Jack returned with Dewayne's big screen television, Ray was pacing the room again and the boy was slumped on the sofa. Jack set the TV on a table in the corner of the room then threw himself into the chair behind his desk. The Beretta dug in his back, but he left it in place. He didn't need Dewayne seeing where he kept it.

Ray lowered himself into the chair in front of the desk. "That's quite a story Dewayne told me. You believe him?" Ray asked.

Jack looked over at Dewayne and nodded. "Absolutely."

"He lied before—"

"He omitted," Jack corrected. He sat forward, elbows on the desk. "Look, he's 15, lives alone, and he was scared. But now we know the truth, so we need to work out a plan to move forward. Ginnie's in the wind. We have an APB out on her vehicle. We need to keep Dewayne in protective custody," he cocked his head in Dewayne's direction, "and we need to locate his mother. I think we also need to put a patrol car outside Franklin's house in case she tries going back there."

"Already done."

Jack nodded. "What about Ginnie's place on Grenard? Obviously, a car on the street didn't deter her, so we need to get a car up on the terrace itself."

"Organized."

Jack thought for a moment, then gazed up at Ray. "I want to know what happened up on Grenard. We had four officers watching the entrances onto the property, so how did any of them miss Ginnie's return?"

"Massie swore no one used the alley," Ray told him.

"What about James? Where was he?" Jack asked.

Ray shook his head. "He claims it was late, he was cold, everything was closed, and he needed to take a piss."

"So he wasn't even at the scene?" Jack exclaimed.

"Around the corner, but technically no."

"Goddammit! So Ginnie could have used the alley, especially if Massie was on her own and her attention was distracted, even for a moment," Jack suggested.

Ray nodded. "She would have had more to contend with . . ." He left the rest unsaid.

If Massie was the kind of officer Jack thought she was, she would not have only been watching the alley, but keeping her eyes open for any opportunists thinking she was a working girl while also watching for her partner who was relieving himself into the garden of some unsuspecting resident. James already had two strikes on Jack's list. This was a strong third.

"Be sure to report all this to Haniford. Let him deal with the incompetence." Ray nodded that he agreed. "The next issue is finding Denise Watkins. Dewayne's been living on his own for the last few months after she stopped coming home. He said he doesn't know where she is but has a history of bouncing between whichever lover has the better drugs."

"You don't want to call CPS and let them handle this?" Ray

asked. "It's not like we don't already have enough on our plate."

Jack shook his head. "Not yet. We'll stake out her known haunts, and if we can't find her, maybe there's an aunt or uncle who can—"

"Dude!" Dewayne exclaimed. "I'm sitting right here."

Jack got Dewayne's TV set up in the corner of the front room so he could play on his Xbox while he and Ray updated the murder wall. It was going on 4a.m. by the time Ray left for home and Jack got Dewayne settled into the narrow bed in the backroom before hitting the sofa. Before he left, Ray called the department to put out an APB on Denise Watkins.

The holidays could be a rough time for families—civilian and police alike. Crime didn't stop, which meant crime stoppers didn't either. Jack knew it was harder for his friend this year because Maria was pregnant. She was getting close to her delivery date and Ray wanted to be home more to help. But no one ever expected a case like this.

He could only imagine what it must be like for Dewayne. Poor kid. They'd talked about his mother, Denise, on the drive over. It didn't seem she'd been home last Christmas, and he wasn't expecting her home this year either. Forget the holidays, Jack wondered what the boy must have to deal with just on a daily basis. All things considered, Dewayne had been looking after himself well enough, even if he was illegally cashing his mother's welfare checks. Big screen TV and Xbox aside, it appeared he'd been using the money to keep a roof over his head—smart kid.

If being forced to be an adult and take care of himself so early in life wasn't hard enough, he was the only witness to a violent homicide, and tonight, the killer had tried silencing him.

Jack turned over and tried getting comfortable. A spring hit him in the lower back like a sucker punch. Any drowsiness he may have been feeling instantly disappeared. He tossed and turned, contorting his body around the offensive spring.

Thoughts tumbled around in his head, from the fuck-up on Grenard to where Ginnie could be holing up. Did she have credit cards on her for a hotel room, or would her face or name open doors for her? Was she sleeping somewhere in her car, or had a friend taken her in? He'd have to ask Franklin about any friends his wife may have or where else he thought she could be.

Fuck this raggedy sofa!

Jack shot to his feet, went to the desk and dropped into the chair. He wiggled his mouse and the monitor came to life. He squinted against the glow cast across the desktop. He checked the time—8:49a.m. He'd dozed longer than he thought he had, but it didn't feel like he'd slept at all.

Then his automatic scheduling app popped up with today's appointment.

Christmas Eve.

Fuck. How had the month gone by so quickly?

He spun the chair toward the window and pulled up the blind. Early morning light filtered through the haze, barely making a dent on the darkness of the room. The city's iconic fog was thick on the ground, but he still made out the spires of St Frank's on the hill.

Fuck-fuck! How had he let so much time pass since he'd seen Nick?

He knew his old friend was an early riser, so Jack headed for the backroom where he quietly showered and grabbed some clean clothes. After dressing, he left Dewayne a note, telling him where he'd gone. And if he was hungry, to get whatever he wanted from Tommy's downstairs.

CHAPTER THIRTY-ONE

J ack never realized how slight Father Nick had become until he saw him lying motionless in the hospital bed.

Jack had become so engrossed in the case, not to mention getting sick in the process, he hadn't realized how much time had passed since he'd last visited Nick.

Today he regretted not having *made* the time.

Gazing into the room from the doorway, it felt like his heart had leaped into his throat and stopped beating there. He swallowed hard several times, trying to dislodge it so he could breathe again.

His friend's rail-thin body was barely visible beneath the light blue colored blanket covering him. If not for Nick's fuzzy gray-crowned head on the pillows and the steady beep of the heart monitor, Jack would have thought the bed was empty.

He willed his feet to move, but he remained rooted where he stood.

From this height, several floors up and at the top of one of the city's many hills, the room was above the fog line. Through the thin shroud, he could just see Hyde Street Pier and San Francisco Bay.

Jack was thankful Nick had a private room, sparse as it was. A single guest chair sat in one corner of the room beside a narrow wardrobe. A TV was mounted on the wall opposite the bed, and a tray table that held a small jug of water and a glass was within arm's reach of the bed.

The beeping monitor at the top of the bed seemed to grow louder the longer Jack stood at the door, as if screaming at him.

Beep! Where have you been?

Beep! Why didn't you make the time to visit?
Beep! What kind of friend are you?
Beep! You've failed. Again.

"You going to just stand there, or are you going to bring me those flowers in your hand?" Nick's voice sounded as fragile as he looked.

It had taken all of Jack's strength to enter the hospital, and sheer will had dragged his leaden feet through long corridors. The heavy feeling in his body didn't ease as he crossed the room to his friend's bedside.

Jack gazed down at the old man. The term *skin and bones* couldn't have been truer. Nick's nearly translucent skin pulled against the shape of his skull. Ruddy cheeks protruded around dark, sunken hazel eyes. Thin, pale lips pressed together above his sharp chin.

He'd known Nick for more than a decade but had never noticed the man age. Jack's stomach twisted at the thought that his friend could be dying.

His heart thumped heavily in his chest. "I wasn't sure if you were awake." He took a deep breath and forced a smile.

Nick glanced at the flowers. "Nice posies."

"I didn't know what you liked, but the florist did a nice job of putting these together." Jack lifted the bouquet to show Nick the arrangement full of cream-colored flowers—roses, chrysanthemums, and delicate Queen Anne's Lace—that were nestled between Dusty Miller leaves and sprigs of Silver Dollar eucalyptus.

"It was thoughtful of you, Jack." He waved a shaky hand toward the water jug. "Stick them in there, then sit down and tell me why you have such a sour look on your face."

Jack removed the lid on the jug and carefully set the flowers into it, then pulled over the chair to the bedside and settled against the tan Naugahyde seatback. He couldn't get comfortable. He crossed one leg over the opposite knee, then shifted in his seat to re-cross them in the other direction. Finally, he set both feet on the floor and leaned forward, putting his elbows on his knees.

"What's the matter, Jack?" Nick's quiet voice was tinged with an undercurrent of melancholy.

"I went up to Saint Frank's to see you, only to find you'd collapsed walking to the confessional on Saturday. Why didn't you have anyone call me? It's been three days, Nick." Jack wrung his hands together to keep them from shaking.

"I didn't want—"

Jack shot Nick a glare. "Don't you dare say you didn't want to bother me."

"Well, I didn't. Don't get yourself all knotted up over this. I'm sorry to have scared you, but I'm all right," Nick assured him, but the waver in his voice told another story.

Jack brooded for a moment. "I'm sorry—" he finally started.

"For what?"

"For not going to Saint Frank's sooner. This case—"

"You don't owe me an apology, Jack," Nick cut in again. "I know what you're like when you're on a tough case. You're either all in or all out. There's no middle ground for you." Nick motioned to the remote hanging on the side of the bedrail. Jack handed it to him. Nick pressed a button that moved the bed into a more upright position.

"If I'd have visited more regularly, I would've known you needed to see a doctor. Maybe it wouldn't have come to this." Could he have prevented his friend from getting so sick? He'd spent a lot of time over the last four years contemplating the *what ifs* in his life. What if he'd *made* the time to visit Nick after Mass *every* Sunday and not just when he felt he needed spiritual guidance? What if he'd paid more attention to his friend rather than focusing on his own problems when he did visit? He might have known more about Nick as a person, and the person he was before he came to the city all those years ago.

Another what if . . . What if he'd got home just ten minutes earlier; could he have prevented Zoë and Trax's murders, and saved his wife?

The last thought widened the hole he felt growing inside him. He inhaled long and deep.

"Are you okay? Is there anything I can do?" he finally asked, hearing the concern in his own voice. He was worried about Nick and scared shitless he'd lose his friend.

"I'm fine," Nick calmly said again. "I'll be here a while longer. I'm where I need to be, so stop worrying."

"Tell me what happened."

"It's just pneumonia."

"Pneumonia! There's nothing *just* about it at your age. You're in hospital for Christ's sake—" He caught himself short at the blasphemy but wouldn't apologize for it. "How long have you known you were sick? Why didn't you see a doctor before it came to this?"

Nick waved a shaky hand in Jack's direction. "Don't get yourself worked up over this. I was feeling a little under the weather and expected it to pass."

Jack grumbled aloud. "I should have known you were here."

"Why should you? This isn't your fault and you couldn't have prevented me from getting sick," Nick told him.

"I could have done—"

"Done what, Jack?"

He ran his fingers through his hair and felt his eyebrows draw tightly together. "I don't know . . . something."

"Well, I'm here now, and so are you. Let's talk about something more pleasant," Nick suggested. When Jack didn't say anything, the man continued, "Nice view they gave me."

Jack didn't have to look over his shoulder to know it was. "Don't get comfortable here. You'll be home soon." Home. Was the church really a home? "Have you ever thought of retiring? Get yourself out of that drafty old building and into a house. I can fix up the Sunset house for you. The beach would practically be at your doorstep," he suggested. He wasn't doing anything else with the house. It made sense.

"I appreciate the offer, Jack. It's tempting, but I *do* prefer the view from the church's bell towers. I can see across the Bay to Angel Island from up there. And the mountains."

Nick's sigh brought on a raspy cough. The monitor's relentless beeping accelerated with his increased heart rate. Jack rose to pour his friend some water, then realized the flowers were in the jug. He glanced toward the door, hoping to catch a passing nurse. But the beeping monitor slowed again as his friend caught his breath. Nick breathed deeply through his nostrils, taking advantage of the tube full of oxygen. Jack's gaze traced the cables peeking out from under the hospital gown to the blood pressure monitor and the oxygen monitor clipped to his finger. An IV line had been inserted into the back of his hand.

The room certainly wasn't part of the ICU—that was on the ground floor—but they were definitely taking good care of the old man, even if he was full of tubes and wires.

Tubes and wires.

Jack's mind flashed to a vision of himself lying in a hospital bed, his attempt to join his family gone wrong and they were keeping him alive by any means necessary. He'd only ever thought about spending that round, not failing in his task. He made a mental note to amend his living will to include a DNR clause. The last thing he wanted was to be kept alive. That opposed the whole purpose of swallowing a bullet.

"There's something about being up in the tower." Nick's voice sounded thinner and he spoke with more effort. "Being closer to heaven and with a view of the island of angels."

Jack went to the door as Nick spoke and asked a passing nurse for a fresh jug of water. "There's a much better view of Alcatraz up there too," he said, returning to Nick's bedside.

"Alcatraz . . . Well, there's a story." Nick gazed away from the window and weakly motioned toward the chair. "Stop fussing. Sit down so we can talk. Did you bring the bottle?"

When Jack had gone up to Saint Frank's, the rector told him about Nick having been taken to hospital, and that Nick had given him instructions for Jack to bring the bottle from his office when he visited. Jack pulled the bottle of aged Jameson from his inside pocket and set it on the tray table.

"Are you allowed to have this?" Jack asked.

"No, he's not, but I won't say anything if ye won't," the pretty nurse said with a wink as she approached the bed with a fresh jug of water and a clean glass. A soft Irish brogue tinged her words. "At least ye have good taste in yer tipple. Lovely flowers, Father." Her tag read Edna. She set the jug on the tray table and the glass beside it.

"They're from my friend here, Jack."

"It's nice to have such thoughtful friends, so it is." After moving the jug of flowers to the windowsill, Edna came back to the bedside to check the monitors and make notes in Nick's chart.

Jack watched as the nurse checked Nick's upper arm cuff then pushed the button on the wall mounted machine to take his blood pressure. A moment later, Edna said, "Your blood pressure has come up a wee bit, Father." Turning to Jack, she added while straightening the blankets, "Your visit seems to have perked him up."

"I was raised by my aunt. Her name was Edna, too. Edna Ellison." He gazed at Jack. "At my age, a few marbles in the memory are bound to roll away, but I could never forget my dear Aunt Edna."

"I'm sure she was a lovely woman. Look how well ye turned out, Father. Now, are ye comfortable? Is there anything I can get ye?" she asked.

"From the old country, Edna?" Nick asked.

Jack saw the gleam appearing in his friend's eyes. With a surname like Morrissey, he'd long assumed the priest had a connection to Ireland. His friend rarely talked about his life outside of the church. Maybe he still had family there. If Nick had family anywhere, Jack thought they should know the man wasn't well.

Edna's cheeks took on a rosy glow. "Not in a long time."

"Surely, they miss you," Nick said.

"Of course. I *am* going home for a visit after the New Year, to see me mam. Knowing her, it'll be a right hooley."

"And why not? Her beloved child is home and I'm sure the whole family will turn up."

Edna laughed. "The whole of the village if I know her."

"What part of Ireland are you from?" Jack asked.

Gazing up at him, she said, "Donegal. Do you know Ireland?"

Jack shook his head. "Just curious is all. Nick, do you have family in Ireland?"

Both heads spun toward Nick. "There were rumors, but who has time to chase rumors? My work at Saint Francis keeps me busy enough."

"Right, Father. I'll leave ye in peace. Ye have yer buzzer if ye need anything." Edna patted Nick's shoulder before heading toward the door.

"Thank you, Edna. I'll remember you in my prayers."

Edna turned with a fresh blush in her cheeks. "*Go raibh míle maith agat*, Father."

When the nurse had gone, Jack settled back against the chair. "You've never really talked about your family, Nick. Has anyone been called since you've been . . . here?" He didn't want to say sick, and he avoided the word hospital. He hadn't been in one since he'd been brought in for observation nearly four years ago. He'd been a hot mess that night when he'd been found slumped against a wall across from where his daughter's lifeless body had been propped in the old highchair. Haniford and Ray both agreed he needed observation for a few days.

Memories from that night were still fresh in his mind. No surprise since at some point every day he retraced each step he'd taken that night, hoping to uncover something he might have missed. At this point, he didn't even care why it had been done to his family, only who did it. Once he knew, he'd exact his revenge. And then he'd take out his Beretta for the last time.

Nick had suggested the mystery might never be solved, but Jack couldn't accept that. Someone had to know what had happened. Leah had to be somewhere. He just wanted the answers to everything before it drove him completely out of his mind.

"No, Jack." Nick's frail voice brought Jack back to the room. "There's no one to call. Any family I had is long gone now."

He couldn't believe Nick had absolutely no one outside the church. How could he be so alone in the world? Then he answered his own question. Aside from Ray and Maria, and Nick, he had no one else in his life either.

"You going to pour us that drink?" Nick asked.

Jack sat forward and poured them their customary shot of the aged whiskey. He knew neither of them would drink until they were done talking, so he pulled the chair a little closer and sat back.

A strange feeling settled in his belly. Something was off about performing their ritual in this sterile environment. Their tradition was the same, but the location wasn't. It didn't feel right.

"Are you sure there's no one? What about brothers or sisters, nieces or nephews, cousins—"

"As far as I know, I was an only child."

"You said you were raised by your aunt. What happened to your parents?"

"Mother sent me to live with Aunt Edna," Nick said in a frank tone.

"Wh-why would your mother send you away?" Jack couldn't believe any parent would do that.

"Mother didn't keep men around long once they realized she had a kid. The last one I remember didn't like me and made no bones about it."

"That's horrible. She chose him over her own son?" Jack was horrified at the thought.

"Sure, but that's how it was. Didn't mean I was happy about it. I certainly hadn't made Mother's life easy. I hated that man she was with and did everything I could to make him leave," Nick confessed.

Jack's eyes widened. "Do you remember much about your parents? Where was your dad in all this?"

Nick laid back and gazed at the ceiling, looking back and forth as if watching a scene before him. "I don't remember anything about my father. All I know is he went by the name of Tommy Tonker. When I started causing trouble, Mother said I was just like him. And that I had his eyes. If he ever came around, I don't remember."

"I'm guessing they weren't married, Tommy and your mother."

Nick shook his head. "Not that I know of. Mother, Thelma Phillips, played the field, as they say. As the rumors went, her men came and went. Eventually one came, Tommy, and gave her a bastard son before leaving. Soon, another man came and stayed a bit longer than the rest, despite her being pregnant. I think they married, as he adopted me and gave us both his name, but he left too, and eventually, so did I."

Jack's heart squeezed at the thought of his gentle friend and mentor having suffered so much as a child. Worse, that he called himself a bastard.

"Do you remember anything about the man who adopted you?"

Nick shook his head. "I only know he was called Morris. I don't know anything else about him; even if he had children of his own. He was gone by the time I was old enough to make memories."

"Was Edna your mother or father's sister? Did she have kids?" Jack asked.

"I don't know how she was related. She could have just been a friend of the family, for all I know. She never had kids of her own—I don't think she ever married—but I'd like to think she loved me like her own son though. At the time, I was just an angry boy and getting into trouble for attention. Mother was never around after I was sent away, and I'm sure I was a lot to handle for my aunt."

"You, a rabble-rouser?" A faint smile crept across his lips. "Doesn't sound like you."

Nick lifted his head and gazed at Jack. "I'm sure none of this sounds like me. But yes, I was a handful and I lashed out at the wrong person. By the time I was fourteen, Aunt Edna put me into state care—an industrial school for troubled boys. I was in and out of institutions until I was drafted in forty-four."

Jack laughed. "Somehow I think you're pulling my leg. I've known you a long time, Nick. You've been nothing but kind, generous, and thoughtful. Nothing about you seems remotely like the boy you're telling me about."

"What about this?" Nick slid down the top of his hospital gown and showed Jack his upper arm. Jack eyed the old red devil tattoo for a moment then fell back against the chair. He watched Nick pull a bony knee out from under his blanket and reveal another tattoo of a star with the number seven above it and eleven below. "I used to have a star on the base of my left thumb and the number thirteen beside it under this finger." He lifted his shaking hand to show Jack the faintest curve where part of the three was just visible under his index finger beneath dark age spots. "Congregants don't need to see that mess on the person they entrusted with their secrets. These others . . . they're my reminders of the man I used to be."

"Damn, Nick. You must have had one hell of a revelation to mend your ways and become a priest. What happened?"

Nick lightly grinned. "You're inquisitive today. Isn't your case keeping you busy enough?"

"You've never said much about your past before Saint Frank's. Your eyes lit up while talking with Nurse Edna. It sounded like you wanted to talk."

"Not really. I just hadn't thought about my aunt in a long time. You never see that name anymore and it brought back memories."

"Tell me about your change in careers, shall we say," Jack urged.

"I'll save that for another day. Tell me how you are, Jack. Your case must be complicated to keep you away so long."

"I have to admit. This one has me twisted in knots. And now I have a fifteen-year-old staying in my place until we can find his mother."

One of Nick's eyebrows lifted. "You fostering, Jack? Does this mean you've moved home?" Nick's voice took on a distinct wheeze and Jack wondered if his friend was getting tired.

Shaking his head, Jack said, "He's my witness. He's the only one who can ID the killer. She's already tried getting to him once. I can't run the risk of her succeeding if he's turned over to state care and they can't protect him. Once we find his mother, Ray will get them both into official protective custody until we close this case." Jack knew that anything he and Nick ever talked about would be kept as confidential as if he'd been in the confessional, so he brought Nick up to speed about the gist of the case without detailing the most gruesome aspects. Including how Dewayne had been living on his own after his mother disappeared.

"Do you think she's still alive?"

Jack shook his head. "I don't know. Ray's already put out an APB on her. If she's still alive, we'll find her. Until then, I'm keeping an eye on him."

"Well, ain't that the damnedest thing? And that woman took an awful chance coming to you."

"I'm still trying to figure it all out. In all my years, I've never met anyone like this before. It's common for some suspects to want to be in on the investigation as a way of controlling things or knowing what the department's next move is so they can avoid capture. But this woman . . . Nick, she was still killing after hiring me." Jack scrubbed his fingers through his beard and rubbed his chin.

"If anyone can bring her in, it's you. Now, I'm getting tired," Nick wheezed. "But I want to talk with you. The last time we spoke, we'd started working on your relationship with God. Have you remembered to take some time out of each day for contemplation?"

Jack shifted uncomfortably in his seat. "I'm ashamed to admit that I haven't made the time."

Nick reached out, his hand shaking more than before. "Take my hand and let's make that time now. Then we'll have that drink."

CHAPTER THIRTY-TWO

Tuesday – Christmas Day

"This was a great idea," Ray said, leaning back in his chair. One course back, he'd popped the button on his jeans and now lowered the zipper before lacing his fingers over his distended belly.

"I know how much you and Ray wanted to cook today, but I also know you've been so busy with your case. This," Maria said, "was amazing. And thoughtful. Thank you, Jack."

Jack gazed at the destruction scattered across the dining table with a satisfied grin.

After his visit with Nick yesterday, he and Dewayne had spent the remainder of the day shopping. Jack was still worried about his friend, but they'd had a good talk, and Nick had assured him he'd be back for Mass on Sunday.

It hit Jack when he got back to the apartment that since he and Ray had been so engrossed with the case, neither of them had had time to think about Christmas, let alone plan an extensive meal. Hell, Jack hadn't even had time to shop for gifts for his friends.

Then there was Dewayne. Jack didn't want to exclude him just because he was his witness. He wondered if the teen had ever had a normal Christmas by the way he'd been checking out things in the shops.

Before setting off for the afternoon, they went next door to the Stinking Rose and placed a last-minute order. Jack called in a favor and arranged a pick-up the next morning before taking everything over to the Navarros'. The remnants of that meal were now laid out before them—leftovers of the full garlic-roasted prime rib roast which Ray had put in the oven the moment Jack arrived, the shattered remaining shells of the two full Dungeness crabs which they'd pulled fresh from the steamer before sitting down to eat, and all the sides and salads he and Dewayne could carry. That included what had once been a whole baked pumpkin cheesecake with a traditional sour cream topping.

With Maria pregnant and Dewayne underage, and he and Ray leaving soon for the Majestic, they'd settled on Martinelli's sparkling apple cider over crushed ice to toast the meal.

Ray sat forward and took Maria's hand in his. "I don't remember the last time I had prime rib this good."

"You'll be scaring away vampires for the rest of the week, *mi amor*." She pulled Ray close and kissed his cheek.

Jack turned his attention to Dewayne who sat suspiciously quiet. "You can thank Dewayne for all this." The teen's head shot up. Jack gave him a wink and looked back to his friends. "When I suggested hitting up Tommy for one of everything, Dewayne said it didn't sound very Christmassy to him. I think he was right."

Maria pulled herself to her feet and navigated around the table to Dewayne's side and kissed him on the cheek too. "*Gracias, cariño.*"

By the look on the teen's face, he relished the affection, but he tried not letting it show. Instead, he said, "When I suggested turf and surf, I meant burgers and fish sticks."

Jack chuckled, tossing his napkin on the table. "Yeah . . . no. That was never gonna happen." Pushing back his chair, he added, "Maria, why don't you and Dewayne relax somewhere more comfortable while Ray and I clean up? We need to talk about tonight, anyway."

"Yo, what about the presents?" Dewayne asked.

The one thing that surprised Jack while shopping with Dewayne was that he wasn't a typical teen. Even though he'd been living on his own for months and had put on a tough exterior to survive, he was actually a sensitive and kind kid. When he told Jack he was uncomfortable going to the Navarros', it wasn't because he felt like he was an outsider, but because he didn't have any money to buy them a Christmas gift. Jack knew there was a gift under the tree for the Navarros and that Dewayne was anxious to give it to them.

"As soon as we clean up," Jack promised. "Zip up, *amigo*. It's time to move." Ray groaned but complied.

Maria disappeared down the hall then reappeared with Butch trotting along behind her. She put a few scraps on a saucer then headed for the living room. Dewayne picked up the dog and followed.

With the two working together, the kitchen was quickly cleaned and the leftovers had been stowed in the fridge.

When the men entered the living room—Jack carrying a tray laden with mugs of coffee and tea, and containers of sugar and milk—Maria and Dewayne looked to be in deep conversation. Butch lay in Dewayne's lap, content with the stroking, and no doubt, a full belly.

Maria looked up with a smile, and any anxiety Jack felt evaporated instantly. She was going to be a wonderful mother, as she was patient and understanding, and a good listener. And Dewayne was opening up to her in ways Jack was sure the teen would never do with him.

Setting the tray on the coffee table, Jack asked, "Who's playing Santa this year?" He flicked his gaze at the small pile of gifts under the tree. Twinkling colored lights flickered against the shiny wrapping paper. Soft holiday music was just audible in the background.

"Can I do it?" To everyone's surprise, Dewayne handed Maria the dog, shot to his feet and knelt beside the tree.

"Sure," Jack said, "but remember there are still a couple things out in the Jeep." He pulled the keys from his pocket and tossed them at the teen who raced outside.

"He's a wonderful boy, Jack," Maria said. "I hope you can find his family soon."

"He's definitely full of surprises," Jack said, settling back in a stuffed armchair, coffee mug resting on a crossed knee.

Ray sat forward. "Are we going to turn him over to CPS if we can't find his mother?"

"I'm really hoping he has family out there who will take him in. His mother has a history of abandonment. Even if we find her, likely by this time next year, he'd be back to living like I found him."

Just then, Dewayne appeared with a large box in hand, which he placed on the floor before Maria. "We brought in the other stuff earlier, but a couple things were too big. This one is for the baby."

Maria handed Butch to Ray before pulling herself to the edge of the sofa. "Help me open this," she said to Dewayne. The two pulled off the paper and Dewayne opened the top of the box so Maria could reach in. Butch barked and growled as Maria pulled out several crumpled pieces of colored tissue paper before extracting an oversized teddy bear with a red bow around its neck. Ray struggled to keep the dog in his grasp.

Gasping, she said, "Oh my! It's adorable." She pulled Dewayne in for a hug. "*¡Muchos gracias!* Our baby will love it. Oh my God, it's so soft," she exclaimed, cuddling the bear to her face.

Over the next several minutes, Dewayne doled out gifts from under the tree. With Jack's help, meaning credit card, Dewayne bought Ray a bottle of tequila and a pair of earrings for Maria. In turn, the Navarros had given Dewayne a gift too. The teen's eyes lit up when the wrapping paper fell away to reveal a new Nintendo Switch.

"You can even hook it up to your big screen," Ray told him.

For a moment, Dewayne was lost for words, but the glistening in his eyes and the quiet *thank you* spoke volumes. Suddenly, he got up and rushed outside.

"He okay?" Ray asked, turning toward the window.

Nodding, Jack said, "He's been through a lot recently. I don't think he was expecting all this, but he'll be fine."

A moment later, Dewayne returned with two potted plants, one under each arm. Jack got to his feet and took one of the pots from the teen. "These are from me. Apple trees for your back yard.

The woman at Flora Grubb said you need two for pollination."

"How nice, my love. More plants." The tone of Ray's voice matched the pained grin on his face. Jack grinned at his friend's underwhelming response.

"Oh, Jack, they're wonderful," Maria exclaimed. "I've been wanting to do something with the back yard, and this will get us started. Ray, open the back door so they can put the trees out back." Ray grumbled, dumped the dog onto the sofa, and went to do as he was told.

Back in the living room, there were three gifts left under the tree.

The first had Ray's name on it. "This one says it's from Jack," Dewayne said, handing it over.

Ray ripped off the paper, revealing a new automatic coffeemaker.

"You're going to need that, brother. Once the baby arrives, you'll never sleep again," Jack said.

Everyone laughed, except Ray.

"Thanks." Sarcasm dripped from the single word. "It makes it a little easier knowing you'll be moving in here soon. You can help with nighttime feedings and diaper changes." Ray grinned.

Jack had hoped his friend had forgotten about that promise. "I'll do the uncle thing, but I don't do diapers."

Before Ray could protest, Dewayne looked up with a small box in his hands. "This one says it's to me from Jack. You already bought me some things." Gazing over at Ray and Maria, he said, "He bought me a bunch of new clothes and these fly Air Jordan hightops." He lifted the leg of his new jeans to reveal the black and white sneakers with a red Nike swoosh up the sides.

"You needed clothes," Jack said. "This is something extra."

Dewayne turned the flat box in his hands. He gave it a shake then removed the paper. The box read *Kryptonite Keeper Bike Lock*. "Thanks, dude, but ain't no one gonna steal my piece of—" he stopped short of saying shit.

"Why don't you go into the garage and see what it goes with?" Jack suggested. For a long moment, no one said anything. "Go on. We'll wait."

Maria stood and pulled Butch into her arms. "I'll show you the way. I have to pee anyway." Jack saw her give Ray a sidelong look.

When they were alone in the room, Jack asked, "What was that look about?" Ray rose and went to the tree. He picked up the last box and handed it to Jack. "What's this?"

Ray sat on the edge of the coffee table and put his elbows on his knees. "Open it."

Jack couldn't think of anything he wanted, and he couldn't remember mentioning anything to Ray. He gave it a quick shake, but whatever was inside felt heavy and stationary. Beneath the wrapping paper, a plain white box revealed itself. He removed the lid and set it aside, then folded back the red paper.

Jack sat motionless, staring into the box. His heart thumped hard in his chest, making it hard to breathe. His vision blurred and he used his fist to scrub his eyes.

"Do you think it'll fit?"

"Fuck you."

"Try it on. If it doesn't fit, I can take it back."

"You really are an asshole, you know."

Jack stood. He grasped the leather jacket and let the box bottom fall away. He slid his arms into the familiar garment. This had been one of the last gifts Leah had given him before she disappeared, and he hadn't seen it in a month since it had been taken into evidence.

He pulled the front around him and noticed how loose it now fit, even after the big meal they'd just had. Had he really lost so much weight since Thanksgiving?

He zipped it up and stuffed his hands in the pockets, feeling the warmth instantly surround him. He hated to admit, the only thing he wanted to do right now was pull his Harley out of the Navarros' garage and take it for a long ride down the coast to Carmel. Maybe even Big Sur. The further from his troubles, the better.

Jack ran a hand over the leather and felt the hole put there by Travers' bullet.

"I had it professionally cleaned. Otherwise, it's as-is, Jack."

Jack was speechless. He was only capable of pulling his friend into a bear hug. "Thank you," he finally said. A long moment later, Jack leaned back and cleared his vision again. "Really, man. Thanks. I've missed this."

Ray clapped him on the upper arm. "I know. I had a talk with Haniford. Since you were cleared off the suspect list so long ago, there's no reason why the jacket couldn't be released from evidence. I've got your clothes from that night too, if you want them."

Jack shook his head. "This is all I wanted. Thanks, Ray."

Just then, Maria's voice from the front yard caught Jack and Ray's attention. "Be careful, *mijo*!" Dewayne was on his new bike and racing it up and down Dublin Street. Butch danced back and forth at the end of his lead where they stood on the lawn.

"It's a good day," Ray said.

"Absolutely," Jack agreed.

"You're not moving in though, are you?"

"Let's solve the case and find Dewayne's mother, or family who can take him in. Once things quiet down we can revisit the move."

"Thanks for the coffeemaker."

Jack turned and gave his friend a pained look. "Man, you really are gonna need it."

CHAPTER THIRTY-THREE

If it was possible, the Majestic Lounge was busier tonight than previous competition nights. Jack was sure the place exceeded legal capacity as set down by the city's fire codes. Patrons stood shoulder to shoulder like the proverbial sardines.

Jack chuffed to himself about how much he'd gleaned in the last few weeks. When he'd first met Chad, he'd said drag was all about the performance, the dramatics of it all. Almost no one went out in drag unless they were performing. But drag was a different lifestyle.

Men occasionally dressing as women, as Franklin did to transform himself into Carol. The old term was transvestism, but common parlance called it cross-dressing.

Those living as women, dressing full time in women's clothing, and even some seeking gender reassignment, were transgender. The term transsexual had been replaced because one's gender had nothing to do with sexual preference.

The difference between trans and drag was that while some drag queens were openly trans, most trans people weren't into drag. Especially as there were a number of straight men who also performed in drag. Even some women. Drag was all theater. Over-the-top theater, but theater just the same, no matter one's sexuality or gender.

Was either lifestyle something he could see himself in? Absolutely not. But it didn't mean he didn't respect the lifestyle choices of others. His mother had raised him to believe a person's true identity was what was on the inside. *"Inside is where the truth lives, Giacomo. The light and the shadows. You must see both to know the real person,"* she had told him.

The thought of his mother squeezed his heart. She had been the only person to call him Giacomo. His father preferred anything but. Jack hadn't heard his given name since his mother had passed away nearly seven years ago, having survived his father by ten years. She'd lived long enough to see him make detective and to see him marry but had died shortly after Zoë had been born. Thank God she hadn't known what had happened to his family. It would have broken her, as it had broken him.

The shadows lurking inside him darkened further at the thought and made his heart squeeze in another way. How would his mother feel, knowing in his darkest shadows, he thought of taking his own life? He thanked God again she she'd never have to see that either. It saddened him that his actions may take him right to Hell, even if the modern belief suggested he wasn't in his right mind and thus not culpable for his actions. Was he in his right mind? Perhaps it depended on the day. He lived in hope that he'd find Leah alive and well and he wouldn't have to find out.

"I don't see her," Ray said loudly over the pounding music as he sidled up beside Jack, pulling him out of the dark place.

When they'd arrived earlier in the evening, Christmas music played in the background, but was quickly replaced once the acts—winners from the previous four competitions—took to the stage for their final performances. Now, the place was jumping with heart-thumping electronic dance music, getting many patrons onto the dancefloor while everyone waited for the announcement of the ultimate competition winner.

Jack had to admit excitement was in the air, and if Leah was home—he still refused to believe she was dead—he knew she would've loved coming here for the event.

He leaned toward his friend to be heard. "Are you sure? Half the city has to be in here tonight."

Ray shook his head. "I've been all over the club. If she's here, she's well hidden."

"What about outside?"

"Harry and Wash are still up front, posing as bouncers. Massie and James are over on 17th checking IDs on anyone using that alley behind the theater. Don't look at me like that. They've been given strict instructions—if either of them so much as thinks about abandoning their post, they're *both* getting written up."

"As his TO, Massie needs to keep her eye on the ball," Jack said. "Let's hope she keeps him in line. Have you seen Franklin yet?"

Ray shook his head. "I wonder what's keeping him. He said he'd be here."

Jack gazed toward the back door to where Rod and his harem were in their usual spot.

Out of professional courtesy, and to not step on each other's toes, Special Agent Roderick Henderson had been invited to attend the task force meeting at the department. Haniford laid it out in clear terms—Rod either went along with the operation and worked with the team to apprehend their suspect or took a night off and stayed out of the club so his team could do their job. Rod's cooperation would make it a win-win for both departments—PD and DEA. He only reluctantly accepted the terms because Jack told him he knew who was dealing drugs in the club and would tell him after they captured their suspect. When Rod agreed, he was brought up to speed on incidents leading up to obtaining an arrest warrant on Ginnie Whitney-Cummings, aka Eleanor Mae Hogg.

Rod's girlfriend, Vice Inspector Susan Sharp, had also been invited to work the case, but Rod explained she had morning sickness. Jack wondered at their sudden engagement.

Sergeant Bill Waters had been roped in to take Sharp's place in the harem, and both he and Rod monitored the comings and goings near the back door. Waters towered behind the special agent, his beefy, dark brown arms crossed, his chest and biceps straining under his tight leather biker vest. Jack knew the man was a big softie, but right now he looked anything but. Gay or otherwise, his intimidating gaze was effective.

Jack caught Waters' attention then and gave a jerk of his head, silently asking if he'd seen Franklin. Waters' reply was a quick shake, telling Jack he hadn't.

He and Ray moved into the crowd again. As they neared the

bar, his gaze caught Officer Amy Chin's. She'd also been pulled in for added surveillance. It was painfully obvious she still had a thing for him, as she'd agreed all too readily to work this case. "Anything you want, Jack," she'd said. So far, she was doing as she'd been instructed, but every time Jack looked in her direction, she was always staring back at him—as she was now. She lifted her glass and wrapped her lips around the straw. Her demeanor was meant to be sexy, but to him, he felt embarrassed for her.

Jack turned his back on her.

"What's that about?" Ray asked, jerking his head in Chin's direction.

"Nothing."

"Doesn't look like nothing to me."

"I couldn't say anything to Haniford when he brought her into the operation. She's been fixated on me practically from the moment Leah—" Jack took a long breath. "I've been trying to ignore her."

Ray glanced toward the bar again. "She's still staring at you."

"Well, then, ignore her," Jack demanded. "She won't take no for an answer and I don't have time to deal with her right now. We have to find Ginnie. She's gotta be here somewhere."

Ray pivoted and pointed through a gap in the crowd. "Wow! Would you get a load of that?"

Across the room, a beautiful, statuesque woman with curves in all the right places was talking and laughing with friends. It was obvious they were admiring her holiday attire by their animated gestures.

There was nothing drag about this woman. From the top down, she was the epitome of style and grace. Long, wavy blonde hair cascaded over her bare shoulders and curled around her breasts. The deep blue, sleeveless floor-length gown was embedded with white sparkling gems and winked in the club lights, giving the garment a starry-night effect that was echoed in her modestly tall heels. The diamonds hanging from her ears and wrapped around her neck and wrists screamed wealth.

When she saw Jack openly staring at her, she strode in his and Ray's direction.

"Looking good, Carol," Jack shouted over the music. "Caitlyn Jenner, move over."

"It's Caroline, now. Sounds more feminine, don't you think?"

"Sure. What about this . . . transformation?" Jack asked, jerking his head at her new look.

"With Chad's help, I took every lesson I learned from the Indian girls and well—What do you think?" Caroline spun on her toes and struck a pose, fluttering her long lashes at Jack.

"Honestly, we didn't know it was you," Jack said.

"Get used to it because Franklin is dead and gone. The tabloids will have a field day with this, don't you think?"

Jack chuckled. "No doubt."

"What do you think, Ray? You're awfully quiet. Will I do?"

Just then, the music stopped as the house lights dimmed. Jack heard Ray muttering to himself. "*Me voy a quemar en el infierno por lo que está pasando por mi mente en este momento.*" (I'm going to burn in Hell for what's going through my mind right now.)

"*¿Es cierto lo que dicen de los amantes Latinos?*" Caroline asked. (Is it true what they say about Latin lovers?)

For once in Jack's memory, Ray was lost for words. Jack wasn't sure if it was because Caroline spoke Spanish, or if it was what she replied to his friend.

Before he could ask, the stage lights came on and Chad flounced up to the microphone dressed as Marilyn. Though, rather than the traditional long pink gown, she now wore a sexy Mrs. Claus red velvet strapless dress. The plunging neckline and short hem were edged in faux white fur, as was the matching Santa hat. Over-the-elbow red satin gloves accentuated her long arms and feminine gestures. Her slender legs were covered with white tights. And her red velvet heels had a white pom pom on each toe.

"Good evening, dahlings!" Chad's Marilyn self crooned into the mic. She blew kisses with both hands and tossed them into the audience as if she was scattering wildflowers. The crowd cheered before she launched into a short monologue about the history of the club and the drag event, the multi-talented contestants, and what winning would mean for that one lucky person, as well as for the city's LGBTQ community.

Jack and Ray had already talked with Chad about what he could and couldn't reveal about the deaths of his friends. Officials wanted the case kept hush-hush. The situation earlier in the year with Travers had been bad enough. The people of San Francisco didn't need the panic of another serial killer in their midst. Especially during the holidays and one targeting gay men.

"For most of us," Marilyn continued, "coming out as gay is a damn tough journey. We're bullied and abused most of our lives, forced to conform to the expectations of others, and when we try living what's in our hearts, we're ostracized, even from our own families—shunned by those who said they loved us. It's been my hope, my *dream*, that this place," she spread her arms wide, "this club, would be a home for all of us. A place where shame doesn't exist and where we're all free to be the person we were born to be." The crowd cheered again, some whistled, while others spun their boas in the air over their heads. "Which is why it pains me to know so many of our brothers and sisters have been taken from us this season. So, before I announce the competition winner, I want us to have a minute of silence for the friends we've lost."

The club lights dimmed and nearly everyone bowed their heads. The room had gone absolutely silent except for the faint rustle of fabric.

After the full minute had passed, soft music came up around the room, then Marilyn began singing. Low at first, then her voice grew stronger as the music rose. She'd chosen Lady Gaga's *Born This Way* and hit every note on key.

Jack was impressed, Marilyn had a set of pipes on her. Jack joined the crowd's raucous applause as she took low, dramatic curtsies, crossing her legs one way then the other.

Marilyn put her hands up to quiet the room. "Now is the time you've all been waiting for. After four weeks of tough competition— believe me, *all* of our performers were just *so* amazing—it's time to announce our winner!" The crowd cheered again. "Get up here, girls," she commanded the final four contestants who trotted up to stand beneath the club's neon sign. "Thank the lord I don't have to choose the winner, or I'd lose my ever-lovin' mind. So, give it up for our totally impartial judge, the Applause-O-Meter!" Marilyn waved to the side of the stage where the arm on the giant meter reacted to the audience's whoops and calls. Below the arm, a digital decibel readout registered the exact noise level. "You, our wonderful and amazing audience, will decide who will walk away tonight with the Majestic Lounge drag queen crown!"

"Pardon me, boys," Caroline said before pushing her way through the crowd toward the backstage door. Ray had already brought Franklin up to speed about tonight's operation. He readily agreed to help, so Jack assumed she was now taking her place behind the scenes.

It was easy getting caught up in the reverie, but Jack forced himself to keep his eyes on the crowd. Ginnie had to be somewhere in the club—but where? As Marilyn called out contestant names, one by one, the crowd cheered. It was the last name that drew the most noise.

"It looks like we have our winner. She comes all the way from bonnie Edinburgh—Australia, that is. Give it up for Bunny MacTaversnatch!"

The crowd went wild. People surrounding Jack and Ray bounced up and down, clapping, punching the air, whistling and cat-calling, and otherwise making their approval known.

"You ready?" Jack asked Ray.

Ray nodded. "See you over there. Good luck." He disappeared into the crowd.

Just then, a deep, almost baritone voice came over the speakers. "G'day!" Jack's gaze shot up and he saw what could best be described as a Scottish Highlander drag queen. And she had to be over seven feet tall.

Bunny MacTaversnatch was dressed from head to toe in red tartan—short bustier crop top with long, cuffed arm sleeves; leggings tucked into long, high heeled pirate boots; and flowing, pleated fabric tied around her waist that swung out behind her like a train. Big, wavy, bright auburn hair framed dark, seductive eyes. Surrounding her bright, ruby-red painted lips was an equally bright auburn beard that even Jack was envious of.

He wasn't quite sure what to make of her. She certainly had the curves and everything one would expect in a woman, but that beard was something else. And that deep voice certainly caught Jack's attention.

He watched a scantily-dressed stagehand in red velvet shorts scurry over with a short ladder and set it up beside Bunny. He assisted Marilyn up the steps so she could place a glittering crown on Bunny's head. Once back on the stage, Marilyn presented Bunny with a large bunch of long stem red and white roses and her statuette—a crystal clear and slightly curved cock on a plinth.

"Congratulations, Queen Bunny!" Marilyn applauded along with the cheering crowd. "Please say a few words before giving us another winning performance." She stepped aside and Bunny moved toward the mic once more.

"I'm humbled and honored to have won this amazing competition," Bunny continued with her thick, deep Australian accent. "I'm dedicating my win to all the drag queens here, and those Down Unda!" She fisted the statuette and pumped it in the air. The crowd cheered again, now chanting "Bun-ny, Bun-ny, Bun-ny."

After relinquishing her wins to a stagehand, Bunny took her place at the microphone to perform the song that got her the win. Once the crowd had quieted, a smooth, jazzy version of Kylie Minogue's *Slow* came over the speakers. Bunny's voice took on a surprisingly feminine tone as she crooned to the audience. The lyrics' *ohs* and *ahs* were breathless and sultry.

When she reached the first chorus, her voice dropped to the baritone that drew Jack's attention moments before. She had everyone under her spell as she pranced back and forth across the stage, using her free hand to dramatically whip her train as she turned.

While the crowd was distracted, and he hoped Ginnie was too, if she were here, Jack took a deep breath and headed backstage.

CHAPTER THIRTY-FOUR

The house was dark and everything was quiet by the time Jack and Caroline arrived at the Sea Cliff property. She pulled the Roadster into its space in the garage and shut off the motor.

"You still okay with this?" Jack asked.

Caroline nodded. "I think so. I just want my life back."

Jack's phone buzzed. He hit the text icon. "Ray knows we're here now. He said he cleared the property and that everything's set up." He looked up and caught Caroline's attention. "Just like we talked about, okay? Ginnie's targeted everyone you've left the club with, so leaving with tonight's winner shouldn't be any different. If she's followed us, and I'm sure she has, it won't be long until she makes an appearance," Jack said. "Ray and his team are set up in unmarked vehicles up Sea Cliff and 27th. When Ginnie arrives, we'll know. Okay?" Caroline nodded again. "When we get out of the car, act normal. You're entertaining a friend. When we get inside, turn on a light or two, put on some music, pour some drinks."

"Are you sure about all this? I've never brought anyone home before."

"Ginnie's already panicking, so if anything, bringing someone home will really put her off her game. If everything goes as planned, taking her into custody should go smoothly. We need to keep you safe though. Look at me," Jack said, needing Caroline to focus. "If it looks like things are going sideways, I need you to go right to your safe room and lock yourself in. Don't wait for instruction. Just go. Do you understand me?"

Caroline huffed. "If she's only going for people I've left the club with, she'll only want Bunny, right? I shouldn't be in any danger."

Jack shook his head. "Right now, we have no idea what Ginnie's thinking. Based on previous behavior, Bunny would certainly be her next target. But things have changed in the last few days. *You've* changed."

"Yeah . . . I don't think she knows yet," Caroline said.

"If she was at the club, she would have seen you, even if it was just you getting into your car with someone she thought was Bunny. She's followed you before, so I'm sure she's followed you tonight. Knowing you've brought someone home this time is certainly going to add fuel to the fire."

"She's already mad as a hornet since I changed the locks on her," Caroline said.

"I bet. And now she knows what we do about her—her real identity and that she's the one who killed those men. She knows we're looking for her. It's my guess that after tonight, she'll leave the city and reinvent herself again somewhere else."

"Do you really think so?"

Jack nodded. "Absolutely. She left Tennessee and reinvented herself as Jennifer Morgan, then again when she married you. She's fully capable of doing it again, so tonight is our best chance of catching her."

"Point taken, but why come here? Why not just cut and run while she can?"

"Coming here makes sense, even if you hadn't brought someone with you. We froze her personal accounts and her credit cards. If she has any money stashed in the house, it makes sense that she'll come here to get it before she leaves the city. Your bringing someone back to a place she once called home will certainly agitate her even more. Wherever she's been holed up the last couple days, she's going to be tired and running on pure adrenaline. She was already unstable and could be more so now, so we have to be ready for whatever craziness she has planned. Promise me you'll follow the plan so we can keep you safe and bring her in." After a moment, Caroline nodded. "Good girl. Now, let's casually get out of the car and go inside. Act—"

"Natural. Got it. But can I be excited about all the drama and scared shitless at the same time?"

He chuckled. "Absolutely."

She pressed the palm of her hand over her chest. "My heart feels like it's going a million miles an hour."

"Mine too. Let's go."

Jack yanked the tartan hood over his head and, once out of the car, pulled himself up as tall as he could to mimic Bunny's height, then made sure the cape was wrapped around him to hide his street clothes.

Caroline came around the car and threw a long arm around his waist and pulled him close. "Act natural," she reminded him with a wink, then led him toward the front door where she punched some numbers into the keypad. Just inside the door in the foyer, she stopped short and pulled Jack into an embrace. Against his ear, she said, "Pretend I'm kissing you. If Gin's already out there and watching, we both have to be believable."

Jack felt himself flush and thanked God they stood in near darkness, but Caroline wasn't wrong. He reluctantly drew the cape around her.

A moment later, Caroline kicked the door closed and released him. "That ought to get her going," she chuckled, kicked off her heels then pulled him into the living room by his hand.

Jack watched Caroline move around the room, doing exactly as she'd been instructed. After tossing her long coat across the back of a chair, she went to the bar at the side of the room and switched on a light. It offered just enough light to locate the furniture, but not enough to wash out the view through the huge picture window. Jack walked over to the wide expanse of glass and looked out at the water.

The Golden Gate was illuminated with lights along its deck and spotlights up the twin towers. A lone tanker passing beneath was just visible on the inky water. The sun had set hours earlier, but the city's famous fog bank was rolling in, obscuring the Marin Headlands and the western night stars. It hadn't reached the bridge yet so the twinkling lights of the city beyond were still clear and bright.

Soft music came on, something smooth and sultry. Jack closed his eyes for just a moment and inhaled long breaths. He hadn't lied to Caroline in the car. He was nervous about the set up. Shit had the potential to get crazy when . . . if . . . Ginnie turned up. He needed to focus and keep his head clear of the darkness that had been hovering in his mind all day.

"Drink?" Caroline asked.

Jack reluctantly opened his eyes. The tanker was gone now. "Sure. Club soda's fine, or coffee or Diet Coke. Anything with caffeine." He gazed at his watch. While the club had technically closed at 2a.m., he and Caroline couldn't leave until the real Bunny had made the rounds and accepted her congratulations. Then she'd been secreted away backstage where Jack had donned her long tartan cape before leaving with Caroline. Now it was after 5a.m. He would rather have been in bed, but was too jacked up to sleep anyway.

For all the comfort talk he gave Caroline in the car, Jack didn't have a good feeling about the situation. In a perfect world, he would take Ginnie into custody quickly and effortlessly. No drama. But memories of his standoff with Travers kept creeping in.

The clink of ice dropping into a glass drew his attention. Caroline poured out some club soda into what looked like a hand-cut crystal tumbler.

Then she lifted another bottle and swung it in his direction. "You really need to try this rare Irish whiskey sometime." The dark liquid glinted in the pale light as she poured a measure over the ice into a matching glass. "I paid over three thousand dollars for it."

"You equate cost with quality?"

Dumbstruck, Caroline said, "Of course. Higher quality always costs more. Just look at me now." She flipped her hair over her shoulder and sashayed across the room to Jack's side with both glasses. "All this came at a cost, darling."

Jack took the offered glass. He wanted to say, *Sure, some cost— probably your business reputation, possibly your circle of friends, and definitely your marriage.* But he kept it to himself.

"Are you not going to offer *me* a drink, *sweetheart?*"

Jack and Caroline spun in unison toward the stairway he knew led to the bedrooms upstairs. "How did she get past Ray?" Jack muttered to himself.

"The stairs also lead to the lower level. She could have come in from the beach," Caroline whispered, then louder, she said, "I don't remember you being invited to my party, but I'll pour you one . . . for the road." Caroline moved toward the bar.

"Don't move," Ginnie said.

In the shadows, Jack just made out Ginnie's outline. She wasn't wearing the wide-brimmed hat witnesses had said the mysterious man wore, but she did appear to be in the long coat, or a matching one. She stepped slightly forward and the dim light glinted in her eyes, and off the *Imura* revolver's white barrel in her hand.

"Get back where you were. Beside . . . *not* Bunny." Her eyes widened when she realized it was Jack in disguise.

He dropped the cape from around his shoulders and tossed it onto a nearby chair. He still wore his black work club suit—trousers and button-down shirt. The matching jacket concealed the holstered Beretta under his left arm.

"Surprise," he flatly said. "Why don't you give me your weapon so we can have a chat?" He took a step forward and stretched out his left arm, leaving his right hand free if he needed to go for his weapon.

"Stay back!" Jack halted. "I actually like you, Jack, but I *will* shoot you if you come near me."

Jack stepped back. "Well then, why don't you at least lower your weapon? We're not going anywhere. Let's talk this out."

She hesitated for a moment and Jack thought she might actually comply. Her hand wavered then steadied again in his direction. "Fine, let's talk."

Jack caught a flash of him standing in another living room with another weapon pointed at him. He suppressed the urge to reach up and massage the scar Travers' bullet had left.

In the shadows, Jack could just make out Ginnie shaking. Probably from her near-manic state, if her wide eyes darting between him and Caroline were anything to go on.

"What do you want, Gin?" Caroline asked. "I know you weren't happy in our marriage. You've been unhappy for a long time."

"You think?" Her voice dripped with sarcasm. "This," she waved the weapon in her direction, "is not what I signed up for."

"I get it. But I don't think you were happy before this. I don't think I was either. If I had been, maybe I wouldn't have been looking for something more . . . something else."

"Are you saying I wasn't exciting enough for you?" Her voice rose. "My God, Franklin. We're rich—"

"*I'm* rich. And please stop calling me that. I'm Caroline now."

Ginnie swayed from one foot to the other; the weight of the weapon gradually weakened her wrist. "*We're* rich," she corrected. "We're married, in case you forgot. What's yours is mine and what's mine is mine and all that."

"As it turns out," Jack said, "you aren't married. You may have married under the name you're known by—Jennifer Morgan—but we all know now that's not your legal name. Without a legal name on the marriage license, the marriage is automatically null and void. None of this," Jack waved a hand around the room, "is yours."

Ginnie pumped the fist holding the gun in his direction then Caroline's. "Damn you, it *is* mine. We had a wonderful life. We had everything we wanted—fame, prestige, friends . . . powerful friends."

"You can still have all that, Gin, and more. You don't have to resort to this," Caroline said, her palms up in a pleading gesture. "Apparently, you still have your condo. I know you still have a sizable bank account since you've been spending *my* money like it was going out of fashion. And you're still beautiful. You can go back to modeling."

"You think any of that matters, that that's what I want?" Ginnie's voice raised another octave.

"If it's not, tell me why you kept your condo after all these years? I don't care about the money, but you had a wonderful home here. You didn't need the condo. You could have at least upgraded your car. Why keep all that old stuff when you could have had new?" Caroline asked.

Ginnie thought for a moment. "Maybe it was to remind me of the past, where I came from, and how good I had it with you."

Caroline's voice lowered. "You could have told me."

"Would it have changed any of this?" Ginnie waved the weapon again at Caroline, as if using it as a pointer.

Caroline shook her head. "No, sweetheart. I don't think so," she said softly. "I felt this way for years before I ever met you."

Ginnie loudly guffawed. "You hid it well . . . *Franklin*."

Caroline flinched but it was obvious to Jack that she held her tongue over the continued use of her birth name. She dropped her arms loosely to her sides and collapsed into the sofa behind her, setting her whiskey glass on the low coffee table. A moment later, she gazed up. "Just tell me what you want, and we can sort it out."

Caroline had Ginnie's attention. Good. Jack slowly pivoted more into the shadows and carefully slid his hand into his pocket. He hadn't put his phone into his breast pocket because of the cape but was now grateful for its location.

He only had a few apps on his phone and even fewer shortcuts on his home screen. He knew from memory where Ray's icon was located and pushed it. He couldn't hear when Ray picked up; it wasn't his normal cell number. But Jack knew when his friend saw the app activated, he'd know Jack was in trouble. He hoped Ginnie's voice came over loud and clear.

"You *know* what I want, *Franklin*."

"I'm sorry, Gin. I didn't mean to hurt you—"

"Hurt me? You didn't hurt me. You *humiliated* me. Big difference."

"Come on, Gin. Let me pour you a drink and we can talk this through." Caroline sat forward on the sofa as if to rise.

"No! I said stay where you are. I'm sure Jack has told you now who I am . . . who I was . . . so you'll also know I can shoot the eye out of a hen at a hundred paces."

"She's not lying, Caroline. I saw her awards. She's a crack shot. I'm impressed," Jack said, gazing toward Ginnie. "You know, if none of this had gone down and I'd known about your shooting prowess, it could have been fun sharing some range time with you. I was the best marksman in the department before—"

"Before you killed your family?" Jack gasped at Ginnie's bold statement. His heart thumped hard. "Yeah, I looked you up. There are plenty of rumors going around about what happened to your family, a lot of speculation that you're behind it. Why else hasn't your wife's body turned up? But your poor kid—"

"Don't talk about my family . . . *Ellie Mae.*" Jack kept his voice low but struggled to stay calm. The slightest mention of his family hurt, but suggesting he had anything to do with what happened made his blood boil. He fisted his hands repeatedly at his sides.

"Why do you think I hired you to follow my husband? Like you said, I could have hired a detective who catered to the wealthy. I didn't want the press. What I wanted was a loser nobody who would keep his fucking mouth shut. If you could keep quiet all these years about killing your family, I knew you'd protect *my* secrets."

CHAPTER THIRTY-FIVE

Through clenched teeth, Jack said, "I didn't kill my family. And contrary to belief, there's no such thing as client privilege in my line of work."

"I paid you to do a job. You work for me."

"Worked," he emphasized. "Follow your husband and get some photos. I completed the work and you paid me, thus completing our contract." He glanced toward Caroline. "Put it this way, if the tables were turned and Caroline had a weapon on you right now, I'm not obliged to protect you."

Ginnie chuckled. "Shut the fuck up. Don't patronize me. We both know that would never happen. Deep down, I know you love me, Franklin."

"I loved the woman I married. In my own way, I did. And I know you loved me. But we're two different people now."

Jack noticed Ginnie's back stiffen. "You're saying you don't love me . . . that you never *really* loved me?"

Caroline nodded. "I loved you, just as a man loves a woman. For a long time, I struggled with my sexuality. I tried playing both sides of the fence—"

"You were fucking men during our marriage?" she screeched. Her hand noticeably trembled. Jack thought she might drop the weapon and waited for his chance to rush her.

Caroline glanced over at Jack. He saw sorrow in her gaze before she looked back at Ginnie. "Once . . . well, one person."

"When?" Ginnie's voice took on a guarded tone. "Who was he? You didn't fuck him here . . . in *our* bed. Did you?"

Caroline slowly reached for her whiskey and downed it in one swallow. "You don't know him. He isn't from the city. We only met when he was in town—at his hotel. I don't even know his last name."

"You were fucking him, and you didn't even find out who he was? Jesus, Franklin!"

Jack thought Ginnie had a point.

"He didn't know who I was either, Gin. It was strictly on a first name basis. He had a family to protect too. But we were both going through the same thing and explored it together."

"That's how you justified your actions." Her tone was accusatory.

"I'm not saying it was the right thing to do. It just—"

"Don't even go there. Just happened. Bullshit! For how long did it *just happen?*"

Caroline shook her head. "It doesn't matter. It was a long time ago."

"How long?" Ginnie insisted.

"A few months. And I don't regret it," Caroline said, shooting to her feet.

"I said stay where you are!"

"You're not going to shoot me and we both know it." Caroline carried her tumbler to the bar, poured herself another shot from the three-thousand-dollar bottle, and downed it in one go. She poured a double before turning back to face the room again.

Jack caught sight of a figure moving in the shadow at the back of the room. He knew the hall led to the garage door. They'd taken it on Sunday to see the cars. He also knew by the way the shadow moved that it was Ray. His silhouette told Jack his friend had his weapon drawn.

Jack focused on Ginnie. "Ginnie, why don't you tell me why you killed the other girls?"

Ginnie spun toward Jack. "Girls? More like little boys dressing in their mothers' clothes."

"Be nice, Gin," Caroline said.

"Tell me why you killed them," Jack pressed, not wanting to waste his breath trying to make her understand just how wrong her statement was. "Last count, there were eight victims who died because of you. The least you can do is explain your motives."

She waved the weapon at Jack. "Would have been nine if you had really been Bunny. And, to be honest," she gazed at Caroline, "I've really been contemplating ten. All this really is your fault . . . *darling.*"

"Why did you do it, Gin? Tell me. Please. They were my friends."

"Friends? They weren't your friends. They were just people you used, like everyone else you use. Fuck 'em and leave 'em and move onto the next person."

"I wasn't sleeping with them. They were—"

"What, Franklin? What were they?"

"They were my friends," he repeated, "and they were teaching me—"

"Teaching you," Ginnie huffed. "Teaching you what? How to be gay? I thought that's what you used your out-of-town friend for."

"No, Gin, they taught me to be . . . me." Caroline waved a hand from head to toe. "Before, I struggled. I couldn't do it on my own, and it was painfully obvious you would never teach me to be as beautiful as you."

"Fuck you, Franklin!"

Jack heard Ginnie sniff, and by the sound of her breathing, he was sure she was crying.

As calmly as he could, Jack said, "It's true. They all had something Franklin needed to become Caroline."

"Like I said, he used them, then threw them away," she spat.

Jack shook his head. "That's not true. As friends, they gave him . . . *her* . . . their help when she needed it the most. The only thing thrown away was their lives. At *your* hands."

"Liars. You're both liars," she shouted.

"Tell her, Caroline. Tell Ginnie what your friends gave you."

Caroline sipped her whiskey then looked at Ginnie, her gaze remaining focused as she explained each of the Indian Spicy Girls' roles in the transformation from Franklin to Caroline.

"That's it? You and the *girls* were sharing hair and makeup tips like a bunch of schoolkids? You expect me to believe that?" Ginnie asked.

Caroline nodded. "Yeah, I do, because it's the truth."

"What about the others? How did you use them too?"

The weapon in Ginnie's hand shook again. She was getting tired. Jack folded his arms in front of him, as if trying to get comfortable. He slowly slid a hand under his lapel and grasped the Beretta. Outside, he hoped he gave the impression he was calm and collected. Inside . . . squirrels fighting in a sack.

"There was nothing there, Gin. Minger . . . Mike . . . offered me some coke. It had been a while, so I followed him home for a couple lines. Pepper . . . Bob. He was in the city for the event. At that hour, taxis are hard to find, so I offered him a ride back to his hotel. Just a ride," Caroline explained.

"And what about that boy? He looked like he was twelve, for Christ's sake."

Caroline went back to the sofa and sat. She never took her eyes off Ginnie as she moved. "Since we're being honest here, he was like the son you never gave me. You knew I wanted a family when we married. You said you did too. But every time I suggested us trying for a baby, you always had an excuse." Even in near darkness, Jack saw that hit a nerve. A big one.

"Damn you!" Ginnie spat.

"I wanted a family. With you. But you were always too concerned about your body and the scars pregnancy would leave behind. Aaron was a sweet boy who was trying to find himself. When I was his age, I needed someone like me that I could trust to show me the way. I wanted to be that for him. I *was* that for him. Until you took him away from me. Like you do everything." Caroline burst into tears. Jack thought she was doing so well keeping her shit together.

Ginnie chuckled. "Maybe you should have competed in that contest because you're such a big drama queen."

"Hey now," Jack interjected.

"I'm just being honest. He's always been a drama queen. It's only taken this," she waved the weapon at Caroline, "for me to realize what it was all about."

"You still haven't told us why you killed those people," Jack pressed. "If Caroline was using them, as you said, it was between her and them. It had nothing to do with you."

"Oh, but it did. Every step closer to that world was another step away from me. I had to eliminate the competition, as it were," Ginnie confessed.

"You thought by killing my friends it would send me running back to you?" Caroline's voice rose with incredulousness.

Ginnie fidgeted a moment, her gaze ping ponging between Jack and Caroline. "Well . . . yeah. I thought if you saw how unsafe it was, it would change your mind. You'd stay home and we could go back to life as usual."

"How can you not see the pure absurdity of what you just said? Do you honestly think I'd want to be with a murder?" Caroline's voice rose in pitch as she spoke.

Jack sidled closer to the window to keep Ginnie's focus on him, distancing him from Ray if she suddenly saw him. "It's obvious you two aren't getting back together. And you've just confessed to killing eight innocent people. I think we all know that the only way you'll be walking out of this house is in cuffs. None of what you've done can be ignored. Why don't you tell us what you want so we can end this now?"

"Please, Gin. Don't let things end this way," Caroline pleaded.

"It's already ended, *Franklin*. You ended it the moment you put on that goddamn dress. You ended our marriage and now I'm going to end you." She raised her weapon at Caroline.

In that moment, Jack withdrew the Beretta from under his jacket and stretched out his arm, taking aim. Across the room, Ray appeared from the deep shadows, his weapon directed at Ginnie too. Jack was conscious of Caroline being stuck in the crosshairs. Who would get off the first shot?

Ginnie spun and fired her weapon. True to her reputation as a crack shot, Ray dropped to the floor with a loud grunt then stilled.

Jack's heart shoved its way into his throat, his gaze ricocheting between Ginnie and his friend. Without thinking, he rushed to Ray's side. "You bitch!" he shouted as he moved. "Ray. Ray! Talk to me, partner." He spun toward Caroline who now stood before the sofa, one hand at her throat and the other arm wrapped around her middle. "Turn on the lights. Dammit, Caroline! Turn on the lights. Now!" The lights came on as Jack felt around Ray's body for the radio he knew his friend carried. He punched the PTT button and shouted into the mic. "Officer down. I repeat. Officer down."

Looking up, he saw Ginnie had disappeared. He had to go after her, but his friend could be dying. His heart pounded so hard he thought it would explode from his chest. Within seconds of the call, the room filled with officers.

"I'm all right." Ray's voice was barely audible above the sudden noise. "I'm just winded. Go after her."

Jack stripped back Ray's jacket and saw the vest. "Thank God, Ray!" He clapped his friend on the shoulder. Nodding, he set off through the house, taking the stairs by twos until he was in the lower room of the house. The patio door was wide open and he assumed Ginnie had gone that way.

He stood in the near dark, the Beretta held close to his chest, and listened for any noise that sounded like it didn't belong this early in the morning. The fog was so thick that even if it hadn't been dawn, he would still have trouble seeing through the haze. It was quiet. Almost too quiet. But he heard the sea below and tasted the saltiness of it on the dew settling on his lips.

There. Something cracked to his right. He sidled that direction, past the steps into the infinity pool, and found a set of timber railings. Between them, steps descended to the beach. The fog clung heavily to the cliffside, but he saw far enough ahead to make out the stairs leading onto Baker Beach. The Beretta in both hands and aimed downward in the direction he traveled, he took the steps sideways, keeping his ears trained for any movement other than his.

Ahead was the sound of feet on the steps. Ginnie wasn't moving as quickly as he'd expected, considering she knew the path better than he did.

Through the mire, he saw her silhouette. She pivoted then disappeared below him. The switchback stairs looked to have been carved out of the granite hillside. He followed, picking up speed.

At the next switchback, Ginnie stopped just long enough to take a shot in his direction. It missed, but not by far as he heard the round whizz past his head. Swearing under his breath, Jack watched her climb over the rail and scramble up the rocks. Below, he saw the tide was in and had flooded the beach. The only direction she could go was back up the stairs, and he blocked her path.

"Come on, Ginnie. Don't do this," he called to her. "There's nowhere to run."

To Jack's surprise, she stood at the top of a rocky outcrop, her weapon still in her hand but at her side. "I missed before, Jack. I said I liked you and I meant it. But if you come closer, if you try following me, I won't miss the next time."

Jack lifted his arms and aimed the Beretta at her. Even in the hazy fog, he wouldn't miss if he were forced to shoot. Her neighbor's patio light cast her in dark relief. "You know I can't let you go. You killed eight people. You held two people hostage at gunpoint. And you shot a cop." He paused for a moment, then added, "If he dies, that's nine murders. A good lawyer could get you life without parole, but killing a cop? That's definitely death penalty stuff right there." She didn't move. "Come back with me. If you cooperate, it'll go a long way to keep the needle out of your arm."

"Catch me if you can," Ginnie shouted as she raised her weapon toward him and fired.

The flash was diffused by the haze as the *Imura* revolver exploded. They were usually only good for one or two shots. This had been number three. There was no mistaking Ginnie's sudden roar of pain and her fall from the cliffside. Her painful cry ended abruptly. Jack couldn't see through the foggy soup, but he heard the distinct crunch of bones.

Alone now on the stairs, silence enveloped him. It was as if the Earth had suddenly stopped rotating and time stood still. There was no sound of the sea on the rocks below, no breeze in the bushes on the upper cliffs, not even the sound of his heart screaming in his ears. The heavy fog seemed to thicken and block out everything within a few feet of him. And for a long moment, he felt he stood in a vast nothingness.

The sharp intake of salty sea air told him he'd stopped breathing. The sound of the world crashed over him like the waves below and blew him backward onto the steps. He laid back and felt the steps bite into his back as he gulped for each breath, trying not to puke.

CHAPTER THIRTY-SIX

Monday – New Year's Eve

"Your friend looks like she's going to pop."

Jack was just old enough to remember Goldie Hawn in Rowan & Martin's Laugh-In TV series, and that's just who Chad reminded him of now. She'd dressed as a '60s hippie flower child, the outfit including a brightly colored paisley skimmer dress with long bell sleeves; daisy tights and knee-high patent leather boots covered her thin legs; her blonde pixie-cut wig had been threaded with tiny flowers; and a pair of round glasses with rainbow colored lenses completed the look. Her makeup had given her a natural glow rather than her traditional over-the-top look.

"Nice outfit. Do I call you Goldie now?" Jack asked.

"You can call me anything you want, sugar. But sure, for tonight, I'm Goldie."

Jack rolled his eyes over the sugar comment but ignored it. "Yeah, Maria is due in a couple weeks. She said this is her last chance to have some fun before the kid goes off to college. Ray's scared he or she will choose SFSU then get a job in the city and end up living at home forever."

"If this is her last outing, maybe she'll give me that amazing dress." Marilyn tipped her head in Maria's direction, indicating the bright pink form-fitting dress that fell just below her knees. Her dark blue shawl hung over her arms, revealing narrow straps and her bare shoulders.

Chuckling, Jack said, "Maybe."

"Do you think Ray would come out with me if I wore it? Look

at him." Marilyn growled deep in her throat. "Meow!"

Ray's pink shirt matched the color of Maria's dress and was open at the collar. His dark blue trousers and single-button blazer were the same color as her shawl. The couple had turned heads when they'd arrived and strolled through the club, with his styled, slicked back hair and now clean-shaven face and Maria's natural beauty and long, wavy black hair.

Jack just chuckled again. "I'm feeling a bit underdressed compared to everyone else here."

Goldie leaned back as much as the crowd would allow and gave Jack the once over. "Honey, there isn't anything underdressed about you. Those trousers are hugging your ass in all the right places, man, and I can see those pecs under that sweater. I love the leather jacket and boots, too. I get a sense you wear a lot of black, but the look you're going for is classic Italian."

"It's a good thing I'm Italian then."

Goldie got up close and said, "I'd love to see what's under all that black." She lifted a hand to silence him when he opened his mouth to speak. "I know, honey, I know. Ain't never gonna happen, but that doesn't mean a girl can't dream."

Jack wasn't sure how he felt having this information, so he turned his attention to the stage. He jerked his head in that direction and said, "Great performance. She's really good."

Bunny MacTaversnatch had been performing on stage for the last half hour—vacillating between singing and cracking a few jokes. Jack had to admit, she was infectious and found himself getting into the performance with everyone else.

"She was a surprise, I can tell you. First time in the city so first time entering the competition. She blew everyone else out of the water. Her win is well deserved. I wish she lived in the city. I'd contract her as a house artist. Look at all these people." Goldie spun and gestured around the room. "If we had Bunny on the books, this place could be hopping like this every night."

Bunny had hung up the tartan and tonight had dressed in what Leah would have called come-fuck-me red. She wore a form-fitting strapless, red-sequined body suit with matching platform red high heels and tule bustle skirt. Her long, shapely legs were clad in white tights and matching white gloves that covered her upper arms. The heavily applied makeup gave her a piercing *I want to swallow you whole* gaze, and her wavy, red-orange tresses framed her beautiful face and hung just off her shoulder.

Bunny's style exuded femininity and sensuality, even with the shock of red-orange chest hairs curling over the low-cut bustier and her enviously thick beard that hung down to her collarbone.

Jack chuckled. He'd met Bunny backstage last week while she was getting ready for the Christmas competition finale. She'd arrived in street clothes. Shed of her Bunny persona, Tyler Dean looked like every other hipster in the city.

Goldie grasped Jack's arm and looked up with surprise on her face. "Did you hear about Isaac?"

"No. What about him?" Jack casually asked. He had heard but wanted to know what she knew.

"He was arrested yesterday at his home. Can you believe it?" Goldie's free hand flew to her mouth. "Oh, my ever-lovin' God! It turns out that Rod was DEA and he thought I was dealing drugs in my own club. Me! Turns out it was Isaac. The rat bastard. I was so good to that man."

"Seriously? Biker Rod? I don't believe it." Jack gasped for effect.

"Seriously! And that Michael Smith who was killed, it turns out he was one of the guys Isaac set up in the club to supply my patrons. I say good riddance to them all. How dare they put my club in danger. I've worked my whole life for this." Goldie folded her arms in front of her, a look of disgust crossing her face.

"You said Smith was one of the people selling in the club for Isaac. There were others?"

Goldie nodded. "At least three. That Smith guy and two of my servers. I just can't believe it. Thank goodness I brought in some temps to work the party tonight or I would have been shorthanded. And," she emphasized, "I've had to hire in more security. I really wish I could hire you full time, Jack. I like you. But more importantly, I trust you. It's going to be hard for me to trust anyone else."

Jack put a hand on Goldie's shoulder and looked her in the eye. "I appreciate your trust. I know how hard it can be to trust again when you feel you've been betrayed, but I'm sure your new security will work out fine. Now that the competition is over and tomorrow starts a new year, you'll have more time to put into getting better security measures in place to prevent this from happening again."

Goldie smiled up at him. "I'm sure you're right."

Just then, someone grabbed Jack by the arm and dragged him backward. He spun to see who it was.

"Maria," he gasped. Her other hand was grasping Ray's arm in a similar fashion, her eyes squeezed shut and her jaw clenched. Jack recognized labor when he saw it. "How long have you been having contractions?"

She gave him a surprised look. "Contractions? I thought it was the excitement about coming out tonight." The softening of her features told Jack the cramp was subsiding.

"Is this the first one here in the club?" Jack asked.

"Why didn't you tell me you weren't feeling well?" Ray asked.

She shook her head, looking at Ray then back to Jack. "I've had a couple little cramps, but really, I thought it was just the excitement. Or maybe something I ate."

"I'm pretty sure you're in labor, Maria." Jack gazed between his friends. "We need to get you to the hospital. Ray, where's your car?"

"Up the road. I'll give you the keys—"

"My Jeep's out back." He gazed at Maria. "Has your water broken yet?" She shook her head. "Good. That means we have time. Are you okay to walk?" When she nodded she was, Jack turned to make his excuses to Goldie.

She waved both hands in a shooing motion. "Go. Go! Good luck, sweetheart." Jack heard over his shoulder, "I'd be okay if you name the baby after me!"

Jack rose and paced the waiting room. They'd arrived hours ago with Maria. While he wasn't allowed into the birthing room, he wasn't going anywhere. He wanted to be here for his friends and meet his new niece or nephew the moment he was allowed to. In the meantime, he was alone with his thoughts. More than once he had to shoo the black dog from the corner of the room.

Jack felt like he'd been in a tailspin the last few days.

If trying to track down the person responsible for killing club patrons wasn't emotionally charged enough, seeing Nick in the hospital bed had been sobering. Standing at the door and looking in at his friend's frail body, Jack had realized how he'd come to rely on Nick always being there when he needed him. He knew Nick was old, but he never thought the old man would go before he did. Until he found those responsible for taking his family from him, Jack needed Nick's friendship and counsel to keep him focused.

Nick had led Jack to believe he'd be released to return to his normal Sunday Mass, and a huge weight seemed to have lifted off Jack's chest and allowed him to focus on the case. He'd promised to attend Mass this time, rather than parking himself outside the doors and waiting for everyone to leave first before entering the church.

However, Saturday afternoon, the rector had called and asked Jack to come up to the church.

"Father Nicholas has left something for you," he'd said.

Confused, Jack asked, "I'll be at Mass tomorrow. Can I pick it up then?"

"I think you should come for it now. Or if you prefer, I can walk it down to you."

"That's okay. I'll be right up."

When he'd arrived at the church ten minutes later after a quick jog up the hill, the last thing Jack expected was to see the coffin at the altar and Nick lying inside it. The rector said some kind words when he placed an envelope in Jack's hands, but he hadn't heard any of it as he gazed at his friend. Shock washed over him and he collapsed into the nearest pew. He took long, deep breaths to calm his racing heart as he willed his friend to sit up and tell him it was all just a bad joke.

He didn't know how long he sat there staring at Nick's profile before the rector returned to ask Jack if he was all right. He'd assured the man he was fine and waited for him to walk away before he allowed his body to start shaking again.

He clenched and unclenched his hands repeatedly before realizing the envelope was still in his hand, now crushed and wadded in his fist. He didn't want to open it, but he forced himself to break the seal and remove the crumpled note inside.

To my dearest friend, Jack,

Please don't be angry with me for not telling you the full truth when we spoke yesterday. You're a vital cog in the machine that keeps this city safe and I didn't want to distract you at such a vital stage in your investigation. I have faith that you've succeeded, once again, in protecting our fellow San Franciscans by capturing your suspect and bringing them to justice. We're all grateful to have you in our lives. The world needs more men like you.

I mean that, Jack. You're a good man, but I know you let yourself go to dark places—your sorrow is immeasurable. You've suffered more than most people, yet you remain strong and determined, even through your worst days. Please know that if God accepts my contrition and allows me into the Kingdom of Heaven, I will seek out your family and tell them of the man I know and of your selfless acts toward others. And of your unwavering love and devotion for them. When it's your time, you will be with them again. But only when it's your time, Jack.

My last wish on this mortal plane is for you, my friend. Find a way through your grief and start living again, rather than just surviving.

Learn to accept that you may never find the answers you're looking for. Life is too short to dwell in the past.

Let others in again. You're not alone. You have only to destroy the wall you've built around your soul and recognize that you are loved and cherished by many people. Lean on your friends and those you trust. And if the opportunity presents itself, find love again.

I've been blessed to have called you my friend and have been honored you've turned to me to help guide you through your darkness. I regret that I'll no longer be here in the flesh to continue filling that role in your life, but know I'll always be here in spirit. You've only to think of me and I'll be listening. I believe in your heart you'll know what my advice will be.

There are many things I'd say to you, and one day when the time is right, we'll meet again and share another drink after a good, long talk.

I spent my youth as a selfish punk who only thought of himself, so I've spent the last fifty-odd years trying to right my indiscretions. But there is one last thing I want for myself. I would be honored if you would say a few words for me on the day I'm laid to rest. I know you will honor a dying old man's last request, so I'll thank you now.

God be with you, my friend.
Nicholas

With the help of the Navarros, Jack had been able to honor Nick's last wish. They'd taken in Dewayne since Christmas—they had the room and the boy was quickly becoming emotionally attached to Maria. Jack was grateful his friends had stepped up to the challenge but was more grateful for his empty apartment when he returned from St. Frank's. He spent the rest of Saturday with a thirty-dollar bottle of Jameson—two zeroes less than Caroline's Irish tipple—and tried coming up with a eulogy for Nick.

Sunday funerals were not commonplace, but as Nick had been one of their own, the church scheduled a special Mass. Jack had retrieved the whiskey and a pair of glasses from Nick's office and stowed them behind the pulpit until it was his turn to talk.

When he'd finally stepped up to say his piece, he poured out a shot of whiskey into one glass as he explained about the tradition he shared with Father Nicholas.

Jack had let the whiskey rest while he'd spoken about the Nick he knew. He'd left out the sad and tragic parts of the man's early life—that was no longer who Nick was. He'd emphasized the man's kindness and generosity, his love of the community and city, and his dedicated spiritual counsel and devoted friendship.

He looked out across the packed pews as he spoke and was

surprised to see Janeen Baker, the manager of Dinish Ranganathan's apartment building. Had Nick been counseling her too? Jack didn't remember ever seeing her leave any of Nick's services.

When he was done speaking, Jack raised the glass and saluted his friend before quickly downing the amber liquid. Beside the coffin, he'd gazed down at Nick through his tears one last time before the lid was lowered for the last time.

"We'll meet again, my friend, and share another drink together."

Jack's legs had trembled under the weight of the coffin as he helped carry it out to the waiting hearse. It wasn't from his burden's weight—the man seemed to have shrunk in the final stages of his illness—but from his overwhelming grief. The last time Jack had felt this weak was the day he carried his daughter's tiny coffin. The weight felt like a ton of bricks; a feeling that had remained with him ever since. Nick's death only compounded things. And he knew that once he found Leah, the overwhelming weight would be too much to bear.

Nick had left written instructions for his cremation, a task which the Church organized, so Jack said goodbye from the church steps and watched the hearse carry away his friend.

Ray and Maria had attended the service along with Dewayne. They asked Jack to come home with them, but he assured them he was all right and wanted to be alone for a while. He'd spent the rest of the day with the remaining whiskey, and his darkness.

"I'm sorry they won't let you in, Jack."

Jack spun away from the window, pushing his dark thoughts aside, as he did the tears he hadn't realized he was shedding.

"Well?" He held his breath in anticipation. It had been a while since Ray had come to give Jack an update on Maria's condition.

He well understood what Ray was going through. While waiting through the night, he recalled every moment just before Zoë arrived—his adrenaline switched on high for hours, the constant pounding in his chest, the ache in his legs because he couldn't sit still. And that moment when he held Zoë in his arms for the first time, it was as if the world had stilled and the angels sang just for her.

He missed the hell out of his little girl but found much of the same anticipation for his friends as they were about to bring a new life into their family.

He waited for a long moment, gazing into this friend's eyes. He looked tired. Jack was sure the same adrenaline that had kept him going all those years ago had been keeping Ray going tonight. But it lasted only so long. His friend wavered on his feet, but Jack wanted to throttle him. "Well?" he repeated more urgently, feeling himself leaning forward to grasp him by the audacious pink shirt front.

A weak smile crossed Ray's face. "It's a girl," he said meekly.

For a moment, Jack stood motionless, letting the news sink in, then he let his body follow its trajectory and threw his arms around his friend and held him tightly. He felt Ray's arms around him and squeezing him back. Jack's eyes burned with emotion and tears rolled down his face. He clapped Ray's back and hugged him again before leaning away and scrubbing his cheeks with the back of his hand.

"A girl?" Jack remembered those words when the doctor had told him the sex of his and Leah's child. They never asked during the scans; they wanted it to be a surprise. He was good either way as long as the baby was healthy. "A girl!" he finally exclaimed.

Ray beamed up at Jack. "I have a daughter, Jack. A daughter!"

Jack clasped his friend by the shoulders. "Ten fingers and toes?"

Ray nodded. "She's healthy and absolutely perfect. Come on. Let's go meet your new niece, *Tío Joaquín.*"

When they reached Maria's room, Jack stopped at the door. She was propped up against the raised bed, her wavy dark hair hanging down around her shoulders, and the blanket barely covering her and the newborn at her breast.

There were no other words for it. Maria was radiant.

Jack knew about the Magic Hour and how important the first suckle was.

Only when Maria finally looked up did he enter the room. He walked around the bed and kissed her on the cheek. "You look amazing, Maria. I'm so happy for you and Ray." He gazed at the baby's profile and blinked back a flash of Zoë and Leah in the Magic Hour. "She's absolutely beautiful."

Despite the early hour and waning adrenaline, the baby's arrival seemed to give everyone a second wind. Maria repeatedly apologized for ruining their night out, but she'd loved the event. Jack assured her the night hadn't been ruined but had been made better by the arrival of their daughter.

The door opened just then and a nurse entered. She moved past Ray to check mother and baby. "How's she doing, Mother? Any trouble feeding?" she asked, fluffing up the pillows and straightening the blanket.

"She's perfect. I think she's fallen asleep though," Maria said.

"It's been a busy day for her. Let's have her and I'll see if she's used her diaper yet." After changing the diaper and firmly bundling the baby in her blanket, the nurse asked, "Shall I put her in the cot?"

Ray stepped forward with outstretched arms. "I'll take her." Once the nurse was gone, Ray moved over to Jack. "Do you want to hold your niece?"

Did he? Jack gazed at the baby and again, images of Zoë flashed in his mind. Was this all too much, too soon?

Before he could decide, Ray stepped closer and nestled the baby in Jack's arms. It was second nature holding the swaddled newborn against his chest. He moved to a bedside chair and sat. He cradled the baby's head in one hand and her tiny body in the other and gazed down at her for a long moment.

This time last week, in similar early hours of the morning, Jack had witnessed the tragic end of a woman's life. Now, things had come one-eighty and he welcomed a new life into the world. And she was perfect.

When he looked up, Ray had moved to sit on the bedside and held Maria against his shoulder. She looked up at her husband and locked her gaze with his.

Jack knew those glances couples shared. They spoke volumes in the silence.

"What?" he cautiously asked. His friends looked up. Jack's gaze moved back and forth, waiting for one of them to speak. "What?" he repeated.

"Jack, Maria and I have been talking about names," Ray finally said. "You know . . . what to call the baby if it was a boy or girl."

"Yeah," Jack drew out.

"We were thinking, if it was okay with you—"

Maria cut in. "You know you're already the uncle to our children, right, Jack?" He nodded. "We'd also like you to be her godfather."

Jack was taken aback. He'd had the last few months getting used to the idea of being an uncle, but a godfather? That came with a whole different set of responsibilities. The biggest one included taking in the child if anything should happen to her parents, God forbid.

"We also want to give her Zoë's name," Maria added.

After a long moment trying to digest what Maria had just said, he turned away from his friends and looked to a point across the room he couldn't see because images of *his* Zoë abruptly raced through his memory.

How did he feel about this? Could he be okay with calling his niece by his own daughter's name? Would he expect to see his Zoë every time he said her name?

He didn't know what to think or say, because he didn't know how he felt about any of it. Sure, yeah, Ray and Maria had been his Zoë's godparents. But nearly four years later, he was still processing the loss of his family and now someone wanted to name their child after his own.

Ray broke the silence and said in a subdued tone, "We're naming her Esmeralda."

"Right. Zoë would be her second name, as a way to remember your little girl through ours," Maria added.

Jack moved his gaze back to the child in his hands and gazed into the dark blue eyes typical of newborns. He knew in time they'd be the same dark chocolate brown of her parents. And over time, she'd start looking more and more like Ray and Maria.

Words from Nick's letter whispered in the back of Jack's mind.

Find a way through your grief and start living again, rather than just surviving . . . And if the opportunity presents itself, find love again.

Was this the opportunity he needed to let love in again? He was sure Nick meant he needed to start dating again, but Jack wasn't ready for that. He didn't know if he'd ever be ready. But could he love Ray and Maria's child as if she were his own?

"Esmeralda Zoë Navarro," he whispered. The baby's big eyes moved toward the sound of his voice and she seemed to look up at him. He whispered the full name again. The edges of her lips slightly curled. "She's smiling," he exclaimed. "I said her name and she smiled."

"She loves you already, Jack," said Maria.

"I love her too." Jack looked up at his friends, warmth spreading through parts of him he thought long dead. "Yeah, I'm good with calling her Zoë. And if anything were to happen, I will protect her with my life."

CHAPTER THIRTY-SEVEN

Saturday – Jack's House, mid-February

Life changes.

Sometimes those changes come in gentle waves that lap at your feet and give you time to accept them before the next wave comes.

Other times, the waves crash over you, knock you on your ass, steal your breath, and threaten to pull you out to sea in a riptide.

The latter always seemed true for Jack. *Story of my life.*

He stood at the curb, looking up at the little Victorian house that had once been his home and felt a rumbling wave approach.

If he didn't know better, he would have sworn he'd been blasted into the past, back to the time when he and Leah had been looking to buy a house and found this one while driving around. It hadn't been for sale, but it wasn't occupied either. It needed a lot of TLC—the original green and white paint had been curling and flaking, and exposed timber was rotting. But they'd been up for it, so Jack had tracked down the owner and asked if they wanted to sell. Within a few months, they'd started remodeling as soon as they took possession of the keys. Within a year, the house was fully remodeled, inside and out. The little Queen Anne Victorian was the freshest house on the street with its cornflower-blue-nearly-violet exterior and pale-butter-yellow trim.

One of their neighbors said the house reminded them of a wild violet, so that's what they'd called it—Violet Cottage. They hadn't put a sign on the house, but they did have a custom door made with a narrow stained-glass panel full of leaves and violets. He remembered how much Leah loved when the setting sun shone through the colored glass and cast purple, yellow, and green prisms across the hall.

Fast forward and the house had returned to its former dilapidated state, his precious daughter and Trax had been murdered, and his wife was still missing. Except for the black hole in his soul where the memory of his family lived, it was almost like the last ten years had never happened.

If it had been funny, Jack would have laughed over the irony that the house looked how he felt—abandoned and neglected. He couldn't help how he felt, but he was the only one to blame for letting the house he and Leah had cherished so much fall into disrepair. Not only was the paint peeling off cracked timbers, weeds had sprouted up anywhere they were able to get a foothold. And now it had probably been broken into, going by the hole in the once-treasured glass door panel.

Something didn't look right though. Jack took a deep breath and headed toward the steps to inspect the damage, sifting through his keys for the one to unlock the door . . . should he need it.

His phone rang as his foot hit the first step. He didn't recognize the number.

"Hello. Jack Slaughter Private Investigations and Security."

A feminine voice came over the line. "May I speak with Mr. Slaughter, please?"

"Speaking. How can I help you?"

"This is June calling from Doctor Rumsun's office."

He'd nearly forgotten about the HIV tests he'd needed after finding Bob Johnson, aka Pepper Mint, bleeding out in the driveway at the Majestic Lounge. Cutter had already called him with Johnson's own blood test results—he'd been virus free, so Jack could relax. His heart rate kicked up a beat anyway, hearing June's voice on the line.

"I'm calling with your test results, Mr. Slaughter. They're negative," she said.

He inhaled deeply as relief washed over him. "Thank you, June. I appreciate the call." He disengaged.

Well, at least that was some good news.

He gazed up at the door, took a deep breath, then headed up the steps.

On the porch, he peered through the hole in the glass. From this angle, he couldn't see where the glass had fallen, but nothing looked unusual in the empty hallway. He tried the door and found it locked, so he slid the key into the deadbolt. The hole in the glass was beside the deadlock but he didn't want to risk cutting himself if he reached inside, nor did he want to taint any evidence that might have been left behind, including prints on the inside thumbturn.

Behind him, he heard a vehicle with a big block motor pull up and turned to see Ray sliding out from behind the steering wheel.

"Hey!" he called, trotting up the steps. On the porch he asked, "What happened to your window?"

Jack chuckled. "Some detective you are."

"Yeah, yeah, it's broken. I can see that. I mean, do you know who did it?"

He shook his head. "I just arrived and found it like this. I was just going inside when you pulled up." He turned the key and pushed open the door. Before stepping in, he surveyed the space.

He groaned aloud. Did he have squatters? There was a faint smell of shit in the air.

"What?" Ray asked.

"Smell it? There might be squatters." He looked around for the glass but the floor was clean. "If there are, they cleaned up the glass."

Ray gazed up at him. "Why would someone break into the house and clean up the glass?"

"Good question. I'm going to check the house. You can check the garage. I'll meet you in the kitchen in a few minutes." Ray nodded and quickly walked to the end of the hall and into the kitchen. Jack heard the garage door open and Ray's boots as he descended the stairs.

Jack took the stairs by twos and stopped at the top of the landing, listening for any sounds that shouldn't be in the house. Did he have squatters?

Cautiously, he searched each room in turn. The place seemed too clean for anyone living here—it didn't look like anything had changed since he was here last—and it certainly didn't smell like unwashed vagrants. But there was a heavy pong in the air. He found the culprit in the bathroom. It had been so long since the toilet had been used, the water had all but evaporated and the smell of the septic had risen up the pipe. He gave the toilet a couple flushes to fill the S bend again and cracked open the window to vent the room before going back downstairs.

In the kitchen, he went to the back door and checked it. Locked. No broken windows. He twisted the thumbturn on the deadbolt and went outside onto the back porch. His heart squeezed as he took the steps down. Leah's garden was no longer discernible from the tall weeds. He wandered the small space, looking for something she would have planted. Even if it were overgrown like the weeds, at least he'd know her spirit still lived in this space. But there was nothing.

"The garage is clear," Ray said from the porch.

"Same upstairs."

"What are you doing out here?"

"Nothing," Jack said.

"Really? You're standing in the middle of ass-high weeds. If you laid down, you'd disappear. What's up?"

Ray had always been perceptive. "Leah used to have a beautiful garden. Curious if any of it has survived."

"After this long and no one taking care of it?"

"Yeah, yeah— Hey, have you found Dewayne's mother yet?" Jack asked, retracing his path through the overgrowth. At the porch steps, he stopped to brush off the sandburs that had attached themselves to his jeans.

Ray shook his head. "No, but I get the feeling he's okay with that."

"What do you mean?"

"All things considered, he's really a good kid. He's been helping out around the house, and he's even taking turns changing Zelda's diaper."

"Zelda?" His short reply was more of a startled reaction than a question.

Ray chuckled. "Yeah, that's what he calls her. He said Esmeralda is too long. Zelda is hipper, or some shit."

Jack couldn't suppress his own chuckle. "Diapers too?" Ray nodded. "Damn!"

"I think if we found his mother, he might not want to go back to the same situation you found him in. Hell, I wouldn't."

"Have you looked for any relatives? An aunt or uncle . . . grandparent?"

Ray shook his head. "*Nada*. We even ran his birth certificate to see who his father was. Came up blank there too. Just said *unknown*. If we can't find his mother, he's got no one in the world. I don't know how he's going to handle going into CPS." Jack grinned. "What?"

"Sounds like he's fitting in really well at Casa Navarro. Check you out, brother. Two months ago you didn't have any kids, and now you've got two, and a dog!"

"Naw! Don't even go there. We're just helping Dewayne because you can't keep him over at Tommy's, and you won't move back here." Ray thumbed over his shoulder.

Jack crossed his arms, silently telling Ray not to go there about moving back to the house. He knew the neighbors had already dubbed the place The Slaughter House, and it was the last place he'd want to foster Dewayne, or any child. Instead, he egged on his friend.

"You said it yourself. He's a good kid and is voluntarily helping out around the house. Come on, man. No one volunteers for diaper duty. That kid's a keeper." A deep furrow formed between his friend's bushy eyebrows. "And remember, CPS will pay you to foster the boy."

"That's not the point."

"Then what is the point? Dewayne's inserted himself into the family since Christmas. You saw him doling out gifts like he was Santa's little helper. He's an only kid from a seriously fucked up family. He knows a good thing when he sees it. And you are good for him."

"Maybe he's just scoping things out to see what he can get away with," Ray suggested.

Jack shook his head. "You're a better judge of character than that. And I don't see him taking advantage of the situation. I think he genuinely likes you and Maria, and it sounds like he's falling in love with . . . Zelda." It was going to take some time getting used to that name.

Ray groaned as he gazed away. "He does walk Butch and cleans up the poop in the yard."

Jack clapped his friend on the shoulder. "There you go. Baby poop, dog poop, *and* he puts up with *your* shit? I'm telling you, he's a keeper."

"They're little poops," Ray pointed out.

"Poop is poop, brother." Ray only grumbled again. "Come on. Let's get to work." Jack took the steps up to the porch and followed Ray into the kitchen.

"Where do you want to start? Maybe some air freshener—" Ray suggested.

"Dried up S bend in the toilet upstairs. I opened the bathroom window. Hopefully this cross ventilation between the front and back doors will help." After glancing around the kitchen, Jack said, "As for this, like I said yesterday, I'm taking everything back to the drywall. The new owner can rebuild and put their own stamp on it. I just want to pull down everything and replace anything that has blood on it."

Ray waved around the kitchen. "Where do you want all this stuff? Should we just throw it all off the back porch or take it down to the garage?"

Jack weighed the options. "Down to the garage. It's a little more work going up and down the stairs, but it won't be an eyesore to the neighbors. And it'll be easier to take it through the garage door to your truck than down the side of the house."

"Good idea. I'm still trying to work off Christmas dinner so I can use the exercise," Ray said, rubbing the mound just above his belt.

Jack chuckled. "That's too many tacos, my friend."

"Fuck you! There's no such thing as too many tacos, *esé*."

He chuckled again. Ray was such an easy mark.

"Where do you want me?" Ray asked.

"The department's HAZMAT team already removed anything they deemed hazardous a few months ago, so we can just start dismantling the kitchen and take it downstairs. The bulk of the job is in here, but it shouldn't take us too long. When we're done here, we'll start on the rest of the house."

"I brought up the tools when I was checking the garage." Ray pointed to the old metal boxes on the counter. A sledgehammer was propped up against the cabinet below them.

"Good thinking."

"Why make two trips when you can make one?" Ray's wide grin made Jack laugh.

Jack looked around the kitchen. A strange feeling came over him. The despair, loneliness, and sorrow were still there, but it was a gentle wave licking at him. The bigger wave he'd felt rumbling outside must have been his overactive imagination.

Nick's last words had encouraged Jack to live again, to turn to his friends when he needed them, and to open his heart. As much as he desperately wanted to find his wife and get some closure to the tragedy that had taken place in this house, he couldn't deny the love he felt for his new niece . . . Zelda. He smiled to himself. The nickname was as cute as she was, so it was growing on him.

Then there was Dewayne. He really was a good kid, and while Jack had been fully prepared to foster him until his mother could be found—he'd even thought about renting a better place to live—he was surprised at how easily the boy had become part of the furniture in the Navarro household.

And this house. He felt good about selling it. There was nothing left here for him. He knew it the last time he was here to clean it out. If not for discovering the highchair, the place would have been gone long ago.

His plan, once this place sold, was to put the money into buying another house. Maybe something over in the Excelsior District near the Navarros.

He hadn't planned on buying another house but to put the money into trust for Zelda. Now, with Dewayne living with his friends on top of them having a new baby, space was at a premium. Ray and Maria had decided to convert one side of the two-car garage into a room for the teen until his mother or family could be found, which unfortunately meant Jack had to find a new storage unit.

It made more sense to put money into a monthly mortgage than into someone else's pocket at a formal storage facility. And when he finally found his wife and the person responsible for his daughter's death, he'd make sure the trust had been set up for Zelda and that she was his beneficiary.

Jack moved toward the toolbox closest to him and grabbed the handle to open it. "Where's Dewayne today? I thought he was going to help out."

"Home. I didn't think he needed to be here for this, especially since there's still blood on the floor. He's had enough trauma in his life."

Jack didn't need to look down to know Trax's blood had stained through the original linoleum and into the baseboard. The linoleum had been removed by HAZMAT but the floorboards were part of what he and Ray would be replacing today.

"Good point. Let's get started." He picked up a flat-sided chisel and handed it and the hammer to Ray. "Let's get the garage door off its hinges. That will make it easier for us to go back and forth. While you do that, I'll get started over here."

Ray nodded and got to work on the door. Jack moved into the dining area. The old table and chairs were still in place, as was the highchair, which he'd left as he found it once he'd realized his daughter's murder had been staged. This would all be removed too.

Jack stepped up beside the highchair for one last look at where he'd found his daughter's body, still warm and oozing blood onto the highchair table and onto the floor. He blinked several times to keep his vision clear.

He looked across the dining table, following arterial spray. His heart instantly kicked up a beat. He forced himself to take deep breaths to calm himself.

Though they'd searched the house, the broken door glass was nowhere to be found. Whoever had done it, hadn't taken anything, or used the place as a party house or place to squat. Now he realized why someone had broken in.

It was to leave something.

At the edge of the table in the center of a pool of his daughter's dried blood was the small pile of broken glass. Beside it, a note simply read: *I'm sorry.*

"What the fuck?" Jack said aloud. He moved closer to inspect the note and saw a dark shadow fill the corner of his eye and he turned toward it. For a split second, he expected to see Trax. But it wasn't the dog.

Jack had heard Ray removing the door and taking it down to the garage, but the sound faded into the background as his heart slammed hard against his ribcage. The rush of his blood spread like lightning through his veins, deafening him to everything around him except for the thundering *whoosh whoosh* in his eardrums.

"Jack!" He barely heard Ray's concerned voice somewhere in the background but ignored it. He felt his friend trying to drag him away by his shoulders and fought to stay where he was. "No!"

Against the wall behind the dining table lay the lifeless body of a man. His denim jeans and jacket, green plaid flannel shirt, and brown boots were covered in the filth of someone who'd been living a long time on the streets. The source of the shit smell was evident from the stains around the man's crotch where his bowels had emptied.

Lying beside the man, a handgun was caught up on the finger he'd used to pull the trigger. From the blood splatter radiating around the man's head on the wall behind him, along with pieces of skull and brain matter, it was evident this man had come here to kill himself.

ABOUT K.A. LUGO

K.A Lugo is a native of Northern California who grew up on the Central Coast, with San Francisco just a stone's throw away.

Like most writers, Kem has been writing from a young age, sampling many genres before falling into thrillers, mystery, and suspense.

Kem loves hearing from readers and promises to reply to each message. Please visit Kem's socials to stay up-to-date on this exciting new series.

FIND K.A. ONLINE

Website
www.jackslaughterthrillers.com

Facebook
www.facebook.com/KALugoAuthor

Twitter
twitter.com/ka_lugo

Blog
jackslaughter.blogspot.com

Goodreads
www.goodreads.com/KALugo

BookBub
www.bookbub.com/profile/1147179734

Tirgearr Publishing
www.tirgearrpublishing.com/authors/Lugo_KA

K.A. Lugo also writes romance as Kemberlee Shortland
www.kemberlee.com

OTHER BOOKS BY KA LUGO

<u>JACK SLAUGHTER THRILLERS</u>

SLAUGHTERED, #1
Release date: November 2018
ISBN: 978-1-910234-34-1

Jack hates missing person's cases. He only agrees to search for missing wife, Bonnie Boyd, because the details of her disappearance closely match his own wife's, Leah. Soon, Jack discovers the city has a serial killer officials have dubbed The Butcher. Could Bonnie Boyd be a victim? More important, was Leah one of his victims? With every clue Jack weaves together, the more his own life unravels.